Mamaw

SUSAN DODD

Mamaw

VIKING

With boundless gratitude to Dana and Marty Kline,
who gave me the hideout, the alibi, the getaway directions . . .
pretty near everything but the horses.

VIKING
Published by the Penguin Group
Viking Penguin Inc., 40 West 23rd Street,
New York, New York 10010, U.S.A.
Penguin Books Ltd, 27 Wrights Lane,
London W8 5TZ, England
Penguin Books Australia Ltd, Ringwood,
Victoria, Australia
Penguin Books Canada Ltd, 2801 John Street,
Markham, Ontario, Canada L3R 1B4
Penguin Books (N.Z.) Ltd, 182-190 Wairau Road,
Auckland 10, New Zealand

Penguin Books Ltd, Registered Offices:
Harmondsworth, Middlesex, England

First published in 1988 by Viking Penguin Inc.
Published simultaneously in Canada

Grateful acknowledgment is made for permission to reprint
excerpts from the following copyrighted works:
The Sound and the Fury by William Faulkner. Copyright 1929, renewed
1957 by William Faulkner. By permission of Random House, Inc.
"Ariadne" from *The Darling and Other Stories* by Anton Chekhov, translated
by Constance Garnett. Copyright 1916 by Macmillan Publishing Company,
renewed 1944 by Constance Garnett. By permission of Macmillan Publishing
Company, Chatto & Windus, and the Estate of Constance Garnett.
Intruder in the Dust by William Faulkner. Copyright 1948 by
Random House, Inc. By permission of Random House, Inc.

LIBRARY OF CONGRESS CATALOGING IN PUBLICATION DATA
Dodd, Susan M., 1946–
Mamaw.
I. Title.
PS3554.O318M36 1988   813'.54   87-40661
ISBN 0-670-82180-2

Printed in the United States of America by
Arcata Graphics, Fairfield, Pennsylvania
Set in Garamond No. 3 and Weiss

For André Dubus

Contents

Women are like that . . . just born with a practical fertility of suspicion that makes a crop every so often and usually right they have an affinity for evil for supplying whatever the evil lacks in itself for drawing it about them instinctively as you do bedclothing in slumber fertilising the mind for it until the evil has served its purpose whether it ever existed or no. . . .

—William Faulkner,
The Sound and the Fury

Prologue

The old woman—eighty if she's a day—distorts perspective, throws off scale. She towers over everything she stands beside. She knocks the world awry.

She steps off the porch, and as she moves away, the cabin, log gussied up with whitewashed clapboard, seems to breathe a sigh of relief, to stand up taller. She follows a path beaten through the grass around to the back, past a smokehouse, to the ragged edge of a sparse wood.

An ancient beehive constructed of mud and bark sits on a makeshift trestle table that leans against the trunk of a cottonwood tree. The huge old woman, a bellows smoker and a hive tool clutched in her left hand, the only hand she's got, walks a loopy line toward her bees.

It is late summer. The morning is hot. The old woman glances slyly back at the house to make sure her granddaughter's not spying on her from the window. Then she sets the smoker and hive tool on the ground, reaches up and lifts the beekeeper's veil from her head. Hot as Hades in there, damn useless thing, and if there's anything she finds fearsome, ain't hardly her own honeybees. She tosses the silly mesh contraption down on the grass, laughing softly. Her toothless mouth, beneath the large burl of her nose, looks not much bigger than an apostrophe.

She starts removing flats, using her bare hand—a glove would not occur to her. "Things goin' pretty good in here, are they?" she says. She leans down close to look, her eyes not being what they once were. The bees' music is thick in her ears. Their crisp, glistening bodies cluster on her fingers, move up her arm. And then the air is blind and black and gold as the bees cover her face, her eyes. . . .

More come. The scout bees of the colony abandon the nectar-heavy meadows and woods to come to her.

The swarming impulse is getting too strong, too capricious. *Means the queen ain't long for this world,* the old woman thinks. "Where are you, you old trollop?" she says. The bees crust her lips, turning her words to a mumble. "How you keeping these days?"

Standing beside the vacated hive, the old woman vanishes entirely. The place where she stood is marked by a six-foot column of writhing honeybees and a buzz you'd swear you could see.

The column throws its head back and laughs, fit to be tied. The air is viscous as honey with the music of the bees and the column's laughter and the voice from another world that sings:

"Oh, there is Honey in the Rock . . ."

It is an unspied miracle: a pride . . . an *exaltation* of bees.

PART I

When I am nailed up in my coffin I believe
I shall still dream of those early mornings,
you know, when the sun hurts your eyes. . . .

—Anton Chekhov,
"Adriadne"

I

The Knowing

1 8 2 5 — 1 8 4 0

The tendrils of memory curl, twist, and tighten around all she knows, all she could possibly know and much she could not.

She knows things in her bones, young Zerelda Cole. The Coles have knowing blood—why, just look how her grandpappy, Richard, knowed when a body was up to anything at all. In the tavern it was a good thing, too, that kind of knowing. The kind of men come to the Blackhorse was the kind usually up to something.

"Up to no good," Grandpappy'd say. He'd set their whiskey and ale and port down so careful in front of them, like the pewter tankards and tumblers was spun glass. All the while he'd be keeping his eyes fastened hard on the eyes of the men who were up to no good. Let 'em see his knowing. Take his knowing to heart. Take their troublemaking somewheres else, far from Midway, Kentucky, far from Richard Cole's tavern and his make-do family and his knowing.

When his son Amos was going to get killed, Richard knowed. "I seen it coming the day before," he told Zerel years later. "Leastwise I knowed we's in for trouble. Didn't know how to head it off is all." A dagger ripped Amos open so wide some of his guts spilled out onto the tavern floor.

Richard's knowing had told him his other son, James, wasn't long for this world, either. "Your daddy got the look of doom about him. I tried to think like he's just sorrowing after his brother, but I knowed better."

Not three months later—Zerelda but two years old, her brother Jesse barely a year—James Cole flew from the back of a horse as he raced across a teal-blue Woodford County pasture. His head struck rock as if aimed for it. He was dead before they fetched him home.

"Reckon Grandpappy knowed he was gonna die?" Zerel asks her mother, Sallie.

They are laying out Richard Cole in the vestibule of the Blackhorse Tavern. He is bathed and combed, shaved under his chin, and got up in a yellowed shirt with a stiff, spotty collar. Grandpappy only owned one shirt collar. He used to put it on Zerel's head for a crown when she was a mite. "Queenie," he called her.

Sallie Cole doesn't look at her daughter when she answers. "Ever'body's gonna die. Ever'body knows it." Sallie studies her father-in-law's face as if trying to figure exactly how much the old man knew.

"Yesterday, I mean," Zerel persists. "You reckon he saw death comin' for him?"

"Don't talk foolish," her mama says.

Mama don't know nothin'.

But Zerel knows. And she knows Grandpappy knowed. Last night he had a faraway look and a faint voice when he asked Zerel to come downstairs to the tavern after supper. "Keep me company," he said. "Don't leave me down here by my lonesome."

Mama didn't like Zerel hanging around the tavern. So many ruffians coming through these days, the girl fourteen now, only looking older with the size on her, growed up, and the old man getting older every day, taking his granddaughter for just a child, never considering she might be taken by some for a woman. . . .

But Sallie was no match for the old man . . . *cuss,* she called him behind his back. No match for the girl, either. Sallie never won. So Zerel was down in the tavern last night when Grandpappy slumped over a table, then slid to the floor, his beard sweeping planks soaked twelve years earlier by his son's blood, leaving a faint sad shadow.

Zerel remembers it all. She didn't see it, wasn't there to see or hear, couldn't understand, only two years old, the shouts, the blood, the shadow. Zerel a baby . . . when Uncle Amos died, when Daddy died. Not there. But her bones know. Her blood remembers. Her knowing is choked by memory until knowing and remembering twist into a single great breathless thing, and Zerel is bursting with it, with nobody to tell it to, now Grandpappy is dead.

A widow at twenty-three, bereft of her childhood playmate as well as her husband (her cousin, James, her dearest, her only friend, who else could she have married?), Sallie Lindsay Cole had been entranced by grief. She'd groped through a week alone, one day at a time, hour by minute by second, as if she had no will, no sense, no feeling. She had two babies, nothing more.

Her father-in-law, her Uncle Richard, had come and got her then, knowing there'd be nothing but trouble otherwise. More trouble. On the eighth day after his son's burying, he came for Sallie and the children and put them in the rooms above the tavern where he'd been mightily pleased to live by himself since his wife had died several years before.

Richard was fond of his niece, when niece was all Sallie was to him. A sweet-tempered thing, easily entertained. But his son's wife—that was a different matter. Sallie done James no good. Too soft. Too comfortable. James needed a woman who'd ride him hard, use reins like they was made for, make the boy a man. Useless as toys, the two of them, Sallie and James. She'd coddled him, he'd played with her, the babies had made no difference at all. James died at twenty-three the same way he'd have died at sixty: an overgrowed youngster tearing up the countryside as if he hadn't a care in the world.

And so the father inherited the son's cares; Richard brought the widow and babies to live with him. He reared them, all three together, and he tried to keep the tavern seemly and safe because now, again, Richard Cole was a family man.

If Sallie Lindsay Cole was a child in her father-in-law's care, she blossomed into adolescence with his passing. Foolish and flirtatious. Heedless. Distracted by frippery. Fractious.

Her daughter, fourteen, is disgusted by her mother's sudden girlishness. Mama works in the tavern with her shapely white arms bared to the elbow, smiles at men who are strangers. A pulse beats fast in her smooth throat, such a naked thing, Mama's throat, when she leans toward nameless men.

"Ain't proper for a lady to keep no tavern," Zerel says.

Sallie's laugh is irritating, dissonant music played for two men at the tavern's corner table as she talks to her daughter behind the bar. "Didn't see much wrong with it when your granddaddy kept you down here, did you?"

"That was different. *He* was here."

"Now I am," Sallie says. She sweeps a strand of auburn hair from her forehead, circles her waist with measuring fingers as she sucks in her breath. The men are watching. Her bosom swells. "Go see what your brother is up to."

Mama's eyes are wandering out onto the road now: a spring evening, still daylight at seven, wanton, extravagant light, and the moon floating weightless along the scalloped green edge of the horizon. The scent of clover wafts in through the open door. Zerel looks, and sure enough, here he comes again, that Missouri farmer Thomason. Coming by near every night, with his red hands and thrust-out belly, now Grandpappy's gone. Buffoon, Zerel mutters to herself. Fat pig. Sow belly.

Her mother hovers over a gleaming tankard, studying her curved reflection in its dented side. She is pinching color into her cheeks, smoothing her hair. "Go upstairs."

"Goddamn," Zerel says softly, but Sallie pays her no mind, no mind at all. Up to no good, Zerel thinks. She walks outside and spits in the dirt like a man. Like Grandpappy. Goddamn. She doesn't deign to notice Thomason when he tips his hat to her. Acts like she doesn't even see him coming. Grandpappy'd run him off, he would, and Mama wouldn't carry on so if Grandpappy was downstairs.

Zerel goes around back and climbs the rickety stairs to the room where a body's apt to forget there's a tavern or anything at all down below.

"Jesse?"

Her brother, twelve, does not look up as Zerel comes through the door. He is sitting before the hearth on a three-legged stool, holding a small tin box between his knees. His face is soft and pink and dreamy.

"You counting them damn coins again?" his sister asks.

"Grandpappy give 'em to me."

Zerel looms over him, staring into the box. "Ain't much," she says.

"More'n you got."

"Mama's got that suitor rootin' around down there again."

"She likes him." Jesse Cole looks at his sister. "Maybe Mama'll get married and she won't have to look after the tavern anymore. Then we could—"

"Seein' as I only got one brother, seems like the Lord coulda give me one with a little more sense," Zerel snaps. "You want to wind up sloppin' Missouri hogs and taking orders from some big-bellied man ain't even your kin?"

"But he'd be our daddy."

Zerel doesn't even think about it, she slaps him. A red splotch seeps across the left side of her brother's face, and his seven coins roll and scatter on the bare wood floor.

Jesse stays stock-still, just looking up at her. His eyes are watering, but he doesn't say a word.

Zerel, though, is the one who cries. "This is *home*," she says. "Don't you understand a thing?"

Her brother stands up and pats her shoulder awkwardly. "I wouldn't pick to leave, Zerel, but it don't look to me like we're apt to have much say in it."

She lifts her hand as if she means to strike him again. Her brother doesn't move, but she sees him wince. He is afraid of her. She drops her hand.

"Maybe you mean to spend your whole life doing what other folks tell you," she says. "But damned if I will."

Jesse stares at her for another moment. Then he bends down and begins to retrieve his scattered coins.

"I ain't going," Zerel says.

Sallie leans into Richard Cole's shaving mirror, a shard of glass nailed to the wall beside the bed where the morning sun comes in. She licks her finger, then twists a tiny curl around it. "What do you mean, ain't going? I mean to marry Mr. Thomason and make my home with him in Clay County, Missouri. I'm going and you are going with me."

"See if I do." Zerel's voice is plain, matter-of-fact, not the least bit huffy. Her dark eyes are steady and sharp.

Sallie turns. Her eyes are a thin, pale wash of blue below her creased brow. "You're just like that old man . . . your granddaddy," she says.

Zerel smiles. "He thought Thomason was no-'count, too. Reckon we was like-minded."

"Now you listen here—"

"Talk all you please, Mama. I don't aim to leave."

Sallie, looking as if she's about to cry, jams her clenched

hands into her apron pockets. "He wants me to be a mother to those youngsters whose own mama died . . . it's what I want. Can't we just . . . be happy now?"

The girl's expression softens. "I don't mean to interfere with your wanting, Mama. I just got my own. You go on, leave me stay."

"You mean to stay on here and run a tavern?"

Zerel grins. "Sounds right fine. But I don't reckon even Grandpappy woulda took to that idea."

"Just what do you propose to do, then?"

"I can stay over to Stamping Ground with Uncle James and Aunt Mary."

"Oh, can you? You're so all-fired sure they'll welcome another child, with eight already of their own?"

"I ain't a child. Besides, they keep me every summer."

"No, you ain't," her mother says. "No natural and proper child."

Sallie argues. But Zerel wins. Regular cuss, Zerel. Shades of the old man.

Sallie Lindsay Cole marries Robert Thomason, a widower, in August and leaves with him for Missouri, taking her younger, more tractable child, Jesse, with her. Zerel is left in the guardianship of her uncle, Sallie's brother James Lindsay, who enrolls her in Saint Catherine's convent school in Lexington for the winter term.

"Goddamn," Zerel says. "We ain't even Catholic, thank the Lord. What do I need with a convent?"

Uncle James is a large ruddy man, his graying hair like a silly disguise above his boyish face. He laughs. "Them sisters may be the only ones can get you to stop cussin', girl."

Zerel, her eyes like broken glass, appeals to his wife.

"Might even teach a young lady not to spit," Aunt Mary says.

Zerel is arguing a blue streak. Uncle James, still laughing, heads out to the barn, his hands clapped to his ears.

Aunt Mary goes right on with her sewing. She's making a new dress for Zerel, attaching some kind of doodads or furbelows around the neck and cuffs. Buttons march up and down the front, fastening nothing.

"You ain't got to fuss like that," Zerel says, looking suspiciously at the dress.

"I don't mean to send you off to the convent looking like a ruffian," her aunt says, pinching a bit of flowered calico between her fingers. "It's time you became a young lady. And you got to start dressing like one."

Goddamn.

Sister Furbelow and Sister Fichu, Sister Gimcrack and Sister Knickknack. Sister Reticule. Sister Snood . . . never saw a more useless, dried-up, dusty herd of old bossies in a single barn.

And the "young ladies" are even worse. Flock of ninnies, twittering their Latin and French, pecking through prayers and hymns and sums. They rustle with starch and flimsy fabrics when they walk. They smell like dying flowers.

Zerel is amazed that foolishness can take so many elaborate forms, that penalties can be so easily come by. The convent is a forest riddled with traps; the sisters are loaded for bear. Zerel crouches in the tangled underbrush of rituals and rules, tries to make herself scarce. But they catch her coming and going, catch her every time. Zerel, going on fifteen, is nearly six feet tall. Zerel is caught, enlarged in their sights.

The chaste, narrow cots are laid out, twelve to a room, side by side in a single row. There are three rooms, not an empty bed. The spiny beds are dressed like the nuns: in stiffened white linen, scratchy charcoal wool. The windows stay open through even the bitterest nights, fresh air as essential to wholesome bodies as oatmeal, grace. Zerel is eternally hungry and cold, wanting.

First thing in the morning, last thing at night, three times throughout the day, the girls kneel in silent prayer. Dark angels loom above, behind, beside them. *Devotions,* the sisters call these hours of torture to knee, spirit, spine. Mass, "the Holy Sacrifice," for starters, before a bite of breakfast. Zerel's stomach growls, ruining sublime contemplations, drawing frowns.

"What am I supposed to do, with all this goin' on?" Zerel asks. Her first week, her last fling of innocence—before she learns to question is to sin. "*I* ain't Catholic."

Sister Tiara, Sister Brooch, Sister Somebody-or-other barely moves her scaly pale lips in reply. "You are not of the faith. All the more reason to pray, child."

Zerel is hectored into dawn, pushed toward the chapel door.

Divine complexity: there are feasts for flowers, feasts for palms, observances with ashes for foreheads, candles for throats, blessings for water and wine and bread and animals. Saints sing as they burn, smile as they bleed, pray as they expire and ride clouds into heaven. Worship: Zerel stands apart from it, yet can't avoid being lost in it, lost, mislaid, unsaved.

Her eyes seek but do not find a wall free of the horrible cruciform—wood and plaster, brass, silver, gilt. The convent is littered with bodies of Jesus giving up the ghost. Corpses line the halls. Thorn-pierced hearts flutter at eye level in the refectory, transforming bread into blasphemy. Zerel grows wan but not thin. She is taught to embroider, to make novenas.

Short of breath, Zerel prays for deliverance:
Goddamn.

One weekend each month Zerel is permitted to go "home"— to Stamping Ground, to the overcrowded house of her uncle and aunt. Her eight cousins cluster around her, the four boys slapping her back and tweaking her skirts, as their sisters examine Zerel shyly. Aunt Mary studies Zerel for clues to ruin: torn shirtwaists, lost buttons, a sallow complexion. James wraps his niece in bearlike arms and swings her around the kitchen in a lead-footed dance. "Our girl," he cries. "Our wild child comes back to the roost!"

They pry and poke and tease and shout and lay down the law like a body's own family, sure enough. The old slave woman, Louisa, even gets in her licks. "You look like a trussed chicken in them skirts."

Zerel welcomes the unmannerly, boisterous moments of arrival with gruff delight, pushing the little ones out of her path, slapping away her overgrown boy cousins. Good to be home . . . it *is* home. But she is barely through the door when she's out again, thighs pumping against the patched constraints of her cousin Joe's britches as her legs part for horse-flesh . . . ah, Lord, she canters, trots, gallops, jumps . . . she craves. The Lindsays got a whole stableful: nags for plows, ponies for young 'uns, thoroughbreds for races, even a Tennessee Walker. Before the weekend is out, there's no critter on the place Zerel hasn't exercised, curried, cozied up to.

"If even *one* of our boys took hold around here thataway." James sounds wistful.

Mary Lindsay pats his hand. "Boys, yes. It'd be right fine. But if one of our girls took on so, I'd put a switch to her."

James kisses his wife. Gentle Mary, she'd like as not use a lace collar, a cologne atomizer to tame a wild girl. Like as not be *right,* too. Honey for flies. But Zerel is piss and vinegar. The wildness in this niece of theirs—James Lindsay is almost sorry the task of driving it out of her has been laid at his door. Not befitting, maybe, but a fine thing anyhow to see, Zerel's wildness.

"You think those sisters in Lexington will teach her how to behave?" Mary asks, sounding troubled.

James grins. "Over her dead body, maybe."

Old Louisa chuckles softly over by the hearth. They'd forgotten she was still in the room. "That child might-could save the whole passle of us some trouble if she breaks her own neck first."

It is Sunday noon. Near time to be starting back for Lexington, but the girl is nowhere in sight. Mary's been calling her from the porch every five minutes for the past half-hour, wasting her breath on fancy filagree in the late November air.

"I'll go out and have a look," James says.

"Might take the ox team along," Mary tells him, "if you mean to haul her back in."

Zerel's red cardigan gives her away at a distance against the bleached-bone sky. She's out in the eastern pasturage, in plain view of the house, knotted in a crotch high up in the lone sycamore.

James waves. "Hull-loo up there!"

Zerel sees him, hears him, but doesn't wave back, doesn't make a sound.

James walks straight to the tree, taking his time. Looking up, he circles the fat trunk.

The girl watches him with narrow eyes.

Finally her uncle raises his arms, jumps ramrod-straight, reaching. He misses and drops back to the ground with a thud.

"Huh," she says.

James jumps again, his thick fingers catching the sturdy limb this time. Twisting his long body into the momentum of his leap, he manages to get astride the limb. The branches shudder and creak. Five feet above him, Zerel sways. She tightens her hold on the trunk, but all signs of unsteadiness are kept from her face.

"Howdy there," her uncle says.

"You lookin' for something?"

"Sure am. A mean-eyed, horse-bustin' gal. Got a call for one in Lexington, I hear."

"Too bad for them," says Zerel. "I ain't going back."

"Do tell."

"I hate it . . . I hate *them.*"

"Hate who—the sisters?"

"Hate everybody."

James keeps his eyes on the house, where he can see Mary's blue Sunday dress moving past the parlor window. "Me, too?" he says. "Even your old uncle?"

"You ain't old."

"I'm older than you."

"Don't care."

"Me, neither. Reckon we can be friends anyhow."

"You think you're foolin' me into somethin'?"

"Hell, no—beggin' your pardon, Sister Zerel. But hell, I say. *Hell, no.* Couldn't fool you if I tried."

"Uncle James?"

"Ma'am?"

"I really do hate it there. Hate it like hell."

He looks up through the branches and smiles at her with his eyes. "Reckon you'll like Missouri any better? Hear your stepdaddy got him a fine place there . . . right sightly."

"You know I ain't going to no Missouri."

"That so?"

"Hell, no."

"Must be time you was heading back to Lexington, then."

She is there in time for vespers, giving the Lord the same silent treatment she's given her uncle clear from Stamping Ground to the convent's black gate.

Zerel: last one in . . . rotten egg.

II

Tobacco Bride

1 8 4 0 — 1 8 4 1

Ollie, ollie-in-come, all-come free!

Sudden spring, the open dormer windows a benediction and a praisesong, fresh air something to be gotten away with, gorged on. Summer plays hide-and-seek with the hills, and Zerel's thighs ache for the tremble of horseflesh between them. The gate slides open to the heat of her desire, and then she is home, her knees spread wide, her hair a wildness . . . *home free.*

She calls it home now, Stamping Ground, makes no bones about it. If this ain't home, what is? She sucks the flesh from peaches, tears into the tender skin of pears with bared teeth. The juice runs down her chin, trickling under her clothes, and Zerel shouts, gallops, stirred, always stirred-up, Zerel. For whole days she disappears into thickets, ravines, hillsides, creek beds, caves. She comes home late to supper, her mouth stained blue and scarlet, her cheeks on fire.

"Ain't she a beauty, though?" Uncle James says.

Mary Lindsay smiles, but looks worried.

She's no beauty, Zerel: man-size girl with boyclothes and no manners. Her nose is too big by half; a cynic lurks around the eyes and mouth. Her voice is deep. Her hands are rough. Thighs you could build a house on. It's hard to know what's best, what to hope for a child like that.

"Stand up straight?" Aunt Mary's orders are so delicate the girl takes them for suggestions easily dismissed. "Head high, shoulders square?" But Zerel, no beauty, hangs her head, slumps in company. She keeps her arms tightly folded across her chest, as if the wealth of flesh gathering there is a downright disgrace.

Zerel slouches over the table, inhales her food, overturns her chair, forgets to excuse herself, bangs the door. Unused daylight after supper this time of year: she's back to the stable again.

James winks at his wife. "Ain't she a beauty?"

Zerel? Hell no, she ain't. But set her on a horse, set her feet to fiddle music, set her to laughing in a certain pure light and the girl is a stunner.

It is the wildness in her, James thinks. Knocks the breath right out of a body, like sometimes a mountain does.

Robert James, though—now there's a beauty. The first time Zerel sees him, every man she's ever laid her eyes on goes pale and puny. Zerel's struck blind and dumb. A pain in her breast throws her shoulders back hard, lifts her head as if the terrible weight of this man's beauty wants to crush her, but she can throw it off, can throw it off if she tries. . . .

She's strong, Zerel, but not strong enough to throw off the weight of the wanting, the awful wanting in her that Robert James becomes the very first moment she sets eyes on him.

The first time Robert James sets eyes on Zerelda Cole, he calls her "young fella."

Zerel is too shocked for shame.

"Beg pardon, young fella. Can you tell me the way to the Bynums' place?"

Early morning on a dismal June day, swirls of ground fog like clammy white fingers clutching the throats of trees. Zerel is glad for the mist, hovers in it, keeping her distance from the beautiful young man who stands at the side of the road: his high, wide cheekbones, his tapered jaw.

Zerel drops Wonder's bridle, thankful she picked on a horse with no mind of its own this morning. "Easy, girl," she whispers, her voice low. The horse shifts under her, then stands still. Zerel folds her arms across her chest, holding in the heat.

"Bynums'?" Place nearest to the Lindsays' on the north, but she doesn't say so. "You cross down here, past that barn, see?" He can't see. The fog interferes. "Well, a gray old fallin'-down barn, anyhow. . . ."

The beautiful young man is looking at her oddly. Zerel roughens her voice, makes short work of the directions. Then she turns Wonder around and takes off at a clip toward where she just come from.

The young man, sounding a bit puzzled, calls after her. "Thank you kindly."

He doesn't say "young fella" this time.

The fog dampens but does not cool her face.

She knows soon enough who he is: Robert James a divinity student at Georgetown College, boarding with kin in the country for the summer. Stamping Ground is his makeshift home, like hers. He is twenty-one.

The next time she sees him, Zerel is dancing. He is still beautiful, maybe more beautiful in light than in fog. But now Zerel doesn't care if he takes her breath away. Zerel pays no mind to anything when she dances. But he can't dance, Robert James. Divinity students got to start acting like men of God while they're still boys, poor things. Robert James, slender and still, watches her from the corner of the room like he's having trouble keeping his mind on the old man who's got his ear.

Rosettes on the modishly low shoulders of her dress, Aunt Mary still at it, goddamn. Zerel's hair piled up in swirls like frosting and cluttered with pink bows. *Hell.* Hot as hell in here. All this to-do about clothes for a homely country dance, Aunt Mary fussing the better part of the day, adding last-minute complications to Zerel's dress, torturing her hair. "You don't mean to wear those dreadful boots, child?"

"I mean to *dance,* not hobble around like I got a split hoof," Zerel said.

Now here not an hour's gone by, Zerel's hot and wet as a horse been rode too hard, bare shoulders, satin rosettes drooping and . . . goddamn hot eyes on her shoulders and hungry doubt in his eyes—Don't I know you?

It only takes a minute and Robert James remembers, the girl finds her proper place in his memory, among the swirls of fog. He flushes with embarrassment. He remembers, all right—"young fella." But he'll never admit it, never mention it.

Hastily excusing himself from the venerable white-whiskered gentleman at his side, Robert James crosses the floor, threading through the spinning dancers. He feels as if everybody's watching him, everybody but the magnificent strapping girl: the melting ice cream of her dress, her crude boots stamping out invisible fires on the floor, eyes so narrowed she might be inspecting her own interior . . . that girl will not see Robert James, not even when he's beside her, tapping her partner's shoulder. . . .

Robert bows slightly.

"May I have the pleasure—"

She looks at Robert James then. Looks hard. *"You* ain't supposed to dance," she says.

He is almost . . . *almost* as tall as she is. Almost as steady of eye. Power is in the span of his back, the curve of his arm. Softness in his mouth.

"Reckon I'll dance if I care to," he says. "I hope it will be with you." He smiles.

So stern, her face, unlovely as a woman can be. No softness, no *give* in that face of hers.

But then Zerel laughs. Wipes sweat from her face with the backs of both hands. "Reckon you'd look a fool," she says, "dancing all alone."

She is . . . fierce, Robert thinks. Something more fearsome than beauty in her. She is dazzling.

When she holds out her large strong hand, Robert James takes it and holds on for dear life. He stands up straight and tall, measuring himself against her.

She *will* have him. She knows it, and he knows it. She cannot be wooed or won, cannot be fooled or tamed or evaded. And so Robert James befriends Zerelda Cole the way he would befriend a wild creature.

She taunts and eludes him, leads him a chase. Not coy, Zerel. Not teasing, but running for her life from the hot wanting in her that she doesn't understand. Doesn't care to.

Robert understands: it is meant to be. He can't say why or how. He only knows it shall come to pass. Zerel becomes an article of Robert's faith, her wildness and wanting somehow part and parcel of the Lord's mysterious will.

Why?

She will help to make me strong, Robert thinks. From her I shall draw that which makes me more fully my own. And God's.

Zerel taunts Robert James. She ridicules him, calling him "Preacher," at pains to conceal her disappointment when she fails to vex him.

"You don't really *believe* all those things they make you

study, do you, Preacher? All them prophets' gloom and doom and brimstone?"

Robert smiles. "If I didn't believe, why would I study it?"

She shrugs. "You're a mighty peculiar person. How should I explain what you do?"

"Don't you thirst to know the God that made this earth, Zerel?"

Zerel, sitting half-turned from him, lifts her face to the August sun. For an instant an unaccountable sweetness molds her expression. Robert, lying on the grass beside her, reaches up and brushes his fingertips down her cheek. She flinches, leaning away from his hand.

"You're a very peculiar person, too," he says softly. "Why must you hide your gentleness, Zerel?"

"Hogwash," she says.

"What a felicitous expression."

"I know worse, Preacher."

Robert laughs. "So do I."

"We're even, then."

"I doubt it. I doubt we'll ever be even, you and I."

"I really do want to know. . . ." Zerel rips a handful of grass from the dry ground, then flings it away. "Why would somebody so *smart* want to be a preacher, anyway? Seems like a puny ambition."

"Don't you believe in God?" He sounds, finally, taken aback.

"Well, *God*," she says. "Don't guess I even know, now I think about it. Only time anybody ever talks to me about God's when they're tellin' me what *they* want, what *they* think. Mama. The sisters. Even . . . well, even my grandpappy sometimes."

"Tell me about your grandfather."

Zerel squints. "That's *my* business."

"You are a bramblebush, girl."

"That's my business, too, I reckon."

Robert laughs. "Whatever you say, miss. Go on about God, then."

"Now *that*," Zerel says, "is *your* business, Robert James. Goin' on about God."

"You really don't believe?"

"Don't know as I do or not. Don't seem like God has much to do with what I want."

"Hah!"

"Oh, never mind one of your homilies, now, Preacher."

Robert sits up and looks directly into her eyes. When Zerel tries to look away, he takes hold of her chin and turns her face toward him. "Listen," he says.

"Don't hear a thing but magpies and larks . . . crows . . . sparrows."

They are both quiet for a moment, his hand still holding her face. Then a languorous call, infinitely sad, floats from a pine grove behind them: *ooah-ooo-oo-oo.*

Zerel shivers, crosses her arms.

"Mourning dove," says Robert, still staring into her eyes.

"Well, glory be! Figured you meant to tell me it's the voice of God."

"It is," says Robert. "It is. Hear Him."

Oh, how could she *love* a man like that? God's own fool, Robert James. And what is love, anyhow? Might just be a mask, for all she knows, a thin disguise for unreasonable demands.

God, Robert says, is love.

But Robert is a fool. Zerel knows it. Anyone can see it.

Zerel fights and fumes and taunts and wonders and burns. Her own body has become a kind of torment, endlessly insisting on itself. Why will he never touch her? If he touches her she'll scream . . . she feels it like a stranger beside her in the bed, her own treacherous body. The nights are long and never silent, never peaceful. Zerel arises peevish and giddy and hollow-eyed to late-summer mornings deafening with the eternal joyful noise of the birds.

He rides as well as she does. Almost as well. He would be her match all right, if only he could learn to be as headlong. Zerel dares him, jumps over fences and creeks and stumps and just dares Preacher James to follow.

And when he does she thinks: *He's going to touch me finally now . . . I'll scream.* Only Robert makes free with nothing more than her hand when they cross rough ground. And when he does, like as not Zerel will snatch her hand away. Why won't he touch me. . . .

Zerel burns.

One day he says to her, very calm and matter-of-fact, "When we are married—"

What? Zerel doesn't hear the rest, his first four words roar in her ears. "Married?" she says.

Robert smiles at her confusion. "You know it as well as I do," he says.

She takes herself in hand. "What makes you think I'd marry you?"

Robert goes right on smiling, just as he does when she tries to shake his faith in the Almighty, and doesn't say another word.

Flesh of my flesh, Zerel thinks, and her face is hot and Robert's eyes are cool and laughing; he is laughing at her, and when she nudges her horse away, away, her knees are weak and watery.

Old Louisa passes Zerel the flapjacks and mutters in her ear, "Best scratch that itch you got, child, lest you never sleep again."

Then summer is over, bitten off like loose thread. Color drains from the fields, the hills, the trees. Even the sky takes on a peaked look. The orchard smells winy, rotten-rich. A cantata of flies. The mornings are effervescent, afternoons lethargic, dusks swift and wan. Robert returns to Georgetown the first week of September. The following week the convent gates open for Zerel like jaws. She is eaten alive with her wanting.

Robert wants to marry her.

Zerel wants . . . Robert.

Not so many miles between Lexington and Georgetown, a pleasant ride, a possible walk. Yet Zerel is behind the gate, Robert a world away. They meet only in Stamping Ground, on occasional holidays. Abbreviated, tangled-up times, those visits, like dreams to Zerel, dreams heady with chaos of others' making, shouts that stick in the throat. Dreams always on the verge of ending before they are grasped.

He writes to her in a fine, sure hand. He calls Zerel "my dear friend," and does not refer to romance, betrothal, marriage. He tells her of his people, a fine old Virginia lineage modest in its accomplishments and assets, extravagant in its beliefs and dreams. He is a dreamer, Robert James, a fool. She wants . . . she *will* have him.

They are married in December of the following year, three days after Christmas in 1841. Robert is twenty-three, Zerel a month shy of sixteen.

"Too young," Aunt Mary says. "Just a child yet."

But she does not say so to Zerel. Too late, far too late for that. The girl knows what she wants, and she will not be denied.

Uncle James does not oppose the marriage, either. But weighed down by the responsibilities of guardianship, he does slow it down, complicate it. A bond, he insists, must be posted to guarantee fulfillment of the marriage agreement.

Robert has nothing.

Zerel has conniptions.

Uncle James acts somewhat sheepish, but remains adamant. "I promised your mama when she left you with us that I'd look after you, protect you."

"Robert ain't hardly the sort of person I'd need protecting *from*." Zerel's dark eyes spark in a way that reminds James Lindsay so powerfully of his Uncle Richard, the old man, that he has to look away if he is to stand his ground. Oh, she is a stubborn cuss, this girl. James wonders if young Robert's got any idea what he's taking on with her.

"No offense to your intended," James says. "Nothing personal at all. But you need my written consent to marry . . . and I need some evidence of good faith."

"Don't it strike you somewhat foolish—questionin' Robert's good *faith?*" Zerel, her face white, is nearly hissing.

"Maybe so. But it also strikes me somewhat foolish getting married at your age. Seems like what I find foolish never mattered much to you all along. Listen, honey—"

But the girl is gone, slamming the door behind her.

Robert tries to calm her. "I'm sure it *isn't* personal, my dear. Your uncle's just trying to—"

"Oh, don't go tellin' me everything he's already waved under my nose."

"I'll take care of it, Zerel."

And he does. A well-to-do classmate, J. J. Milliken, agrees to co-sign the bond with Robert. Fifty pounds of tobacco is the security.

The bride is in a snit.

"Never mind now," Robert says. "It's all been seen to."

"An outrage and a insult's what it's been," says Zerel.

"For your own good," Uncle James says, miserable over the whole business; such hard feelings, still, on the wedding day.

His niece gives him a terrible look. "Exactly right," she says. "My *own* good."

"Be nice now, Zerel," Robert says. "Don't talk to your uncle that way."

"I'm sorry." James Lindsay looks at Robert. "I truly am."

"Don't pay him no mind, Robert," Zerel says.

"You needn't apologize, sir. It's all settled now."

"I ain't never going to forgive—"

"Be reasonable, Zerel."

"Be *still*, Zerel." Aunt Mary has to stand on a footstool to fasten the gardenias—coaxed into bloom indoors, a living miracle, those flowers—in her niece's hair. "Do stop tossing your head that way."

"Zerel . . . honey?"

She turns abruptly toward her uncle, jutting her chin at him. Two alabaster petals float to the floor. Aunt Mary groans.

"I ain't talkin' to you."

"Zerel, for goodness' sake—"

"Never you mind, Robert James. This is *my* family. You keep out of it."

Robert sighs, smiles hopelessly at Mary Lindsay.

"Child, will you *please*, for the love of God, stand *still* for a moment?" Aunt Mary mumbles, her mouth full of pins.

Uncle James is waiting, looking up at her with his blue boy-bridegroom eyes. "Honey girl?"

"You may kiss the bride," she says.

James Lindsay takes her large, rough hand and tucks it in the crook of his arm. "Let's get you married first, Sister."

"Wait, the veil . . ." Aunt Mary teeters on her footstool, reaching once more for Zerel. "Oh, you shouldn't be seeing this, Robert. What was I thinking of?" She pins the lace, a panel cut from her one good tablecloth, to Zerel's hair.

"Enough icing. The cake is done." James shakes out the flounces in Zerel's skirts. "Let's get the I-do's done before this bridegroom changes his mind."

Old Louisa, upon a signal from Mary Lindsay, opens the parlor door. As Zerel passes her, the old woman whispers, "You gonna get rid of that itch now, girl, I promise you!"

Then they are all laughing, moving out of the kitchen

toward the parlor, the preacher, waiting neighbors and kin. James is pulling Zerel behind him, herding Mary ahead. Robert is smiling, standing back and watching and smiling at Zerel as if she has done something astonishing.

"I, Robert, take thee, Zerelda . . ." *So young,* Robert thinks, *she is only a girl. Is this the Lord's doing, or am I grown reckless, headlong?*

He looks into Zerel's eyes.

She grins at him.

"I, Zerelda, take thee, Robert . . ." She is half scared to death.

Mary Lindsay presses a swatch of linen to her eyes. James is pale and solemn, the smaller Lindsay girls wide-eyed. . . .

And then it is done.

She has him. Home free.

It's going to be fine. Zerel knows it in her bones.

III

Missouri Light and Dark

1 8 4 2 — 1 8 4 3

June 1842

Come summer, they head for Missouri.

Zerel fights the trip tooth and nail. Robert, exhausted after six months of trying to manage his new bride and his ministerial studies all at once, is nearly defeated. But their two-room lodging in Georgetown is stuffy, cramped, lacking privacies of the most basic kind.

"You don't want to pass the summer *here*, surely?"

"We can go to Uncle James and Aunt Mary," Zerel says.

"They hardly have the room—"

"They'd make room for kin. You know they would."

But Robert, somehow, stands his ground.

"I've never even met your mother."

"You ain't missed much."

"Wouldn't you like to see your brother?"

"Bet he already forgot me."

"You know that's not true, Zerel."

Finally, to his surprise, she gives in. "I could do without

❖

the visit to Mama," she says, "but I do kinda hanker to see Missouri." *The West* is how she thinks of it.

They travel on horseback, almost everything they own in their saddlebags, only Robert's growing library left behind. At night they unroll two blankets, one to cover the ground, one to pull over them, and they sleep under mild skies. The weather blesses most of their passage. When occasional rains fall, they manage to find farm families willing to lodge them for a night.

It is mid-June when they reach Clay County, sticking close to the river, steering a wide path around St. Louis, Jefferson City, Kansas City. "We ain't fit to be seen in town." Zerel sounds downright pleased about it.

The land in western Missouri, green and bragging of plenty, unrolls as far as the eye can see, not quite flat, but winding, rippling like a bolt of fancy goods displayed in haste and pride. Suggestions of hills remind Zerel of Kentucky, making her feel at home. She squanders her attention on endless sky, fields that seem to lay thmselves out with an almost foolish generosity.

Robert, too, is smitten with Missouri at first sight. "Such bounty," he says. "Such freedom."

"If I'd stayed cranky, Robert, like I was at first, would you gone on anyhow, left me behind in Kentucky?"

They are skirting Excelsior Springs, a short ride now to the Thomason place. In a nearby oak a cardinal's wing flickers like a flame.

Robert laughs. "I'd a mind to."

Zerel sniffs. "You'd have missed some of your most highly favored comforts without me, Preacher."

"I would at that."

Blue as blazes, the sky, fields an eye-lacerating green hemmed in by the dusty road. "Wouldn't miss this ride for anything," Zerel says.

"Does that mean I might hope for you to listen to my future suggestions more readily, dear wife?"

"Don't reckon I'd count on it, were I you."

"That's my girl," Robert says.

Oh, it is fine with only the two of them, something blessed fine. But just mix them up with other folks and the whole thing goes awry. Mama is still a regular flibbertigibbet, only foolishness sets worse on her now she's grown plump. Got one new baby already, another coming along from the look of her. "You'd think the six he got without her'd be plenty," says Zerel. "Already used him up one wife."

Robert hushes her, but Lord, it is the only time they can talk in private, at night in their bed.

Thomason's still fat and bossy and not near so smart as he thinks. Can't get out of Mama's house soon enough, Zerel, a married lady herself now, with Mama nattering and fussing over her like Zerel can't hardly be expected to dress herself. And Sallie takes a shine to Robert, goes all flirty with him. "Cryin' shame," Zerel mutters, "growed woman carryin' on so."

Still, summer passes swift and high, so much to see, to do. Robert, long indentured to studies, is only too happy to be given a horse, a hoe, a field. Zerel rides out with him early in the morning, waving off his protests about womanly behavior and pitching in along with him. The soil is rich, well-tended, full of warmth and promise.

Once, during a playful scuffle in the young corn, Robert scoops up a handful of fine black soil and rubs it on his wife's sunburned cheek. To his amazement, she suddenly lies still beneath him, then slowly turns her face, inviting him to dirty the other side. He starts to pull away. She grabs his hand, pries open his fingers, and takes some of the earth into her mouth. Her sigh, when she swallows, is blissfully content, the sound she makes in their bed at night when she is finally ready for sleep. Oh, the appetite in her, the young husband thinks, the will to devour. He is shamed by the passion rising in him as he looks at the muddy corners of her mouth.

Robert pulls away, jumps up and starts brushing at his clothes.

Behind him, on the ground, Zerel is laughing. "You're apt to bust your trouser buttons," she says.

It gives her a powerful appetite, this land. It feeds her wanting while it cuts her down to size. Zerel understands, now, the swell of her mother's belly. There is a fertility here that will not be denied, a vitality that's almost indecent.

In the months since leaving Kentucky, Zerel's brother Jesse has taken on heft. This year, on Thanksgiving, he will turn sixteen. They're so close in age that Zerel can't account for the short time when she didn't know this boy. Yet he's become a stranger, a beautiful golden-colored stranger, preoccupied with learning to carry a man's body, a man's share of work. She finds herself thinking what a wonder, that a creature like him should be born of woman.

"I've missed you," she tries to tell him. And she doesn't realize until she says it how deeply and painfully it is true. Not Uncle James or Aunt Mary, not even Robert can be to her what her brother is, what Grandpappy was, what her daddy might have . . . something in the bones and blood, a likeness a body can't do without, even when they got to.

Jesse flushes. "Reckon I missed you, too, Zerel." He tries to sidle past her out of the barn.

"Jess?"

He pauses, looking miserable.

"Do you wish, ever, that you stayed behind with me?"

"It ain't bad here," he says.

"No, reckon it ain't. Only . . . You still got them coins?" she asks.

Jesse grins, sheepish. "Got thirteen now."

"Getting mighty prosperous. Don't know how you put up with that stepdaddy of ours, though," she says. "I seen shoats with more wit."

Jesse laughs. "He speaks right kindly of you, too, Sis."

"He works you like a dog, don't he?"

"I like to work, Zerel."

"Reckon I do, too. Only I like to have something to show for it, something's my own."

Her brother glances into a filthy stall, reaches for his pitchfork. His pale eyes are peaceable. "It ain't forever," he says.

It feels almost like forever: a delectable, enchanted summer . . . in spite of Mama and Thomason and fits of rain and temper now and then, it seems like it could last. Long days in the fields with Robert, long nights with him in the bed they soon improvise in the barnloft. Zerel sheds her boots and dresses, confiscates an old pair of her stepfather's coveralls, never mind what Mama says about how a wife should look. Zerel goes fishing with Robert and Jesse, rides every horse on the place. Zerel rides bareback, shucks corn, grabs hold of Missouri with her long naked toes.

And thinks later, *Well, surely, it was just too good.* Summer up to no good, turning her head so she wouldn't be on the lookout for winter's treachery.

"This is the goddamn worst thing's ever happened to me!"

Robert looks down where she lies in the bed—not in the barnloft now, in Mama's own room, hers and Thomason's, so sick has she been, poor Zerel.

Please don't curse when folks can hear you right on the other side of the door, the doctor barely gone yet, have some thought for your mother . . . is what Robert wants to say. But he knows better. Besides, she is so pale, so feverish yet.

❖

"It *seems* like the worst," he says. "Seems so to me, too. Do you know how I'll miss you?"

The fever came on the day before they were supposed to start back for Kentucky. Robert has one more year at Georgetown. For a few days Zerel was so sick Robert's leaving was unthinkable. He wondered, they all wondered, whether she would live. But she is strong, Zerel, strong as an ox. She could have told them there wasn't need for worry of such magnitude. Anyway, she wishes she had . . . wishes she *would* die now. It would be a damn sight better to get buried in this luscious ground than to spend a whole year in Mama's house, almost a year, with Robert gone back to Kentucky without her. She tells herself: *It ain't forever.*

"I'll be back before you know it," he says. "It's no use, anyway, distressing yourself. It's bad for you. You've got no strength. The doctor said you couldn't withstand the trip."

"But if you'd just wait a few more days. . . ." Zerel's eyes fill with tears, and Robert tries to remember if he has ever before seen her cry. No, surely he'd recall if he had.

"Days won't do, Zerel. It will be *months* before you are fully recovered. You need someone to look after you, and your mother is good enough to do it."

"Don't go, Robert."

"My dear, you know I am very late as it is."

"I don't care."

"Yes, you do. We both do."

"I know." *Goddamn.*

"When I come back, we'll have enough money to get a place of our own. I'll find a pastorate here and . . ."

Zerel closes her eyes, as if she is sleeping. She is not sleeping. Zerel is reaching down deep, gathering the force of her will. But when she opens her eyes, only Robert is there, Robert who didn't do this and can't change it . . . her husband.

August 1843

She is awed by her own amplitude. Now, with the child growing in her, the abundance of Zerel's flesh suddenly seems purposeful, benign. She glories in her girth, standing with her legs planted far apart as she runs her hand over her belly. If Robert could see me, she thinks.

He came back in early spring, found him a church, leased them a place. Yet most hours of most days Robert isn't there to see; Zerel can do as she pleases. Zerel is growing a child. She carries it high. A boy that means, one of Robert's church ladies told her. None of her affair, old crone. Still, Zerel hopes the old woman knew what she was talking about. Oh, she did, surely she did. Zerel knows, too: it is a boy. Zerel's boy is coming.

And Robert does sometimes see her, catches her hand caressing the mound of her own front, joy and pride naked on her face. "Mighty pleased with yourself, aren't you, Mrs. James?" he says. "Yet do you so much as acknowledge that I had some part in this wondrous turn of events?"

"Oh, I'll allow, Reverend, as you had to do with it. Are you feelin' overlooked? Perhaps I should stand up at church next Sunday and tell your flock, since they seem so all-fired curious about our business, just how—"

"Never you mind."

"Reckon some of them ladies might be downright tickled to hear the details, how you talked Georgetown College into lettin' you out early so you could hightail back here and carry on like a April fool." She is laughing, Robert trying not to; she can always curtail him with his own embarrassment. "Don't believe you were in Clay County two nights before this deed was done." Zerel pats her belly.

She crosses the room to the table where he is sitting, a Bible open before him. "Put your hand there," she says.

Robert looks up, eager, embarrassed, frightened all at once. "Is it kicking? Should it be so soon?"

Zerel takes her husband's hands and presses them to her. He feels the heat, the weight of her, but no movement. Taking one wrist, she moves his right hand down low, below her belly. He looks bewildered. "I don't feel anything different."

"Didn't say you would. Just like your hands on me, is all."

"Zerelda James—"

Awkwardly, she bends down, holding both his wrists now, and molds his fine cool hands to her breasts. When she lets his hands go, they remain there. Her nipples grow taut beneath the thin cambric of her nightdress. Slowly he lowers his head and presses his face to her belly.

"Ain't it a wonder," she says softly. "And my mama said I'd never amount to much."

They call her Mrs. Pastor James. They bring her the fruit of their trees, the flowers of their gardens, preserves from their cellars, cakes from their ovens. They send their sons to help with chores, to chop her wood and carry her water as Zerel grows cumberson with the child. Their husbands come to reassure her when peril is about, fierce weather and rumors of Indians. The pastor is often away on the Lord's work. The ladies of the church see to Mrs. Pastor James, see her through the confinement.

And they are there with her, two of them, when the child announces itself.

Alexander Franklin James dawdles over his arrival, makes it unnecessarily complicated. Zerel, in labor for thirty-seven hours, is so stupified with pain and exhaustion that she hasn't sufficient attention for fear.

Robert, however, is terrified. Mrs. Emmaline Wickens, the local birthing virtuoso, and her sister-in-law, Mrs. Sponable, make every effort to dissuade, dismiss, assure, and shoo the

Reverend away. But Robert will not be detached from his wife's bedside. Even when the ladies are tending to things no gentlemen should see or know about, he is there. Throughout the ordeal, perhaps in part to master his own terror, Robert sings to Zerel—Kentucky mountain songs, Virginia ballads, sweet simple hymns. Once in a while Zerel laughs or sings along with him, which the ladies find unseemly. He speaks tenderly to his mightily laboring wife, as if the other women simply are not there.

More than once Zerel loses consciousness. She curses now and then, but so softly that the ladies take it for prayer.

"I didn't raise a ruckus, did I?" she asks Robert later. "Not in front of . . . them?"

"Never," Robert swears to her. "You never once cried out."

The pain batters her. She is tired, so tired, and she can't remember why. Isn't she supposed to be sleeping?

"Come to bed with me, Robert," she says. She is a great white heat on the bed, and if Robert would just lie with her . . . "Not over *there*," she says sharply. "I need you on top of me," and the ladies turn away, scandalized, and Robert is smiling and red, why? Why on earth is Robert smiling while something he is not bears down, forcing her thighs open and the stabbing pain is coming from there, she knows it, even though it is everywhere, the pain, and she is dying of it and can't even remember for God's sake *why?*

But comes a moment when she does remember—oh, Zerel recollects the whys and cares nothing for the how, even the when is small, and her mighty thighs part until she could hold a continent between her knees, and she bears down and keeps Robert in her eyes, no one else there, no, no one should see this, what she recalls now, it's just between them, Zerel and Robert. She knows why and she bears down and forces her legs to open wider to the wanting of what is struggling to come now . . . tearing . . . bearing down . . . not crying out. . . .

"Please," she whispers, "don't let it be a girl."

"Dreadful creatures, girls," Robert says. Oh, how can he smile that way? "Such weaklings."

"Won't be long now," Mrs. Wickens says.

"Oh, do hush," says Zerel, "Robert, come to bed, I want you so."

"Sh."

It is the second day, the second dawn.

Zerel bears down. Ah, God . . . oh, Jesus. Her mouth opens in a scream without sound, a pain beyond bearing, an ecstasy of wanting. Her tongue is bitten nearly in half, but Zerel doesn't care. The world is between her thighs now and she opens wider, just a little bit more, because there must be room for the tiny head there now, and she shoves the world aside and makes room for it, for him, there.

Frank James is born just in time to witness the sunrise.

"You have a son, praise be," Mrs. Sponable says. "A beautiful baby boy."

"I should hope *so*," Zerel says.

The Reverend's laugh is edged with hysteria. No wonder, all that time carrying on singing with no sleep and his wife's scandalous tongue.

Zerel's tongue is swollen and bloody.

Their boy is a brick-red squirming thing about the size of a small country ham. Mrs. Wickens lifts him by the heels, suspending him for a breathless second before the square coral swatch of a January dawn. Then, with the sound of a cracked whip, she swats his backside none too gently. "Poor little lamb," she says.

"Tell her to keep still," says Zerel.

"There, there." Robert smiles foolishly at Zerel, then looks at his new son. "If you aren't a regular miracle," he says.

The baby screams.

"That's right," says Zerel, "You tell the Preacher."

IV

Tending the Fires

1 8 4 3 — 1 8 4 5

Robert: on a wing and a prayer. Robert on a mule, carrying the Word to far-flung hamlets, the grubby villages and mud-towns the Lord ain't seen fit to visit yet.

Zerel: on her high horse. *You git yourself back here and stay put. I had about enough of this business.*

He has a way about him, Robert, has every half-baked Baptist here to Kansas City eating out of his hand: his flock, pecking him clean like a bevy of crows.

"And what about *us?*" Zerel says.

Robert smiles, oh, Robert is always smiling these days, what with the Lord's work being a boom business. "We are the lilies of His field," he says.

"I ain't one of your crows," says Zerel. "You expect me to swallow that?"

"Crows?" Robert says.

"Never you mind them birds and lilies. Your wife and your boy is the subject here. High time you paid us some mind."

" 'Did you not know I must be about my Father's business?' " He looks to Zerel for a smile and gets the wrath of God.

39

"And what about that place you promised, place of our own so far out of town them church ladies got the gall to call me Sister can't come snoopin' around every afternoon? Just answer me that," Zerel says. Her mouth puckers tight, and her face gets puffy, like a stuffed drawstring bag, Zerel's face.

"Our place . . ." Robert's damnable smile stretches out like angel wings as his wife works up fire and brimstone. "I did promise you such, didn't I?"

"Indeed you did. That was before you started promising everything you got to everybody else," she says. "Before you gave your soul to the New Hope Church and started dividing what's left between two *more* churches, your infernal North Liberty Baptist Association, and some harebrained scheme to found a college. When's *our* account come due, I'd like to know?"

"Bear with me, Zerel."

"I'd say I done that already too long by half."

"Yes." Robert nods. "I suppose you have."

"Then why are you lookin' so pleased with yourself, Preacher? Is that smile crackin' your face in two supposed to humor me?"

"Zerel, I've got a surprise."

"Don't tell me—another church. Another gussied-up hen-house with a pointy little steeple on top?"

Robert laughs. "A chicken coop is involved, I confess."

Her look is hard as nails, yet a flicker of hope betrays her. *I've been letting her starve,* Robert thinks.

"Zerel," he says. "I got our place. We take over the deed next week."

Goddamn: two hundred and seventy-five acres of Missouri all her own. Zerel's fingers itch, her mouth waters, she can't sit still . . . beside herself, Zerel, plumb beside herself.

"It's not new," Robert cautions her, "not large. Nothing fancy."

A creek is a stone's throw away. "It'll do," says Zerel. *A creek.*

The cabin, built of logs, squats in a cleft backed up by a grove of young pines. Sturdy and plain as a chunk of Kentucky limestone, that house, like something the earth coughed up. Two fair-sized rooms. A chimney rises between them, asserting itself against the slate winter sky. A barn. A smokehouse. Coops. Zerel barely looks, yet takes it all in. A cabin out back. Zerel is down on her knees, studying the soil, frozen solid. She scratches, she sniffs like a hound. Zerel would, were Robert not watching, roll over on her back and howl.

"Reckon it'll do," she says, "for starters."

She scrambles to her feet, gazing past the hand her husband offers, out toward the western pasturage. She sees a sea of oats yet to be planted. She can feel the rich, oh, almost sickening sinful-rich earth between her teeth, in her throat. Zerel swallows hard.

"Don't you want to see inside the house?"

He's ready to laugh; she knows he is. Robert always knows what's in her. Robert can taste the dirt in Zerel's mouth.

"Inside don't hardly matter," she says.

"I know," he says. "I know."

Plain, hard, dry as a rusk, that house. Naked log walls, a floor of mud. Just what Zerel expects. "Just what I wanted," she says. The hearth is broad and homely and rough, door sturdy, windows stingy. There are no ornaments, but a few rude furnishings—a table, a pie safe—have been left behind for the taking. An iron poker leans in the corner. A battered tin cup lies sideways on the sill. The kitchen fireplace is clogged with ash.

Zerel stands in the doorway, clutching the jamb. She is trembling. "Beautiful," she says. "So beautiful, Robert." She is not looking at the room, but out from the house to the southwest corner of the yard, where a coffee bean tree shudders in the wind.

"The bedroom's back here," Robert is saying. As if she couldn't find her own way through a two-room house. *Her own house.* Zerel turns slowly from the door and follows him. "If we put the bed here, we'll see out first thing on summer mornings with the shutters open. And that trap up there? There's a fine loft, room for plenty of children once they get big enough to climb a ladder."

Zerel smiles vaguely. "Frank," she says.

"Children," Robert repeats, touching her arm. "All kinds of room up there."

Zerel is at the window then, trying to pry loose the shutter, nailed tight against winter.

"All kind of room," she murmurs, her long fingers seeking a chink in the rough-hewn planks.

She is thinking of curtains, Robert imagines. Dreaming of the things she should have, the small strokes of beauty and comfort a woman craves about her. He really shouldn't leave her alone so much. She's right . . . *things will be different here. . . .*

But he cannot, not always, tell what is in his young wife's mind. Robert James imagines white muslin, delicately hemmed, drawn back upon dawn. . . .

Zerel pictures a curtain of green grain fluttering in the wind, walls of corn, a carpet of beans and alfalfa. *Maybe we'll even coax cotton out of this earth hereabouts,* she is thinking. *Some say we could . . . and an orchard.* Greenings, Zerel thinks, russets and pippins, Jonathans and Limber Twigs, branches brought low with fruit, bowing to harvesttime.

"I'll lay an oak floor for you," Robert says.

Zerel's feet are rooted to the frozen mud floor, as if she means never to relinquish it.

". . . finish the walls in here with batten board . . ."

His voice is far behind her. Zerel is moving toward the open doorway, her eyes long gone from the house. "Suits me fine like it is," she says. "It will serve."

———

Crossing the narrow threshold to sleep takes her no time at all. Trying to slow sleep down, to savor and survey her days, Zerel counts. She counts in acres and furrows, bushels and bales and head . . . all she and Robert have, all they are, what they have come to, an embarrassment of riches.

Zerel counts: 275 acres, 30 sheep, a yoke of oxen, 3 horses, a mule, 6 cows. More chickens every day. A dozen hogs, more or less, depending on the season, the state of the smokehouse. Seven slaves. A hive of bees. A son . . . a boy to love and tend these fields alongside them. Their boy.

And then there are the buildings, the house and the barn and the cabin out back where the slave family . . .

And then Zerel is sleeping and can't count, can't reckon with the plenty that is hers, hers and Robert's and Frank's. The James homestead, the James place, out beyond Kearney.

So much in the palm of her hand, so much of her wanting filled now, Zerel scarcely remembers how to dream. But that is what the children are for, Frank and the one she carries now, carries high. Zerel is riding high, and dreaming for the children's sake, dreaming of more children who will come as all good things come: to Zerel who waits and Robert who prays, sleeping sound at night in the tight-fisted cabin of her dreams.

Frank is a whiz. Oh, just a mite yet, to be sure, and not what you'd call a lovely-looking child. Ain't walking yet, acts like he don't care if he ever says a word, hardly ever smiles. Got a start on his mama's nose. But he's smart. Zerel can tell by the way his eyes follow her around the cabin. He's figuring her every move. When she tickles him under the chin, he fixes a look on her that says, "Behave now." A baby who brooks no nonsense, Frank.

And stubborn? The boy's stubborn as a mule. Doesn't eat or sleep unless he's a mind to.

"Takes after his mama, I guess," says Robert.

"Cross a brood mare with a jackass, a mule's what you got to expect." Zerel smooths her apron over her rising belly. "Reckon it's clear which of us is which."

Sunday morning. Snow is piled past the church steps, drifted near up to the windows on the north side. Two dozen men and women huddle with their children in the first few pews. Robert looks down and sees stern, pale, expectant faces appealing to him through the clouds of their own frozen breath. Craving what no man has to give.

"And the way shall be made smooth," Robert says.

Zerel, little Frank propped up on her lap, sits alone, four or five rows back from the rest of the congregation. Her face, ruddy and bright, is almost disreputable against the stark backdrop of the rude church, its wan occupants.

She looks straight at him, her husband up there on the pulpit, his blue fingers gripping the spine of a worn Bible. Something in her eyes, something like a dare, makes Robert forget for a moment what he means to say.

"The way *shall,* the Book says, be made *smooth.*" He struggles, stalling for time. He lifts his hands, as if appealing to Heaven.

Zerel is staring.

Someone coughs.

"Smooth," Robert murmurs.

Zerel's eyes narrow. He can almost hear her:

Prove it.

"Why do you look at me that way in church?"

"Look at you what way?"

"Like you don't believe a word I'm saying."

"Maybe I don't," she says.

Robert sighs.

"Oh, it ain't the faith I find so hard," Zerel says. "I reckon

I got that, even if I can't find the words for it like you do. It's my patience won't hold up, Robert. All these folks thinkin' like they own us."

"I *am* theirs, Zerel, in a way."

"Well, I ain't," she snaps.

"And I don't expect you to be." He takes her hand. "I just wish you could . . . I don't know, *bristle* less, perhaps."

She makes a sound of disgust and pulls her hand away.

"Can't make no silk purse outa me, Preacher. Try, you'll only wear yourself out."

"I'm not asking you to transform yourself, Zerel. Just allow people to befriend you."

"Befriend me? Them stiff-necked ladies can't abide me."

"That's not true. They feel you can't abide them."

"Maybe smarter than they look, some of them."

Robert shakes his head slowly. "A little Christian charity . . ."

"Oh, I'm just fooling. No need to make a sermon out of it."

" 'Love thy neighbor,' " he says. "It's the simplest commandment of all."

"I'd find it a good bit simpler if my neighbor kept her nose where the Lord intended. If it ain't in my business, it's up in the air. A wonder that Miz Shively don't fall flat on her face walking past me."

"Now wasn't it Mrs. Shively who was by here only last week, bringing us some of her fresh-made sausage?"

"That sausage was just an excuse to come snooping."

"Noticed you didn't mind eating it." Robert laughs. "Mrs. Shively's 'excuse' was mighty tasty."

"It was at that." Zerel grins, "Wisht I could say as much for her sister's chow-chow. Kept me up for a week."

"And you kept *me* up for a week."

"So I did, Preacher. But that wasn't no indigestion I was inflictin' on you in there." Zerel inclines her head toward the bedroom.

Robert tries to look stern. At twenty-seven, he still blushes. "I'm a regular angel at night, ain't I?" Zerel says.

"And a devil by daylight."

"Maybe we should have us a little nap, Preacher. See if I can't disprove this theory you got about me."

"They don't know you at all, Zerel. That's all I'm asking you to do, give them a chance to know you."

Zerel, almost eight months pregnant, raises the front of her apron. "I give you that chance, and look what you done."

"Robert?"

It is late, he's almost asleep, thought she was, too.

Beside him in the bed, Zerel's body throws off a wonderful heat, a scent like grass. He rolls over and touches her face in the dark.

"What is it, Zerel? Are you all right?" His voice is gentle.

"How come you got to go now? You know I need you here."

"The revivals are in the summer, dear. This is my work. I can't alter the seasons."

Her voice is more bewildered than angry. "Well, neither can I. The child will come. . . ."

"And I'll be back by then. I promise you."

She is quiet for a moment, until he nearly believes she's asleep again.

"You know what I said to you that time, when you ask why I look at you somehow in church?"

"I remember." Oh, Robert remembers, all right, her words like a chill he can't rid his bones of. But faith is not a thing a man can ask of someone, he thinks . . . not even his wife, especially not his wife. He strokes her hair, waiting.

"It wasn't right, what I said. It ain't that I don't believe, Robert. I do, mostly. Maybe I just don't care like you do."

"But, Zerel—"

46

"Let me say, Robert. Let me say this one time. Then if you don't want to hear, I'll never say it again."

"Go on."

"When I see you up there, when I hear the beautiful way you got in moving folks to be something . . . well, something finer than they know how to be on their own, what I'm thinking is, you ought to be somewhere better than these little no-'count churches. Somewheres more folks could hear you tell things a body needs to . . . to make their way." He hears her take a deep breath. "In *this* world, Robert. Not the next."

She is trying so hard to be gentle, reasonable, kind. Robert hears effort in her voice, feels it in her rigid body. She doesn't mean to hurt, diminish him . . . that is what hurts and diminishes him so.

"Zerel," he whispers, "this is God's work I am doing."

"I know."

"What better work could I possibly do, what better place than where people need me?"

"Ain't it all God's work, though? I mean, when we're out in our fields, planting something in His earth . . ."

"Yes, that is God's work, too, surely it is But to harvest souls for the Lord . . ."

"Don't reckon I'll ever be quite able to take it in," Zerel says.

"This work is like a fire. I don't ask that you burn with me, Zerel. Only stand near . . . beside me."

"You know I will," she says softly. "Only I reckon you got to forgive me if I look at you that way in church sometimes. I see how you shine up there, and I swear, you might be Governor, Senator . . . you ever think Missouri might need your fire more than the Lord does?"

The moon slips from behind a cloud. Faint silver light filters into the small room between the open shutters. Zerel sees Robert's smile, tired and sad. "Maybe one of these boys of ours will choose that path," he says, taking her into his arms. He feels the beating of her heart strong against his chest.

"You reckon this one's another boy?"

"As sure as the Lord allows a man to be."

"Let's hope he favors his daddy in disposition," Zerel says.

"But not in vocation?"

Zerel sighs, "Reckon this one'll have his own fire, with or without our say-so."

Mid-July: just a few more weeks, the child will come. Zerel's breasts fill with milk. Zerel feels each hint and nuance her body whispers now—the baby is lowering himself, readying himself, readying her. A sharp ache lodges in the small of her back. Her legs swell. Her breasts, so heavy she sometimes feels she cannot straighten her spine, are taut and tender, overfilled . . . already too full, Zerel. Full to bursting.

Robert is home for only short stays, then off to preach again. Zerel, managing without him, is exhausted, yet sleep eludes her when she needs it most. She is so tired now that to walk, to see, require an almost inhuman self-mastery.

On the morning Robert is to leave for the Kansas Territory, Zerel lies beside him, fully awake, waiting for dawn. She has been sleepless for hours, flattened against the lumpish ticking by the pain, the weight of her breasts.

Robert is close, on his side, facing her. His breath is even and shallow, his sleep profound.

Suddenly she cannot bear it another moment, her fullness. She moves carefully onto her side, closer to Robert, her head above him. She unfastens the tiny mother-of-pearl buttons at the front of her nightdress. Then she lies very still, listening to her husband's breathing, yes, he is still asleep.

Very slowly, very carefully, she cups her swollen right breast, raising the nipple to his mouth. He sighs softly, then presses his lips together. Lightly, ever so lightly, she traces his lower lip with the nipple's hardening tip.

He sighs again, deeply. Zerel holds still, breathless. His breath is warm on her skin. A fragment of a smile hovers on his mouth. But his eyes are closed, his breathing light, he is sleeping. . . .

Again she nudges Robert's lips. They part. Then his mouth is fastened to her, sucking, and she feels the milk begin to flow out of her and into him. She hears him swallow.

The tightness, the fullness begins to ease. Finally Zerel pulls gently away, refastens her gown. She rolls away from Robert and she sleeps.

When she wakes, Zerel feels shriveled and cold.

Beside her, her husband blinks awake, innocent as the new day. His mouth is tender, his eyes untroubled.

"I hate to leave you," he says.

But there is gladness in his step as he moves from the bed and makes ready to go.

"Right nice of you to come by," Zerel says. She steps reluctantly back from the doorframe and motions to the visitor to enter.

"I was just goin' past," Clara Shively says, "and I thought to myself, why these must be dim days indeed for Mrs. Pastor James, this dry heat and her time drawin' near and all." Her eyes sweep the cabin side to side, top to bottom. In the corner of the kitchen, beside an empty washtub, little Frank sleeps on the bare planks of the new oak floor. His face is dirty, his thumb in his mouth. Mrs. Shively lowers her voice.

"Figured you might be glad of some company, dear."

"Right kindly," Zerel says.

"Don't reckon the Reverend's back yet from Lawrence?"

"I expect him tomorrow."

The old woman is inching her way farther inside, clearly

❖

awaiting the offer of a chair and refreshment. Zerel is damned . . . damned if she will, never mind what Robert . . .

"Please sit down," she says. "I got some cold tea."

Clara Shively lowers herself into one of the two chairs at the table, looking triumphant. "Don't discommode yourself, Sister."

"No bother."

"Reckon it must be hard on you, the Pastor havin' to be away for so many revival meetings just now."

Zerel turns her back, begins looking for the only glass. ". . . Lord's work," she mutters.

"How's that?"

"Work of the Lord," Zerel says loudly.

"Yes, indeed."

Ain't that just how they are, Zerel thinks, getting you to say what they want so's they can act indifferent about it.

"Reckon you know," the woman says, "Miz Wickens and Miz Sponable gone to St. Louis? Left yesterday."

"No." Zerel's voice goes weak, uncertain. "No, I didn't know."

"Funeral." Mrs. Shively nods, as if approving the circumstance. "A brother, I think it was."

"I'm sorry to hear it."

"Figured you would be. Guess that puts you in a fix, them bein' gone for a couple of weeks at least. When was it you're due?"

Oh, she didn't want them hovering about her anyhow, old buzzards, circling her body like they're just waiting for her to . . .

"About now," says Zerel. "Any day."

"Well, don't you worry none. Miz Shively's gonna be right here to help you."

"Don't reckon I need help. I done it before."

Clara Shively laughs humorlessly. "Sister, ain't a woman born don't need help."

Late afternoon and the heat is stupifying. Bees drone in entanglements of wood sage and fogfruit, ground cherry and touch-me-not along the low creek bank. The false lettuce is tall and stooped. Bright blue-violet blossoms wink between the toothy leaves of Venus's looking-glass. The birds sound lethargic, as if intimidated by the sun's glare.

Zerel slips into a small oval clearing above where the creek forms something resembling a pool. There has been little rain these past weeks, and the water is miserly, muddy. Still, it has to be cool, cooler than the hushed, relentless air.

Zerel unbuttons her loose gray dress—more sack than dress, she thinks, nothing else would cover the mound she's growed into—and pulls it over her head. She is already barefoot, and naked beneath the dress.

She stands in the clearing for a moment, stock-still. A raven rustles a branch above her, gives one short, dazed-sounding cry. Then it is so quiet Zerel can hear herself breathing, ragged and slow. She squints at the sun—a big eye staring down on her, bold as brass.

Resting her hands low on her belly, she walks down and squats at the edge of the creek, her heels against a smooth rock. She dips her cupped hand into the water: lukewarm.

Handful after handful, she scoops up the water and pours it over herself—face and neck, arms and legs, breasts and belly. Her broad thighs are pressed tight together. The water pools there. Struggling to keep her balance, without rising, Zerel forces her thighs apart and the water runs down between them and falls to the ground.

When the water no longer seems even a little cooler than her skin, Zerel stands and climbs awkwardly from the creek bed to the level ground of the clearing. The grass there is sparce and tough. She spreads her dress out flat, then lies on it as if it is a blanket.

She lies on her back, her eyes closed, listening. The eerie silence of the afternoon is the very sound of heat.

Zerel feels the heat fondling, lapping, then penetrating, possessing her almost like Robert does. With the soles of her feet feeling their way along the rough ground, she raises her knees, then parts them slowly, opening, offering herself to the sun. Her hands curve, reach, enclose, lift her breasts. Zerel's breasts rise into the stroking of the sun. So heavy and hot . . . hot. Zerel is nearly asleep. Her thumbs move slowly, tenderly, caressing her nipples, measuring the fullness, the almost unbearable glorious fullness . . . she opens her thighs wider to take in the sun, and her breasts are . . .

Then she is cold, so cold. A cloud has covered the sun.

Zerel rises, shivering, and struggles into her gray dress. She stumbles toward the house, to the sound of a child's ravenous screams.

V

Dittany and Doves

1 8 4 5

"No two ways about it," Zerel says. "His name is Robert. Robert James."

Her husband, holding the hour-old infant, smiles. "Very well. But you know then, what I'll insist upon for our first daughter . . ."

"Over my dead body." Zerel, exhausted, shuts her eyes. "So very small," she says softly.

"Babies usually are," Robert says.

"Frank wasn't."

"You've just forgotten. Try to sleep now."

"So small," she whispers.

"Nothing more than the season," Mrs. Shively says. The woman comes by every day. "This heat. He's a mite on the puny side, I'll grant you, but—"

Zerel clenches her jaw, eyes casting a threat across the room at Robert: *Get her out of here quick or I'll . . .*

"May we offer you a glass of buttermilk, ma'am?" Robert says. "Maybe with a piece of this nice cornbread you brought us?"

Zerel turns her back on the woman, on Robert, and bends

to the cradle. The infant is like marble, like the cool, smooth, pale marble in the chapel at Saint Catherine's. A bluish white with faint mottlings of lilac and rose. The down on his soft skull is gold, surrounding his pinched face like a halo's shadow, nothing like Frank at all . . . so small . . . he worries her. . . .

She doesn't hear Mrs. Shively coming up behind her, doesn't know the woman's there until she feels the clawlike hand on her arm. "Be right as rain in no time, Sister. Don't fret."

Zerel looks at her coolly. Small and tough as a prairie chicken, that woman, she thinks. Her voice disturbs the quiet like the hollow sound of someone blowing into an empty bottle.

"Won't serve no good to coddle him," Mrs. Shively says.

The child is a month old when the fever comes upon him. His skin turns a scorched scarlet color, and his cries are sharp and thin. He will not take Zerel's milk. He will not stop crying. A crust of bright yellow mucus forms perpetually around his eyes, his nose, his mouth.

Zerel dissolves a lump of alum in a cup of sweet boiled milk, making a poultice for the baby's eyes. He screams when she touches him, then abruptly quiets, his eyes closing. His eyes are crusted white. He looks dead.

August, thank the Lord, the ditanny is in bloom. Zerel leaves Robert with the babies and rushes to the woodlands northeast of the cabin, where the flimsy purple flowers grow low and thick on square tough stems. She returns with a tangle of flowery branches. The scent of mint clings to her hands and the dark cloth of her dress.

As best she can, Zerel dries the leaves and blossoms before a scathing unseasonable fire. Robert, pallid and wet, watches. They are both streaming with sweat. Little Frank, not yet three, has been sent off into exile with Mrs. Shively.

When the dittany tea has been brewed and cooled, Zerel

pries the baby's mouth open and slides droplets of the cloudy liquid from her fingers onto his tongue. He whimpers, struggling weakly, then vomits up a greenish clot of phlegm.

Zerel weeps.

Robert goes for a doctor.

Night falls and still Robert is not back.

The child, soundless now, still burns.

Zerel holds him, standing in the doorway of the cabin. Listening for the sound of someone coming up the road. The air is heavy and hot, stirred only by a light percussion of cicadas. Holding the babe is like cradling glowing embers to herself, branding her useless laden breasts.

The old slave woman Louisa once told Zerel how a child who died of fever was brought back to life. A dove was split open with a knife. Its heart still beating, the bird was laid on the dead child's breast. As the dove's heart expired, the child's heart began to beat again.

"Who killed the bird?" Zerel asked.

"Why, the baby's mama, of course," Louisa said. "Aint nothin' any natural mother wouldn't do, child."

Standing in the doorway with her newborn son heavy in her arms, Zerel weeps for want of one small bird, a living sacrifice.

When Robert returns, leading the doctor through the dark maze of midnight, the baby Robert is dead.

Zerel sits on the kitchen floor beside the cradle, dry-eyed and silent. The child is clutched to her, close to Zerel's hectic face. Day breaks before she will let Robert take their son from her arms.

The dawn is bluish-white, mottled with lavender and rose, spattered with gold. The heat has not abated. Zerel has not spoken a word.

A wastrel profusion, the dittany, clinging to September as if it were June. Wild geese reel across the sky, yet the days remain warm, a libelous summer. The night air, cooling, is filled with a fragrance very much like mint, only more biting, bitter. Zerel, like the creek, is silent and dry.

Her face goes gaunt and gray; her mouth is a withholding. She will not eat, will not even try, as if sticking to some hard bargain, some formal rate of exchange, words for food. Neither does she give or take, Zerel. There is no commerce with her. Her eyes, darkening, fasten on some hopeless inner distance. An emptiness. Her waist, long concealed by the child, emerges. Then her ribs. Like the creek bed, Zerel.

But she is not empty, not dry. Her breasts continue to fill, to leak, to burst with the needless milk until her nipples crack and bleed.

There are measures, Zerel knows, that might be taken. Creams and ointments, implements and practices. She might be relieved of the leakage, the overflow. She tries to recall whispered woman talk: old Louisa bending to Aunt Mary, taking the white child, soft and fresh, in her rough gnarled hands. Dark as coffee beans, the nigger woman's hands and female secrets like magic.

Then Zerel imagines Robert's hands on her, Robert's mouth . . . but she will not be touched, Zerel, will not touch herself. She lies on her bed in the room shuttered against the sun, pulling the hot blankets up to her shoulders so no one might see stains, the milk that leaks but will not leave her.

"Just try to eat a little something, my dear." Robert's voice gentle, but his eyes wild. "Some bread, some broth . . ."

Zerel's body flattens itself below the comforter as she turns her face to the wall.

There is something murderous in her grief, Robert thinks. Her dreams, fragmented, urgent, are an affliction now:

children, always children, running up ahead, catching up behind, enclosing her all around, their faces round and white
as snowy owls. . . .

Zerel is surrounded. The children run nameless, shrill, full
of hunger and wanting and warning.

She chases them: *What do you want?*, yet the children are
always following her. They pluck the hairs from her head and
toss them to the wind. Zerel's hair silver, and the wind weaves
a nest for the children, a noose . . . not for the children, no,
a shroud . . . a winding cloth for Zerel . . . what is left of Zerel.

They pluck out her eyes.

Every corner is blind.

They sing to her, the children, a sweetness in the dark.

Her skull is naked, her body a mountain, crumbling, and
still she runs after them, scattering bread crumbs of comfort,
shaking the salt of wanting on their tails . . . *there now, there
now.* . . .

Their cries pierce her skin, peel it away: *Mamaw! Mamaw!*

Zerel hurtles through the air in a slashing of wings, of
claws. Her skin falls away in shreds. Her limbs are torn from
her. Caught in the high branches of an iron tree: Zerel, a
cage of bone.

She is pried open.

Zerel's heart drops to the ground like a windfall apple and
is devoured by the birds.

Zerel is eaten alive, torn limb from limb by the dreams,
the children, the wanting. . . .

She speaks only in her sleep, soft, desperate callings from
inside an assault of snow-colored birds:

"Small . . . so small . . ."

It cannot go on. Robert listens to Zerel's dream cries, her
long mute days, and thinks, *she will die this way.*

At last, in October, Robert takes Zerel to Kansas City.

She is pallid, limp, unresisting. Zerel is *docile:* Robert is horrified.

He takes her to his mother's second cousin, Miss Louella Kinney, who is known for her ways with healing, with sorrow, with illnesses of spirit. Robert barely knows this kinswoman of his—she visited once when he was a boy in Kentucky, once again for his mother's funeral. Robert hasn't seen Miss Louella since he was nine.

Within the James family Cousin Louella is regarded as more than a little peculiar, perhaps even harmlessly mad. Her faith and gentleness, however, are legendary. She has heard of her cousin's misfortune and written to offer her vague help. Robert accepts because he hasn't the slightest idea where else to go. Beside him on the buckboard seat, Zerel sways perilously and keeps her eyes on the floor.

Miss Louella occupies a bleak, narrow, two-story house on the northern edge of the city. Her street drags like a muddy sash along the river. A sagging porch looks northwest, upon Kansas. Tradesmen's carts move sluggishly through but do not linger in Miss Louella's neighborhood.

She is, Robert thinks, the sort of woman whose kindness is the only thing to make a lasting impression. Even when you are looking right at her, her features seem to dissolve. She is perhaps sixty years old, yet unlined, unbent, uninitiated. A brown crepe dress hangs limp on her bony frame. Her graying hair is confined in a snood, tiny coral beads trapped in its webbing.

"Dear child," she says to Zerel.

As the old woman reaches up to touch his wife's hollowed cheek, Robert waits for Zerel to flinch, perhaps even to swat Miss Louella's hand. He starts toward them to intervene. *She does not bear touching. . . .* But his cousin lifts her other hand, waving off interference. She is looking steadily into Zerel's eyes. "My poor dear child."

Zerel's gaze is riveted on the unfamiliar face, so close,

raised to hers, waiting, knowing. She does not seem to feel or notice the hand that rests on her. For a moment Zerel looks as if she is trying to decide something very complicated. She blinks. Then she darts to the corner of Miss Louella's dim parlor, folding her arms across her chest.

The ocher parlor walls are cluttered with crude pastel drawings of prairie scenes and animals. Zerel, hugging herself tightly, studies one. Her intensity is palpable across the room.

Robert, embarrassed, opens his mouth to speak, but Miss Louella shakes her head.

Zerel's voice, tucked into the corner, sounds childlike, frail. "Old nigger woman name of Louisa told me once if you dry jackrabbit's turd and make a tea of it, fever will break in no time."

"Zerel—" Robert is flushed, frantic.

Miss Louella, however, seems completely unaware of him now. Unshocked. She crosses the room and touches Zerel's shoulder.

Slowly Zerel turns around. "But where was I to find me a jackrabbit?" she says. "Where on earth . . ."

"I know," the old woman says. "I know, child."

The day after Robert goes, a doctor comes. He is very young and tall, very much like Zerel, only his shoulders are not broad and his eyes are blue. He looks sad and lost and afraid, and he speaks to her slowly and kindly. She does not hear his words, but she hears the sound of him and the sound tells her better than words that the doctor will not hurt her and he doesn't try to touch her; he just talks. She lets him and listens to his sound as she sits in the straight chair in the corner of the flower-papered room upstairs in back where Miss Louella says she can stay as long as she likes, not a soul to bother her if only she'll eat a mouthful of something now and then.

The doctor keeps talking. "I know of your sorrow," he

says. "Miss Louella has told me, I hope you don't mind. She thought I might be able to help."

Zerel reaches over and pulls the coverlet from the bed and wraps herself in it without leaving her chair.

"I understand your silence, you know. I won't try to talk you out of it." He smiles, and Zerel stares at his face without expression. His smile wavers, then dies like a candle flame; still he goes on talking.

When the doctor has run out of words, he seems sadder than ever. His eyes have turned grayish in the room where everything is the pale pink of evening primroses. Zerel looks at him and sees that he is somehow very beautiful, not like a man is beautiful, like Robert. The doctor is beautiful more like a child: his softness could so easily get crushed and spoiled.

Zerel pulls the faded rose coverlet higher, covering her arms. Her wrists press down hard and she feels the milky dampness, soaked through her chemise into her shirtwaist.

"What is your name?" she says suddenly.

"Dr. Aldrich," he says. "Benjamin Aldrich."

"Benjamin." Zerel's voice is uncertain. "Like in the Bible, David's friend?"

His eyes are on her, just on her face, the rest of her gone, and his eyes are cool and sweet like witch hazel on skin inflamed by a surfeit of sun. "My brother's name is David." His smile is so frail. *He knows about terrible things,* Zerel thinks.

"It's good to have a brother." She thinks of Jesse, the manly muscle of his neck, skin the color of toast. Her brother: foreign in his contentment, yet known to her blood.

Dr. Aldrich nods. "It's good to have a friend," he says. "It would please me to be your friend."

"I thought you was my doctor."

"Yes, that." He bows his head. "But doctors don't understand as much as they think they do. Friends understand more."

"Maybe so," Zerel says. "Don't guess I'd rightly know."

The small room is dim but not dark. The dark seems to move a little way away, outside somewhere. Zerel feels like sleeping.

"You're tired," Benjamin Aldrich says.

She looks at him, struggling to keep her eyes open.

"Come." He holds out his hand to her. She studies it for what seems like a very long while. "You lie down now. I'll come again tomorrow."

She takes his hand. His fingers are so fine, with pale soft down above the knuckles, skin you can see through, see the bones . . . so easily crushed. . . .

"Tomorrow?"

And then Zerel is sleeping in the cool white space where grief cannot, for the moment, find her.

Zerel finds something in the silence. What is it? *A place,* she thinks. *A place where I can stay.*

Miss Louella is good. She does not try to take Zerel from the place she has found. Sometimes Zerel smiles at her. And she tries to eat a bit. She does not taste what she swallows. Her mouth is dry. But the food is not bad, not nearly as bad as losing her place in the silence. Zerel eats to keep the peace.

The doctor comes nearly every afternoon. Benjamin. Miss Louella brings him up to Zerel's room, taps softly on the door, leads him in, then leaves him there.

The doctor talks to Zerel, does not touch her, does not give her medicine, does not seem to mind if she does not answer. She wonders if he knows she does not hear the words he says to her. She likes the sound of him. His voice comes into the place where she can stay and does not make her leave it or lose it, does not disturb the quiet.

The doctor does not talk to Zerel about herself or the baby or Robert or death or God. Sometimes he doesn't even ask how she's feeling. She likes that about Benjamin very much, how he sometimes looks at her first thing when he comes into her room and his eyes can tell how she's feeling and so he does not ask. Sometimes she smiles at him.

Benjamin tells Zerel things about himself, things he has done and seen and thought about. The sound of his voice is soft, but the edges of his words are sharp. He is not Missouri-born, not Kentucky either. No, from Boston, he tells her, in the East. He studied to be a doctor at Harvard College, in Boston. Then he got into trouble of some kind because of things he thought, and then he went to Italy, where there were beautiful paintings and green hills, and then to Austria, where there was beautiful music, and then to England, where it rained for a whole month and he got homesick and came back to Boston and found it wasn't his home anymore, and then he came to Kansas City because his uncle was a doctor there and said he would help him and he did.

Sometimes when Zerel is feeling very safe in her place, she comes to the edge of it to ask Benjamin a question.

"What were their names?" she says.

He looks startled. "Names?"

"The songs you heard in that place."

He smiles. "Oh, Vienna."

"That ain't the place you said."

"Austria?"

"That's it. What songs? Did you dance?"

When he laughs, Zerel cringes, pulling back inside the place. But then Benjamin speaks of symphonies, madrigals, concerti, and Zerel can't conceive of them, yet savors the sounds of the words on his tongue, words with soft edges.

"Say that again."

"Cello," he says.

"Chella?"

"Cello. And listen to this: *diminuendo*. Can there be a more marvelous word than that?"

She smiles at him. "What does it mean?"

"Fading away to nothing." His eyes dim.

"But why didn't you dance?"

"I watched people dance," he says. "Surely you've heard the songs . . ." His eyes bright again, he hums a Viennese waltz.

Zerel shakes her head.

"You would like it," he tells her, "such music."

"With the law?" she says, days later.

"What?"

"The trouble you got into at Boston, was it with the law?"

"No, with the doctors, a hospital . . . my family, too, you might say."

"What did you do?"

"I didn't do anything. I just didn't keep still."

"Been in that kind of trouble myself," Zerel says.

Benjamin laughs. "You? I'd say you keep uncommonly still."

"Nossir, not always."

Then Benjamin Aldrich starts telling Zerel how he got notions while he was studying to be a doctor that people sometimes take sick of the spirit and it's really not their fault, hardly different from sickness of the body, only other folks act like it's sin instead of sickness. . . .

"Folks'll do that," Zerel says softly.

The doctor blinks. "What?"

"Put the name of sin to what they can't understand."

He nods slowly, staring at her. "And sometimes it's belief in sin that's the sickness."

Zerel turns away, her gaze darting to the window as if she needs to escape from what the doctor knows, what he may see in her. Behind her, his voice unwinds like silken thread, telling how in Boston there was something like a trial with a doctor for the judge and doctors for the jury, doctors who bore witness against him, Benjamin, because he said a murder could come of sickness, not sin, so they told him he couldn't be a doctor anymore, and he wouldn't keep still even then, and so his own father, also a doctor, said to him: you are not my son. . . .

But he can't do that, Zerel thinks. Your child is still and always your child, no matter what he does, even if he has . . . *no.*

Zerel listens to the sound of the doctor's sad voice and watches the October light wane in a red-gold branch that brushes up against her window.

"Are you trying to save souls?" she asks suddenly.

Benjamin Aldrich shakes his head. "Just to heal them . . . so they can save themselves."

"Maybe some souls don't care to be saved," she says.

The places where her breasts cracked and bled have healed, the scabs fallen away, leaving faint white scars. But the milk does not stop. December, January, and the milk yet flows, and the branch outside the window is bare and black and icy.

Robert comes to visit at Christmastime. He brings Zerel a package wrapped in thin white paper and tied with silk cording of deep rich green the color of pine boughs. The present is a dainty reticule, petit point, black strewn with pink flowers not much larger than pinheads. The brass clasp is shaped into fancy scrollwork.

Zerel sets the purse on her lap, on top of the coverlet she has wrapped around her. She looks at it. She doesn't look at Robert. She doesn't want to hurt his feelings. She wishes he would go away.

Robert talks to her. He talks and talks. His voice is like Benjamin's, gentle, kind. Robert's words have soft edges, Kentucky. But she wants him to keep still, wants him to go away, because he is trying to pull her from her place with his talk about little Frank and the church and the homeplace and Zerel: *we wish you would come home.*

"Not a soul to bother you," Miss Louella promised. But

Robert's is a soul to bother Zerel. She would see it plain in his eyes, all she means to forget, if . . . she cannot look at him.

And she is afraid he is going to touch her. What if Robert wants to be her husband and then he would see how the milk still . . . why doesn't he touch me?

But he doesn't.

There is a cherry chiffonier in the corner of Zerel's room, with a small time-darkened mirror in a gilt oval frame hanging above it. Below the window is a cherry washstand, carved to resemble the chiffonier. A large pitcher and washbowl of white china sit on the washstand. Each evening when she brings Zerel's supper up, Miss Louella's hired girl, Bess, takes the pitcher away. Each morning before breakfast she brings the pitcher back, filled with hot water.

Zerel does not like to bathe. Mostly she just washes her face and hands. Zerel doesn't like to take off her clothes. She doesn't want to see herself, touch herself.

But when she can smell the stale, sour smell of her own body, then Zerel supposes Miss Louella and the doctor will smell her, too. Then she washes quickly as she can, keeping her eyes closed, her head turned away.

She wonders if the girl tells Miss Louella about the stains on the front of Zerel's clothes.

It is late January. Miss Louella comes to Zerel's room after lunch. "I must go out this afternoon, and I have sent Bess to town for something. Will you be all right here by yourself, Zerelda?"

Zerel smiles.

Miss Louella looks worried. "Well, then . . ."

"What about the doctor?" Zerel says.

She still speaks so seldom that the sound of the girl's voice startles the old woman. "Oh, my word, yes. What about him?

I shall leave him a note on the door to explain. He can come again tomorrow." She looks closely at Zerel. "Will that be all right?"

Zerel smiles, looking down at her hands. Miss Louella goes out.

Zerel can smell herself, stale and sour. She has not bathed in a very long time, and she needs to put on a clean shirtwaist.

She waits until she hears Miss Louella leave. Then she goes to the washstand and dips her hand into the pitcher.

Although it has been standing for several hours, the water is still warm, heated perhaps by the bright winter sun that pours through the window, through the cold glass . . . hot . . . the sun. . . .

Zerel strips off her shirtwaist, then slips the straps of her camisole over her shoulders so she is naked to the waist. Looking away from herself, she takes a small linen handtowel, wets it, and begins to bathe.

The water, only slightly warm, is scented with lemon. Zerel's skin tingles. Slowly, she raises her eyes and . . . don't, no, don't . . . she looks at herself in the mirror.

Her breasts are still swollen with the milk that will never leave her, still faintly golden with the sun that possessed her last summer, at home when . . . before . . . *if only she had not . . .*

And then Zerel is not safe anymore, she is inside the dark glass, not in the still white place where . . . she drops the wet cloth and then her hands are clawing, gouging, trying to get the milk out, release it, make it leave her and the pain is terrible, she bleeds, but the skin her breasts all torn are not where the pain is and she hears the words with hard edges and the screams making her lose the place she has found and held to, held safe in, tearing herself open Zerel and the screams coming out and . . .

And then he is there. Benjamin. He has come into the house somehow, up to her room, and he sees her there before the window in the sun, Zerel, bright red and fading gold all torn, tearing herself apart and the almost clear milk and the water running down and tears and screams, everything pouring out of her, Zerel, and he is holding her, touching her, his tongue taking away the milk and the water and the blood . . . and the milk doesn't stop . . .

And he does not stop.

VI

Diminuendo

1 8 4 6 — 1 8 4 7

Benjamin:

He touches her . . . in the pale gold afternoons with Miss Louella downstairs in her innocent ocher parlor, and the carts rattling past the front door, and the girl in the kitchen fixing supper, Benjamin is touching Zerel, kissing her, lifting her from the hard stiff chair in the corner and carrying her to the bed and touching her, and his hands and his tongue and the milk . . .

Zerel touches Benjamin. Clings to him in the pale golden afternoons in the back room upstairs because she has lost the place where she thought she could stay and can't get back there now it is closed to her and she is cold and feels things now and remembers and the milk will not leave her and she has to stay someplace and it is Benjamin.

The down on his chest is reddish gold and thicker down there where he . . . and on his legs darker . . . but silver in his hair, silver white so fine Zerel wouldn't see unless holding his head in her arms she . . .

"How old are you?" she says.

"Thirty."

❖

"I am twenty-one," she says.

"I know."

"But you," she says. "You are just a child."

"No," he says.

Zerel smiles. "Just a child."

He rolls away from her onto his back and covers his eyes with his arm. "A child is not what you need. Not now."

A child who burns who screams who fades away to nothing who . . . "No," Zerel says. "Not a child. Not a man, either, I reckon."

"I know."

"This ain't right," she says.

"No. No, it isn't right at all."

"Is this what you . . . how in Boston, when . . ."

"No, it was never, I swear . . . never."

"This ain't healing?"

"I didn't intend . . . but maybe it is. Or saving? I don't know."

Her skin still golden from the sun, old gold. His belly hard and flat and white. Her skin is warm when he touches her. He touches her all over, warm. Burning. He does not stop. Benjamin . . . his mouth . . . the milk . . .

He knows, then, knows she cannot be healed?

"Not this," he says. "That is not what this is." And his mouth . . .

He is hungry, Zerel thinks. He is starved. Benjamin . . . just a child. There is no healing, no saving, only feeding and . . .

His coat is gray, a finer stuff than any wool. "Cashmere," he says. From England where it rains. Cashmere, Zerel takes the word into her mouth and swallows. Benjamin's coat slides from the bed to the floor.

He calls her "my darling." No one has ever called Zerel such a thing. No one, Zerel knows, will ever call her so again.

She listens: Zerel takes in the words with soft edges, and

they are like something she can hold in her mouth, a sweetness on her tongue. *My darling.* And Benjamin's tongue is . . .

The smells of pallid city vegetables, overboiled, float up the stairs. Zerel hears Miss Louella singing, as the late milky light fades away to nothing in a room the shade of evening primroses.

It is April, then May, and the fading to nothing, to almost nothing, is slower now, and sweeter, and Zerel has no milk, the milk is gone.

Benjamin brings an extra horse, a buggy sometimes, and takes Zerel to the country. Miss Louella's smile is like a blessing. "The air will do her good, the sun . . ."

"I'll go home soon," Zerel says, not healed, not saved, but strong, stonger now.

"You needn't go, you know," says Benjamin. "You mustn't go unless you're ready. You needn't go at all."

"My husband," Zerel says. "My boy."

"I could be your husband," Benjamin tells her, glancing away.

You could be my boy. She slips her fingers inside his loosened collar and touches the red-gold down on his chest, wanting the thicker there where he is no boy, surely not, and her wanting is . . .

"You know we couldn't," she says.

"I wouldn't have thought so, no. But now . . ."

"Leave it be," Zerel says.

"Yes. I know."

Benjamin leans back on the grass, and the sun is on his white throat, then something dark, a reddening dark and Zerel shivers. *He will not live to be a man,* she thinks, the thinking so strong, so certain, that it is like a voice, and the thing she sees is . . . knowing.

"My darling," she says, the words' edges not soft on her tongue, words too hard for her, Zerel, the shapes of tenderness all wrong for her tongue, and she hears how she fails and knows she will not try again, but Benjamin, he . . .

"My love," he says, and he smiles, and she knows that it is a kind of saving to make him happy for even a moment before the dark reddening thing reaches his throat and she swallows the shame of her failing.

In July, the countryside ablaze with butterfly weed, day lilies, wild mustard, Robert James leads his wife home.

"Soon goldenrod," Zerel says, "and ironweed."

"Hawkweed," says Robert, leading her on. "Prairie dock."

Zerel thinks of the seasons she has missed: henbit and lousewart, buttercups, wild crab . . . the things she has forgotten. Long lost days in the fields and woods, on the prairie, Robert teaching her to name the wildflowers and birds.

"Soon Frank will be four," she says.

"Just wait till you see him. And hear how he talks."

"You reckon he'll remember me?"

Zerel's voice is uncertain and sad. Robert reaches for her hand, raises it to his lips. "We didn't forget you for a second," he says. "Sometimes I could almost see you, Zerel. Feel you there with us. Most especially late in the day while . . ."

"Forgive me, Robert."

"Forgive you?" he says. "You are blameless."

"Forgive me for all we've lost, the time . . ."

"We will not speak of it. Now you are yourself again."

Zerel, herself again, goes home. A place where she can stay.

The cradle is not in the kitchen anymore.

Frank James stands beside the table. He looks up at his mother, without blinking, through the rungs of a ladderback chair.

She takes a few steps toward the child. He backs away, dragging the chair with him.

"Don't you want to kiss your mama?" Robert says.

"No."

Zerel comes no closer, but leans down low to look her son in the eye. His gaze is cool and knowing. He doesn't trust her.

"Franklin?" Robert says. "It's your mama, boy."

"Never mind," Zerel says. "Give him time."

Robert looks at her uneasily. "I'm sure he'll—"

"I know."

"Mrs. Shively's been a Godsend, looking after him. . . ."

Zerel walks to the doorway and looks out at the eastern pasturage, an endless sweep of green. Above it, the day's light is draining from the sky.

She can feel the child's eyes on her back, hard with suspicion and blame.

Zerel is surprised, at night, in the bed with Robert, how easy it is to forget Benjamin, to forget everything. Robert: still occupying reaches Benjamin never crossed, a memory her skin recollects with ease and joy. Where she belongs now, Zerel knows what she is supposed to do with each hour of the day. It is only when she catches the hard glance of her small son upon her that she thinks of Benjamin Aldrich and the touch that did not heal, the feeding that did not save . . . Benjamin the holding . . . Robert the healing . . . *heal so they can save themselves,* said Benjamin.

The child in his way comes around, not affectionate, not trusting her still . . . perhaps never quite trusting his mother. But he speaks to her now, his sentences lengthening with his curiosity. Frank is a whiz. And he lets her, when need be, touch him. He calls her "Mamaw."

One night in late November, when the harvest is finished, the fields and garden stripped bare, Zerel, in the bed with

Robert, dreams of Benjamin, his throat black-red and torn and silent. She wakes to the sound of a screaming wind.

Benjamin is dead. Zerel does not know how where when, just knows. She sees his throat laid open and hears a howling not Benjamin, hard edges of death without words and . . .

Zerel knows.

A few days later Robert comes back from Excelsior Springs and tells her how he heard there a terrible thing: the young doctor who was so kind to her in Kansas City . . . a man gone mad there and taking the neck of a broken ammonia bottle left carelessly on hospital stairs and the jagged glass like teeth in the throat of the kind young doctor who once wrote to him, Robert, of the healing of spirits sickened by grief . . . and now he is dead, that poor doctor.

And Zerel sickens, turns white and cannot speak.

"I wish I didn't have to tell you," Robert says.

But she knew . . . she knows, Zerel. And she sits on the cold ground behind the house for a while, with the sun sinking fast and Robert understanding without knowing and leaving her there, Robert always understanding . . . never knowing. In the blue twilight Zerel remembers the rose-gold light of the small room and the down on the backs of his hands. . . .

And then she goes inside and starts supper, as the light fades to nothing.

The child is conceived in December, days after Dr. Benjamin Aldrich is buried in the Missouri soil outside the city where he was not born.

The child is Robert's, Zerel knows. But the striking of the spark of life just now . . . it is a kind of saving. Her body gladdens to the carrying of life, the milk that will come again, the child that will heal.

She imagines the new life inside her as something Benjamin has given, a beautiful boy. And she carries him high.

Jesse Woodson James is born with an almost spectacular grace and ease on the fifth of September, 1847. He is a golden child, long of limb and delicate of feature. A beauty. His eyes are violet-blue, his hair the pale amber shade of honey.

This time Robert James is not present for the birth of his son. He has crossed the river, again to spread the Word past the eastern edges of the Kansas Territory.

"I'll be home before your time comes," he said. "I shall be here."

But the babe has a time of his own. Arriving ahead of predictions, Jesse makes his first appearance to a roomful of smitten womenfolk.

"Will you look at them eyelashes? And him a boy . . ."

"That hair's gonna curl, just see if it don't."

"Hush," Clara Shively says. "You'll turn him cocky first thing."

Zerel groans.

"Poor thing, her husband still away and all . . ."

It seems to Zerel that fully half the ladies of the church are there, though in fact there are only four. Mrs. Wickens is in charge again, Mrs. Sponable assisting. But Clara Shively ain't about to be shunted aside. She brings her daughter Elspeth along, just to even things up.

"Time the girl learns what she's in for," Mrs. Shively says. "A woman's life ain't no ice cream social."

Elspeth, thirteen and faintly green about the gills, stays in the kitchen and boils water. Zerel is glad for her sake, the girl's, that the ordeal hasn't lasted too long.

The squalling infant is handed to his mother. "Jesse," she whispers. "You gonna be my new little brother now? Oh, we're gonna understand each other fine, you and me."

The day after Jesse is born, Zerel is on her feet again, strong as an ox and ornery—she wants them harpies outa her house. The only way to run them off is to prove they're not needed.

"I can manage, I tell you."

"Well, it's your lookout, I reckon." Miz Shively is the last of the reserves. "I'll send Elspeth around again towards suppertime, though. Guess by then you'll have some of the wind let out of your sails."

Zerel looks toward the prairie and imagines herself floating across it, billowing white. "No need," she says. "We'll make out fine."

Clara Shively huffs away, predicting dire collapse.

Frank James, not yet five, looks at his mother. "Maybe you should mind her," he says.

"Now you listen here, young man. I had enough buttin' in from them ladies. Don't hardly need your say-so too, do I?"

"Suit yourself," the child says. A schoolmarm in knickers, that boy, Zerel thinks. Then she laughs . . . he's only a baby, looking at her with dark broody eyes.

"What do you think of this brother of yours, Franklin?"

"He's all right. Don't cry much."

"No, he don't. He's a little man, just like you."

"Mamaw?"

"Yes, boy?"

"You be goin' away again now?"

"What give you that idea, child?"

Then Jesse is fussing to be fed and Zerel goes to him, the question forgotten, and Frank trudges out to the yard and stirs a mudhole furiously with a long, bent stick.

The September afternoon is warm. Zerel thinks of the creek and feels a terrible thirst, a hankering for the water and sun. The past few weeks have been uncommonly rainy; the water should be high. Frank is having his nap. Jesse, five days old, lies in the cradle, eyes like morning glories, just biding his time before raising a ruckus.

Zerel studies her new son. Too soon for the baby eyes to

focus on much of anything, she knows. Yet she'd swear he's looking straight at her, taking her in.

"You got a thirst?" she says.

He makes a gurgling sound.

"Figures. Best come with me, then."

She sweeps the blanket aside and lifts him from the cradle, surprised at the weight of him, no bigger than a minute.

Along the pathway that cuts to the creek the blue lobelias are in flower, shored up by scaffoldings of silver spider webs.

Zerel hears a noise behind her. She turns around. Charlotte, the slave woman, is hanging bedsheets on a line that runs from the smokehouse to a tall cedar post in the dooryard.

All signs of blood and borning already scrubbed away, Zerel thinks.

Behind the flapping wet white cloth, along the wall of the slave cabin, sunflowers stand six feet high. Did Charlotte plant and tend them? Or did they just grow by themselves?

Zerel, without acknowledging Charlotte, hurries on, holding Jesse fast. "Just wait now, little brother," she whispers. "We're gonna have us a time, you and me. Ain't got a need for nobody else."

The infant's eyes, blue as delftware, are fixed on hers.

Zerel lays the child on the grass, slips off her dress, then moves Jesse onto her skirt before taking off his diaper. He is dry. "Good boy," she says. His knees curl up toward his chest and he flails tiny fists at her. She scoops him up in her arms.

And then they are in the water, the cool greenish water that comes clear up to her waist. She holds the baby away from her body, then lowers him slowly down, very slowly, just wetting the back of him a little bit, tipping him so his feet dangle first, then the back of his head.

She waits for him to scream. But he doesn't. His gaze is steady on her face. The he opens his mouth, twisting his body strenuously in her large hands, and he laughs.

❖

And Zerel laughs. What a glorious child.

She holds him just under the arms now, his head against her, letting him hang in the water to his shoulders. Zerel lowers herself until she, too, is submerged to the top of her chest, and the water is the coolest, sweetest thing that has ever touched her. "Ain't it fine?" she says. Jesse smiles at her.

The water is a torpid green, rippling only where Zerel and the child set it in motion, eddying away from them. Patches of yellowish algae skim the surface. Here and there a beetle skates and skitters.

Zerel slaps the surface of the pond hard with the flat of her hand, delighting in the baby's startled wonder. The splash takes him by surprise, but not fright. This boy ain't scared of anything, Zerel thinks. The water recovers from her small violence and smooths out again.

Zerel stands very still. Jesse stops squirming, then she feels a warm current against her belly as he pees in the water and they both grin.

The water is almost perfectly still when she sees something long and dark and sinuous a foot away from her shoulder, from the baby, moving toward them.

"Well, lookee here," she says. "I am really going to show you a marvel now." She shifts the infant into her right arm, cradling him against her breast, and reaches with her left hand for the snake.

It is thick and greenish-black, perhaps three feet long. Zerel grasps it just behind the head. It's eyes pierce her with needles of light, and it flicks its tongue as she lifts it out of the water.

The snake coils around her upper arm, but she keeps a firm hold on its forepart, bringing the shining hissing head up close where Jesse can touch it. Oh, he sees, all right. She sees his seeing. He reaches out with a tiny hand and grabs at the snake, his fingers on its tongue as the snake rears back and hisses, fangs showing, eyes spitting light, and don't that give him a good laugh, young Mister Jesse James.

The sun is sinking now, red behind them, red as fire. The baby's eyes are gleaming, his mouth open wide, like the snake. Zerel looks at her new son and throws back her head to laugh and . . .

That is when she sees Robert, standing paralyzed on the bank above the creek. His suit is blacker than black against the tangled flowers. His face is white and cold as snow.

Zerel drops the snake, flings it from her like poison. It slithers into the murk and disappears.

Jesse wails, his hands clutching furiously at Zerel's dark distended nipple. For a moment Zerel freezes, caught there before the fiery sky. There is a sound like roaring in her ears. Then it dwindles, dies away.

And that is the first time Robert James sets eyes on his boy Jesse.

VII

Fugue

1 8 5 0

A popular legend

On an early March morning in 1850, when Robert James
leaves his wife and children for California, he is nearly dis-
suaded by his son Jesse. At the final moment of farewell, the
little boy hurls himself at his father's knees and clings there,
sobbing: "Don't go. Please, Pa, *don't!*"

Robert James falters.

Zerel burns. She pulls the child roughly away from his
father's legs. "Don't," she says.

Jesse James will never again beg for anything.

A personal legend

As Robert James turns and rides away from his home and
family, setting off toward the gold-studded hills of California,
his three-year-old son, Jesse, stands beside his mother, watching from the doorway. The child's eyes are bright and very
blue, his mother's very dark, yet the two pairs of eyes are
similar: hot and dry.

Reaching the crest of the small hill that marks the boundary
between his own land and the county road, the Reverend

James reins in his roan mare, turns in the saddle, and lifts his black hat high against the early morning sky in a last gesture of farewell to his wife and son.

The woman turns from the door and busies herself at the hearth.

Standing alone now, the child slowly raises his hand. Taking careful aim, he shoots his deserting, dreaming father through the heart with one pointed finger, tiny and utterly merciless.

A fact

When Robert James leaves his home for California early in 1850, his son Jesse, age three, is sound alseep in his bed and will continue to be for more than an hour after his father has vanished over the small crest that marks the western edge of the James land.

Robert James has insisted, over his wife's objections, that the smaller children's sleep be undisturbed. They have lived in a stormy atmosphere for weeks.

"Why distress them?" he says.

"You can't look them in the eye," Zerel says.

"I haven't the heart to explain what children could never understand."

"I can't understand either," she says.

A memory

She recalls a cold windswept morning in early March. The sun, a pale half-circle the color of cider, seems poised at rest on the eastern horizon as Robert makes ready to leave. The fields are starkly bare, overlaid with a lacy pattern of blue shadow and gold light. Here and there a patch of snow has taken refuge in the shade of a rock or a tree. The children sleep. She and Robert have, by this daybreak, very little to say to one another. Their silence is a madness, formally expressed. The rites of departure are enacted with extreme care.

A fact

Departure is delayed not by Jesse, but by Frank, Robert's firstborn, then seven. The few belongings the Reverend James will carry west with him—clothing, a bedroll, a Bible, a coffeepot—are packed in his saddlebags. His roan mare, Charity, the recent gift of a prosperous congregant, stands hitched to the garden fence. Anxious to make tracks, she paws the half-frozen ground and whinnies like an impatient child.

Robert, too, is anxious to be off. His party will be waiting for him near the schoolhouse in Liberty. He is late.

He is detained by young Frank, who is out in the privy behind the house. The boy has been out there for quite a long time.

Perhaps he is weeping? That cannot be known for fact.

Finally, in order to say good-bye to his son, Robert must go out and fetch him. What he says to comfort the boy cannot be told.

Memory

A February without mercy. Late at night, the children long asleep, Mamaw recalls waiting for the new baby, Susie, to wake with soft cries for the breast.

Outside, a blizzard that started at sundown is burying the snug farmhouse. The roads may not be seen again for days, a prospect that contents Zerel. Robert looks tired. Now he'll be forced to stay home and rest.

A high wind rises, shrieks, then drops to a moan. When it quiets, the cows can be heard lowing nervously in the barn.

Zerel is mending one of Robert's shirts. He should have new ones, she thinks; these patches won't last for a season. Needlework has always tried her patience. Now, with three children so young, she can easily neglect the sewing for months. Only dread that continued dereliction might lure the church sisterhood to her door with bundles of perfectly topstitched linens for her disheveled spouse has goaded her to the sewing basket this evening. The ladies of Robert's flock express their contempt for her by way of extravagant kindness.

Robert paces back and forth before the hearth. His hands, clasped behind his back, fidget. So roughened by the fields, the winters, Robert's hands. Once they were smooth and pale as the pages he fingered. His volume of Horace lies face-down on the rude planks of the table.

"You are restless as a wolf," Zerel says.

He smiles absently, his gaze on the discarded book. " 'No ascent is too steep for mortals,' " he murmurs. " 'Heaven itself we seek in our folly.' "

Zerel glances up from her work. Seeing her husband's troubled face, she fixes her needle to the shirt collar and sets her sewing on the table within the circle of the oil lamp's light. As she waits for Robert to speak his mind, Mamaw thinks how she mustn't forget to put the mending back in the basket before she goes to bed. She pictures Jesse with a silver needle lodged in his small, tender throat.

"What is it, Robert?"

"There is a mission I must . . . I have decided something, Zerel," he says.

She is pricked by fear, cold and sharp and fine.

"This may be hard for you to accept at first. But I have prayed over it. I have truly prayed. . . ."

Zerel hasn't a prayer, of course. Zerel gave up prayer years ago, a form of begging.

"I must go to California," Robert says.

A number of Clay County men have already been lured westward by promises of gold in the hills and streams of California. Several belong to Robert's church. Zerel knows them, knows they are driven by desperation, not simple greed or adventuring. Fools all the same, she thinks. Damned fools.

Now, with winter's hold on the prairie about to loosen,

another party is preparing to set out. A fools' paradise. Fools, yes. But Robert?

Robert don't believe in that kind of paradise. It isn't gold that draws him, but his flock. Straying far this time, far from the comfort and safety of home and family to wander in valleys the Word of God has not yet penetrated. Robert hears their bleating and will go running after them as if he himself has no family, no sense, nothing better to do. . . .

He calls it "a mission."

Zerel calls it like she sees it: "Desertion," she says. "To chase after idiots."

"My dear, these are godly men," Robert tells her.

"Fools and dreamers often are," Zerel says.

Dreamers, but perhaps not such fools after all. They are able to do what Zerel cannot: they claim the allegiance of Robert James.

She will fight, of course. Zerel is both prepared and practiced. She has fought the land, the weather, the town, the church. She has fought God Himself for the devotion of Robert James.

Zerel burns.

"Forgive me," Robert says.

Zerel freezes. *I am going to lose.*

A popular legend

The Reverend James is driven off on this unfortunate mission by a difficult, unsympathetic, faithless wife. A cruel and unmannerly woman who has hardened her heart against her husband, knows too little of obedience and humility, too much of sensuality. A woman who deafens her ear to the Commandments, blinds her eye to the illuminations of faith, turns her countenance from all propriety.

Robert James leaves brokenhearted: his wife has been promiscuous and indiscreet. His children—some say that pretty boy Jesse ain't even his—are being reared like wild animals. The Preacher's gifts have been trampled, his spirit and pride broken, by the scorn of his own helpmeet.

The Reverend Robert James, a desperate man, leaves his home on the threshhold of spring 1850, possessed of an undernourished hope that Mrs. James, left to her own devices on the prairie for a year, may come to her senses, soften, repent.

A *fact*
She does not know.

Zerel does not know what measure her stubbornness, ill temper, eccentricity add to the scales when Robert weighs the call to the godless, goldless hills.

Zerel has been faithless. Only once, and surely Robert does not know of her betrayal, but Zerel knows.

Robert leaves.

A *personal legend*
Robert is haunted by the vision of his wife in the water one afternoon three years earlier: all unbound flesh and hair, uncontained, elemental.

The infant, his tiny hands grasping her dark distended nipple, was a satyr.

A snake coiled familiarly around a vast womanly wanting, exultant flesh.

The water roared, and the sky behind mother and child flamed.

Robert James saw Satan that day, in several guises.
And he fled.

A *memory*
Spring approaches, yet there is no thaw. No pardon. No reprieve.

She weeps only once, the night he first tells her. Then he takes her in his arms, pressing her hot, wet face to his chest as she pleads with him. "You can't leave us," she says.

But if Reverend James interprets his wife's tears as sorrow, he misconstrues them. At heart, Zerel is murderous.

A month later, on the morning of his departure, Robert soundlessly climbs the ladder to the loft where the children sleep. Frank is not there. Zerel follows Robert, watches him from the hatchway. Her husband stands above Jesse for a moment, gazing down on him, but he does not touch his son.

When Robert lifts Susie from the cradle, she does not wake. He holds her close to his face. His beard, newly grown, brushes her brow as he traces his finger over her lids, her tiny unformed nose and delicate mouth. He uncurls the fingers of her right hand. His lips move as they do when he prays.

Robert bends to kiss the top of his daughter's head as he gently lays her down again and covers her with a wheat sack softened by many washings. When he turns toward Zerel, his face is streaked with tears, honest and silent.

Zerel knows, with hindsight, that Robert must have been forming his resolve back in autumn. Yet he waited to tell her until several months after their daughter, Susan Lavenia, was born. The little girl's birth in early November was even easier than Jesse's. Zerel was completely recovered and already starting to think about another child by the time Robert's journey was announced.

Susie, like her brother Jesse, is a remarkably pretty creature. She is small, meek, well-behaved. A joy to tend, Susie, but she lacks her brother's spark.

Mamaw's feeling for this new infant falls short of fascination; there is nothing to tame in her, a mere bundle of blankets. But Robert loves this little girl with a passion his sons do not rouse in him.

A fact

It is six-thirty in the morning on Monday, the eighth of March, in the year 1850, when Robert James leaves his homestead in Kearney, Missouri, for the hills of California.

The word of the Lord is on his lips.

The contents of his heart are unknown.

The rise he crosses is still spattered with blue and gold after he can no longer be seen.

Legend. Fact. Memory.

Each, finally, obscures what was. And Zerel is left with remnants: what might have been.

From old Fort Carney
April 14th, 1850

Beloved Wife,

At last we pause, to rest our weary limbs and restock our dwindling supplies, to regather our spirits. Had I but known the rigors of our journey, I wonder indeed whether my courage for the task would have held fast. I can only, now, thank the Good Lord that I did not know. My heart was sufficiently heavy, upon setting out, with the sorrow of departing from you and the children. I doubt I should have been able to bear doubt and fear as well. . . .

I pray that this difficult separation strengthens the union of our spirits in measure equal to what it demands of them. I entreat the Father hourly to keep you in safety, to lend you the comfort of His eternal peace. I have asked so much of you already, yet I urge you now to raise up your children in the nurture and admonition of the Lord and live a christian life yourself. The Almighty will protect and strengthen you in these efforts.

Give my love to all inquiring friends and take a portion of it to your self and kiss Jesse for me and tell Franklin to be a good boy and learn fast and say to my

precious Susie . . . ah, but there are not words in my
poor pen for her . . . nor for you, Dearest Wife. . . .

May 1st, 1850

Beloved Wife,

I write from Grand Island (though I have seen nothing
grand about it so far), near Old Fort Carney. We are on
our way. At the moment, however, I fear I do not look
like a man who is likely to go anywhere, since in order
to write this letter, I am forced to sink to my knees
below the sagging mule hide, this rude tent which is my
temporary domicile. The table seems a refinement which
has not yet found its way to this part of the world. There
are many other such deficiencies, but the new May skies
are generous, and cinquefoil flowers dot the prairie like
butter.

I long for the sight of you, my dearest wife, and our
children. To leave you afflicted me, and I am heartsore
at the thought that twelve or eighteen months may pass
before we are reunited. Only these brief and necessarily
hurried letters bring me true consolation. I intend to
dedicate myself wholeheartedly to the mastery of this
art of writing in the months to come, for I believe with
practice, we can through our letters meet and converse
as if face to face.

I beg your prayers now, as I have begged your good
faith and indulgence heretofore. I send you my devotion, also to the children and our loving friends. If we
meet no more in this world, may we meet in Glory, and
may the Lord bless you as fully as I love you.

Hangtown, California
July 19th, 1850
. . . At last we have arrived at the object of our journeying,

❖

the encampment which is to be my pastorate for such of the future as the Lord gives me to see. . . .

In the five days which seem somehow to have passed since our arrival at this crude and unpopulous destination, my time has been largely given over to the requirements of setting up some semblance of a shelter. Hides and saplings are the foundations of our settlement. A strong gale could blow us away. Poor Charity, too, seems quite frail and done in by our travels. I daresay her sense of propriety is as insulted as her hoof is worn . . .

Otherwise, I have been occupied with the disheartening, confounding, essential task of trying to locate those stalwart Clay Countians I am to minister to. Finding someone here amid profligate rock and unmarked trail is truly the Lord's work, as only the Deity Himself could do it. So I stumble about, awaiting His direction as I grow lost on my own. . . .

Here is a curious report which, albeit shamefacedly, I offer in hope of bringing a smile to your dear disapproving face: yesterday afternoon your deaconish husband prospected for gold. Indeed I did. I washed but one pan of dirt, a pan I regret to say did not yield the telltale glitter. I would not have gone so far, I confess, had I not been teased into it. William Stigers, who as you know is this venture's greatest enthusiast, goaded me saying I should one day have to confess to Franklin and Jesse that I was a mere bystander at the making of history. "This is the *Gold Rush,* Reverend," he said, "and you right here in the belly of it and haven't got the gumption to lower a pieplate into a stream!" Well, how could I resist a challenge put that way? I washed my little pan of dirt and now I can say I was one of them, these men who were willing to cart their hopes so far from home. But I beg you not to reach the conclusion your preacher husband will return hitched to a wagon of gold. I have much to learn from these brave men, Zerel, about faith, about hope. . . .

Faith and hope are as elusive as gold. No wagon returns, no husband.

A short time after writing this letter, Robert James falls sick. The precise nature of his ailment is never revealed to his wife, though she can make an educated guess: many men in those hopeful, hellish mining camps succumb to the fevers. Typhus and other fatal afflictions flourish in contaminated water, unsanitary dwellings, tainted food. He must, by then, have been so worn, she thinks. He must have felt so far removed from all he knew and loved, all but his persistent, imperious God. He must have burned much as small Robert did, but without the coolness of her hands, her lips. . . .

Fact
Robert James dies on the eighteenth of August, 1850. He is thirty-two years old. The word of his passing does not reach his wife, twenty-five, until nearly a month later. By that time he is at rest in an unmarked grave near Maryville, California. Years later his eldest son will travel there to seek his father's grave, but it will not be found.

Robert and Zerelda James have been married not quite nine years. At the time of his death, their children are seven, three, and ten months old.

Memory
Zerel imagines Robert's end with such clarity that she will never again be able to treat death as a stranger. She sees the way her husband's flesh has wasted away, leaving nothing but hair and bone and the eyes that burn with a fever he calls God. She presses his lids down, and her fingertips are seared. When she touches her lips to his cheek, she tastes and smells the stench of the rotting that is death. She begs.

Zerel realizes her presence could not have prevented Robert's dying, perhaps not even eased it. She is not a woman from whom ease naturally comes. Still, she longs to have been with him. She imagines how she would scour the California hillsides for healing plants, steep them in clear spring water, cool her husband's brow . . . there is dittany, there are doves.

She is there. Zerel is with Robert, beside him, giving ease when death comes. And Robert, in death, emanates forgiveness and the sweet scent of earth. . . .

Then recollection loses its shape, escapes its unreliable confines. Reality freezes, burns, expires. Memory passes away for burial in some lost distance. Memory is interred but will not decompose. Blue and gold shadows stretch across the empty places left by its passing. . . .

Legend. Fact. Memory.

Legend is born long after the fact. Often there is no intercourse between them. In that respect, legend perhaps constitutes something of a miracle.

Memory, like love, is an act of imagination, an abandonment and a possession.

Memory is the bastard child of unholy union between legend and fact: shameless, illicit, a crime of passion.

Memory is, finally—after the fact, above the legend—all that is real, all that endures.

Memory, fact, legend

Zerel hoards the scraps, the strands from which she will weave the tapestry of her life.

A personal legend, her own

Robert James, a perfect fool . . . God's fool.

Robert loves Zerel. Zerel loves Robert. May they meet again in Glory, where forgiveness abounds.

VIII

Taking Up the Slack

1 8 5 0 — 1 8 5 5

They call her, now, the Widow James, like it's a profession.

Widowhood: even from the depths of her fresh bereavement, it seems to Zerel a station she is naturally suited for. She has never fit the shapes others have cut and expected her to adhere to. She believes (forgetful with grief, Zerel) she has never been young. She is twenty-five, possessed of her own code, her own instincts. Expediency is her native-born talent. She will be a match for sheer necessity.

Mourning at the New Hope Baptist Church is showy, yet—the widow acknowledges it   profound. A man like Preacher James is not easily come by. Zerel graciously accepts the ornate condolences of neighbors. Even a measure of solicitous interference, to a point. For Robert's sake. It will not last. She knows shortly she'll be left in peace, cut loose. Uncoupling has outlawed her.

And—perhaps this too for Robert's sake—Zerel makes her bow to God. She does not stop arguing with the Almighty, but she owns up to Him: He won fair and square. She knows, Zerel, when she is whipped. The Lord is a small comfort, but a comfort just the same.

May he rest in peace, she says. *Amen.*

Two years, two hundred and seventy-five acres, three children. The boys run wild and Zerel runs down.

Robert gone two years now, two years and four months, when in September 1852 Zerel again marries. Zerel promises to honor and obey, knowing even as she does so the wrong-headedness of it. *I am addled,* she thinks, *unsteady.*

Zerel's new husband is a neighbor name of Simms. A farmer of modest means but much method. Zerel covets her neighbor's way with livestock and land. Simms is short and stocky and rock-ribbed, but his corn is lithe, his fields lush, his milking herd curvaceous and sweet-natured. Mr. Simms (his given name Benjamin, but damned if she'll call him that) is sixteen years older than Zerel and every bit as ferocious. He admires her economy of word and motion, her surplus of girth, but he does not much care for her children. Them boys is a regular handful, he'll tell anybody who'll listen.

Zerel is her neighbor's wife but a few unyielding months when she hears, one afternoon, a ruckus behind the barn. Frank's voice thins with outrage in the biting air.

Zerel, holding tight to the broom she has been applying to the front stoop, runs out back to see. . . .

And there is Mr. Simms, red-faced and grunting like a pig, applying his belt to the backside of her boy.

Mamaw: she rears up and roars, in such fury Simms don't think twice before letting the brat go.

Frank, tugging at the straps of his overalls, trips fast into the trees, his white tail vanishing like a rabbit's.

"That cussed boy of yours was—"

Zerel won't hear of it. She cuts off Simms's explanations with the rough end of her broom. "You will leave, Mr. Simms," she says. "You are halfway off my place already."

"I will have my supper first," says Simms.

"Very well. But it shall be your last meal here, I promise you."

Mr. Simms, his bride towering behind his chair, partakes of his final repast hungrily, takes his own sweet time. The yam is fibrous and tough. The greens are boiled to a fare-thee-well.

Mr. Simms is back to doing his own cooking by sundown.

"Mamaw?"

"What is it, Franklin?"

"When you reckon he'll be back?"

"Who?" she says.

"Why, Mr. Simms. Who else?"

"You won't be seeing that man around here again, son."

"You mean you run him off?" The boy looks oddly disconcerted. "For good?"

"You got some objection?"

"Reckon I done what he said I done."

"What?"

"I cussed him."

"Then you shall be whipped," Mamaw says. "But I shall be the one to do the whippin'."

From the day Simms retreats, Zerel refuses to carry his name. The first few times folks call her Miz Simms, she gives them the fish-eye. "Miz James," she says. Word gets around soon enough, then Simms is like something never happened to her.

Almost like. She means to divorce him. It will be an embarrassment, but not near so big a one as being his legal wife, his chattel.

Before she has gone so far as to engage the services of a lawyer, however, Simms up and dies.

"First kindness he ever showed us," Mamaw says.

Then comes the time of Bleeding Kansas, The Troubles.

"We got that so-called Congress in Washington to thank," says Mamaw. "Bunch of filthy scoundrels, if you ask me.

Musta pickled their own brains with all that toilet water they use."

Jesse hoots.

"What's toilet water?" Frank says.

"One stink to cover another one," Mamaw tells him.

Oh, they really done it this time, them politicians. Open up Kansas to white settlement like it's uncomplicated as bread pudding. Nothin' to it.

And there ain't, of course, long as they dodge the big question: slave state or free, that's what folks around here'd like to know.

"Well, why don't we just leave that up to the folks who settle out there?" Got all the answers in Washington, they do, them in their satin breeches and slick-toed boots. Abolitionists start movin' into Kansas like it's the Promised Land, wagons loaded down with Boston do-good money. . . .

Missouri raises its hackles, its ire, its dander. Raises strenuous objections and militia and arms. Let them abolitionist vermin set foot . . . it is a time for conscience, for courage, for spit. An era for the fierce. Mamaw's in her element.

Kentucky blood runs hot in her veins, Kentucky pounds. For once, Mamaw's not alone. The neighbors are like-minded, Kentucky-born, too, most of them. You don't go back on a bargain. Missouri been a slave state long as it's been a state at all.

"Illinois, Iowa . . ." A sweep of Mamaw's arm takes in the midsection of the country and then some. "Ain't bad enough we got them free-staters surrounding us on two sides and Arkansas too far by a long shot to help a neighbor out," she says. "Now they mean to hem us in to the west? Well, they got another think comin'."

"This is politics, Zerel," her stepfather tells her. "No concern of yours."

Mamaw fixes a jaded eye on him. "You huff all the way

out here to tell me that?" Thomason has never paid her a visit before.

"Folks is talkin'. It's got your mama worried. Your brother, too."

"Tell 'em it ain't none of their account. Yours neither."

"It just ain't a lady's place, carryin' on so."

"You see any man around here to take up the slack?"

She knows her place, all right, Mamaw.

The Kansas-Nebraska Act's the last straw. Free elections. "Free, my foot!" says Zerel. "Ain't nothin' free about this mess. We been turned into hostages."

Her eldest son studies her thoughtfully, always figuring the angles, Frank. "What's got everybody so riled up?" he asks her. "Who gives a hoot, anyhow, what goes on over in Kansas?"

"You listen to me, boy. Jesse, git over here. I want you to hear this, too."

Jesse, seven, hasn't got a notion what all the fuss is about. Mamaw's mad all the time and it ain't at him, is all he knows. But the boy loves a sniff of brewing trouble. He comes and sits on the floor at Mamaw's knee.

"Let me put it to you boys like this," she says. "What if there was a regular family, like us right here. Decent folks who loves their country and works their land, tryin' to make something of themselves and mindin' their own business. . . ."

"Like us," Jesse says.

"Right. And let's say they got an empty room in their house."

"How come?" Frank says.

"Never mind. They just do. Anyways, they figure that spare room oughta be good for somethin' and some extra money wouldn't hurt, so they decide to take somebody in, a boarder like."

"Or a hired man?"

"Yes, son. Like that. So, they're all ready to let this room and they start lookin' for . . . well, for a body who's *suitable.* You understand me?"

The two boys nod, beginning to look bored. Jesse tweaks the rawhide lace on his brother's boot. Zerel reaches down and slaps his hand away.

"So there they are, lookin'," she says, "when one day some man they never seen before rides up to their place. Got him a gun and a huge horse, a whip maybe . . . real mean look on his face."

"Who is he?" Jesse asks.

"That's what I'm tellin' you, they never seen him before in their lives. But he got this gun and . . . 'Look here,' he says, 'We got this fella, shot up the town yonder, killed him a whole houseful of folks, got a pack of uppity niggers with him, too. We got to put 'em somewheres, and I hear you got this spare room and . . .'"

"He can't do that," Frank says.

"A killer?" Jesse cries. "We ain't gonna—"

"You got to, is what the man on the horse tells 'em. And seein' how he got this gun and don't mind usin' it . . . well, you can see there ain't a thing that poor family can do."

Mamaw looks at Frank and Jesse, her eyes gleaming in the firelight.

"Mamaw, you mean Kansas is like our spare room?"

"Almost like under our own roof. A body ain't safe . . ."

"But they can't *do* that," Jesse says. His small hands curl into fists.

"They can try," Mamaw says.

Ink barely dry on the infamous, foolhardy decree, and blood starts to flow. Armed to the teeth, Missourians with swift horses and stout hearts begin the lightning raids on Kansas. They cut through the border like a hot knife through butter, striking while hot, striking to kill.

Bushwhackers, is what the Missouri guerrillas come to be called. Mamaw savors the word, conjuring up visions of quick and canny men endowed with a wrath like beauty. Mamaw keeps as keen and partial an eye on the Bushwhackers' doings as she does on the progress of her children, the yields of her land.

The sides square off. From Kansas come odd-lot fighters every bit as brave and brutal. Their raids into Missouri are swift and merciless as acts of God.

"What's a Jayhawker, Mamaw?"

"Ain't no such thing," she says.

Frank and Jesse dig a bunker in the woods. They gather stones and sharpen sticks. Mamaw contributes a fractured broom handle to their arsenal. The James boys will hang John Brown in effigy before Harper's Ferry's been heard of, will hone their spelling skills on Pottawatomie . . . pee-oh-double-tee. . . . Tree stumps are named for famous Jayhawker commanders: Jim Lane, Charlie Jennison, Dan Anthony . . . and suffer barrage. The James boys bring down mythical birds, take aim at the moon and stars. They shoot varmints full of holes, bring body-counts to the supper table.

Ain't no such thing as a Jayhawker. . . .

Mamaw's dreams are an amalgam of desire and dread. Oh, she too would ride, would strike . . . then pictures her boys, the whiz and the beauty, pursued by creatures half-bird, half-man, thighs bulging in red morocco leggings. . . .

And she wakes, stokes the fire, starts breakfast. She pulls a plow at midday. Mamaw reaps and sows. And she tells herself: . . . *long over by the time my boys come of age, there will be peace by then.*

She prays for the cooling, Mamaw, but she feeds the fire.

Kansas has been warned. And, just in case the raids seem ambiguous, Missouri says it loud and clear, black on white, right in the Kansas newspapers: " . . . we will continue to lynch and hang, tar and feather and drown, every white-livered abolitionist who dares pollute our soil."

The towns get the worst of it. Terror sweeps the streets. But the farms aren't much safer: harder to find, easier to hit. There is burning, looting. Honest men are accosted between fresh-carved furrows, accused of harboring traitors, passing secrets . . . simple farmers blown across their own fields like bloodstained scarecrows brought down in a sudden gale.

Zerel's dreams are fewer now; now she witnesses bitter curses upon what she'd taken for a God-blessed land. To sleep, to dream amount to unconscionable negligence. For who, should Mamaw close her eyes, would defend the children when the enemy strikes in the darkness? She keeps herself awake with visions of muscled red legs creeping toward her door, trampling her crops, sneaking through her barn. She imagines her three children, asleep in the loft, suddenly seized by sharp-beaked mythical birds, borne off to arid western spaces like so much loot.

Have I left us defenseless? she wonders now and then. *No, defenseless is the last thing I am.* But alone, Mamaw and her youngsters, *alone.*

It was a matter of simple arithmetic, Zerel letting go the slaves after Robert died. Seven mouths to feed every day of the year, while their seasons of usefulness were so short. Jesse and Frank getting big enough to work soon, plenty of hired help meantime, for the months she needs it. Self-taught in economics, but no slouch, Zerel, trading some no-'count niggers for ready capital, for tools and seed, even for another few acres while prices were favorable.

And two of the Negroes have freely chosen to stay on.

Charlotte and the man she calls her husband, Jonah. Best of the lot, them two. So there's a girl to help in the house, a hired man.

We make out, Mamaw thinks. *We'll stand up to what comes.*

January 1855 brings the most merciless cold spell Zerel has ever known. The wind whips down from the north and punishes everything. A body can't breathe through the nose. When you open your mouth, the air tastes like copper pennies, makes your teeth ache. Heartless.

The week after New Year's, a nigger field hand down to Purdy's, less than a mile from the James place, was out bringing in some hogs. Somehow he fell and broke a leg. By the time they found him, he was frozen to death, lying in the snow-blown stubble, half his face eaten away. Everything hungry out there now, on the prowl.

"Just for little while, Mamaw, a couple minutes leastwise?" Jesse's voice is pitched high, gearing up to wear her down.

"No, indeed," Mamaw says. "You ain't goin' out in this weather."

"Aw, Mamaw—"

"I told you what happened over to Purdy's the other day. That nigger's nose is in some critter's belly now. You want to wind up like that?"

"But—" Frank wants in the act now.

"Keep still, the both of you. I said my piece and I don't mean to change it."

Susie, five, has been down with croup since the day after Christmas. Her deep cough has loosened now, but she is fussy and fully of complaint.

"Mamaw, my head hurts. Jesse was hittin' me."

"Never mind now."

Susie, her claim summarily dismissed, opens her mouth in a convalescent wail.

"Baby," Jesse says. "You gonna mess your pants now?"

Frank mutters. The sound of scuffling. A ripping of cloth. The child's screams. . . .

Mamaw leans into the hearth, stirring a pot of peas and ham hocks. Her fingers tighten around the handle of the ladle. Never mind them children, just lettin' off steam, we all been cooped up too long . . . and her back aching and the wind howling like wolves at the door, and we're gonna run out of firewood if this cold don't let up soon . . . chilblains on her fingers and Susie pestering the life out of her, tugging on Mamaw's skirt from behind thataway, it's a wonder I don't . . .

Mamaw turns around fast, brandishing the ladle. "Can't you give a body a moment's peace?"

It seems like a long, long time passes then, Mamaw standing there with that ladle in her hand, before she realizes . . . grasps what she has done.

Below, not waist-high to Mamaw, Susie James stands with hot broth and grease running down her small face. And she can't think or move, Zerel, with the child's cries so urgent now and Mamaw still holding the hot ladle like a club and not a sound from the two boys across the room, Frank grim and Jesse worse: curious, holding back judgment, looking at his mother with that wondering: *What would make a person do such a thing?*

Mamaw, caught in the act, frozen, and Jesse amazed at destruction—unwarranted. Red welts rise already on the little girl's cheek and brow, her anguish fills the house.

Still she cannot move, Mamaw, and Frank turns his eyes from her helpless look like slamming a door in the face of her need, Frank twisting his hands, then crossing the cold kitchen floor to pat his sister in the helpless way of a man with comforting, and Jesse watching as if it's all a spectacle. . . .

"Oh, help me," Mamaw says. "Frank—" and then she is, finally, thawed. She drops the ladle and bends to the scalded child, who cringes from her. "Please help."

Frank's words are slow, Frank always hesitating, weighing. "Reckon we could put snow on them burns." His voice is cold and crackling-thin.

"I'll head over and fetch Dr. Samuel." Jesse's hand is already on the door.

Zerel turns from her daughter. "No! Not in this weather . . . I told you what happened to that man."

Susie is sobbing.

"Mamaw, we got to do something. Can't just stand here and jaw about it."

She thinks of the other child, taken by burning, gone.

"I won't have you out there freezing to death." *Gone.* She turns to Frank. "You go."

"Frank and me go together, we can't get lost."

"No. You're staying here with me."

Frank looks at his mother for a moment. Then he pushes the door against the battering wind. *Gone.*

Mamaw, if we was all out on the river and the boat tipped over and we was going to drown and you could save just one of us . . .

The question is unthinkable.

It is an interminable half-hour before Frank returns with the doctor.

Susie James is bundled into Mamaw's bed, a red quilt wrapped around her. She lies still now, in shock. The welts on her face have blistered white. Jesse hovers by the bed, pressing a muslin packet of snow to his sister's forehead, where the burns are worst. Mamaw paces before the fireplace, her eyes wild and unseeing.

The door opens. As two sets of footsteps cross the kitchen, Mamaw keeps moving, back and forth, her skirts fanning the fire. Her broad shoulders are hunched in a coarse black woolen shawl, her eyes cast down.

"Mamaw?"

She does not stop, does not look at her eldest child.

The doctor follows Frank into the room. He sees her, the huge dark shape of her bent and spattered with shadow and firelight, stalking the hearth. The doctor has seen her in her fields, driving a mule, once pulling a plow with the traces over her own wide shoulders. He has seen her in town, watched her proud gait past smaller women in finer clothes. Once, she even bested him at a livestock auction, her hand more certain and alert than his own. She isn't fair or soft as women are supposed to be, but there is something handsome about her.

Now, though, the handsomeness, the pride have deserted her. Her eyes look wild, her shoulders defeated. *She is walking the very edge of madness,* he thinks. *What keeps her from falling in?*

"Miz James?"

Her expression is vague for a moment. Then she snaps to, stands still. "Thank you kindly for coming, Neighbor Samuel."

She is struck by his whiteness, an unearthly pallor that belies his second vocation: the doctor is a farmer. Surely he has seen the light of day, yet so pale . . .

Reuben Samuel is a man not small, but of modest proportion—or modest disproportion, perhaps. His legs are short and slightly bowed. His narrow shoulders seen barely equal to the weight of his head and the beaverskin cap upon it.

Dr. Samuel removes a pair of small rimless spectacles from his overlarge nose and wipes steam from the lenses. His eyes, pale gray, are tranquil. "Pleased if I can be of help."

She hears Kentucky in his voice. "It was an accident," she says.

"Ain't a house got young 'uns in it don't have them," he says.

Frank, still unnoticed by his mother, turns away. "Guess I'll see to the horses," he says.

It is Reuben Samuel who replies: "Thank you, son."

Jesse steps forward, man-of-the-world. "Got our hands right full here, Doc."

The doctor smiles. "I can see that. Yes, indeed." His gaze is on the little girl. "Can you hold on there for just a shake, child? I best warm my hands before I touch you or you might succumb to . . . reckon you know what affliction I mean?"

Susie, staring at him, shakes her head slowly.

"Why, the shiverin'-willies," Reuben Samuel says. "They can be mighty grave."

The child's smile is tenuous.

The doctor flexes his fingers over the grate. They are long, delicate, as if all the pale disparity in the rest of him comes to perfection in those hands. Zerel feels a pang of familiarity, sharp and sweet: Benjamin, the holding, the healing.

As Dr. Samuel approaches the bedside, Jesse draws back.

Susie begins to whimper as the doctor comes near.

"There now, sweet darlin'." He drops to one knee beside the bed. The child quiets, yielding something over to him with her steady gaze.

"Got him a regular knack, don't he?" Jesse says.

The white wet pillow of melting snow still rests on her brow. The muslin has stuck to her blistered skin. Reuben Samuel removes the pack with his gentle white fingers. His beard brushes the pillow as he bends and whispers to the child.

Susie does not cry out. She does not flinch. She does not move. Her eyes, even as her skin is torn away, rest on Reuben Samuel's homely face.

"Forgive me, child."

Zerel hears the words; they pierce her heart, then cleanse the wound: *Forgive me.*

Though the burns are severe and slow to heal, they leave no scars. *Recovered,* Mamaw thinks, and she tries to tell herself she only imagines flickers of wariness in the lingering glances of her children.

Long after unguents and dressings and laudanum cease to provide cause, Dr. Samuel continues to visit the James place. "You are always welcome here," Zerel tells him. She spots delight and eagerness in the way her children usher him up to the porch, display their small proficiencies and passions. The doctor does not shower them with gifts. Barley sweets do not line his pockets. He is staid, though still a youngish man—younger than Zerel by a few years, not one for rough-housing or chatter.

"Jesse, git in here."

He pounds into the kitchen, flushed with spring. Snippets of weed cling to his hair, grass stains on his shirt.

"What mischief are you up to while your brother's out plantin' like a useful citizen of this county?"

"Figured I'd trap me a rabbit for our supper."

Mamaw grunts. "Day you trap a rabbit's the day I'll walk to town on my hands."

Jesse grins. "You best be gettin' a start then, Mamaw."

"Never mind your smart talk. I need you to do somethin'. Take these-here jars of relish and conserve over to Dr. Samuel . . . and ask him can we borrow that fine-tooth saw this afternoon."

"Why don't you go?"

"Don't get fresh."

"Wasn't meaning to be fresh, Mamaw. Just reckon the doc'd rather see you than me."

"Stand there winkin' like you got a tic. You gonna get goin', or am I gonna git you goin'?"

"I'll go. Right glad to. But see if the doc's face don't fall when he finds only me come tappin' on his door."

Zerel sighs. "The Lord seen fit to visit this family with a pure-blooded fool."

"He's sweet on you," says Jesse. "See if I ain't right."

"I don't aim to stand here all day discussin' your daydreams, boy. I need that saw."

"Guess you're a little sweet on him, too," Jesse says. "I'm goin'."

"And don't dawdle coming back. Who knows what riffraff's on the road these days?"

Reuben Samuel loves lemonade. Nothing better in the late heat of a July afternoon. And now that the train makes a stop in Kearney, a body can even get a fresh lemon now and then, providing they can meet the price. Not this week, though. Ain't a lemon to be had, and Reuben coming this evening for supper.

Mamaw fetches some cider from the cellar, spikes it with vinegar for tartness, and picks some sprigs of wild mint from the edge of the north pasture.

"Try this," she says. "It's a Missouri julep."

If this ain't the cleverest woman, Reuben Samuel thinks. Zerelda James plain tickles him sometimes.

"Ain't you going to have one?"

"Don't mind if I do."

She goes back to the kitchen for a minute. When she returns to the porch, she has a tin tumbler in her hand.

She sinks down on a wood plank bench beside Reuben. "Nice to have a chance to rest my feet 'fore them youngsters come stampeding in here."

"I don't know how you keep up with 'em."

She laughs. "I don't . . . scarcely even try."

"Oh, I seen you got things pretty well in hand around here." Reuben Samuel smiles bashfully. "I think a lot of you, you know."

"Well, we think of a lot of you, too."

Reuben clears his throat. "I didn't mean it just right like

that. I . . . what I'm trying to say is, I seem to have you on my mind a good bit . . . and I mean, you know, *you*. Not y'all."

"Oh," Zerel says.

Reuben is sweating. He loosens his collar a little with a forefinger. "Seems like there ain't a day anymore when I don't get a hankering to come over here . . . see if the snow's got you under or the heat's got you down, I don't know what-all."

Zerel is looking at her drink, kind of absent, but the look on her face doesn't appear exactly pleased. *Well, I am really putting my foot in it now,* Reuben thinks. *Likely about up to the anklebone.*

But suddenly Miz James is giving him a big, toothy, handsome grin, and it seems to have a touch of mischief in it.

"You just keep on coming as often as you can stand it, Reuben," she says. "I'm downright grateful to see a body with some sense around here."

Reuben's smile stretches off toward his big ears.

"Besides," Mamaw says, "this family got a call for a doctor's services near every day, anyhow."

Zerelda James marries Reuben Samuel on September 26, 1855, in a private civil ceremony on the outskirts of Kearney. The morning is fair. The Justice of the Peace, a widower himself, provides a sister and a stableboy for witnesses. His parlor seems alive with dust motes. There are no flowers.

Reuben and Zerel are attired in fresh but ordinary clothes. Her concessions to ceremony are a round hat of black glazed straw and a crocheted ivory collar affixed to her black broadcloth dress. Mamaw doesn't own a "best dress," but this one's as good as she's got. Reuben wears a paisley silk cravat, purchased years ago in St. Louis on the brief, whimsical conviction that something extraordinary might befall him someday.

Zerel, as far as Reuben is concerned, is extraordinary.

They talk little as they drive the wagon back to the James place. (Always and ever will it be "the James place," though Reuben Samuel will occupy it five times as long as Robert James ever did.) They stop by Reuben's farm, to be let now, to pick up the few effects he intends to bring to his bride's household—clothing, doctoring bag, a few medical books, and his precious tools. Reuben treats the implements of farming and carpentry with the same tender and meticulous care he accords his medical instruments. They are wrapped, for the brief journey, in chamois cloth and laid in wooden cases.

Zerel looks at the motley pile of goods and grins. "Quite a dowry you got yourself here," she says. A cracked gladstone bag with a busted clasp spills out a trail of socks and galluses. A much-darned union suit drags in the dust.

Reuben blushes and stuffs the underwear back in the bag. "My trousseau," he says.

The bride nods. "Right dainty."

Zerel pokes through the barn while Reuben is loading the wagon.

"Your plow's better than ours," she says. "Reckon we could exchange 'em before your tenant takes over here?"

Reuben smiles. A practical woman. "I don't see why not," he says.

Susie and Jesse wait on the porch, hands shading their eyes, when Reuben and Zerel reach the rise in the road. At noonday the September fields look like beaten brass in the hot, high sun.

Jesse spots the wagon. His whoop can be heard clear down the road.

"Ain't he just runnin' with sap, that boy?"

Mamaw smiles. "He is at that."

Frank comes out the door, wearing a purple shirt Zerel's never seen him put on before. She made it for him last Christmas. "Too notice-ish," he'd said, then kept right on wearing the faded blue, the tattered gray.

Something red as a tanager feather flutters in Susie's doe-colored hair, a ribbon of some kind. Where would the child get a thing like that?

"Bound and determined to carry on over this, seems like."

"Reckon you know I love these youngsters like my own," Reuben says.

"Reckon I do," says Mamaw.

As they alight from the wagon, Jesse showers them with handfuls of oats. Frank offers his stepfather a handshake, manful and self-conscious. Then, after a bewildered pause, the boy shakes his mother's hand as well. "Felicitations," he says.

Zerel laughs.

"Thank you, son," Reuben says soberly.

Susie holds out what appears to be a tangle of weeds, broad bristled leaves of silvery green around small blue-violet flowers: blue devils. . . .

Viper's Bugloss, Robert said, to drive out melancholy and exhilarate the heart.

Frank grabs Susie by the waist and raises her so she can place the bushy wreath on her mother's head. Mamaw, bowed under the flowers, looks at her children and cannot speak.

"Flowers all over the place inside, too, Mamaw."

"And a wedding feast!" Jesse cries.

"Well, now"—Zerel's voice is faint—"ain't that fine."

The kitchen is shot with gold: mums and asters and saw-tooth sunflowers and goldenrod buzzing with bees.

Susie takes a flower from a crock on the hearthstone. Shyly, she fixes the yellow pinwheel in Reuben's buttonhole.

"My own brown-eyed Susie," he says gravely. "Thank you, my child."

"Reckon we can eat now?" Franks says.

The wedding repast, laid out on the table, consists of cheese grits, roasted ears of corn, pound cake, and cherry cordial.

"Reckon you know who made this cake," Frank says.

"The bride's ownself would be my guess," says Zerel. "How'd you manage to find it?"

"We don't miss much," Jesse says.

"Seems I'm rearin' a den of thievin' rascals. I been saving that cherry liquor since I don't know how long."

"Lucky that bottle turned up, ain't it?" Jesse says.

Mamaw nods. "Right lucky."

Frank reaches for an ear of corn, then withdraws his hand when his brother glares at him and raps on the table.

"And now, lady and gentleman, if we might ask your indulgin' for just another minute here, the feast will kick off with some musical entertainment."

The three children scrape their chairs away from the table and arrange themselves before the fireplace.

"This here's a love song I wrote specially for today," Jesse says. "I call it 'Hang Old Jim Lane.'" Started up with a hum and signal from Frank, who conducts, they sing in three-part harmony.

Mamaw claps and whistles when they've finished. "Prettiest sentiments I ever did hear," she says.

Reuben, at a loss for words, stamps his feet, which Jesse takes for an ovation. The encore, by popular demand, is a family favorite:

> *Throw out the life-line! Throw out the life-line!*
> *Someone is drifting away.*
> *Throw out the life-line! Throw out the life-line!*
> *Someone is sinking today.*

Reuben takes a gulp of cherry cordial, which goes down the wrong way. Frank and Jesse pound his back.

Mamaw looks at her new husband. "Hope you ain't goin' down for the third time," she says.

It is growing late. Mamaw listens, her head tilted to one side. There isn't a sound from the loft above. "Thought them youngsters never would settle down."

Reuben leans over the table, supporting his head on one hand. "Good bit of excitement. I'm about done in myself."

"Figured you might pass out before dinner was done, way you was suckin' up that cherry liquor." They both laugh softly. "I'd plumb forgot that villainous potion existed."

"Took me aback, I can tell you. Never figured my bride for a drinking woman."

"Beg pardon, but any fool could see that bottle ain't been touched till now."

"How'd you come to have such a thing, anyhow?"

"Brewed it myself," Zerel says. "From ground cherries. Years ago. I was just a girl."

"And a pastor's wife, to boot."

"Reckon that's why. No harm in it. I just wanted to see what the pastor'd do, finding spirits in his own house."

"What did he do?"

Zerel looks away from Reuben, staring into the sooty glass chimney of the oil lamp. "Didn't do a thing," she says. "Told me to go on and drink it myself if I'd a mind to. Which of course I didn't."

Reuben smiles. "Well, maybe it was meant to be kept for today."

Zerel reaches across the table and pats his arm. "Maybe so," she says. "I just hope them boys didn't acquire the taste. They got enough of the devil in them already."

Then they are looking at each other, uneasy, grave, nothing left to say.

"Reckon you're tired, then. . . ."

"I am, a bit." Reuben's gaze is drawn toward the bedroom doorway, then he sees Zerel watching him and his face turns red.

"Feels right awkward, now it comes to this," he says.

Zerel smiles. "We get on pretty well, you and me. Don't guess the rest of it ought to be any different."

She rises from her chair, takes the oil lamp from the table, and starts for the bedroom.

Reuben follows her.

IX

Exigencies

1 8 5 8 — 1 8 6 3

Jesse and Frank grow tall, secretive, savage in their games, their chores, their rivalries, their beliefs. Frank is the easier of the two, no doubt about it: a favorite with the teacher at Pleasant Grove School, the best field hand Mamaw ever had. Jesse does less and makes more noise about it, makes nothing easy. His energy is brutal. *Like fire,* Mamaw thinks: *handled right, ain't nothing that boy can't do.* And Frank keeps an eye on him—she'll say that for her first child, got the sense he was born with and then some.

The day after Christmas 1858, Reuben and Zerel married three years, Sallie Samuel is born. Delivering the baby, Reuben is steady and cool, every inch a doctor. Until he holds the fact in his hands: his own child. He acts giddy and dazed.

"Just what I need," Mamaw says. "Another fool to suffer."

Reuben smiles at her. "You ever think there may be a contagion in your household?"

"Could be. It does seem . . . I don't know, foolhardy like, bringing a helpless little critter into a world where folks shoot and set fire to one another's houses," she says.

"But what would the world come to if we did not . . ."

Reuben gazes at his infant daughter and his expression is peaceful, sure.

"Reckon you got more faith than I got," Zerel says.

"Hope," says Reuben. "Just hope."

Jesse, Frank, and Susie James are enchanted with their new baby sister. On the day she arrives, Jesse begins to call his stepfather "Pappy." A little joke. But it catches on. Reuben Samuel will, on the James place, never again be known as anything but Pappy.

The world, just down the road, keeps on unraveling at an alarming speed.

Mamaw is carrying another child by December 1860, when the news of South Carolina's secession reaches Kearney.

Pappy is saddened, worried. "I don't like the look of things."

"High time somebody took a stand," Zerel says. "I almost envy them."

"You don't mean that, Zerel."

"No, reckon not, exactly. I hope it don't come to that kind of pass, but . . ."

"You oughtn't let the boys hear you talk so."

She shrugs. "Don't hardly know anymore what those boys need to be told to get by in this world."

But she tells them a thing or two, she gives it to 'em straight, Mamaw. And a few months later, when fire is opened upon Fort Sumter, her frenzy is a thing to behold. Not much more than a month away now, the borning time, and Mamaw resembles a volcano.

"Ain't bad enough decent Southern boys got to risk their necks down there and we got this lily-livered legislature in Jeff City. Now damn Lincoln—"

"The President," Pappy corrects her mildly, glancing at his stepsons.

"President in a pig's eye. Man's got the brass of a fancy

candlestick and about as much brains if he thinks Missouri'll be providing troops to raise arms agianst the Confederates."

"Now don't excite yourself so," Reuben says. "I told you it ain't good for the baby when you get overwrought."

"Reckon it ain't none too soon for him to hear this, nei-ther."

"Oh, *him,* is it?"

"You wait and see if it ain't."

"Least the Governor told 'em what they can expect from us," Frank says. "When Washington City sees this-here Home Guard, they'll wish they never mentioned the word 'troops' in these parts."

"Guess General Price'll run them little-boy-blues off so far their own mamas won't never hear from 'em again." Jesse grins. "Wish I could join up."

"Reckon we might change the subject?" Pappy says. "We got a woman in a delicate condition here."

Mamaw snorts. "Delicate my foot. Wisht I could join up myself."

A few days later, on April 20, a band of Confederate sym-pathizers, perhaps tired of waiting to see what will happen next, raids the Federal arsenal at Lexington, an hour's ride from the James place. Four cannons and a wealth of small arms are delivered triumphantly to Governor Jackson's new-born fighting militia.

Frank's had it with hesitation. "Well, that about settles it, I'd say. Time I started helping out."

Zerel sinks, slow and heavy, to a milking stool. "Son—"

He holds up his hand. "We both know I'm going, Mamaw. Why don't we take a shortcut around the argument, save us both a lot of wear and tear."

"If you'd just wait another year. . . ."

"A year from now . . . Mamaw, what difference would it

make, 'cepting they might not need men so much as they need 'em now?"

"Men." Mamaw shakes her head. "You got any idea what you're getting into, son?"

Frank grins. "You bet I do."

"This ain't gonna be no lark."

"Mamaw, I do believe you're jealous," Franks says.

Gone.

She doesn't know where Frank is by May 10, tells herself he couldn't possibly have got as far as St. Louis by the time a crowd is massacred by Federal militia at Camp Jackson.

There is still no word from him two weeks later, as Mamaw gives birth to a boy she names John.

For a month afterward, though the labor was short, the delivery easy, the child strong, Mamaw is listless, black-spirited, always cold, never hungry.

"We'd have heard by now," Reuben tells her, "if something happened to him."

"I should have tried to keep him," she says. "Unpersuaded him." She raises the new infant to her breast without looking at him.

Finally, in late June, an overgrown boy in a tattered make-do uniform stops by the homeplace at dusk, doesn't even get off his horse. Zerel sees him talking to Reuben in the yard, his scabby stallion pawing the dirt. She rushes out into the dim twilight.

"It's all right," Pappy calls as she runs toward them, making the boy's horse skittish. "It's word of Frank. He's fine."

"Where is he?" She looks up at the boy.

"I can't say." He stares down on her with odd opaque eyes, greenish and somehow spiteful. "He ain't harmed is all I'm supposed to tell you."

Mamaw makes her own eyes steely. "Who are you?"

"Name's Younger, ma'am. Thomas Coleman Younger."

"You kin to the Jackson County Youngers?"

The boy nods, his face stony. Then, without another word, he wheels his horse around and takes off, spewing dust like a trail of smoke behind him.

"Hard, ain't he, for such a young 'un?" Reuben sounds like he's talking to himself. His eyes follow the swirl of dust rising on the road.

"That Younger family been hounded near to death," Zerel says. "No wonder he ain't interested in passing the time of day."

"Told me he's the oldest child of that man got his livery stable burnt out."

A breeze blows up from the pasture. Mamaw is soaked with sweat. She shivers. "Boy like Frank got no business with men like that, Pappy."

"I don't reckon that Younger boy's much older than Frank, Zerel."

"Not in years, maybe."

"Never mind, now. Frank's all right is the main thing."

"For today, anyhow . . . or last week, more likely."

They never know till afterwards where Frank has been, what he has done . . . they will never know what Frank has seen. When General Sterling Price is triumphant at Wilson's Creek, Frank is there. The Union forces are soundly defeated, losing more than thirteen hundred men. To hear the Missourians tell it, Price's troops barely suffer a scratch. A few weeks later, when the Union is put to shame at Lexington, only forty miles from Kearney, Frank is among the victors.

It is not quite suppertime, a mild September dusk. Jesse and Mamaw, finished with evening chores, sit on the porch steps watching the road for Reuben to return. He's gone into town

❖

to call on a sickly bride who has taken to her bed since her young husband, frisky from nuptials and spring fever, lit out for the Lexington arsenal several months ago.

The breeze, still warm with sun, shifts slightly, ushering a sweet, rich fragrance toward the house.

"Pears are fine this year," Mamaw says. "Shame we got but two of them trees."

Jesse grunts for an answer. He has been moody since his birthday a few days before.

"What's eating you?" his mother says.

"I'm tired of sitting around here like old folks."

"Well, sir, we got plenty of pastimes on these acres to keep you from having to sit and rock too much."

"Wisht I was with Frank."

"Bein' all of fourteen now," she says dryly.

"I could fight and you know it."

"Lord knows I know it, seeing you tear into your sister like you done this morning."

Jesse looks abashed. "Yeah. Reckon I been sort of touchy. But shoot, Mamaw, who *ain't,* when things got so's they come in there and run our own Governor out?"

"You don't have to tell me, little brother." Mamaw, she's been a mite touchy herself since Lincoln ousted the feisty Governor Jackson and replaced him with his poor excuse for a "provisional government." Only tad of enjoyment she's had lately is hooting at the new Governor's name: Gamble. Seems like this President's too dumb to read his own handwriting on his own wall.

"Ain't none of us exactly busting to pieces with joy these days," Mamaw says. "But listen here, son, it don't change a thing for you to be taking on so."

"I know it, Mamaw. My birthday just got me thinking how long it's apt to be yet before I can *do* anything." He looks over the darkening pasture toward the road. "Somebody's comin'."

"Pappy said he'd be back in time for supper."

"It ain't Pappy."

Instinctively, long accustomed to wariness, they both stand up.

"One sorry-lookin' horse, that is," Jesse says.

The figure reaches the entrance to the James place. As he turns in, he waves.

"Glory be!"

"Mamaw, that's Frank!"

He dismounts like an old man, stiff and slow. "Greetings, loved ones," he says.

"The hero of Wilson's Creek!" Jesse cries.

"And the first word outa his mouth sarcastic," says Mamaw.

Frank awkwardly embraces his mother. "Reckon a measure of irony's fitting," he says. "The hero's been sent home with spots on his face."

Zerel and Jesse study Frank in the dim twilight, now noticing how thin . . . his peaked face is covered with small pink welts like insect bites.

"What on earth got after you, boy?"

"The horrors of battle is many and various, ma'am."

"Looks like measles," Mamaw says.

"Told you if you come too close to them Yankees you'd get some disease," Jesse says. "Lucky it ain't worse."

A man now, Mamaw thinks. Never told her much to begin with, now he tells her nothing.

Within a few weeks Frank is well again. He takes up the farming work, tolerates Jesse's pestering and Susie's adoration, shows a surprising tender interest in the little ones. He doesn't say a word about if he'll stay, how long he'll stay, what he might do next. He is weighing again, Mamaw thinks, always weighing, Frank. He looks like a man come more from defeat than victory: beaten down, flinching at noises, hiding

❖

from visitors. He is waiting for something, but he won't tell her what.

Frank won't come in for supper.

"Ain't hungry, he says." Mamaw can tell from Jesse's injured voice that his brother has been snappish with the boy again.

"Pappy, you see to it these children eat like civilized folk. I got to talk to Franklin."

She finds him behind the smokehouse, sitting on a stump. "How-do," she says.

He nods. "Mamaw."

"Parole," she says. "Let's have us a talk about that."

He jumps. "How'd you find out about it?"

Mamaw found out with no trouble at all, just kept her ears pricked up in town.

"Hell," she says, "they even got a notice about it nailed up by the postal window."

Seems the boys who come home from fighting Missouri's good fight are seen as traitors now. They want to linger in Clay County longer than to pack a bag and borrow a horse, they got to swear loyalty to the Union and post bond to back up their word.

"So you know all about it," Frank says.

"How come I didn't hear about it from you is what I'd like to know."

"Nothing you can do about it."

"And what about you? What are you going to do?"

"If I knew that, I'd be off doing it."

"You best do something if you mean to stay here much longer."

"I know." The setting sun is behind her. He looks up, squinting. "Reckon you heard if I turn myself in I got to swear I won't . . . 'cease all manner of aiding and abetting the enemy's' how they put it, I believe." He kicks up some dirt with the toe of his boot. "You imagine that, Mamaw? The enemy—ain't nobody but us they're talking about."

Mamaw touches his cheek. Her fingers seem smooth against his skin. Whiskers. Well, of course. But what particular day when Mamaw wasn't paying any particular attention did those . . .

"I ain't here to tell you what you ought to do, son. Don't rightly know what I'd do myself, were it me. But I figure I might help clear up the choices."

"How's that?"

"By reminding you there's only two—either you go along or you get going. You ain't safe here, the way things are. And neither is this family."

Frank looks down at the ground.

"Don't take this for shaming, Franklin. I don't blame you for needing to think and wanting to come home to do it. But there ain't much time."

"I know that, Mamaw."

"There's something else. I know it ain't just the . . . the promise they ask that's bothering you. They want a thousand dollars besides."

He picks up a stone and scales it at a dogwood, hitting the frail trunk hard. " 'Good behavior bond' is the name they give that part . . . highway robbery's more like it."

"Well, never mind. The money's the least of it. I just wanted to tell you, you need it, you come to me."

He looks up, startled. "Don't tell me you got a thousand dollars, Mamaw?"

"Ain't nothing you need to know except I'll take care of it."

He watches, speechless, as she starts back toward the cabin. At the corner of the yard, she looks back at him. "Son?"

"Yes, ma'am?"

"Promises can be broken," she says. "If need be."

The following week Mamaw and Frank ride into Kearney in the wagon, wearing their church clothes on a Thursday afternoon. Frank, looking neither at his mother nor the administering officer, takes an oath of allegiance to the Union. Mamaw hands over the money.

"It's a fine thing to see," says the officer, grown voluble on cash in hand, "a mother who's willin' to take responsibility for her son's erroneous ways."

"Indeed I am," Mamaw says. "Willin'."

"You keep an eye on this one then, ma'am. Next time he might not get off so easy."

"I got things in hand," she says.

"You listen to your mama, young fella."

"Yessir."

They are silent in the wagon, Frank and Mamaw, until they've passed through town. When they hit the straight flat stretch out to the country, she begins to hum "Hang Old Jim Lane."

"Ain't you ashamed," Franks says, "setting such a disgraceful example for your young 'un?"

"You enjoy my performance back there?"

" 'Just a' ignorant farm boy.' " Frank raises his voice to a plaintive pitch. " 'No daddy, and his pore mama tryin' to scratch a meager mouthful outa the dirt.' Mamaw, you were priceless."

"I was, wasn't I? Kinda wisht Jesse been there to see it."

"Good thing Pappy wasn't, though."

"Reckon so."

They reach the top of the rise. Mamaw looks down and sees the homeplace, the sturdy little cabin squatting before a backdrop of evergreens, the symmetry of fields around it. "Tell me something."

"What's that, Mamaw?"

"When you take that oath back there . . . you cross your fingers?

Frank, keeping his eye on the road, smiles the way Robert James used to when Zerel questioned the existence of God.

Two-fisted fighting now for Missouri: as the nation, top to bottom, gears up for civil war, the border battles with Kansas continue. Two all-out wars side by side and all mixed together till you can't tell one from another. Now more urgent . . . everything more urgent now. Decent boys are branded turn-coats. Peaceable citizens are granted no protection. Private property's fair game. Everything heating up. The summer of 1862 is, in Missouri, a firecracker. Hot as a pistol, Clay County.

Amid the screams and bloody rending, Missouri labors to bring forth legends: heroes are born. Little Arch Clement, no bigger than a flea and decked out in the stained blue coat of a Union officer, sneaks through enemy lines and leaves all corpses, no tracks. Jo Shelby paralyzes the enemy with his black unblinking eyes. George Todd makes Jayhawker mincemeat. A boy name of Anderson turns threats into prom ises and is rewarded with the name "Bloody Bill" for keeps.

But they are all harmless tykes—Clement and Shelby, Todd and Anderson, mischievous boys in short pants—when lined up next to William Clarke Quantrill, the most savage guerrilla fighter to run a raid or sit a horse. Some say he is a spy, a devil, a genius, a god: a fighter brave to the point of madness, and he's loved for it.

When Frank has finished weighing and made up his mind, Mamaw can tell. One day at the end of August she sees him standing taller, sees the hunted look gone from his eye. He sticks around long enough to help with the harvesting. Then he heads out to join up with Quantrill's guerrillas. He has made his choice.

❖

"Had my choice made for me," he tells her.

Mamaw needs no explanation. A few weeks earlier Missouri's provisional government—Lincoln's lackeys—ordered all Missouri men of military age to enlist in the State militia. To fight against the Confederacy. For many it comes down to no choice at all.

Frank James is nineteen when he rides off after William Clarke Quantrill, "the bloodiest man in American history."

X

Calculated Risks

1 8 6 3

Mamaw sits on a sunny patch of grass behind the cabin. A few feet away, on the cinder path to the smokehouse, fat is heating in a cast-iron pot over a small fire. As she waits for the fat to melt down so she can add the lye, Mamaw turns her face up to the generous midafternoon sun and feels a surge of nameless hope. *I ought to know better,* she thinks.

But the stillness, the warmth, are seductive. Susie has gone with the younger children and a loaded picnic hamper to Reuben's old place. The tenant, Joe Heacock, says the brook's bubbling with trout just now. Got the youngsters all excited till he didn't hardly have no choice but to invite them. Jesse is plowing a field out east of the house. Reuben's around front, replacing a weak plank in the porch floor.

"You seen these dandelions out here?" Zerel calls to him.

"Dandelions?"

"Got us a bumper crop this year, Pappy. Thinkin' I might go into the wine business again."

His laugh comes around the corner on a breeze. "Well, you just let me know when it's tasting time," he says.

The fat is beginning to bubble, the scent of pork both

❖

appetizing and incongruous in the fresh flowery air. Dead meat and ashes among the flowers . . .

Necessity, Mamaw thinks. Always upsetting the natural order of things to get what we think we need, to keep what we hope we got . . . beautiful clear-eyed boys with bloody bullet holes in their foreheads . . . tired old women watching men they've never seen before, will never see again, turn rooms where children been bred and reared and fed into ash heaps. *Why can't we just leave things be?* she thinks. And it makes, for this moment, perfect sense.

But there ain't no perfect sense anymore, no sense to things at all. Frank Lord-knows-where, in Texas last thing she heard, fighting . . . setting fires himself, for all she knows. Jesse, still half-child, a messenger and lookout for armed guerrillas. While she, Mamaw—about to bear her seventh child—not only gives her blessing, but her help, her roof and table to strangers, boys with blood on their hands. By the book, treason . . . traitors, Jesse and Mamaw. What sense in that? Aid and comfort, she thinks. Necessity.

Mamaw frets and wonders and waits . . . fat hisses and spits in the pot and Mamaw waits to add the lye to make the soap to scour the grease to . . . sooner or later it all sinks into the ground again, the natural order of things.

At first the sound of hooves pounding up the road doesn't alarm her. Seems like folks do more visiting these days, when they ought to be sticking closer to home. Neighbors stop by on the thinnest excuse now, as if they just want to see others who, like themselves, keep up the age-old daily steps as the world goes up in smoke.

"Looks like we got company, Mamaw." Something in Reuben's voice puts her on her guard. Horses, too many of them moving too fast . . . now Mamaw knows trouble's likely on its way, coming to find her when she stops looking for it.

She struggles to her feet, fighting the bulk of the child,

imagining Frank torn and trampled somewhere in Bleeding Kansas . . . she brushes the grass from her skirt.

Before she can make her way around the house, the thunder of hoofbeats skids to a stop in the yard. A harsh cry, "There!" and a scuffle of dismounting, running. Then Reuben's peaceable voice:

"Gentlemen. Some service my household may do you?"

Mamaw is about to round the corner of the cabin now, moving into view.

"Never mind the Southern gentleman routine. We ain't much interested in you. It's your spying whore of a wife and her boy—"

"Now look here, son—"

Zerel hears the sound of a blow, then Reuben's soft groan.

"No, you listen, mister. We know what this family been up to. We know who's been sleeping in this house. If you're such a gentleman, maybe you best be more choosy about who you sleep with."

A brutal laugh. "He got anything else on him the size of that nose, ain't a wonder his bed's so busy. You got anything else that big, little man?"

"Wouldn't touch him myself, but . . . say, you got gloves, Jack. Why don't you undo them trousers, give us a look-see Il what he's got in there's puny as I expect, we could carry it back with us . . . folks in Kansas won't hardly believe a thing could be that bitty 'less we show 'em."

Mamaw stands beside the woodpile, hidden by the corner of the house, frozen. She can't see Pappy or the men. The sound of abuse rises, insults punctuated with fists and boots, Reuben's soft gasps and moans.

(*Just yards away guns in the house, only the door's out front . . . windows shut against the heat of day, neighbors help by the time she got there, even halfway there where while the ruffians bastards finished with Pappy finished long gone . . .*)

Mamaw doesn't move or make a sound. Crouches like an animal. She smells the boiling animal fat and wonders how long before they notice too and come around back . . . and she wonders why she cannot move, why she's thinking *like thinking has some bearing on what they're doing, what Reuben's suffering Reuben screaming and she not breathing not even thinking now but seeing: Jesse alone half-naked plowing out in the open no protection this earth . . . and Frank on enemy soil even more in the open less protection and she sees herself, too, Mamaw: invincible striding out into sunlight bearing down treading on their shadows bloodying blinding the lye a storm blown from her hands and them firing shooting blind and the youngsters hearing the shots over beside the brook bubbling with trout . . .*

And she stays where she is: concealed, murderous, safe. Mamaw stays put and doesn't dream of making a sound.

And then they are gone.

She runs from behind the house and at first she doesn't see Reuben because she is looking for him on the ground, his body flat and dim as a shadow.

Up in the sunlight Reuben hangs from a limb of the coffee tree in the southeast corner of the yard. A stout rope clings to his neck. The worn soles of his boots are only a few inches above the earth. A pattern of leaves spatters his face.

Mamaw runs inside for the butcher knife. She slashes at the rope three times: it scarcely frays. She hears screams of rage and isn't sure whether they are in her throat or her mind. Holding Reuben against her with one arm, trying to raise him up, she saws the blade of the knife back and forth, back and forth, urgency made patient until the heavy rope is severed.

She tries to keep hold of Reuben as his weight is released, but she doesn't have a good grip on him. He falls at her feet in the dry dirt at the base of the tree.

Mamaw drops to her knees and takes his head in her lap.

His face, pressed to the slope of her belly, is absolutely colorless, raw burns at his throat. He is not breathing.

"No," she says. Her voice quiet and firm. "No." She hold her husband's face between her hands and leans down close to him. "Do not give them this," she says. "You hear me?"

Reuben, then, makes a small choking sound.

"Oh, God." She quickly loosens his collar, then holds his face again, moving his head from side to side, slowly. She opens his eyelids with her thumbs . . . pennies, she thinks, *pennies on the eyes to keep them closed so they can't see how others still have life while they are dead, so the living won't spy their own likeness in the dead eyes that become like mirrors where we glimpse at last how small we are, how faint our prints on the earth. . . .*

She turns Reuben's face to the left, where he might open his eyes to grass, to earth, and she goes for water. As she pours the water over him, as she dips the hem of her apron into the water and bathes Reuben's throat, she says to him over and over, "No . . . don't give . . . they shall not have . . . shall not . . ."

At last, Reuben opens his eyes.

"Pappy?"

He cannot speak. He raises his hand, then lets it fall again.

"It's all right," Mamaw says.

There is no thought of weights and measures, distances, possibilities, as she carries him to the house. Mamaw carries Reuben as if he's one of her children. Out of the sun she carries him, out of the dirt, and lays him gently on the bed.

His black doctoring bag sits on the floor in a patch of sunlight beneath the window. She finds a jar of burn ointment and rubs it lightly over the ruined flesh of his throat. When lying flat seems to trouble his breathing, she rolls a coverlet and works it under his head. Still he does not speak, watching her with empty eyes. She raises the window to let in air. Then she sits beside him on the edge of the bed, chafing his wrists, stroking his hands. "It's all right . . . going to be all right now . . . "

"Four times." His voice is raw, a whisper. "Four."

Mamaw, too, whispers. "Never mind."

"They pulled me up four times."

"It's all right now."

Reuben's eyes fill. "I let them," he says.

She feels something collapsing in on itself like a star until nothing is left of her: Mamaw, a dark vacuum. She gets up slowly, supporting herself on the bedpost, and moves away, turning her back to Reuben.

"*I* let them," she says.

"Nothing you could do," Reuben says. "You come out, they'd only—"

"Don't," she says. "It can't be absolved."

She is still standing silent in the corner of the bedroom when they hear a heavy tread on the porch.

Mamaw reaches to the mantel for the one shotgun that's always kept loaded. Then she crosses the room without making a sound.

The barrel is sighted straight on the door, at a fair estimate of a tall man's head.

The door swings open with a creak. Her aim holds steady. Jesse looks past the barrel of the shotgun at his mother.

"You're welcome to what's left, Mamaw. But it ain't much, I'm afraid." He turns around; the back of his faded blue shirt hangs in bloody tatters.

Mamaw lays the shotgun on the table, still pointed toward the door. Wordlessly she takes hold of Jesse's arm and leads him into the bedroom.

Reuben's eyes are closed, his breathing ragged.

"They been here, too." Jesse says.

Mamaw nods.

"Pappy all right?"

"He will be," she says.

Gently as she can, she removes her son's shirt. A few patches of blue cloth stick to the drying blood on his torn back. She helps him to lie, face-down, beside Reuben.

Midnight: she rocks . . . into three o'clock, then riding toward dawn. The night is long and loud: screams of rage, threats of revenge. Terror is a baying. Mamaw's lips move in prayers of remorse and thanksgiving, soundless howls at the moon. Within her, she feels the coming child's first gesture . . . or fancies she does.

It was the brink of darkness when Susie and the babies came home, sunburned, their dirty hands festooned with a string of iridescent fish.

Mamaw met them on the porch, told Susie as much as she needed to know.

"You get these little ones fed and put down out here, sleep in the kitchen for tonight."

The girl, fourteen, got weepy for a moment. "Let me see Jess and Pappy."

"Do like I say," Mamaw told her. "There's times men don't want to be seen."

Not a sound comes now from the blackened kitchen, where Susie, John, and Sallie lie on a makeshift pallet on the floor. Mamaw rocks, keeping watch over the men. A creak in her chair marks time like the ticking of a clock.

Occasionally Reuben whimpers in his sleep. "Never mind," Mamaw says, bending to him, whispering close to his cheek. "Never mind."

Jesse, too, sleeps, but only off and on. Mamaw sees his eyes on her, drawing a hard light from the single candle that burns beside her chair.

Once each hour Mamaw leaves her chair to bathe and salve Jesse's wounds. He winces when she touches them. His skin is feverish. She covers the wounds with leaves, mullen gathered by the last of the daylight. The leaves are grayish, covered with a fine hair to draw the fever out.

When Jesse lapses into sleep, he talks up a storm. His threats are so detailed Mamaw finds it hard to keep hold of the fact that he is asleep.

Finally, as dawn starts to lighten the sky, Jesse quiets. He lies on his side, facing the door. His eyelids flicker, and his tender young mouth is set in a hard, grim line. He looks, as he dreams, like a dangerous man.

They'll be back, she knows, like starved dogs to the site of a kill.

Not two weeks have gone by when they come. This time Mamaw is alone.

She is scattering chicken feed in the yard when she sees them, three this time, cutting in from the road. She has time to go to the house for the shotgun, but she doesn't. She stands waiting for them, her massive stillness making their reckless speed ridiculous. They tear into the yard, raising dust, scattering chickens, trampling flowers.

"Where's your boy?"

The tallest one seems to be the leader, though he isn't twenty yet. Likely none of them are. His sparse red beard looks like it still needs some coaxing.

"Ain't here," Mamaw says.

"Reckon we're supposed to take the word of a lying bitch like you?"

"Believe what you like. Only boy here now is a two-year-old having a nap . . . don't guess that's the one you're looking for?"

The tall one dismounts, the other two quickly following suit, surrounding her, coming so close she can smell sweat and bad food and last night's whiskey . . . and fear, she thinks, just scared boys. . . .

Their pieced-together uniforms are so ragged and filthy she imagines them filched from the dead. "You boys smell worse than your horses," she says.

The smallest of the three, a towheaded youngster with oddly pale eyes, raises a hand as if to strike her.

She splays her fingers across the swell of her belly. "You won't lay a hand on me," she says.

"True enough, ma'am. Wouldn't touch no rattlesnake, neither."

He is nearly a head shorter than Mamaw. She takes a step closer, looking down on him. "That's a good boy."

"Keep a hold on her, Tommy. I'll go have a look inside."

The blond boy grasps her arms roughly, holding her as the others enter the house.

"You needn't clutch at me that way," she says. "I certainly don't intend on lightin' out just because three half-growed banty roosters strut into my yard. Where do you boys go to school, sonny?"

The boy reddens, his free hand going to the Colt navy revolver stuck in the waistband of his britches, but he doesn't answer her.

The other two come back out of the cabin. The leader carries the family shotgun, the other a plucked chicken Mamaw was preparing for supper.

"Big game hunters," she says. "Guess you seen my boy in there. He tell you what you need to know?"

"We seen him," the leader says. "Seen the girl, too. Now you go in there, old woman. Get them brats up and ready to travel, and if it takes longer than two minutes, all three of you'll be resistin' arrest."

"I will not. Those children are two and four years old. What's wrong with you boys?"

"Beg pardon, ma'am, but it's what's wrong with you. You are, for one thing, a fat foul-mouthed pig. But I wouldn't hold your race against you, nossir. The problem's the company you keep . . . and this habit you got of droppin' traitors to the Union out of that big belly of yours."

"I try to do my part, sonny."

"I don't doubt it for a minute, ma'am. Now go get them kids and hustle back out here. Don't rightly know how I'll explain this to my sweetheart . . . but I'm afraid I can't bear to go off and leave you behind."

"I ain't leaving here."

The butt of her own shotgun comes up hard under her chin. "We getting through to you now, ma'am? You're under arrest."

Blood runs from the corner of Mamaw's mouth. "For what?" she says.

"For what you are. For a spy."

XI

Not Before Strangers

1 8 6 3 — 1 8 6 5

The jail in St. Joe is an abandoned slaughterhouse. Its walls and floors retain the stench and stains of its former use. A soiled Union flag droops from the crumbling smokestack of what was the fat-rendering plant, a low brick structure now serving as officers' headquarters. Inside the main building, where the butchering was once done, a maze of stalls and trenches houses the prisoners.

It is early afternoon, the day following her arrest, when Zerel and the two young children are brought to the prison and practically thrown through the door. They have spent the previous night locked inside a windowless, rat-infested shed at an abandoned farm somewhere along the Little Platte River, making the rest of the trip to St. Joe this morning.

Neither she nor the young ones have had so much as a sip of water since they were dragged from the homeplace. The air has shimmied with heat since dawn, and they have ridden in the back of a rough wagon through thick clouds of dust. Mamaw is frightened at the condition of Sallie and John. They are so dehydrated they've stopped whimpering. Her own head is swimming, and her legs buckle when she is pulled from the wagon. But she doesn't fall to the ground. She has both children in her arms.

"We got a lying place all ready for you, whore." A guard unlocks the door and shoves her so hard that she stumbles through, barely keeping hold of the babies. Her eyes need time to grow accustomed to the dimness inside; she is yet blind when she feels the weight of the children being lifted gently from her arms.

Sallie screams in terror at being taken from her mother. A guard slams something hard, a club or rifle butt, against the door. "Shut the hell up in there or I'll give you something to yell about!"

Zerel, struggling to see, gets a vague sense of chalk-white faces swirling about her like fog. Someone touches her arm. "It's all right . . . sh, now . . . it's all right."

And after a moment they start to come into focus, her fellow inmates. There are perhaps four dozen of them— grandmothers and young girls, bewildered youngsters, some only infants.

"What on earth—" Mamaw whispers. But they are all silent, all staring at her, their eyes full of pity and fear and questions. One older woman with matted gray hair slowly shakes her head at Zerel, then moves away.

It is an unimaginable assembly, these captives. Too weak for harm, too innocent to grasp what is being done to them . . . to *us,* Mamaw thinks. She wonders if they live under some arcane rule of silence in this grim cloister, for still no one says anything.

But they are just giving her time to get her bearings. Soon the older woman is beside her again. "Do you need some water?"

"My youngsters—" Zerel whispers.

"They're all right. Catherine and Maryrose are seeing to them. You just catch your breath . . ."

Zerel starts to sway. "Water?" she says.

"Yes, dear."

The children scatter, the circle of women parts. Someone grasps Zerel's arm and starts to lead her to a wooden water-bucket set on the floor a few feet away. Mamaw feels herself going down, helpless . . . *not before strangers,* she thinks. She wrenches free of the unseen hand and drops to her knees, then she is crawling toward the bucket, lowering her face into it. . . .

"Stop her. She oughtn't—"

But she is drinking, like an animal at a trough. The water smells fetid and tastes worse. She feels something hard in her mouth and spits out a cockroach but doesn't care. . . . Mamaw cares for nothing now but her thirst, her terrible scathing thirst, and she keeps on drinking until she starts to choke. Then she lifts her head out of the bucket and vomits on the floor beside it.

Everything goes black and when she can see again, she is lying on the ground beside the bucket, her own vomit pooled beside her head, the sour smell the air she breathes now . . . and the white foglike faces drifting close again.

"Just lie still now. You'll feel better in a minute." Rough filthy cloth rubs her chin, someone cleaning where she has messed herself. "Sh."

And then everything is black again, and Mamaw is concentrated into one single small mass of being: the womb that encloses in darkness the life it is hers to carry, conceal, protect.

There is very little light in the prison in daytime, none at night. Zerel can hardly tell one of her fellow captives from another; their faces get no chance to imprint her memory. She doesn't know most of their names, but she doesn't need to. She knows who they are: the wives and mothers, the sisters and sweethearts, the children of the men who ride renegade with William Clarke Quantrill. If the Bushwhackers are impervious to ambush, perhaps this confiscation of their womenfolk, their offspring, will make a greater impression.

A few of the women are interrogated, but none are beaten. The children are not touched; they are hardly even noticed. Mamaw wonders if a vestige of decency in the Union soldiers precludes physical harm . . . or do they simply know how little we matter, how little we could tell? In either case, captivity itself, survival like animals, inflicts sufficient suffering.

Some women are kept for a night, some for a month. Some are questioned, some are not. A few never even know whether they've been properly identified, as their presence simply is never acknowledged after they're brought in. There are days when three rude meals—oatmeal, milk-sopped bread, field peas—are shoved through the door in wooden buckets. Other days there is nothing but supper. Occasionally there is more than enough to eat, but usually far too little. It is as if the men outside have never even bothered to count the captives they have taken or set free.

Filthy buckets of rotting oak with frayed rope handles deliver water and food. There is no distinction between drinking and washing water, no provision for human waste. When the water has been consumed, the bucket emptied, it's used as a communal chamber pot. At some incalculable time— today, tomorrow—it will be removed, refilled, only possibly having received a rinsing.

Nausea and fevers abound. Vermin and insects thrive. Morning after morning Mamaw is amazed to find no one has died during the night. She tries not to wonder about the baby she carries.

Zerel has been in the prison for only a couple of days when she sees a woman break, right before her eyes. Woman . . . she is hardly past girlhood, but already a wife, a mother. Zerel doesn't know her name, but she comes from over by Chillicothe; her young husband has been joined up with the Bush-whackers only a matter of weeks.

The prisoners have just had buckets of some kind of gritty greens for a midday meal, the children are mostly asleep now, many of the women too. All of a sudden a piercing shriek . . . Zerel doesn't believe it's human until she sees this girl in the corner of a stall making it.

The girl's face has no color to it at all; even her eyes show nothing but white. But her lips, pulled back and stretched wide, are bluish. Her scream splits the air in two; it sounds like the end of the world.

Only a few seconds pass before half a dozen women have her in tow, getting her settled down a little bit. After a while the girl is quiet, but her body stays rigid. She just huddles in that stall corner, looking thin and stiff as a knife blade. Even days later, she doesn't say a word to anyone or show a bit of interest in the one-year-old boy she's got. The other women take turns caring for him.

Zerel watches this pathetic young woman from a distance. Seems like each time she looks at her, Mamaw can hear that scream. *Not me,* she thinks. *I ain't going to let that happen to me.*

It is the end of the second week, in the heat of noon a few days past the summer solstice. Zerel is sitting, feels she has been sitting forever, on the edge of a bloodstained trench where thousands of hogs and cattle have been butchered, countless gallons of animal blood have flowed. The air is suffocating, thick with flies. Sallie lies on the floor nearby, her fingers in her mouth, her face wan and listless. Scabs show through her fine hair where lice and ticks have been pulled away.

Mamaw holds the frail body of her son on her lap, gently pressing his head to her belly as if he and the unborn child can console one another.

Suddenly a guard's voice thunders from the other side of the door.

"Mrs. Zerelda James!"

Zerel knows by now they use that name to clarify her connections and her crimes . . . knows her time at last has come . . . knows the rest of the words before she hears them:

"Bring your brats with you!"

She clambers to her feet. No one speaks to her, and Mamaw does not glance back as the door is opened. She forgets the faces of the other captives—women, children, girls—before they are out of view; she has no desire to feast her eyes on their envy or even their hope. She simply forgets them. But she remembers, will always remember, the filthy buckets, the trench worn smooth by torrents of blood.

She walks out of the slaughterhouse carrying both children in her arms. The light of day batters her eyes, but she keeps walking. Reeling under the weight of the children born and unborn.

When her eyes have adjusted to the noonday sun, she sees Reuben. He is standing behind a cordon of ragged blue uniforms, reaching out to her with his gentle, impossibly white hands.

On the way out of St. Joe—the babies asleep on feedsacks in the back of the wagon, Reuben speaking softly as he drives—Mamaw begins to bleed. She says nothing. *Home,* she thinks. The child will be all right if only we can just get home.

"Where is Jesse?" she says.

"Made him stay behind. Wild-eyed. But I convinced him we'd be begging trouble to leave the place untended when they're bound to know we'd be away."

She nods. "It's best. He might have—"

"What I figured," Reuben says. "The boy's been half-crazy."

Mamaw laughs weakly. "Always been half-crazy." She leans back on the seat, closing her eyes. Her neck is stiffened against the jolting of the wagon, her expression held impassive against the pain, the blood she feels flowing out of her faster now, faster. . . .

"Faster," she says.

"Don't worry. We'll get there before dark."

She is barely conscious when they arrive, but Pappy thinks she's just been dozing. He alights from the wagon, goes around to the other side, touches her arm. "Home, Mamaw," he says.

She sways when she stands, starts to fall, and it is not until he catches her that Reuben Samuel discovers her blood-soaked skirts. Then Jesse is running out of the house, lifting her, carrying her through the door. . . .

The bleeding slows after she is put to bed, but it doesn't stop for several days. By then it seems hopeless that she should carry the infant to term, bear it without catastrophe. Even after she begins to recover, Reuben watches over her with worried eyes. Throughout that summer and early fall, Susie runs the house, annoying her mother with the bossiness of an ancient nursemaid. Mamaw fusses right back at the girl, but knows she is a godsend.

Pappy tries to prepare for the worst. "This birth, Zerel," he says. "This child ain't likely to be . . ."

"It will be fine," she says.

Mamaw will not hear of doubt or loss. The body has its own way of doing, and she has perfect faith in the mindless, insuperable will of blood and muscle, a womb long accustomed to fighting for its objects.

"A girl, I reckon. She will be fine," Mamaw says.

Reuben smiles at her and prepares himself for grief.

But the unborn child concerns Mamaw far less than Jesse does. Mamaw knew it even before she and the babies were carted off to prison. *There will be no keeping him now.*

Jesse waits two days, but she knows, Mamaw already knows: he intends to join Quantrill immediately.

She lies in bed, a bloody rag between her legs, and looks at her son.

"You ain't old enough."

"I'm near seventeen."

Mamaw smiles. "I'm quite aware of the circumstances of your birth."

"Reckon you're also aware what's been going on in this part of the country?"

"Don't be fresh."

"All right, sorry," he says. "But look here, Mamaw, you got no right to hold me back."

"I say I do. Until you're eighteen, at least."

"That's more than a year from now."

"You do right well with numbers, for a boy failed arithmetic not long ago."

"I'm serious, Mamaw."

"So am I, son."

"You expect me to stick around and plow so's I can get the britches beat off me by any Union boys feel like some exercise?"

Mamaw winces.

"Be honest, why don't you," Jesse says.

"You know I never lie to you, boy."

"Then answer me this: What would you be doin' right now if you was me?"

Mamaw looks past him, staring through the window. The two weeks she spent in near-darkness have raised up the grass bright and green. The pasture looks soft as a mattress. She doesn't look at Jesse, no need. She sees him, a boy yet bright and soft, sees his body plumb out of life and luck, torn beyond mending. . . . sees the light fade from his blue, blue eyes. . . .

"Keep your head, son," she says.

"I will, Mamaw."

"Find Frank. You boys stick close together."

. . . sees the first spadeful of dirt falling on his face, filling his eyes . . .

"It's the right thing, Mamaw." Jesse touches her hand, but she is staring out the window, does not turn her head for him to see her eyes filled.

"Reckon I can see that, too," she says.

The next morning, before daylight, he is gone.

And three days later, back again, hot as an overstoked stove. He's seen Quantrill's lieutenants at Liberty. Too young, they said. No two ways about it.

"They'll see," says Jesse. "Just you wait."

Mamaw waits.

He takes off for a couple of days. "I'll be back." He's borrowed a horse from Reuben, so Mamaw knows he'll keep his word. Jesse'd never take a thing didn't belong to him.

Two evenings later he rides into the yard wearing triumph like the dazzling halo around a Roman saint. He whoops his way into the house. "The hell with Quantrill. Bloody Bill don't think I'm no youngster."

Eyes like blades they say faster than bullets his hands hotter than flame taste of blood like lust on his tongue so you can just see it and hate is a thirst parched that boy till he's wild a wild beast Bloody Bill Anderson . . .

"You seen him?" Mamaw's voice goes faint. "You seen Bloody Bill?"

Jesse waves detail away like a fly from his nose. "Not himself, of course. You think he'd be sittin' around here? But I got in, Mamaw, don't doubt it. I'm in it now. . . ."

And gone.

For days after Jesse leaves, Mamaw stands on the porch facing west, her eyes full of him. His hair, darkened the past few years, still runs with bright veins of gold. She recollects his father . . . Robert, riding over the same rise, carrying so

❖

much more knowing, into a lesser gravity, she thought. . . .

And she didn't look after him as he went.

And he didn't come back to her.

Over and over again she watches Jesse ride away, a slight, straight figure on the back of a chestnut stallion, gold glinting on his head.

Time and again she sees him: Jesse, growing smaller and smaller.

Mamaw keeps her eye on him, long past the vanishing point.

In autumn Mamaw brings forth another child, without a hitch.

Reuben chooses Fannie for the new baby girl's first name. For her middle name Mamaw gets to pick:

Fannie Quantrill Samuel, born October 18, 1863.

Frank and Jesse: Mamaw doesn't see either of them again for a full year and the most part of another. Sometimes they ride together, sometimes apart. Texas, Arkansas, Kentucky, Kansas . . . they cross entire states like roads, don't want to miss any of the fireworks. They gallop and shoot alongside the bravest and most brutal of men: George Todd, who tore up Texas in Missouri's honor . . . the daredevil Clay County son Dave Pool . . . Jo Shelby who, folks say, done so much killing and drinking by now he'll sometimes foam red at the mouth . . . Bloody Bill . . . and himself: Quantrill. Oh, they're in with quite a crowd. Frank and Jesse fit right in. Hot bullets lodged in their flesh, improvised bandages beneath their improvised uniforms, the James boys ambush and escape. They are a terror.

And terror's all the rage. "The war to the knife, the knife to the hilt!" is the cry. Massacre is the fashion. Quantrill's raid on Lawrence, Kansas, is a very model of annihilation: 150 civilian males skinned like rabbits and left lying in the street, thanks to the joined forces of Quantrill's best boys: Anderson, Todd, and that close-mouthed Younger boy.

A warehouse in Kansas City—being used for a jail similar to the one Zerel was in—collapses. Anderson's sister is among the casualties . . . a sweet fair thing, a lamb. With that, such humanity as might remain in the heart of Bloody Bill is gone. There's hell to pay in spades.

And in retaliation for Lawrence, that most despised Kansan, General Jim Lane, dreams up new punishments for Missouri. Order No. 11 is handed down, evacuating most of Jackson, Cass, Bates, and Vernon counties. Murder and arson follow the banished and create the infamous "Burnt District," a scar of desolation that will deface Missouri for years.

Encamped in Texas for the winter, Quantrill begins to lose control of his men—or so some would have it. Folks say it's Todd and Anderson running things now. They trail back from Texas in springtime to start raising Cain along the Missouri River, where they slam down Federal patrols like pesty mosquitoes.

On September 27, 1864, Anderson and Todd lead a frisky entourage to Centralia, not far from Columbia. The inhabitants are trampled in the dust, the railroad depot set afire. The train pulls in—twenty-five Union soldiers—nice uniforms, but no arms to speak of. They're stripped to their drawers on the town square. Then little Arch Clement starts firing point-blank, soon followed by his friends.

Sometimes Mamaw gets word of the boys' well-being, never their wounds, rarely their whereabouts. She learns where they've been long after they leave: Frank (called "Buck" now, she hears) with Quantrill at Lawrence, Jesse with Anderson in Carroll County, at horrible Centralia, both of them. Mamaw can't keep up. She counts victories. . . .

And defeats: each time the enemy suffers, she takes it for a sign of her sons' safekeeping.

And for her own safekeeping, she adopts a kind of madness. Yes, it is that, she thinks, *mad to maintain balance as the world bucks and tilts, to see with perfect clarity when all is darkness and distortion....*

But she sees. She knows. Mamaw sees her boys rip through brush and gunfire, evading the hands of death. She knows they kill what would kill them, and their killing makes a kind of living for her, too.

Later Frank will tell his mother of Centralia, how his friend Frank Shepherd rode beside him. "Laughing," Buck will tell her. "Both of us laughing. Next thing I know, I'm looking down where his blood and brains is splattered all over my pants."

"It was his time, son," Mamaw will say. "Must have been."

And he will say, "I know it. But laughing," and Mamaw will know then that Frank, Buck, will never be quite the same, after Centralia.

But Jesse's is the life most surely changed that day, in that battle. For it is Jesse James—all of seventeen, mind you—who fires the shot that kills the enemy commander, Major Johnson.

Even Bloody Bill stops and takes notice of Jesse James. "Not to have any beard, he is the keenest and cleanest fighter in my command."

And it is one of those things, what Bloody Bill says about Jesse, that folks just can't let go of. Like that nickname he gets when he shoots his own fingertip off: Dingus. They carry it around and pass it along and blow it up till you'd think they'd get right sick of it. Only they don't, they can't let it rest.

"Our Jesse's a hero now, seems like," Pappy says. "They're all talking about him in town. Lawyer Collins come up and pump my hand like I own the bank."

Zerel grins. "Jesse was never likely to get lost in no shuffle." Then she busts out laughing. "He oughta be in knickers still. A hero!"

A hero's what she expected Jesse to be, all right. Only she never counted on how being a hero makes folks feel they got a claim on you and all that's yours, until they got you surrounded and pressing in so close your whole shape's apt to get changed. She listens to what folks say about Jesse— no man yet, her boy, but a marked man just the same. Because Jesse's a hero now, folks altering his life to suit themselves till a body can't hardly see what they're taking as they build and lay claim and won't let go. . . .

A getting, Mamaw thinks, *with too much giving up in it, this hero business. Like angels and martyrs and kings.*

"I only hope that boy don't start *believing* all this hooey," Mamaw says.

The following year, spring just an undertone in winter's shortening breath as green shadows materialize around dancing branches, comes the inglorious Palm Sunday: Appomattox.

The news has been expected for days. Reuben's face is set and white as he delivers the word to Mamaw. Confirmation of defeat.

They sit quietly at the kitchen table for a while, and Mamaw permits herself a few tears because the children are outdoors and cannot see her.

She hears them out there, the children, laughing in the pasture, crying out, abandoned to their game.

> *Bushel of wheat, bushel of rye,*
> *All not hid, holler I.*
> *Bushel of wheat, bushel of clover,*
> *All not hid can't hide over!*

" . . . can't hide," Mamaw murmurs. "How does a body explain to youngsters how what's right ain't usually what happens?"

Pappy looks for a moment as if he's forgotten where he is. "It was a good fight and it's an honorable surrender."

Mamaw's eyes are cold. "There's no honor in defeat," she says. "None at all."

Off beyond the coffee bean tree Sallie and John laugh with delight pure as air. And above their laughter, Susie calls out, "Whistle or cry, let the game die!"

"I ain't even sure I know what honor is anymore, Pappy."

"Everybody will come home now," he says.

"What's left of it," says Mamaw.

There isn't time to absorb anything, to bring grief to its saturation point, to try to distill some grace or even some sense from it. A body could drown. Lee's ink still wet on the paper surrender when Lincoln's lying in a pool of blood . . . Good Friday . . . theater . . . madness.

The President is dead.

"First good news I've heard in months," Mamaw says.

"Zerel!" Reuben's eyes are welling. "He was a man," he says.

"He was an animal," Mamaw snaps. "Tore this country in two, chewed us up and spit us out."

"Where is your pity?"

"Where was his?"

Reuben looks away, shocked, ashamed of her. Maybe she's even ashamed of herself, a little. It's hard to know what to think, to feel, with history stampeding over you like a wild runaway stallion.

She walks over to the window and puts her hand on Reuben's shoulder. "Easy to forget a body's human when you got in the habit of hating."

Pappy nods, still not looking at her. His gaze is locked on the coffee tree.

"Reckon I get a bit carried away sometimes," Mamaw says.

"It's over," says Pappy. "It's over now, Zerel. Let it rest."

XII

All Over But the Shooting

1 8 6 5

But even if they could—let it rest, put the fighting past them—
Clay County lies beyond the pale of peace. For the Bushwhackers, Appomattox has settled nothing.

Seems Lee's white flag didn't cover the situation in Missouri. The men who fought out of uniform and came up on
the losing end—they got to turn themselves in again. One
at a time. In person. They're expected to swear loyalty now
to all they fought . . . *to kneel,* Mamaw thinks, *for an absolution
they don't believe in. One surrender ain't enough.*

Quantrill is in Kentucky, still raising hell like he knows
Appomattox had nothing to do with the war he's been fighting. Bloody Bill is gone, ambushed in Ray County last year,
just five days after George Todd died at Independence. Lead-
erless now, many Missouri boys remain at large, hiding out
in other states, wandering like lost, exhausted youngsters.

In the first weeks after the surrender, Frank James is in Kentucky with Quantrill, still fighting. Jesse has been with Quantrill's lieutenant, George Shepherd, in Texas through the winter.

"Wish them durn boys'd stay together," Mamaw says. "Things
is bad enough."

Jesse and his comrades don't learn of surrender and its contingencies until they get back to Missouri. "Well, it's over," they say, not quite looking one another in the eye, not quite half sorry. "It's done."

They're almost home . . . hell, they're in Missouri, ain't they? One of the surrender points is Lexington. Jesse, his friend Jess Hamlett, and a few others start off for there, may's well get this over with.

It is April 23, 1865. Jesse and his companions are approaching the Burns schoolhouse in Lexington, to turn themselves in, when five men on horseback cut in on them from the Salt Pond Road. The riders ask no questions, give no warning, they just start firing.

Jesse is shot to pieces: twice in the chest, once in the leg. Jess Hamlett has his horse blown right out from under him. He manages to jump on behind Jesse, and the two light out on a single horse.

"Looks like you got it good, Dingus."

"All over but the shootin'," Jesse says.

A soft May night in Kearney. Mamaw and Pappy sleep with the window raised on a black velvet sky and the sound of peep toads by the creek.

Then Mamaw is awake before she knows it and she hears a scratchy noise and it takes her a minute to figure out that's no peep toad, no raccoon or possum, that sound, and it's around the front door.

Pappy hears it too. "You stay where you are." His whisper is urgent in the dark but she ain't about to take orders, ain't about to cower in the bed with somebody skulking around her place and she is on her feet and halfway to the door before Reuben's got his hands on the shotgun.

Jesse, she thinks. Somebody bringing word from him or maybe Frank, but something tells her *no, it's Jesse, all right, and it ain't good* and her hands are shaking so bad she can hardly get the lantern lit maybe she shouldn't even bother with it only she wants she needs to see the face of the person bringing the news because no matter what he says she will have to see the face before she can tell how bad it is. Then Reuben is there with the shotgun and Mamaw raises the lantern up high and opens the door at the same time she hears Reuben's voice saying, "For God's sake, Zerel, *wait!*"

The hero Jesse James, her son . . . oh, she's had her eye on him all the time, all right, now here he is and she wouldn't hardly know him. Pale as a specter and nearly as thin, leaning against the porch post like he can't stand on his own two feet. The blue cap of a Union cavalryman sits backward on his head. He is holding a willow switch, a soiled white handkerchief on the end of it, raised above his head. But Mamaw hardly sees it, doesn't get the joke. She is staring at his left hand, clutched to his bloodied shirtfront: the tip of his middle finger is gone and its absence holds her attention in a grip so like iron that she misses near everything else about him and can only hear herself saying where is the rest of your finger when she isn't of course saying anything at all.

"I'm turnin' myself in." Jesse grins as if he knows he is a legend now, is getting the hang of it, will work at it till he's ready to drop. And he starts a slow slide down the post that's been propping him up almost like he's melting, but the grin stays right there on his face, his hand on his chest right there over his heart where she still can't take her eyes from that snipped-off finger and can't say a word or move a muscle, so it is Pappy who makes the first move, Pappy the doctor catching Jesse before he melts into the porch floor with his grin and blue cap and white flag and red shirtfront.

Mamaw can't seem to snap out of it. Reuben takes on Jesse's weight, hitching the boy's arm over his shoulder, grasping his waist, half-dragging him into the house and over to the bed still warm with sleeping. Mamaw moves behind them like she's walking in her sleep, good for nothing but light, the lantern she's forgot she's holding.

Reuben eases Jesse down onto the featherbed and starts removing what is left of his shirt, the improvident bandages he finds underneath. "Set that light over here where it will do some good."

Mamaw moves dreamily, doing as she's told, then stands speechless and still behind Reuben. A shadow.

"You been seriously damaged here, boy. I wonder you're alive. How long ago'd this happen?"

"Got to enjoyin' myself so much, reckon I lost track of the time." Jesse still working on his legendary grin, only it gets all ruined with Pappy's poking in his chest that way till the hero lets out a sound that's somewhere between a moan and an outright scream.

"Sorry to be hurting you this way, son. I'm afraid it can't be helped."

Jesse winks at his mother. "Don't guess you can do much worse than the Yankees already done."

Reuben is silent, tight-lipped, bent near double over the boy as he probes the larger of the two wounds with pale, delicate fingers yellowed by lantern light.

"Mamaw, you're a sight for sore eyes." Jesse's voice is faint.

"Hush, now," Reuben says. "Stop trying to talk." His voice is low, gentle. "Zerel?"

Her eyes are caught by Jesse's left hand, now pressed flat to the bed. She appears not to hear her husband . . . the doctor. . . .

Pappy straightens up and turns from the bed. His voice is so harsh he doesn't sound like himself at all. "Zerel, fetch as many lamps as we got and bring them in here. Candles, too. And set some water to boil. *You hear me, Zerel?*"

Shouting at her, Reuben, in that voice almost like Mr. Simms . . . she nods, a glazed look to her eyes.

Then Reuben is Pappy again, a doctor, not Mr. Simms, not . . . "You got to help me here, Zerel." He is taking her by the shoulders, steering her toward the door, and then she is moving again and then she is all right. "Water," she says.

"That's right. Go on, now . . . and hurry." He is being kind to her now and she knows what she is doing and it's all going to be . . .

She waits for Reuben to tell her, like he always tells her: *It's all right now, Zerel, never mind now, it's going to be all right.* . . .

But all Reuben says now, again, is *hurry.*

She pieces together what she can of the story from snippets Jesse hands her out of fever, delirium, excruciating pain as she sits at his bedside. She can never be certain which fragments come from truth, which from dreams. And maybe the legend gets mixed up in it as well. Mamaw listens to rumors of her boy, brave as a lion, and she thinks *but a fool,* just a cub, knowing that somewhere between the legend and the mother's knowing is a truth that is Jesse. She listens and she pieces things together as best she can, and what she cannot use she keeps, she saves . . .

The Hamlett boy was with him at first, then somehow not. They slept in an abandoned cabin, a couple of barns, a ditch, and even a coal mine. They . . . or perhaps it was he, by then, alone—he, Jesse, bleeding so steadily that that alone should have killed him. Went for days without food or water. Traveled many miles when he should have stayed in bed. A few days after the shooting—maybe it was a week—at one time he was patched up by a doctor, a Union man at that, in Lexington. The doctor told Jesse in no uncertain terms: stay put. Keep moving around like you been, these wounds can't do a thing but get worse. The doctor even offered to hide him, look after him for a few days. But Jesse wasn't having it . . . maybe didn't want to stay in no Union household or didn't trust that doctor too far, except maybe he wasn't no Union man in the first place, Mamaw might have got lost following Jesse, his voice gone woolly, eyes all wild. He left, anyhow. He thanked the doctor kindly, Union or not, Jesse always a mannerly boy, and went right back on the move again.

"For a hero, you are some terrible fool, boy," Mamaw says.

Jesse's eyes are nearly closed. He might not hear her. What difference will it make, him hearing her now, anyway? Mamaw pours some cool chamomile water from the pitcher beside the bed and holds the tumbler to her son's lips. "A God-awful fool," she says.

Jesse scarcely moistens his tongue, then pushes her hand away. "All I could think was to get home, Mamaw. I knew I'd be all right if I could just . . ."

She recalls the wagon ride from St. Joe, nearly losing Fannie that way when she got out of jail. . . .

"I'll never understand how I come to raise such a reckless, muleheaded child," she says.

"I'd tell you, Mamaw, but I don't guess you're in much of a reasonin' mood."

"Be still now," she says.

Mamaw sits down again in the chair next to the bed, thinking *I am, though . . . a more reasoning mood than I ever been. I would promise anything, would bear anything, if only this boy comes through.*

But Jesse is weakening with each day. Mamaw could read it on Reuben's face if she wasn't already seeing it for herself in the wounds that do not heal, the bleeding that will not stop, the inflamation. Jesse is slipping away.

Reuben inserts a tube in the boy's chest to drain out the poison of infection. Mamaw envies him, Reuben: his potions, his precise instruments, his graced hands.

"You know why I married you, I reckon," she said to him once, long ago, perhaps the first year they were married. "All

156

the scrapes and broken bones these children bring on themselves, all the sicknesses, if I had to *pay* a doctor we'd starve
in this house." And they'd laugh about it, Mamaw and Pappy,
how she married him for his doctoring bag and his tools. But
there was a mite of truth in it. Reuben, their peacemaker and
healer, knowing how to fix things . . .

Only Pappy's not the fighter, she thinks. And Mamaw is
terrified because Jesse is burning up and wasting away and
can hardly talk or even swallow now, and the only way to
keep his life is to fight, and Pappy's got all the weapons now
Mamaw comes up empty-handed and Reuben's no fighter. . . .

It is after midnight, ten days since the boy got home.

Reuben and Zerel sit in two ladderback chairs, facing each
other across the bed. Up above, the other children are asleep,
and Mamaw has extinguished all the lamps. Two candles burn
on the mantel, another on the small table at the side of the
bed. The May night is cool, a breeze coming in from the
west. Lithe branches skitter along the side of the cabin now
and then. The sound is oddly comforting as Mamaw and
Pappy struggle to keep awake.

Jesse is unconscious. They take turns, every few minutes,
bathing his fevered face

Mamaw lets her eyes close . . . only for a few seconds
now . . . ain't about to fall asleep. Next thing she knows,
Jesse is crying out, his voice so weak, and her eyes open like
something that can fly, and she sees Reuben leaning over the
bed.

"You best help me hold him still, Zerel. He thrashes around
this way he's apt to pull the tube out and start the bleeding
up again." And it seems like there's no midway place with
her leaving her chair, moving to the bed, taking hold . . . she's
just all of a sudden there, pressing down his arms, while he
tries to fight her off and looks at her with those trapped-
animal eyes—*I don't know you*— and Reuben bowed over his

chest doing something with the tube, and his blessed hands almost like a sacrament. . . .

"Settle down, son. Got to shift this thing a tad. You hold on—"

Then Jesse somehow pulls one arm free of her grip and he strikes out at Reuben with more force and speed than a body'd believe was left in him.

"All right, now, this is only going to pain you for a second."

"No," Jesse says.

Mamaw looks into his face as she catches his flailing arm again and holds it down, and she sees him seeing her and knows he's come back now from wherever he's been.

He stops fighting and lies still. "Stop it, Pappy," he says.

Reuben smiles. "Don't look to me like you're in much position to be giving the orders now, boy."

Jesse stares at him steadily. "It's enough," he says. "You done the best you could, Pappy, and so have I. Now I'd thank you kindly if you'd just let me be."

"Don't talk like that," Mamaw says, and she feels her hands shaking, and she lets him go. Always so stubborn, and now if he's decided that dying's the thing . . . there is something she's supposed to say to him now, but she doesn't know what it is.

She sees Reuben looking at her, like he's waiting, too, at first, only then he sees she doesn't have the words or whatever she's supposed to have this time, *this moment like something she's already lost and doesn't know where to start looking.* . . .

"Never mind, Zerel." Then Reuben's eyes are on Jesse, and that's when she sees what she didn't ever expect to see: Reuben is a fighter. He is fierce.

"You want your mama to fetch that puny white flag you carried in here, is that it?"

Mamaw waits for her Jesse to turn Pappy's words into the joke he surely means them to be, even though they come out sounding so mean—oh, that's how he is, her boy, turning anything you please into a good joke, but he hasn't even got a smile now, like the legend's slipped right off him and he's lost the moment too, can't find it and just says, "I'm tired."

Reuben rises up taller, like he's trying to grow into his own long shadow on the wall. "Reckon you are. But being tired ain't a thing a man's got a right to die from."

"Pappy, I got nothin' left."

"That so? Well, I do. And so does Mamaw and all the rest of us. Everybody but you. Don't make you much of a hero now, does it?"

Jesse cries out, childlike, as if Reuben has slapped him, "Can't you see I'm dying?"

Mamaw's voice is a wail: "Stop—" But Reuben, fierce, stays her with a raised hand as if this fight's all his now, his and Jesse's, and Mamaw's got no place in it. Still holding her back with his lifted hand, Reuben Samuel speaks in a voice like thunder, a voice like God *if only God would speak,* she thinks, *if only . . .*

"The hell you are!" says Reuben.

It seems like the echo of Reuben's thunder is still rising, still rolling through the air so that Mamaw can hardly hear when, touching her shoulder, he says, "Never mind, now. It will be all right . . . it's going to be fine, Zerel."

By mid-June Jesse's strong enough to get out of bed sometimes and sit in the sunny yard. The chest wound still acts up off and on. He is weak and suffers from fainting spells. But the boy's coming along nicely, Pappy says.

Only it's Jesse's spirits got Mamaw worried now. There is a bitterness in him, deeper and less readily healed than any insult to flesh. Jesse came home in defeat, but ready to pay the price. The attack on the Salt Pond Road outraged his sense of honor and killed his hope of a peaceable life.

"No forgiving, no forgetting. Talk all they like about amnesty. They don't mean to let up on us, Mamaw."

She wants to argue, knows the bitterness does him no good. The way infection keeps returning to that wound seems like the very pus is formed of his resentment, fever the burning of his rage. But how can Mamaw argue? He's right, she thinks, they ain't about to let us be. If Frank would only come home, but . . . *no safe passage,* she thinks.

"Things will die down," Reuben tells her. "Give it some time." But he, too, looks worn out, almost as if the life he's forced back into Jesse has been siphoned out of himself.

Reuben is depleted, and Mamaw, she just can't talk Jesse out of bitterness when she's full of it herself.

PART II

... he had seen grief ... where he had not
expected it or anyway anticipated it, where
in a sense a heart capable of breaking had
no business being. ...

—William Faulkner,
Intruder in the Dust

XIII

Migrations

1 8 6 5

The terms of surrender turn more bitter than Mamaw or
Jesse ever dreamed.

At the end of June the Samuels, along with several other
families of widely advertised Confederate loyalty, are ordered
out of Clay County . . . exile, pure and simple, and blacker
than any vision Mamaw has entertained.

There is no recourse or appeal, no indication when or if
they might come back. They are simply ordered to go. One
week is given to comply, "to secure their premises and prop
erty" and to clear out.

Seven days after the order is received, carrying what they
can, Mamaw and her family board a steamboat at Lexington
to be carried up the Missouri River to Rulo, Nebraska. Reuben has kin who will help them, somehow, to settle there.

Sallie, Fannie, and John look solemn and completely bewildered. Reuben, clutching the black valise overfilled with
medical supplies and small tools, seems almost as confused
as the children. Susie has gone to Kentucky to stay with
Lindsay cousins. Maybe she'll see Frank . . . still in Kentucky,
Frank, last they heard.

Jesse, his chest inflamed and bleeding again, is too weak
to walk. He is carried aboard the steamboat on a pallet.

Mamaw ships out, wearing a face like rough gray stone.

"Don't know how folks live in a place like this. Ain't a breath
of a breeze."

Mamaw stands peering out the window of Jesse's sickroom
like there's something to see. Nothing but the backside of
another stiff-necked, narrow-shouldered house. "Nebraska'd
be enough to cut the heart right out of a person," she says.

Not that Jesse hears her. Six weeks here and he's sunk so
far inside himself that when he speaks or looks at her now,
seems like a flat empty mile stretches between them.

Mamaw picks up a paper fan shaped like a seashell. It has
a short bamboo handle, a snippet of black silk ribbon hanging
from the end. The printing on it advertises some Omaha
company that sells coffins . . . *as if we don't all make our
own,* Mamaw thinks. She waves the fan back and forth above
Jesse's face. Just stirs up hot air, but at least it keeps the flies
moving.

Sweat stands out on Jesse's forehead, runs down his temples. The tube is in his chest again. Pappy had to put it back
in last night. Mamaw dips a cloth in rosewater and bathes the
boy's face.

"No," he says, without opening his eyes.

Mamaw keeps fanning him. "Sh. It's all right."

Then his eyes are suddenly on her, eyes usually wide and
clear blue as a midsummer sky, now narrowed and dark,
almost violet . . . tornado-colored, she thinks.

"Where's Mamaw?" His voice is suspicious. "Where's she
gone to?"

"I'm here, son. Mamaw's right here."

"You ain't . . . no, I . . . maybe it's . . ." His chin quivers
and his eyes start to water. "Stop asking so blamed many
questions!"

"That's right, child. No more questions. You go on back to sleep now."

He closes his eyes for a few seconds, then looks at her again. "Are you my sweetheart?" His smile is terrifying.

"Why, it's me, Jesse. Your Mamaw."

"Hell, I know that. Just seems like a wounded soldier ought to have him a sweetheart." He laughs softly.

Mamaw touches his hand. "You been dreaming, son."

"What makes you think so?"

"You just asked was I your sweetheart."

"Well, are you?"

Such crazy talk, yet when she looks into his eyes it seems like he's there.

"You think I gone off my head," he says.

"Never mind."

"I'm awake. I know we're in a place called Rulo, Nebraska, only I wonder if it ain't really hell . . . far as I'm concerned, ain't much difference." He laughs again, and she knows that he knows, now, just what he's saying.

"You had me worried for a minute there, boy."

"Mamaw?"

She stops waving the fan.

"You know this is me now? I ain't dreaming . . . nothin' like that?"

"I know," she says.

"I got to tell you something. And I want you to listen . . . you got to help me."

"I'm listening."

"Mamaw, I need to get home."

"You know we can't go home. Besides, what you need is to get well first."

"I can't. Can't hardly stay alive in a place like this."

Mamaw tries to smile at him. "I can't either," she says. "Only I reckon right now we got to."

"Please," Jesse says.

"We'll get home, son. But right now we got to get you strong."

"What if I can't, Mamaw . . . what if I just plain can't?"

"But you can, Jesse, because you got to."

He closes his eyes, shaking his head weakly. "I might die."

"I won't hear that."

"I know you won't. Won't hear nothin' you don't like. But you know it just the same. I could die here."

"Sh. Hush, son."

"No." He opens his eyes and looks at her severely. "You got to hear me now."

"All right," Mamaw says quietly. "All right."

"You think I'm scared to die. But I ain't. If I got to . . ." His voice is fading to nothing.

She leans over him. "Jesse? Son?"

"Take me home, Mamaw. It's the only thing . . ."

"Sh."

"Promise," Jesse says, not asking, not leaving her any choice.

There is no sense to it: Jesse far sicker than when they came, Clay County—home, forbidden to them. But the whole family starts back, by way of Kansas City, the following week.

Again they cross the Missouri River by steamboat, moving downriver this time. They put in at Harlem, north of Kansas City. They seek refuge with relations: Robert's sister Mary and her husband John Mimms make room in their crowded household for Mamaw and her family.

"Been so long since I had time to think," she whispers. "To remember."

Wearing nothing but her chemise, Mamaw lies on a bed in the middle of the afternoon counting the moments of peace as if they are precious stones, shiny and smooth, beyond price. Sunlight is amber, filtered through lowered shades like ivory. Sounds from the rooms below are muffled as if the walls are lined with fur.

"You rest, Zerel," Mary Mimms tells her . . . Robert's sister, Robert's soft mouth smiling out of Mary's broad, plain face. "Looks to me like you're worn down to nothing, all this trouble you had about home and lookin' after Jesse. Just go up and lie down. Zee's doing perfectly fine with the boy."

She is. Mary's daughter, Zerel's namesake, only they call her Zee for short. The girl is only a couple years older than Jesse but handles him like she's already raised a family of her own. Gentle and shy as she is, it's a wonder she can keep him still, now he's feeling better and always wanting to get up.

Mamaw hears them laughing softly beyond the thin door, Jesse and Zee, as she drops into sleep.

Waist can't be but eighteen inches, Mamaw thinks. Maybe nineteen.

She watches her niece bend to the stove, turning corn cakes with a wooden paddle with one hand, as the fingers of her other hand fiddle with a stray curl at the nape of her neck.

"You in need of another hand, girl?" Mamaw asks.

Zee Mimms straightens her supple, narrow back and whirls around, startled as a small animal that's been tracked to the edge of its hole.

"Aunt Zerel! You scared me!"

"Then you scare too easy, child."

Zee purses her mouth, a little huffy, and half turns back to the stove. " Can I get you something?"

"Just thought I might help you ready supper."

"I can manage. Mama says you're here to rest."

Zerel makes an effort to soften her voice. "I know you can manage. I seen how you do around here. But a old workhorse like me gets nervous with too much grazing."

The girl smiles. "Maybe you can store up some ease for when you get back to your place, Aunt."

"Life don't work that way. Who knows, anyhow, whether I'll ever get back home?"

"Oh, you will." Zee's rosy, tapered hand reaches again for her hair. "Cousin Jesse says you're bound to be going home any day now."

"Says he. The boy's a dreamer."

Zee looks away, a small, peculiar smile hovering tentatively on her mouth. "He does seem to know his own mind, does Jesse."

"He knows what he wants, but don't always know what's likely. How do you manage to put up with him these long days?"

"I'm glad if I can help." Zee is tending the griddle again, so Mamaw can't see her face. "Aunt Zerel?"

"Yes, child?"

"Jesse really is going to be all right, isn't he?"

"Right as rain, or my name ain't the same as yours."

Zee sighs softly. "He's been through too much . . ."

"He tell you that?"

"Well, he hasn't said those words. But he tells me, sometimes, about the fighting and all. Some nights he can't sleep for what he remembers."

And how, Mamaw thinks, does this girl get him to tell what he won't hardly mention to his own mother? Her voice is cool again, hard, when she tells her niece:

"Don't do the boy a bit of good to keep bringing up what's past. I'd be grateful if you'd not egg him on when he goes on about it."

"But—"

Zee's soft voice is lost on Mamaw as she turns and stalks out of the kitchen.

Won't hardly be no living with the boy if he starts to take this wounded-soldier-hero business too serious. Especially not if he's getting encouragement from a wide-eyed romantic girl cousin with a waist hardly bigger around than her gardenia-tender neck.

The Samuels have been in Harlem for about a month when Reuben is able to glean hope from the news of home.

Two of the other exiled families have already returned to Clay County, not waiting for permission, and no reprisals have been made.

And Frank is back at the homeplace now, looking after things. Paroled in Kentucky in late July, seems he slipped into Kearney just after the family left. "Don't exactly hide myself," he writes, "but I ain't showing my face in town much, either. Plenty to keep me occupied here anyhow. Corn don't look too good what with such bad heat and no rain but it won't be the worst year this land has seen. And I thank the Lord you got out of Nebraska in a hurry."

"We can go home!"

Jesse shouts so loud when Mamaw reads him Frank's letter that three of the Mimms children come tearing up the stairs to see if he's been shot again.

Zee hovers at the foot of his bed, smiling, but her eyes look wounded.

Reuben is doubtful. "Maybe we ought to wait a bit longer. . . ."

But Jesse and Mamaw bury Pappy's caution alive. Two days later he sets out with the children. Zerel and Jesse will linger one more week, just to give the boy time to gain a little more strength.

The day before she and Jesse mean to start back, Mamaw is sitting on the front porch enjoying the sunshine of a September morning when she hears music. Unlikely as a dream, only she knows she hears it coming closer: horns and harmonicas, flutes and drums, a piccolo. . . .

Mamaw runs down the walk to look where the music seems

to be coming from. Brass and nickel, gold epaulets and polished leather flash in the sun. A marching band is coming up the street right toward her.

There are perhaps a dozen players. They look, from what Mamaw can see, like mere boys. They are neither blue nor gray, but a rainbow of royal colors: scarlet and purple, carnival figures in orange, yellow, green. The music is a proud Southern march Mamaw taught Frank and Jesse when they were babies just learning to walk.

A vision, she thinks. A visitation. Right out of nowhere, seems like. As the band moves toward her up the street, people run out of their houses to see, to hear . . . a wondrous commotion. Fanfare for a new era of good news, Mamaw thinks.

She dashes into the house and up the front stairs. Jesse loves music and pageantry so, he's got to see . . . she stops short at the doorway to his room.

Jesse stands at the window, laughing and tapping his bare toes. He's thin as a scarecrow, legs like sticks poking out at the bottom of Pappy's old nightshirt. His hair stands straight up in the back, unruly from days of being pressed to a pillow.

Jesse, framed by a bright window, leans on his cousin Zee. His arm circles her waist. The parade is passing right by the house now. But the two young faces are turned to one another, the morning sun in their eyes.

Mamaw is, at last, taking Jesse home.

She drives a mule and wagon borrowed from John Mimms. Jesse insists on sitting up beside her as they leave. Little wonder, with the whole Mimms family seeing them off from the porch, almost like another parade.

He's mighty quiet, though, once they're out of sight. All he can do to sit up, she thinks.

Mamaw waits until they've passed through the city streets. Then she stops the wagon at a quiet place on the road.

"You get down there in back now, before you're all wore out."

Jesse nods, but doesn't move. "That girl Zee," he says.

"Your cousin."

"My wife, if I got anything to say about it."

Mamaw hoots. "You ain't eighteen years old yet, not to mention in no condition . . . I swear, I think the fever's come back on you, boy."

"I'll marry her. You wait and see."

"*You* wait," says Mamaw.

Jesse grins. "I will. Reckon I got to, for a while. But my mind's made up."

"Don't hardly *know* your mind, young as you are."

"Don't reckon I'm supposed to mention how you was fifteen when you married my daddy?"

"Never mind about me. Them days was a different world. Anyhow, I didn't marry my first cousin."

"No. But your mama did."

"And not much good come of it, neither. Now you get back and lie down with that blanket over you. I'd like to have me a last few peaceful hours before I see what your brother done in the way of damage with nobody to keep an eye on him."

It is one shade away from true darkness when they reach the farm. The western sky unfurls like a bolt of charcoal wool, its frayed lower edge touched with violet and gold.

Mamaw pauses for a minute before turning in from the road, just looking at her house. The kitchen window, a light glowing inside, is a sharp-edged square of copper. The trees behind the cabin look drawn in India ink upon the sky.

Jesse sits up in the wagon bed. "Listen."

Mamaw spots a V-shaped shadow crossing overhead. Wild geese.

"I love them crazy birds," Jesse says.

She listens to their curious music, slipping southward. When they can no longer be seen, she gives the reins a shake and heads for the house.

"Seems like they always got to make themselves so scarce until it's time they leave," says Mamaw.

XIV

The Boys

1 8 6 5 — 1 8 6 8

"The Boys" is how she thinks of them, not just Frank and Jesse now, but a dozen of them at least. No, more than that. Two dozen. They come and go until she can't keep count, showing up and taking off, and the house always crowded.

The Boys: clustering around her fires and eating her food, muddying her porch and tossing their blankets on her floor until Reuben, who can't hardly get a good night's sleep anymore, makes a kind of spare room for them out in the barn.

Even when she's looking at their faces right across the supper table, it's hard for Mamaw to keep in mind they're scarcely more than youngsters, these friends of her sons. So hard and quick, their eyes and words and bodies. What shows all over them is how they fought with Quantrill and Todd and Anderson, not how young they are. Defeat is like a patina on their faces.

Mamaw listens to them talk and talk into the night, catches every nuance of their ruined hope and belief, each bitter syllable of rage they drop like crumbs through her house. Why, I am just soft soap, she thinks. These youngsters are scathing as lye. Full of poison, The Boys.

And she wants to say to them, *Maybe we ought let it go, all*

❖

of us. Maybe we need to close the book because this account will never be settled anyhow and now we have . . .

But they have so little, have suffered so much. Bad enough to come up empty-handed, but to come up with your hands tied, too . . . no, Mamaw won't be the one to tell them *you just got to take it now,* take some more and more and hope maybe someday they'll tire of beating us.

"The law," Robert used to tell her, "is an instrument. Yet look how wrongheadedly we speak of it. We 'keep' or 'break' or 'observe' it. A law is 'passed,' like mashed potatoes at the dinner table.

"But we're supposed to *use* the law," he'd say. "Use it in wisom, in generosity . . . to build something with it."

What would Robert James say now, Zerel wonders. The law's being used, all right. Used against us, a weapon, an instrument of torture: a new State Constitution that disenfranchises anyone who aided the Confederacy, forbids the practice of law, teaching, even preaching the Word of God, if a man refuses to take their damnable "Ironclad Oath."

Mamaw's with The Boys every step of the way: *if we're rebels it's because they made us such,* their arrests and exiles, their looting and lynching till *treachery's about all we got to keep alive on. . . .*

And it sometimes seems as if God Himself is hell-bent on punishing Missouri. The weather turns against the crops, farm prices drop to nothing. And before a farmer can get to his feet, he's got the banks and railroads bleeding him, the Homesteaders breathing down his neck.

Mamaw, listening to The Boys around her table, thinks, *I don't know the half of it.*

Should be nothing can throw Mamaw now. Yet when in late fall it comes clear she's with child again, Mamaw's about done in.

Well, what did you expect . . . knew you was still . . . ain't but forty years old . . . no miracle about it. Still, it seems impossible to her . . . *ain't got another child in me.*

Only, it seems she does.

Zerel recalls one time, when she was a young girl, hearing the old nigger woman tell Aunt Mary—voices low, nothing for children's ears—how tea brewed of tansy could . . . "put a stop to things," was how she put it. "Why, it's a mercy," old Louisa said, "that's what tansy be."

Mercy don't grow around the homeplace, though, far as Zerel knows. She takes this particular bit of business to Excelsior Springs, no use advertising her private affairs in Kearney.

"Tansy?" she asks the old man in the Excelsior Emporium.

He gives her a knowing and commiserating look. "Got a touch of the rheumatism, have you?"

She nods, clamping her jaw tight.

He reaches for an apothecary jar on a high shelf.

"Fix you right up, this ought," he says. "Providing you survive the taste."

Mercy: the brew is bitter, vile, the very flavor of depravity. Mamaw drinks just one cup and finds remorse in the dregs. She runs to the woods, drops to the dirt on trembling knees, and jams her fingers down her throat. But the stuff will not come up again. One small cup—what harm could come, what destruction? She cannot bring it up, cannot.

She scatters what is left of the tansy over the kitchen fire as she cooks the midday meal, a burnt offering. That night she tells Reuben of the coming child, as if to seal its future in certainty.

"Another child." There is little surprise in Pappy's gladness. Mamaw wonders at her own amazement . . . that the war, putting an end to so much else, did not put a stop to this, too. That is what shocks her so.

As if hearing her thoughts, her protests, Reuben murmurs, "A child of peace . . ."

Mamaw thinks of mauve blooms of gaywings, to come again in May. Milkworts, old Louisa called them, swore their very presence in a house would make the breast fill and flow. Mamaw fixes her eye on the gaywings and coming spring, the carrying of milk and breath and life, and she will be a vessel. *One small cup,* she thinks, *what harm . . .*

As the weeks pass and the child continues to grow within her with no evidence of trouble, gladness is a story she tells herself until she comes to believe it, almost every word.

The winter of 1866 is as bitter as surrender. The snow comes early, one blizzard after another bearing down from the north like an avalanche, until western Missouri is stunned with hardship. Livestock freezes. Travelers are lost. Influenza has a field day.

There are three days of thaw in mid-February, but anyone can see another storm's coming. Around noontime on the third mild day, the sky roiling with new assaults, the town of Liberty is struck by an occurrence so unforeseen and unheard of that no one even knows what to call it.

Ten men, their faces concealed, ride into streets emptied by dinner hour and threats of heavy snow. Two of the strangers, attired in the blue coats of Union soldiers, enter the Clay County Savings Bank. Their companions wait outside.

Inside the bank, the cashier, Greenup Bird, and his son William are making use of the lull by working on the account ledgers. When the two visitors enter, William asks how he might serve them. Next thing he knows, a revolver's pointed in his face. William and his father are forced to pack all the bank's holdings into wheat sacks and hand them over. The two men in blue then lock the cashier and his son in the vault.

"Hear they got sixty-two thousand dollars," Jesse says. "Hoo-boy."

Mamaw sinks to a chair. "Imagine," she says. "Didn't hardly know there was that much money in Missouri."

"That ain't the worst of it," Reuben says. "A boy got killed. Wasn't doing a thing but passing by."

"Who was he?"

Frank snickers. "Unluckiest person in the world."

Reuben shoots his stepson a severe look, which seems to strike the boys even funnier. "His name was Wymore . . . a student at the college, they say."

Mamaw shakes her head, thinking how Robert worked so hard to start that school, give young men a chance to better themselves, and now here . . . "Why didn't nobody stop them?"

"Ten of 'em?" Jesse says. "Or something like that number, anyhow. And they was shootin' like Bull Run, I heard."

"Sent a posse after them," Reuben says. "But then with the storm come up and all . . ."

"Got clean away," Frank says, slapping his hands together sideways.

"You notice how Buck don't look real sorry about it, neither," Jesse says. "Can't say I'm sorry myself. Them blood-suckin' banks . . ."

"I'm ashamed of the both of you," Mamaw says. "Your daddy bein' a founder of William Jewell College and a boy from there, rushed to his grave . . ."

Jesse flushes a bit. "It is a shame, that part," he says. "But it happens. Just like in war."

Mamaw growls, "This ain't a war."

"Maybe it oughta be," Buck says.

"What's for supper, Mamaw? We got meat?"

"There's some fatback in the greens."

"Ain't what I call meat."

"Naw, Mr. Greenup Bird and his boy is havin' them some country ham about now. Bet that sixty-two thousand puts 'em off their feed some, though."

"Now you two boys quit trying to get your Mamaw riled

up," Pappy says. "Keep on this way, we'll get no supper at all."

Mamaw bears her eighth child, Archie Payton Samuel, without harm, on July 26, 1866.

"Eight," she says, shaking her head.

Pappy smiles. "That's you. Me, I'm just getting started."

"Hope you can get along without me, then," Mamaw says. "Reckon I've about had it."

Eight children, two of them men, one an infant . . . and if that ain't enough, she's got The Boys.

Suppertime of a mild autumn evening, and the family sits down to eat with the door open upon twilight.

Lord only knows what he done with his horse, if he even came on one, how he could get right up onto the porch without a body hearing a sound but a few crickets.

"Evenin', folks."

Mamaw nearly jumps out of her skin, only nobody notices, with Jesse and Buck laughing to beat the band.

"His Eminence, he do cover the territory on bitty rabbit paws!" Frank says.

"Bet he slithered up here on his belly like a snake," says Jesse.

"Snake that swallowed a bullfrog, maybe."

Cole Younger has become a big-boned, portly man with unkempt chin whiskers, red hair, and a high forehead that's the start of baldness. The Boys call him "the Bishop"—nothing boyish about him. No, Mamaw thinks. It's as if Cole Younger, wrathful and devout, brings a heavy darkness into a room with him.

"You had supper, son?" she says.

"I could do with a bite," he says.

A place is made for him at the table. Mamaw hands him a plate.

Cole looks at the pot and two bowls in the middle of the table. Then he picks up one of the bowls, mashed yams, and empties it onto his plate.

"Don't hold back now," Mamaw says.

He bows his head, his lips moving through a blessing before he eats.

The Bishop.

"You know I always make your friends welcome here," she tells Jesse and Buck. "I always will. But them Younger boys is about more than I can stand."

Four of 'em, Mamaw can't keep them straight but for Cole, the oldest. She knows the others' names—John, Bob, Jim—but can't get the names attached to the faces. They are, all of them, large, loud, loutish.

"I never seen worse manners," she says. "And they're about to eat us outa house and home."

Buck smiles a bit, but Jesse's laughing right in her face. "Ain't like you, Mamaw, showin' so little kindness to pore orphan children."

"Orphans got nothing to do with it. Them boys come in here chompin' and struttin', next thing you know it's like a plague of locusts passed through. Only difference, Cole chews louder."

Her sons hoot and yip and slip out the door. Mamaw lets them go. The Youngers'll be around no matter what she's got to say. And they *are* orphans, their daddy murdered by Federal militia while Cole was off fighting with Quantrill. A short time later Mrs. Younger was tortured, made to watch her own house burnt up like kindling. *If these boys got rough edges,* Mamaw thinks, *it's likely because they been treated rough. Reckon I can put up with their appetites.*

The assault on the bank at Liberty was too singular, certainly, to be forgotten. But when half a year goes by with nothing of the kind happening again, that's just what everybody thinks: singular . . . Liberty was a one-shot deal. So on the thirtieth of October, when five men take two thousand dollars from the banking house of Alexander Mitchell and Company in Lexington, the shock hits like lightning.

This time, though, nobody's killed. Ain't even any gunfire. The bandits slip away like greased pigs.

"Don't know why you sound so happy about it," Mamaw says. "What I hear is, your friends the Pool boys was leading the posse went after 'em." Like Jesse and Frank, John and Dave Pool are local heroes, worshipped for their brash guerrilla feats with Quantrill.

"Reckon you know," Mamaw says, "plenty of folks been saying it's Bushwhackers doing these terrible things. I'd figure you might be glad to see some of your own come out on the right side for a change, put a stop to that kind of talk."

"Ain't nothing'll do that," Frank tells her.

"Buck's right, Mamaw," Jesse says. "Don't you know they let us back into Clay County only so's they'd always have somebody to blame for everything? They mean to shine their boots on us from now to Judgment Day."

"Don't reckon you're far off there," she says.

"Maybe Judgment Day come sooner than they think," Frank says.

"Lexington paper says it was Kansas redleg robbers got that bank," says Pappy.

"Well, praise be!" Mamaw says. "Sounds like somebody over there still knows a weasel from a setting hen."

The boys are off visiting for a couple days—"just around," Jesse said—in early March when Mamaw and Pappy hear of the bank robbery at Savannah.

"Why, that ain't a dozen miles from here," Mamaw says. "How much they get?"

"Not a cent," Reuben tells her. "Judge McClain slammed

the safe and took a few shots at 'em and they lit out empty-handed."

"Well, good for the Judge!"

"Not entirely. He got shot up pretty bad. Looks like he'll lose an arm."

Mamaw pales, setting down her fork . . . *lose.* To have a part of you cut off that way . . .

"Wisht the boys was home," she says.

"Now, Zerel—"

"I know," she says. "Just seems like ain't no place that's safe anymore, Pappy."

"Don't get yourself all worked up."

"Who'd *do* such things?"

Shaking her head, Mamaw starts to eat again, but her appetite's gone. *Who'd do such things?* The question seems to hang in the room, over their heads, and Mamaw finds herself picturing Cole Younger, large hands grasping what he wants, jaw working furiously while he reaches for more . . . and more. . . .

Then she thinks, *For goodness' sake, the boy says grace before he eats! Don't that make me the fine Christian, thinking slander about a friend of this family? And a war hero to boot.*

Five or six men held up the Savannah bank. People who see the robbery at Richmond say at least a dozen come along this time.

It is May 22, 1867. The men ride into town from different directions and meet on the square in front of the Hughes and Wesson Bank. Four go inside; the rest wait on the street.

They only get four thousand dollars, but this time is different, worse . . . this one's a bloodbath. The Mayor is fatally shot in the chest as he runs at the robbers with his pistol drawn. Then a young boy taking aim with a cavalry rifle from behind a tree in the courthouse yard is shot in the middle of the forehead. The boy's father runs to help his son, and he,

too, is shot dead. Amid gunsmoke, blood, and screams, the
horsemen fly away, a posse on their heels.

"They come close this time," Reuben says.

"Close?" Zerel's face looks white and soft as dough.

"The posse. They actually caught up with them at sunset,
but there was woods, and what with the darkness coming
on . . ."

The darkness on their side, Mamaw thinks. And then she
cuts off her own suspicion: *Whose side? Just who do you
think you're talking about here? This ain't your concern . . .
ain't a thing you know can help you understand the nature of men
who'd . . .*

"Zerel, where's the boys? They be home for supper?"

"What?"

"Buck and Jesse, where—"

"Off gallivanting somewhere like usual. Don't guess they'll
be back for a day or two."

Reuben looks into her eyes for a moment, his lips parted
like there's something he's getting ready to say.

Don't. Don't say a word. He turns away with downcast eyes,
and Mamaw thinks, *Don't don't you dare, these children are
mine, these doubts this darkness and you'd have no right to shame
not you not even if it were so. . . .*

"Zerel—"

"Reckon it's time I got out and done the milking," she
says.

"Let me do it."

"No," she says. "No need for you to take on my part of
things."

A new moon is stuck like a splinter in the tender pink sky
as Mamaw walks slowly toward the barn.

Know? she thinks. *You don't know a thing.*

And it's true. Mamaw has no more than an inkling. The
darkness is still on her side.

By early '68 Jesse is sickening again. All the brightness leaves his skin, his eyes. Even his hair is dull. He grows gaunt, silent, hollow-eyed.

Frank sleeps like a baby, eats like a horse. Beside his darker brother, Jesse looks like a jumpy shadow. He develops a wracking cough. Mamaw leaves Reuben to fuss over that. The trouble, she thinks, is not from war and wounding, but deeper within.

Jesse is the only one in the family who goes to church with her.

March 20, 1868. Kentucky this time, as if they think she won't notice them there. Five men in cattle dealers' linen dusters escape with twelve thousand dollars (some say more) from the Nimrod Long & Co. Bank in Russellville.

Mamaw is outside the Kearney general store, looking preoccupied with fat, slovenly sacks of seed as she listens to the men swap accounts of the travesty. And as she hears their claims—righteous, yet strangely delighted—she can almost see the whole thing happening like a dance: intricately choreographed, delicately performed. One of the robbers, talking fast about longhorn breeding and feed prices, looks over the premises the day before, charms the britches off everybody . . . next day, when the bandits flee, a corps of ten sentries leap from the wings to stymie pursuit. The charmer's laugh is scattered behind him like silver as he rides off. One banker is grazed by a bullet, but no one is seriously injured. The outlaws' horses sprout wings . . . oh, can't you just see it?

It is beautiful.

Pappy draws the wagon up alongside the store, tips his hat how-do to the knot of men on the steps. Zerel heaves a sack of cornmeal into the back and clambers up on the seat beside him.

"You hear?" he says.

She waits until he giddyaps the horse, until hoofbeats and a snippet of road muffle her reply. "A filthy business," she says.

But beautiful . . . somewise such daring must be beautiful to behold. She can almost hear the charmer's laugh dropping a trail of bright silver coins in the dust behind her, and she recalls a phrase of the music language Benjamin taught her so long ago:

Con brio.

"Jesse, it must be three o'clock in the morning. What are you doing out here?"

He crouches at the kitchen hearth, the orange underlighting of the embers scooping out the hollows in his face. He pokes the fire with a crippled stick. His bare feet are terribly white against the rough, dark hearthstone.

"Mamaw." He doesn't look up from the fire. "Could you sit with me awhile?" he says.

"I could," she says. "Only you been choosing lately to sit with yourself, seems like."

"Don't guess I like it all that much, being alone with . . ."

"Don't," Mamaw says.

He looks up at her.

"I can't stop what you do, boy, but the time comes when I got to stop you from telling me."

"I need to talk to somebody, Mamaw."

"Well, be careful who you pick."

"Who'd you suggest, if not my own mama?"

"You might try God," she says.

Jesse laughs softly, and she has to smile herself.

"It's what your daddy'd tell you," she says.

"My daddy." Jesse shakes his head. "Can't hardly imagine what he'd make of things these days."

"You remember him—on your own, I mean, apart from what I tell you?"

"Seems like I do, only the yarn gets kinda tangled. It's like you hear a thing so many times you start believing you saw it?"

Mamaw's voice is soft. "I know."

"Mostly, I reckon I remember his eyes. On my own."

"Your daddy had eyes a body wasn't apt to forget. Truth in them eyes of his."

Jesse stares into the fire.

"Don't ever forget whose boy you are," Mamaw says.

He laughs. "You recollect the first words you taught me to speak? You'd say, 'Whose boy are you?' Then I was supposed to say—"

"I know. Mamaw's boy." She sighs. "Reckon I left off half the story."

Jesse stands up, his face darkening as he moves out of the firelight. "Whose boy am I now?" he says.

"It ain't even a question," says Mamaw.

A few weeks later, with his mother watching impassively from a pew toward the back, Jesse Woodson James presents himself for baptism at the Mount Olivet Baptist Church.

"Must be a right proud moment for you, sister." The deacon, a man named Clement Farlow, pumps Mamaw's hand up and down.

"Happiest day of my life," she says. Her lips part like something sliced by a sharp knife.

The blood is in his lungs, as if drawn there from his hands. There is poison in him. Food won't stay on his stomach; one ear is so badly infected it seems likely he'll go deaf on that side. The bedclothes where he lies are stained with mucus and pus and smell of corruption.

"Anemia," says Pappy, "among other things." The cough deepens. Consumption. A proper name, she thinks. Something is consuming him.

❖

Mamaw begins to sit beside him at night again. She dozes, and in rushed, abbreviated dreams she places her lips to his chest and sucks the poison from him and swallows, consumes it.

Jesse pretends to sleep. She touches his head with pure water, as if reenacting the baptism that brought no salvation, that has changed nothing.

In late April Jesse quits Missouri for California. One day he tells her, next he is gone.

The morning of his leaving, Mamaw's in a fury. She slams breakfast on the table, as if the whole household's in cahoots with him. "For your health," she says. Scorn drips over his plate like syrup. "For your *health* you should stay put where you got folks to look after you."

"The climate—" Reuben says.

"You keep out of this!"

Her husband suddenly looks bewildered and frail. He raises his hands and looks at Jesse. "Dingus?"

Frank leans across the table and pats his stepfather's arm. "Don't be scared, Pappy. I'm stayin' behind to protect you."

The boys laugh, Mamaw slams her hand down on the bread board, and Pappy looks as if he could cry.

"Reckon you think you're quite the sight," Mamaw says.

Jesse jumps up from the table and strikes a pose, leaning his elbow on the mantel. He wears a modishly cut tan suit, brand-new, and a brocade vest the shade of sweet butter. A royal-blue bandanna is knotted at his throat.

"Don't want Uncle D. W. and his rich California friends to think I'm some pore country boy."

"Circus boy's more like it," says Mamaw. "Brim on that hat's so wide you could hire out as an umbrella."

"Cut me up all you like, Mamaw. Zee gets a look at me, I'm bound to recollect how sweet a woman can be."

His mother glares at him. "So Zee's in on this, too? I mighta

186

known. Was there anyone in Missouri you didn't tell 'fore telling me?"

Mamaw runs on and on, working up to a pitch. Mamaw makes a regular spectacle of her displeasure. . . .

A diversion. She don't mean half what she says. The name California just scares the life out of her, is all.

XV

First Frost

1 8 6 8 — 1 8 6 9

The first frost comes early that year. The second week of September Mamaw has to strip the tomato vines. Five crocks of hard green tomatoes drown in brine along the north cellar wall. The late raspberries are a stingy leaving for the birds. The start of October sees snow on the ground. It's a good year for tubers, pumpkins, gourds. Missouri seems bound for a rugged winter.

But in late October Indian summer traipses in, more seductive than the falsest false spring.

For the first time in many years, Mamaw steals a few afternoon swims. She takes Archie, two now, to the pond with her. He doesn't like the water; his mother's naked body frightens him. Purple veins writhe beneath her skin. Her forearms are ropy and knotted like an old man's. The flesh hangs from her, loose and unseemly. *I almost frighten myself*, she thinks.

Archie plays with roots and stones along the embankment, his back turned on a vision larger than life. Zerel splashes in the water, but it's so cold she soon comes out. She stands on the bank, kneading mud between her toes like rich, overmoist dough, as the weak sun dries her skin. Pleasure, now, is a mild thing, but pleasure just the same.

In the midst of this mock summer, Jesse returns.

Mamaw hears him calling to her from the yard late one morning: "Kill a chicken . . . company comin'!"

Her heart pitches at the sight of him in the doorway. He is rose and gold, broad in the shoulder, curved in the cheek. He looks taller . . . that can't be. His eyes are round and vivid as blue poker chips.

"A beard," she says. "Where'd you get that?"

The wooden spoon slips from her hand and clatters to the floor as he picks her up and whirls her around . . . *like I was slight as Zee,* she thinks.

"Set me down! My nursing ain't been called for since the day you left this house. I got no interest in catering to no fool with a crippled back now."

"Knew you'd be tickled to see me," Jesse says.

"Took a shine to California, did you?" Pappy says.

"Plumb crazy about her," Jesse says.

"Who?"

"Why, California, brother."

"Figured you was talkin' about some loose woman in one of them saloons."

"Salooo!" Archie cries, beating a spoon on the floor under Jesse's chair.

"That's enough, Buck. Mind how you talk in front of children."

"I ain't a children," Johnny says. "Did you see real cowboys, Jess?"

"See 'em? I been one." He looks at Frank, then at Mamaw. "And I didn't see no ladies, neither. Still got the only girl for me right over by Kansas City."

Mamaw flashes him a wicked smile. "A fine thing, I say, when cousins is devoted to one another."

Jesse smiles back at her, squinting. "I am that," he says. "Devoted as the day is long."

"What are they talking about?"

"Ain't nothin', Pappy. Pay no mind to it."

Reuben, looking lost, shuffles to the doorway and stands staring out into the yard. Mamaw casts a severe look at all her children, big and small. "Come back here now, Pappy, and finish your supper. I made these dumplings for you."

"I forget things, Zerel." His voice is wispy.

"Well, we all do, Pappy," Jesse says. "But I ain't forgot you. I bring you some things from California, in fact."

Reuben starts cautiously back toward the table. "A present?"

"Why, I don't rightly know as you'd call anything so useful a present, exactly."

Pappy's eyes are glistening now. "Like something for my toolbox, you mean?"

"Like that, kinda . . . how about some new things to put in your doctoring bag?"

Reuben looks dubious, a little disappointed.

"Wait now, just give me a chance to show you."

Jesse's cracked leather portmanteau, left behind by Robert James, is still sitting by the door. He opens it and brings out some small paper packets and several amber vials, a cobalt bottle. He returns to the table and sets them down in front of his stepfather's plate. "For you," he says. "For Pappy. Got something for you too, Mamaw . . . something for everybody, only I'm gonna have to root around in here some before—"

"Dingus?"

Everyone looks at Pappy. His eyes are swimming with tears. "I been sick?"

Jesse glances at Mamaw in confusion and alarm.

"Pappy gets tired sometimes, son," she says. "Addled."

A sad, uneasy silence falls over the table. Pappy wipes the corners of his eyes with his napkin and won't look at anyone. Zerel reaches past the dinner plates to pat his hand. On the floor under the table, Archie begins to cry in a soft, thin wail.

Jesse gets up and goes around the table to squat down beside his stepfather. "Look here, this ain't medicine for you to swallow, Pappy." His words are slow and gentle. "It's some special kinds of doctoring things I learned about in California. Nature-doctoring. They got these herbs and minerals and such that ain't around these parts. I bring 'em to you because you're a *doctor*."

Reuben looks at his wife for a minute. His face is stern. Then suddenly he starts laughing, very quietly.

"You see?" he says. "I'm a doctor."

Then Pappy comes back to himself again as Jesse explains about the wonders of "nature-doctoring." They sit up half the night, Reuben learning the names and purposes of all the vegetable and mineral compounds. Pappy doesn't forget a one.

The restlessness runs deep and wide in Jesse now, after California. There is a mother lode of dissatisfaction in this boy. She hears him pace the kitchen floor at night, watches him disappear in the morning, riding off as if he means to arrive at the edge of the world before noon.

"A ranch is what we want to get us," she hears him telling Buck. "A thousand acres for a song, and we'll build us such a herd . . ."

"Brother, California give you the worst case of one-track mind I believe I ever seen."

"California?" Jesse says. "Why, there's better places than that even. Argentina . . ."

Buck slaps his knee. "The Argen-tine! Now that is rich."

"You bet it is. Rich and ripe and ready. Met a cowhand at Uncle D.W.'s place who just been down there. Told me them

Argentine horses are the fastest in the world. Beautiful ladies with big black eyes and lace dresses . . ."

"Thought you had your lady picked out already."

Jesse grins. "It's you I had in mind, brother."

"Mighty thoughty of you. Reckon I'd as soon look here, though. I lean towards a girl who speaks English. Maybe even one who reads it, I get lucky."

"Have it your way. All I'm tellin' you is, we get us a stake and we can own a piece of the *world* down there. Buy the stock, they give you the land for a present."

Mamaw, listening from the bedroom, waits for Buck to laugh. But he doesn't. Both boys are quiet for a minute or two. Then Buck says, "How *much* of a stake, you figure?"

A few weeks later, on the seventh of December, two men hold up the Daviess County Savings Bank in Gallatin. They only get a few hundred dollars, but the hue and cry are louder and longer than ever before: Captain John Sheets, principal owner of the bank, is shot straight through the heart.

"Finest man that ever walked this earth," folks say. "Wasn't even raising no fuss, just doing like they said. Shot out of pure meanness . . ."

"What I heard is, they took him for Major Cox . . . that they was Bushwhackers after a payback for Bloody Bill's gettin' killed."

"That don't make a lick of sense. War's been over a good while now. . . ."

"Not for some it ain't."

Mamaw hurries past the store. Such a crowd in there this morning. She ain't one for crowds.

This time Missouri gets hot under the collar. Matter of fact, things been heating up for a while now. In the months before Gallatin, several suspects in earlier robberies were arrested and lynched before juries could be rounded up. A sorry business, but enough is enough, even in Missouri. Big rewards are offered.

And this time the bandits, whoever they are, don't get away with it so easy. Gallatin fights back. As the outlaws are ushered out of town to a fanfare of gunfire, one of their horses goes into a panic. Its rider, his foot caught in a stirrup, is thrown and dragged a good way down the street. Finally the second man frees him and the two ride away on one horse.

The handsome, skittish mare left behind is later identified as the property of a boy from Kearney, name of Jesse James.

"What happened to you?" Mamaw says.

Jesse's face is scraped up but good, ugly blue bruise on his forehead. Mamaw pushes his hair back to have a better look, but he ducks out of her reach.

"Mamaw, I'm ashamed to tell you," he says.

"Never mind the preliminaries."

"Got suckered," he says. "Youngers bet me I couldn't ride this mule they got . . ."

She walks away before he can really get started. If she don't want to hear a tale, she shouldn't ask questions.

The boys have been home for two days—sticking close together, close to the barn. Seems like they've got an eye out on the road most of the time.

It's getting near four o'clock, the light beginning to fail. Mamaw comes out into the yard, a shawl tied fast against the wind as she scatters chicken feed over the puddle of feathers she stands in. "Don't get uppity," she says. The pullets squawk and peck at her skirts. She glances at the barn. Strings of light separate the planks of the tack room wall.

Then she hears horses approaching from the road. As the two men ride close to the yard, she recognizes John Thomason, the Deputy Sheriff, and his son Oscar. "Just what we need," she says. "A couple of Thomasons come nosin' around."

Sheriff Thomason is a graying, large-bellied man, his small, hard eyes pouched in fat like buckshot in a risen loaf. He tends to an elaborate politeness with more than a hint of bullying in it. Mamaw despises everything about him, all the more because he's kin to her mother's husband.

She brushes the last of the feed from her hands, pulls her wrap tighter, and waits, chickens eddying around her feet. A picture of Jesse's bruised face rises up, but she slaps it down hard. *You don't know a thing.*

The Thomasons remain mounted, the boy's horse sidling up to his father's as if for protection.

The Sheriff lifts his hat and manages a bow from the saddle. "Miz Samuel, a pleasure—"

"Sheriff." Mamaw nods. "Oscar."

The boy, perhaps eighteen, does not acknowledge her.

"Beg pardon for this unannounced call, ma'am. I am sure that with your many duties as wife and mother—"

"What is it, Sheriff? Something I can do for you?"

"I'm sure we needn't disengage you . . . if we might just ask as to the whereabouts of your two eldest . . . ?"

"Frank and Jesse? What do you want with them?"

"I'd be greatly obliged ﹖"

"They ain't in yet."

"In, ma'am? They been away, then?"

"They been workin'," Mamaw says. "Like always." She waves her hand vaguely to her right. "They was headed out that way somewheres after dinner, I believe."

Thomason's piggy little eyes follow the flick of her fingers, squinting into the gloom.

It comes to her then, cold and sharp, in the instant whose silence is filled with wind and the echo of her last word, believe . . . believe . . .

❖

I have lied for them. I am in it now.

"You're welcome to come inside and wait." Mamaw's smile looks like a pulled thread.

Before Thomason can reply, the barn doors fly open with a thunder of hoofbeats. The Sheriff and his boy turn around in time to see two riders waving hats above their heads as they gallop over the pasture toward dense woods.

Without lingering over the niceties of departure, the Thomasons light out after them.

Mamaw stands in the yard, staring past the point where there is anyting to see. A few minutes after the sound of their horses dies away, she hears a single shot, like the crack of splitting wood. Then nothing.

Holding herself stiffly, she returns to the house. Her black woolen shawl is bunched close around her shoulders and neck, and she is shivering.

"Mamaw?"

"Yes, son?"

"We heared a noise." The whites of Johnny's eyes look big as eggs in his small, windburned face.

"Ain't nothing," she says.

"A *bad* noise, Mamaw. Like thunder."

"Maybe that's what it was, then."

"Where's Jesse?"

"Him and Frank ain't in from working yet."

"But—"

"Never mind, now."

The boy looks resigned. "Can I have a apple?"

"It's too close to supper."

"How come you got your shawl on in the house, Mamaw?"

She hears Archie crying in the bedroom, then the voices of his sisters trying to hush him. She starts to remove her shawl.

"Archie's crying from the thunder," Johnny says. "But I ain't scared."

"No," Mamaw says. "Ain't a thing to be scared of. You scoot now, let me see about supper."

She pushes down the dough in the pans and sets the bread on the hearth for its second rising. She pares turnips, sets plates on the table. It seems that a very long time goes by. Then she hears what sounds like a single horse moving slowly into the yard. She does not go to the door.

"Miz Samuel? Ma'am?"

She walks without haste, measuring her steps to the rapping of knuckles on the door.

John Thomason seems grayer, fatter, older.

"Come in, Sheriff."

Beyond the porch, the boy, Oscar, looks like a statue of a war hero, mounted against the sky. A faint trickle of red seeps between the clouds low on the western sky behind him.

Mamaw, shivering, closes the door.

The Sheriff is breathing hard. "May I sit down for a moment?"

"Please," she says.

He cannot look her in the eye. "I know you are a good Christian woman, and I hope you won't let hard feelin's . . ."

"For God's sake," she whispers, "What is it?"

"Them durn boys . . . somebody, I mean. They shot my horse," he says.

Mamaw turns away. "You don't mean it?"

"Right out from under me, ma'am."

When she faces him again, her face is suitably arranged. "I call that a pure disgrace," she says.

"Yes'm." Thomason looks down at his pudgy hands, twisting them into a lover's knot. "The thing is . . . I'd be much obliged if you and the doctor could loan me a horse?"

"Shame my boys ain't home yet," Mamaw says. "They might have been some help in getting after those . . ."

Thomason smiles at her miserably. His whole face seems to have collapsed under the weight of his indignity. "Yes, them boys of yours can ride," he says. "They surely can."

They surely can. Them boys can ride places you'll never see. But understand—you're in it now.

"Did you ask me somethin' just now?" Mamaw says.

"A horse?" Thomason whispers. "I need to get home."

"Sheriff, our pleasure," says Mamaw. "This family'd be honored to serve the law."

Most mournful-looking man I ever did see, is what Mamaw thinks the first time she meets Major John Newman Edwards. A disappointing figure, after all the boys have told her . . . how Edwards fought at Jo Shelby's right hand straight through the war and even afterwards, refusing to admit it was over, cutting across Texas to go and fight another losing battle in Mexico.

"On the *Emperor's* side?" Mamaw says. "What kind of American's that?"

Buck laughs. "Same kind as you, Mamaw. The Major loves a lost cause."

"He's a decorated war hero," Jesse tells her. "Not to mention our friend. You be polite now, Mamaw, when he gets here."

Just who do they think they are, these boys? Getting right full of themselves. Talking her ear off for three days beforehand, like she wouldn't know how to treat a guest under her own roof . . . fancy friends . . . now this fella shows up who bears a strong likeness to a coon hound. . . .

"How do," Mamaw says.

Edwards drops to one knee, grabs her hand, and kisses it. She shoots the boys a look: *What kind of American . . .*

When Major Edwards stumbles back to his feet, there are tears in his eyes, and what with that moustache dripping down his chin . . .

"Forgive me for being so deeply moved, ma'am. But to meet in the flesh the revered mother of these . . ."

"My pleasure, sir."

"Admiration and awe leave me speechless, ma'am."

"Maybe you'd best sit down and catch your breath," Mamaw says.

Jesse steps in, seeing that Mamaw's about to bust out laughing. He narrows his eyes at her and she coughs, covering her mouth.

"Reckon you know, Mamaw, the Major here's the editor of the *Times* in Kansas City? Wrote him a book, too."

She nods. "So I heard."

"I assure you I'm not always such a fool, Mrs. Samuel. But if you understood what these sons of yours mean to me—"

There's something downright disarming about this fella, she's gotta admit it, she's warming to him. . . .

All three men are looking at her now with anxious eyes. Mamaw's laugh takes the chill off the room. "Major," she says, "these boys get me to actin' a bit foolish myself from time to time."

She gives Edwards a cup of tea, pretending not to notice when Frank adds something from a small bottle he slides out of his coat pocket. Hardly surprising the man needs shoring up. There's something defenseless about him, she thinks, like he carries hope unguarded in his eyes and expects somebody to swoop down and pluck it out any minute.

John Newman Edwards is only a few years older than Frank, yet he seems as worn and whittled down as Reuben. Not, Mamaw thinks, one of The Boys, not this one.

"Will you be stayin' with us?" she asks him.

"No, ma'am. I just wanted to make your acquaintance . . ." He gives Buck and Jesse a questioning look, and they nod at him. "And perhaps to ask your help," he says.

"Mine?" says Mamaw.

"With your permission," he says.

"I'm listening."

◆

"This unfortunate Gallatin incident," Edwards says.

"Now hold on a minute here—" She starts to rise, but Jesse grasps her arm, holds her down.

"If you mean to start in about that horse folks are saying was Jesse's—" She looks above Edwards at her sons, standing now like bodyguards at either side of his chair. Their faces are pale, shifty-eyed, shocked.

"Hah. You think I ain't heard that story by now?" she says. "Folks may keep their voices down, but your Mamaw's ears are pretty good. Eyes, too. Way I been looked at in town lately, I start to feelin' like Grant's mother."

Jesse's grin breaks out like something he's been saving up for after dark on the Fourth of July. "Shoulda known we couldn't fool you, Mamaw."

"And I'd thank you not to forget it," she says.

"Miz Samuel—"

"Never you mind, Major. You're our guest here and I mean you no disrespect. But if you come expecting to tell me how to raise my own young ones—"

"We're hardly young ones." Frank's voice is dry, cocky.

"Well, you been acting like a couple ten-year-olds with wasps in your britches and tapioca for brains, boy."

Frank and Jesse are trapped between amusement and shame.

"Well, what have you got to say for yourselves?" She turns to John Edwards. "And what business *you* got in this mess?"

Edwards looks mortified, astounded, yet strangely determined. "I feel, as I'm sure you do, Miz Samuel," he says, "that these fine boys, these *patriots,* are being unjustly accused."

"You don't need to gild stinking benjamin and tell me it's a lily," Mamaw says. "My nose is still working, too."

"Yes, ma'am. But I want you to know I am making it my business—my personal crusade, if you will—to make your sons' innocence publicly known."

"Innocence!" Mamaw snorts. "You're looking for innocence, you're in the wrong household."

Jesse laughs. "John, didn't I tell you she's a handful?"

But Edwards is in a fever now. He looks at Mamaw, only Mamaw, appeal in his deep-set eyes. "I am asking you to venture . . . *out,* to step forward in the sight of all the world and to say plainly and honestly what you and I both know: that Frank and Jesse James are exemplary, brave, heroic . . ."

Mamaw's ready to talk turkey now. "You want to cut the flowers?" she says. "Reckon we'll get somewheres sooner if we speak plain."

John Newman Edwards stares up at her with his tragic hound's eyes.

"Don't get me wrong." Mamaw lowers her voice. "You talk real good, Major, got quite a gift. Only maybe we could move things along?"

Edwards hesitates for a few seconds, looking like he might weep again. Then a shy smile breaks across his face. He places both hands on the table and, leaning forward, tells Mamaw exactly what he has in mind.

The following week, ringed by open-mouthed reporters in the blazing lobby of a Kansas City hotel, Mamaw goes public. High time, too. If folks think she's apt to sit around and keep still while her boys is accused of . . . well, they just got another think coming.

"Begging pardon, ma'am, but . . . well, where *were* your sons, exactly, on the day in question?"

"Where any decent boys would be," she says. "At home with their family."

"But the horse—"

"That horse ditched at Gallatin, reportedly my boys'? Well, I am here to tell you that very same horse, a mare she was and kinda tetchy, got sold a week—*one full week*—before this

terrible event, this scandal. A man from Topeka, he was—
or so he said, anyhow—slapped down five hundred dollars
like small change, and we can use the money, too, believe
you me. This family ain't got much, but what we got's our
own and honestly come by, I can tell you that. . . ."

Reuben and Susie, wreathed in the light of a crystal chan-
delier, stand behind her as Mamaw meets the press. Pappy
and Susie her chorus, but Mamaw's the prima donna, no
doubt about it. She confounds logic with her aria of exon-
eration, drowns out suspicion in grace notes of detail. The
crystal prisms sway and tinkle to her tune. She brings the
audience to its knees.

Mamaw's first recital gets rave reviews in all the major dailies,
especially in the Kansas City *Times*.

"Bravo," Major Edwards cries. "A magnificent acquittal, a
flawless delivery."

"Did you think I'd just stand by and listen to slander?"
Mamaw grins. "What's a mother for?" Reuben and Susie keep
still and stick close, like captives chained to her.

The boys have already seen the papers by the time she
gets back from Kansas City. Buck's grinning ear to ear.

"Don't start gloating," Mamaw says. "You ain't off the
hook."

Jesse is crowing. "You were a living glory!"

"Kind of a pleasure," Mamaw says, "having somebody listen to me for a change."

Gallatin: minor as bank jobs go. Two bandits, one casualty,
seven hundred dollars. One small-potatoes savings and loan
alongside a piss-poor stream cutting out from the wide Missouri, calling itself the Grand River. A short shot from the
homeplace, fifty miles maybe. Nothing to get flustered about,
Gallatin.

Still, it slices like a knife, cuts her life in two. Gallatin divides everything. Because after that she knows. Gallatin marks the spot where Mamaw can't pretend anymore. Can't wink or blink. She just plain knows and everybody knows it, and there's no use in her acting otherwise, after Gallatin.

She corners Jesse in the smokehouse. His hands are full of soaked corncobs, and he patiently banks the fire: a slow burn. There is soot on his forehead, a dark smudge that reminds Zerel of Ash Wednesday in the convent. *Dust,* she thinks, *thou art dust . . .*

Two sides of a hog, one fat wild turkey, and a haunch of venison hang from blackened iron hooks behind him. He resembles some pagan god of the hunt, bowed down before those carcasses.

His insolence, too, when he looks at her, is rather godlike. "Mamaw." He licks his lower lip and smiles a little, looking her over the way a man might look on a woman he's used and enjoyed and had done with, she thinks. His own mother.

"I got to talk to you." Her voice is thick and acrid, like the smoke.

"Figured you'd get 'round to it," he says.

"Don't get smart, Jesse. I'd hate to see you start believing all that legend-hero business the Major been decorating you and your brother's sorry hides with."

"You done some pretty fancy hide-covering yourself, Mamaw."

"I did at that. But it oughtn't give you the idea I believe everything I say."

Jesse laughs quietly. "We all gotta do some fast talking, I reckon. Me and Frank's just lucky you got such a talent for it."

"Don't mean I'm proud of it, though." Mamaw draws a deep breath, pressing her arms to her sides. "I want you to clear out, you and Buck." Her stare is steady and aggressive, daring him to talk back to her.

"You do, huh? You're turning us out of our own home?"

"I am telling you what I'd think you'd figure out for yourself. You boys can't stick around here anymore."

Not so sure of himself now, is he? Jesse's smile fades, his eyes narrow.

"We live here," he says.

"You don't live anywhere," she tells him. "Now you never will."

"You really want us to leave?"

"No," she says. "I don't want it, I never wanted it. But you didn't ask what I wanted. Being on the dodge is what you and your brother picked."

"We didn't pick nothin'. Things just happen. You know that."

"I don't aim to split hairs with you. What's done is done. However it got that way is the way it is. You just can't stay now, is all."

Jesse spits on the fire, a small hiss. "Never thought to see the day you'd care what folks thought."

She laughs harshly. "You think that's what this is?"

"What is it then, you mind me askin'?"

"I don't mind. I'm only surprised you need to be told. They'll get you if you stay here. I don't aim to see it, Jesse. You clear out now."

"You told Buck?"

"You can tell him. He does whatever you say."

Jesse shakes his head and wipes the back of his hand across his eyes. The smoke is rising up thicker now. "A body could choke to death," he says.

"You might go to Kentucky," his mother says. "My people would see to you for a spell. Or Pappy's."

"Might go anywhere. What difference does it make?"

"Not much, I reckon," she says. "Kind of life you're living now will follow wherever you go."

She walks out of the smokehouse, Jesse behind her. The

air in the yard is thin, brittle. Sinewy pumpkin vines writhe around the edges of the plucked garden. Mamaw unpins the long gray coil of her hair and sets it loose in the breeze, shaking out the smoke. Sunlight spattering her dark skirts, she walks back toward the house.

Jesse stands leaning against the corner of the smokehouse, watching her walk away.

Mamaw does not look back at her son before she goes inside. The bitter taste of smoke coats her tongue and clings to the roof of her mouth.

His eyes tear.

The following morning the boys are gone. They leave her a love note on the kitchen table with their dirty dishes, muddy tracks on the porch. It is coming on to Christmas, but the ground has thawed for them, as if to soften the blow of their leaving.

They leave her low on coffee, sugar, and cornmeal. A cast-iron skillet, just large enough for two, is gone. Some blankets. Two tin plates and cups. Two of Mamaw's children are missing. She has, cold comfort, five more. Things will never be the same.

XVI

Home Remedies

1 8 6 9 — 1 8 7 4

Their absence settles in her bones like an ache. She doesn't know now where they sleep, who they're with, how they live. She doesn't know what gets into them, what they see in Cole Younger and his like. "How can you pick such friends?" she said to Frank once. Her son gave her a sour grin. "Pretty much like you pick an ox or mule or plow horse, I reckon. Only you try not to be so obvious when you check his teeth."

Oh, full of wit and trouble, her boys, and she'll never know what they're up to now until they've had done with it. She only knows what she reads in the papers. And she knows they are gone.

Reuben tries to smother a sigh of relief, disguise it as a yawn, that morning when she tells him, "They are gone." For better or for worse. "Gone for good," Mamaw says, sounding chipper, sounding casual, sounding like anything but a body's just had a part hacked clean away and carried off God-knows-where.

Pappy's smile is wry. "Gone," he says. "But not forgotten."

———

❖

Where are your boys now, how they making out, and when will they grace Clay County again? Everybody's interested. It shouldn't surprise her, yet it does.

Neighbor children follow her like she's the Pied Piper. Even though they're afraid of Mamaw and whisper that she's a witch. They dare each other to brush up against her skirts and offer to carry her packages in town, as if sorcerer's dust encloses her and they want it to coat them, want it to cake between their small fingers and settle in their fine hair.

Sometimes the nameless children hover just outside her cabin. Their heads appear above the windowsills, eyes wide and dark in the shade of the porch overhang. Their faces float pale before the bank of gaudy hollyhocks. They watch Mamaw cook as if magic seasons her butter beans and breathes in her salt-rising bread.

Out in the yard, as she boils the laundry in a copper kettle, the children conceal themselves in the limbs of trees, wary lest she toss their bodies in along with sprigs of rosemary to scent the linens. Mamaw feels their watching all the time, even when she's alone.

The children cross the prairie to surround her like a plague of grasshoppers—devouring eyes, surreptitious fingers. Things vanish. They loot the barn and comb the yard for relics. *Genuine bark from the original tree where the authentic James Boys' one true Mamaw* . . . They would pluck out her hair, build nests of it, she thinks, if she stood still.

Mamaw is under watch, all right, but the children are the least of it.

Every week now the trains bring strangers to town. Their eyes give them away. Never been here before, they say, yet they study the town as if it's their long-lost home. They remember names too readily. Their questions are too round-about, too careless. They care too much, these strangers.

And Mamaw, for once, is rattled. Truth is, she feels like a target. Oh, she's been the target of snooping and suspicion and blame before, had Baptist do-gooders and Jayhawkers and county sheriffs, in-laws and even her own mama sticking fingers into her pies all at once. But nothing in her life has prepared her for the kind of pursuit closing in on her now. *My boys finally brought me into a game I don't know how to play,* she thinks. *These men ain't no fat lazy local boys, no women whose worst weapon is snippiness. Jesse and Frank set real dogs on my tail this time.*

Because her boys, since Gallatin, are wanted men, men with a price on their heads. And each time they act up again, each time anybody even *guesses* the James Boys might have done another piece of mischief, the price goes up another notch.

Under threat from outsiders, Mamaw forms an alliance with the children. Instead of evading their curiosity, she cultivates and harvests it.

"Don't guess you seen that man staying at Miz Tibbetts' place—one says he come from Kansas City?"

"Sure, I seen him," the boy says. "Got a big red chin whisker and a gold pocket watch, some kinda tooth on the chain?"

"That's the one. What brings a man like him here, I wonder?"

"That's simple. I ask' him and he says he come to look over some land hereabouts."

"Land, that so? Well, now. Don't suppose he'd be telling anybody, seeing as how businessmen don't go in much for idle talk . . . don't guess a body could know what piece of land this fella's got his eye on?"

"He don't say, ma'am. But I figure Sheriff Thomason'd know. The two of 'em's always talkin' together in town. And the land must be out this way . . ."

"What makes you say so?"

"You ain't seen him? He passes by here pretty-near ever' day."

The brightest of the bunch, this lad, Mamaw thinks. She troubles herself to learn his name: Cletus Birdsall. He nearly puts her in mind of Jesse sometimes, not missing a trick. Knows how to keep his mouth shut, too, when he's handled right.

"Don't reckon you'd be looking to earn some money," she says.

The boy's eyes glisten.

Mamaw strikes a bargain: she'll give Cletus Birdsall a penny for each newspaper story he brings her about her boys. She can't fetch the papers herself. Doesn't want to look too interested.

"You got yourself a regular job," she tells Cletus. "Only I hear you gone and mentioned it to anybody, the deal's off."

"I ain't much of a talker," the boy says.

Good as his word, young Cletus. He slips her bits of newsprint when nobody's looking. He doesn't say where he cadges the papers, and Mamaw doesn't ask. She keeps pennies in her apron pockets at all times. The clippings pile up in a tin box under the bed.

When they first take off, the boys go to Kentucky—at least she's pretty sure that's where they must be. Lots of houses in Kentucky'd be right pleased to offer shelter to friends of Quantrill and Bloody Bill . . . not to mention cousins. So Frank and Jesse lay low for a spell, and likely live high while they're at it.

"And here's us," Mamaw says to Pappy, "left holding this big unlucky bag of snakes they left behind."

The worst of the snakes—at least of the ones Mamaw knows about—is this red-haired detective from Louisville name of D. G. Bligh. Ever since the Russellville robbery, he come nosin' around Clay County every few months, asking a lot of fool questions, thinking he's being sly when ain't a soul in Kearney finds his purposes less obvious than the wart on Lincoln's face. Why, even a child like Cletus Birdsall can see what the man's up to, his gold watch chain glinting in the sunlight to announce him a quarter-mile before he gets where he's going.

But the James Boys keep well out of sight, keep quiet, for a year and then some . . . it gets so's Mamaw almost enjoys seeing Bligh come to town. She and Reuben pass him on the street before the Kearney House one day, and she whispers to Pappy, "Quite a sight, ain't it, the detective bein' the one got his hands tied?"

Reuben hushes and hustles her home.

But the boys can't stay still for long; she never expected they would. In June of '71 they rob a bank in Corydon, Iowa. A brand-new bank, ain't been open but a week, left with a safe as empty as a cookhouse the raccoons got into. Then they're back in Kentucky again, shooting up the Columbia Deposit Bank and leaving a dead cashier in their wake.

It's Missouri they save the real show for, though. Come harvest time of '72, they hold up the Kansas City Fair. Ten thousand people looking on . . . oh, Jesse musta ate that up, Mamaw thinks. She hopes it wasn't him shot that little girl, even if it was an accident. No, one of them Youngers musta done that, she thinks.

Things are quiet until spring. Then a bank in Ste. Gene-vieve is cleaned out. The papers talk about "suspects . . . hooligans," mention no names.

But Mamaw would know her boys anywhere. As the rob-bers fled, they let loose a Bushwackers cheer.

"Surprised they didn't stop to sign autographs while they was at it," Mamaw says.

❖

July 21, 1873. Adair, Iowa.

Robbing a train: a milestone, a first. Never mind them Reno boys, Indiana. It'll be the James gang makes the fat railway profiteers sit up and take notice.

The Chicago, Rock Island and Pacific train is derailed, by false signal and man-made landslide, near Council Bluffs. John Rafferty, the engineer, is crushed and scalded when the engine topples on him.

"Dead?" Mamaw asks.

"Squashed like a bug," Pappy says.

Johnny races into the kitchen. "Who was?" His face is sweaty, his freckles gleam like gold dust.

"Never mind, son," says Reuben.

Johnny looks to his mother. "Nobody," she says. "Nobody we know."

The boy dashes outside again.

"Regular blessing sometimes," Pappy says, "how youngsters can't seem to pay attention to a thing too long."

Mamaw pressed her lips together. *Scalded . . . crushed . . . I can't pay too close attention, either; none of us can.*

The train robbery is, it seems, an idea whose time has come. Thanks to the James Boys. The legend grows, the rewards are doubled, tripled, pursuit faster and closer, everything's getting out of hand. The Boys still rob a bank now and then, waylay an occasional stagecoach, just to keep in trim. But the trains are where the big money is: passengers' purses, along with express company safes, mailbags. A gold rush on wheels, them trains.

January 31, 1874. Gad's Hill.

Five men, ten guns, a small flag station of the Iron Mountain Railway a hundred miles south of St. Louis.

212

The train is flagged down at 5:40 P.M. After dark. Estimates of the take range from two thousand to twenty-two thousand.

As they rifle the train, the bandits examine the hands of each male passenger. Those bearing the marks of hard labor are not robbed. "We don't steal from workingmen . . . not ladies or Southerners, neither," one outlaw says. The legend, insatiable, grows fat on such.

The rewards by now total up to a fortune, ten times what the boys ever carried off in their wheat sacks to begin with, bigger sums than Mamaw, maybe even Jesse, could calculate in dreams. And the strangers who saunter into Kearney now, their sharp eyes on all those inflated reward dollars, are no sloth-toed men weighed down and made obvious with gold watch chains. The men who circle the homeplace like coyotes these days are the Pinkerton men.

Something don't smell right. Above and beyond the usual, that is. It's mostly small things, hard to name, what seems out of kilter . . . and surely nobody *says* anything to make her suspicious. Mamaw steers clear of town now much as she can. When she does go in, does have a word with somebody, they're apt to talk so careful she could barely get the time of day out of 'em.

"You know that new hired man's workin' for Mister Askew acrost the road?" she asks Cletus Birdsall.

The boy, getting more surly since he's in long pants, says, "I seen him."

"You ever talk with him?"

"Nope." The boy gives her the once-over with eyes that seem to be turning so beady he hardly ever reminds her of Jesse anymore. "How come you want to know about him?"

"I don't," she says. "Just checkin' to see are you staying sharp is all." She turns and walks away, knowing the boy is studying her with a skeptical expression.

Maybe I'm getting a little carried away with all this spying and conspiracy business, she thinks. A neighbor ought to be able to hire a new hand without me going all to pieces, peeking in bushes. But Mamaw sees Askew's hired man, young, too fine somehow for farm work, standing down near the road sometimes and staring at her house like he means to see right through the walls.

It's them Pinkertons and their damn rewards, she thinks. *Best stop being so jumpy or I'll lose what sense I got left.* And she tells herself, *Steady now, ain't a thing in this world you got to do but keep your eyes open and your mouth closed and wait and see.*

Still, there are strangers everywhere, an infestation of strangers getting into everything, like cockroaches.

Well, there are certain remedies, Mamaw knows. . . .

Mamaw sprinkles hellebore, the winter-blooming buttercups dried and pounded to a powder, on the floor at night. Flour of brimstone with potash drives off the ants. The bottle of pennyroyal oil, left uncorked on the windowsill while the family sleeps, staves off mosquitoes, bloodsuckers. Rags saturated with cayenne in the cellar to keep rats and mice from the stores . . .

Mamaw doesn't miss much.

In the disturbing seasons when the meadows grow rambunctious with wild and half-tame blooms and color runs riot on the prairie, she thinks of Robert. Not her husband, the preacher, the father of the boys. Her lover. Memory keeps Robert as Zerel's lover, letting the rest of him go.

Zerel's lover knew every weed and wildflower this immediate earth would bear. He filled her mind with their beauties and poisons, their legends, how they came by their names.

Now, when the oaks' shadows are enlarged by an expansive sun, the bright yellow hawkweeds appear. Like daisies they are, only tougher. Their dark hairy stems are crude.

The hawk sharpened his eyes with the juice of this plant, Robert said . . . did he say which part of the plant? She can't recall. The parts missing from memories, why must they always be the parts she needs to know?

Mamaw tears the hawkweed plant, whole, from the dry, tenacious soil. She strips off two leaves, three petals, a bit of the stem, and crushes them between her thumb and forefinger. There is so much she needs to see from vast distances. The sting is, for a moment, blinding.

When her vision clears, Mamaw looks up and sees a hawk wheeling high above her.

Or thinks she does:

Its dark wingspan is unimaginable. It blocks out the sun, and the whole prairie cringes in its shadow.

Reuben and Johnny come home all excited from a day's trip to Liberty. She hears them calling to her out in the yard. "Mamaw, news!" Oh, Lord, been feeling something dark on her like a stain since yesterday. Now she's about to find out the shape of it.

"What's wrong?" she says.

Pappy holds up his hand to stave off her alarm. But the boy is shouting, leaping from the wagon. "Dead but good this time!" he cries.

"What in the name of God—"

"Them Youngers run into some real trouble now," Reuben tells her.

"Yeah, Mamaw, and that John's dead as a post!"

"The Youngers," Mamaw says faintly.

"You remember which one was John, Mamaw, the one you never liked?"

"Just the Youngers, Zerel." Reuben wafts calming signals past his son's shoulder. "Just them."

Mamaw turns to the boy. "Ain't a one I do like," she says.

"Well, one less to get your goat now, I reckon. Them Pinkertons took care of that."

"What happened?"

"Johnny," Reuben says, laying a hand on the boy's shoulder, "see to these horses, will you? I'll tell your Mamaw the rest."

"But—"

"Do like Pappy says." Mamaw slaps her hands together smartly. "Git."

"Yes'm."

She waits till their son is halfway toward the barn. "The boys?"

"Not even there, so far as anybody knows. The Youngers—John and Jim it was—had a run-in with a couple Pinkertons over to Osceola yesterday. Only one of the four walked away. That was Jim."

"Two less Pinkertons to hang around here, anyhow." Mamaw, her knees weak as clabber, sinks down on the old buggy seat that leans against the porch wall.

"That dead boy musta had more than a regular Younger portion of the devil in him, though. Had a bullet in his neck, likely already giving St. Peter his alibis, when he gets hold of a shotgun and empties it into one of them detectives."

"Wonder which of 'em got into hell first?" Mamaw says. "I hope they spend eternity sharing a set of leg irons."

A few weeks later Cletus Birdsall slips Mamaw a ragged half page of the St. Louis *Republican*. She mashes it in her pocket. When she tries to give Cletus his payment, he refuses it. "Just a little bonus," he says.

Well, she can see why—Frank and Jesse ain't even mentioned. The clipping marks the literary debut of Cole Younger, a eulogy:

Poor John . . . hunted down and shot like a wild beast, and never was a boy more innocent. But there is a day coming when the secrets of all hearts will be laid open before that All-seeing Eye, and every act of our lives will be scrutinized, then his skirts will be white as the driven snow, while those of his accusers will be doubly dark.

"Wild beast is right," Mamaw mutters, tossing the smeared scrap of newsprint onto the kitchen fire. "Now them Youngers is in the legend-peddling business, too. Well, they are welcome to it."

An almost balmy midnight, and Mamaw kneels in the garden, planting potatoes by the light of a waxing new moon. An owl calls softly to her from the woods behind the cabin. She looks up and smiles. "Hoo to you, too," she says. Her fingers, bare, rake the damp earth tenderly. *One for the rook, one for the crow, one to die and one to grow . . .*

"Mamaw."

He'll startle a body out of her wits, the way he just springs up sometimes. So light on his feet . . . she tends to forget. She hasn't seen him in a spell, then all of a sudden his honeyed voice, and she looks into the empty dark, only he is filling it and it seems plain impossible this boy with the dancer's feet and the singer's voice has seen men die, made men die, made men want to kill him.

"Jesse! I didn't know you was here. How did you—"

"Takin' my time." He laughs softly. "You know me, Mamaw. Easy does it."

Her suspicion ripens. "Where's Buck?"

"Ain't he here? He was supposed to come yesterday."

"Oh, son—"

"Now don't get all het-up, Mamaw. You know Buck and his caution. Probably didn't like the odds he saw when he got here."

"He'd be right." She sounds fretful, panicky. She knows it and is ashamed. "It ain't safe."

❖

The white of Jesse's teeth gleams in the darkness. "So many Pinkertons around, we could pave the whole county with 'em if they'd just lay down."

"How can you make jokes when your own brother's missing?"

"Mamaw, Buck can take care of himself. C'mon now, let's you and me have us a dance here in the moonshade . . ." He is holding out his arms to her, grinning with that professional bad man's squinty charm. She hates it and can't hold out against it, knows he's getting ready to cut her off at the knees, filching her bloomers while he's about it. Ain't a thing she can do. She knows that, too. She steps into his arms.

"Are you all right?" she whispers, her lips brushing his ear. *Are you still in there, Jesse? Is this you?*

"Better'n all right," he says. "I bear glad tidings."

"Oh, no," she says. "What now?"

Jesse pinches her cheek. "My mother ain't no romantic fool. Don't let nobody say different."

"Romantic!" She sniffs. "I hope you ain't planning to start in on your Robin Hood–Sir Galahad ruckus. I read enough of that in your friend's newspaper."

His face eases, rounds out: no badman, no bandit, just her boy again, her blue-eyed baby boy, it's him.

"I come on the business of romance." The corners of his mouth go soft. "The real kind. Zee's finally gonna marry me."

She looks at him. He is breaking her back again, only this time he doesn't know it, he really doesn't see.

"Well," she says.

"I waited nine years, Mamaw. Can't say I'm too young now, can you?"

"Don't guess I can. She's still your cousin, though."

"Yep. And still the only girl I ever loved."

"And she loves you?"

"You already know it. You've knowed it all these nine years."

"I hoped it might prove out to be something else."

"Will you come?"

She is looking past him, into the pitch-black woods where trees rustle softly, smelling of flowers so strong that your nose could start playing tricks.

"What?" she says.

"The wedding's tomorrow evening at Zee's sister's place. Right here in Kearney. Uncle William's coming from Kansas City to say the service. You'll be there to stand by me, won't you, Mamaw?"

"Of course. I'll be there, son."

But she is not. The wedding is delayed for hours because the uncle of both bride and groom, the Reverend William James, takes the opportunity before vows are exchanged to read Jesse a Methodist riot act about his life of crime, and Jesse's not going to stand for that, not from no Methodist, not from his uncle, from nobody. The marriage is very nearly off.

But then it's on again, only Mamaw's not there to see it. At the last moment she sends the younger children over to the home of the bride's sister, Mrs. Browder, with a note of regret: "Pappy is feeling poorly, son. Please excuse us and trust that I am there in spirit. Why don't you and Zee come by here afterwards? With a blessing, Your Loving Mother."

Pappy *is* feeling poorly, no lie. Pappy's been feeling poorly ever since Union militiamen wrung his neck like a chicken's.

"Zerel . . ." His voice is querulous, alarmed. "Zerel?"

"I'm right here, Reuben. You dozed off. Why don't you take yourself to bed?"

"Where are the children, Zerel?"

"They've gone to Jesse's wedding. I told you about that."

"Oh, yes." He leans back in the chair and closes his eyes. "Shouldn't we be there?" he murmurs.

"You got to feeling poorly, remember?"

"I forgot."

"It's all right, Pappy."

"I know," he says, snappish as an old man. "I know it's all right."

She sits staring at the fire, forgotten mending piled in her lap, thinking, *Too old, we're too old for this. Jesse's not too young anymore. We got, all of us, too much of life behind us now, too little ahead for . . .*

"We must give them a present," Reuben whispers as if afraid of being overheard. Reuben loves surprises. "You reckon Dingus needs another horse?"

"Why don't you ask him?" says Mamaw. "I don't know what he needs."

Jesse brings his bride by for breakfast the next morning. They are on their way to Texas.

"Honeymoon," Jesse whispers to his mother. He winks.

She leans close, as if she means to kiss him. "Hideout," she whispers. "Getaway."

He laughs. "That, too," he says.

Mamaw turns to her new daughter-in-law. "Congratulations, child."

"Thank you, Aunt Zerel." The girl—but she's no girl by now, is she? Zee already looks the worse for wear, as if the years of waiting and refusing him and wanting him and trying to straighten him out have already used up whatever she might have had. Her expression is wary and slightly dazed. There are folds of pale lilac under her eyes. She stays right close to Jesse and blinks whenever he speaks. She'll go blind, so close to him, Mamaw thinks. A month or two, she'll be paralyzed.

"I wish you happiness, the both of you."

"Right kind of you, Mamaw."

Zee blinks.

"You need a horse?" Reuben asks.

"Well, right now I guess not, Pappy. Maybe after our weddin' trip, though. Then me and this lovely lady plan to settle down for good."

Zee's smile is blind and bland and hopeless.

"Son, why don't you and Pappy have you a little walk, give me a chance to talk to my new daughter-in-law, while we get breakfast on the table?"

Jesse's smile is warning. "We won't be long."

"Might be." Pappy winks. "Them birds and bees take a lot of explaining."

Jesse laughs. "Well, let's get going, then."

The two men go out the door. Mamaw sighs. "I don't guess you're after an easy life, are you?"

Zee looks around as if she just now realizes Jesse is gone. "I don't know what I'm supposed to call you anymore."

"Call me what you please. Aunt Zerel, like you always called me, is fine."

Zee pinches the edge of the gingham tablecloth into fine pleats. "I never wanted a thing but Jesse," she says. "I'll take what-all he brings with him, I guess."

"For better or worse," Mamaw says.

"Yes." Zee smiles vaguely. "That's right."

"I guess you know I didn't exactly take to the notion of you and Jesse . . ."

"I know." Zee nods. "It made me sorry, too. I take no pleasure in opposing you, Aunt Zerel."

"And you'll take no pleasure in opposing Jesse. That's why . . .

"I know."

Zee's thin, bluish fingers knot the corner of the tablecloth.

Mamaw picks up a wooden spoon and scoops a fist-sized lump of congealed bacon fat from a small dun-colored crock. She flings the fat and it hits the hot skillet with a ripping sound.

Zee rises from the table and walks over to the cookstove to stand by her mother-in-law. The young woman, though

on the tall side, is nearly a head shorter than the older one.
Zee James is twenty-eight years old; the blush of youth is
gone—if ever there was such a thing on her. Pretty enough,
but a pale creature, Mamaw thinks . . . that's what I have
against her, what I've always had against her. This sweet faded
woman's no match for my boy.

Zee's eyes clear for a moment. "I know what I'm getting
into, Aunt Zerel."

"I hope so, child. Or maybe I hope not."

Zee's sudden smile snaps like a spark. "He'll tear my heart
out, won't he?" she says.

A couple of months later—probably in June, likely out West,
possibly in Omaha—Buck, too, marries. His bride, Annie
Ralston of Independence, is twenty-two, ten years younger
than Buck. Her family so violently opposes the match that
Frank and Annie are forced to elope. The bride leaves her
mother a note: "Dear Mother, I am married and going West.
Annie Ralston." *Period.* Sharper than a serpent's tooth . . .

Mamaw doesn't even get a note. She reads of Frank's marriage in the Kansas City *Times.* It shouldn't, she thinks, surprise her. Buck's played second fiddle in the brotherly band
all along. Follow the leader. Who is this Annie, anyway? The
girl Jesse's been teasing Buck about lately, no doubt. She
plays a mean game of croquet and has a meaner older brother
is all Jesse's telling. Buck, as usual, hasn't much to say for
himself.

So now he's married too, and Mamaw wonders if the former Miss Annie Ralston has a bit of backbone, and Pappy
wonders would Frank be pleased to get a new horse for a
nuptial gift, but the subject never arises because Buck and
Annie are out West somewhere . . . maybe in Texas . . . possibly with Jesse and Zee.

The papers otherwise bring very little news.

Cletus Birdsall has raised his price to two cents per item,

take it or leave it. He takes his time bringing the papers. There is no awe in his eyes these days. He has turned sixteen. She doesn't trust him.

Still, she keeps them all, each torn and tattered scrap of newspaper that means to tell the world, tell her, who Jesse and Frank James really are.

Mamaw steals soundlessly into the room where Reuben lies sleeping and removes a tin box from under the bed. She takes it to the kitchen, sets it on the table, finds her snuffbox in the back of the pie safe. She goes through all the fragments of newsprint, grown thin and soft and faded from too much handling. The snuff, a rare indulgence, makes her upper lip look swollen, as if someone has hit her. There are bruises of fatigue below her eyes, and she squints in the poor light, trying to pick out the parts that might be true.

On Saturday evenings after supper Mamaw sees to it that the children have baths. They are all old enough to bathe themselves now, even Archie. Mamaw just keeps the hot water coming. She makes the soft soap herself. It melts like butter in the old zinc tub. Clouds of steam make the kitchen ghostly.

When the children, warm and clean, have been bundled off to bed, Mamaw bathes Reuben. He, too, could bathe himself, of course, but everything seems hard for him. Ten years now, a bit more, things been hard for Pappy. He has never got over being baffled. *Feeble,* folks say. *Not quite right.*

"Now you just ease on down in there." Mamaw pats Reuben's withered white haunch. "Squat, that's right." He approaches the hot water with fear. So much fear in Pappy all these years . . .

But he is so good. "Yes, Zerel."

She strokes his hairless, narrow chest with her strong, slippery fingers, soft soap.

While his skin is still damp, she rubs every inch of him

with glycerin and rosewater before she takes him to bed with her.

Both the boys got wives to see to them now . . . maybe that will make them less reckless, keep them safe . . . and nobody should sleep alone.

Mamaw gathers the wood ashes from the fireplace, dumps them into a cone-shaped container with a tin scoop, then pours in water from a brown clay jug. As she watches the lye start oozing slowly from the funnel opening at the bottom, she is thinking about a small child, a neighbor's boy, who pulled down a crock of lye from a high shelf . . . now he is blind, can't see his own hand.

How would a body live without seeing, she thinks, *with every danger multiplied a hundredfold, with nothing on this earth left innocent, harmless? Yet sight a thing so easily and irrevocably lost . . .*

The lye is seeping out steadily now. *Blind and worthless,* Mamaw thinks. She steps out onto the porch, dragging a shawl behind her. December, already the light near gone at four o'clock. She looks down the road, but she can't see the children yet; they ought to be along soon. Her gaze slides up to the top of the rise they'll cross.

Two men standing there, not far from the gate to Askew's place, heads bent close together. Then she sees Neighbor Askew coming toward them. Three of them talking together now, an innocent enough scene, and it ain't all that cold for December, but Mamaw is shuddering, and she thinks, *Nothing on this earth left innocent, harmless. . . .*

Daniel Askew and his hired man, walking close together, start off in the direction of the barn. The third man stands alone for a moment, his head turned toward the James place. Then he walks quickly to a stand of trees at the corner of Askew's land and disappears behind the flounces of an old pine.

Mamaw goes back inside, chilled to the bone. The fire is getting low. She stokes it up. The youngsters should be here any time now, probably with wet feet and not enough clothes. . . .

She sets a tub down and fills it with water. She grates some potatoes into the tub. They are cold as December earth in her hands. She skims the top of the water. When the white sediment settles in the bottom of the tub, she'll remove the starch and set it out to dry, so white. . . .

Blind and white and full of harm, December cold as death and failing light, and soon the snow, white and blinding. So much to get in the way of her seeing, so much to preoccupy her. Blinding the lye, but lye is not soap and starch no shirt fit to cover a boy. December will finish the year, but Mamaw will never finish, never get to the bottom of things . . . she can't see how. . . .

She heats some tallow, sets wicks in the mold, hurrying now. She can hear the voices of the young ones coming up the road at last. The tallow is melting quickly. They are down to two candles and daylight is running out, darkness falling so fast these days.

XVII

Grecian Fire

1 8 7 5

Daniel Askew stands in his barn, examining by lantern light an old horse collar, trying to decide whether it will tolerate one more mending. Perhaps he should just give in, throw it away. It is near suppertime and his stomach grumbles.

Another mending, he thinks. Nothing lost but a little time if it comes out badly.

Jack Ladd, the Pinkerton operative who's been posing for several months now as the Askews' hired man, comes into the barn behind Daniel. He is nearly at the farmer's elbow before he is noticed. "Great horned toads, Jack, you made me jump!"

Ladd is a slender, wiry man still in his twenties, who goes about his work with much seriousness, yet always looks as if he's about to bust out laughing. Now he does permit himself a chortle. "I learned to walk from an Indian," he says. Then he looks at Askew more soberly. "You getting skittish?"

"Only an idiot wouldn't be, his nearest neighbors being desperadoes."

"Desperadoes." Ladd spits on the barn floor, then rubs the evidence into the dust and stubble with the toe of his boot. "That's newspaper talk."

Askew looks sheepish. "I know it is. But you can't blame a man for being jittery. It's all this waiting . . ."

"You aren't getting ready to back out, are you?"

"Hell, no."

"That's good. I told you you don't have to come in on this. You've already done enough, letting me stay here. But I'll feel a damn sight better having somebody along who knows every tree on this land."

Askew smiles. "And I'll feel better sticking behind a body learned to walk from an Indian."

Starting the next afternoon, a number of strangers unusual even for Kearney starts showing up. But the curious immigration is not really registered, since the men drift in singly, by different directions and means, and only two—who appear to be salesmen not previously acquainted—avail themselves of the comforts of the Kearney House.

Daniel Askew that night has a full house. Frail candlelight escapes between the warped barn boards, but doesn't get very far, what with the snow.

"So, boys, how's Cowtown?" Jack Ladd says. "What's new?"

"Paid a call on your wife and youngster last evening, Jack." The man takes a small crumpled parcel out of his pocket. "Hope these really are socks like the lady said. If they're cookies, they ain't what they used to be."

Ladd smiles. "She send a kiss for me, too?"

"Not by this messenger she didn't!"

"I brought you something, too, Jackie-boy." Indistinct in shadow, another man unstraps a bulging saddlebag and brings out a rounded burlap parcel. He peels away the covering to expose a black iron object about the size and shape of a musk melon.

Jack Ladd rounds his hands over the black ball, caressing it. His voice is fond. "Grecian fire," he says.

"What?" Daniel Askew, who has been quiet and shy with

the new men until now, leans close to Ladd's shoulder. "What in the blazes is that contraption?"

"The boss—Mr. Pinkerton—he calls it Grecian fire," Ladd tells Askew in a slow, easy voice. "You light this wick here, see, and when it gets down to the black powder inside, it throws off a great light."

Askew's face is white as tallow. "Light's the last thing we'll want," he says.

"On us, yeah. But we put this through the window of the James place . . . you see how the bottom's weighted here? No matter how you roll it, it lands right side up. Then we can see what's going on over there."

In a dark corner of the barn loft, one of the other men laughs.

The next day, early, a few more Kansas City men make entrances into Kearney, quietly. Now there are nine. Plus Daniel Askew, who's been there all along, no stranger. The city men are not the sort folks'd be apt to notice, not spread out and keeping their heads down the way they are. Besides, it's so cold not all that many people are out roaming around. Indeed, it would be a fine time for Frank and Jesse James to slip into town and have a visit with the homefolks. But in fact they are far away, not even thinking about a trip to Clay County until its weather turns more hospitable.

"I got it." Ladd's voice is low but full of triumph.

"What?" Daniel Askew twitches, holding a royal flush, and now it's waving in his hand like a fan.

The other men tip their cards to their chests as they look at Jack Ladd's face, popped up through the trapdoor in the barn loft floor. He looks like a kid just found a candy box, Askew thinks.

"Confirmed report, all nice and official, from the Kansas

City office. Mr. Askew's favorite neighbors must have reached home sometime last night."

"And us right across the road and never seeing a thing." A man named Tisdall throws down his hand. "I fold."

"You'll see plenty tonight," Ladd says.

January 26, 1875

It is just past midnight. The wind, black and sharp as a razor blade, slashes Missouri from the north. The trees around the farmhouse cower and moan. Frail pines seem to genuflect amid dervishes of snow. But the sky is clear now. The road is, too. The wind has gained the upper hand over everything.

Reuben is dreaming. It is always warm in Reuben's dreams. His face is hot. He wears no clothes. He is twisted through the branches of a green, green tree. He is white and long and flimsy. They have wound him through the leaves like a strip of gauze. He is white and spotted with blood.

Caught there, exposed, he tries to cover himself. Reuben twists and knots, blotting the blood in new places. Above him, in the highest branches, the vultures are still as onyx ornaments.

Below, on the ground, Zerel: dressed in mourning, long and black and still. The sharp curve of her nose is turned away, toward the house. She looks like the black shadow of a vulture cast down on the green, green grass.

Reuben is naked. He must cover himself. He frees one hand, starts to slip. It is a long drop to the ground. His white fingers curl, choking the branch above him. His other hand creeps between his legs. His fingers enclose something small and soft and warm. In a nest of fur. So small, so warm. A harmless creature.

Zerel is watching now, as Reuben strokes the place where it is soft and warm. Cool and dark on the grass, his wife: a memorial, a marker. Her nose, curving down to a sharp tip, is an archangel's wing. The warmth beneath his hand flutters, a dove.

"Reuben?" She shakes him, her talons digging into the flesh of his shoulder. "Wake up."

He falls with a thunderous crash and the sound of ripping wood. "What is it?"

Then they are both on their feet, struggling to cover themselves as they run to the kitchen, stumbling in the dark where nothing is warm anymore. The dark is tinged with green.

Flame in the kitchen, smoke dark, and the bright, sharp, hot smell and hiss of kerosene. Bright, his eyes fill with water for the brightness, and Reuben scares himself with a cough like an explosion.

"They're trying to burn us down."

His feet cover broken glass, lay a trail of blood across the oaken floor planks, a trail for the vultures.

"What in God's name is it?" His voice is small and soft.

The floor is littered with sparks and splinters. Everything shines, snaps, burns.

But Zerel is black. Zerel looms black over the fire, a poker raised high above her head. Zerel, a monument, beats the fire. . . .

And then the thunder of another explosion. The brightness goes blinding red. Gold shadows shimmer like cottonwood leaves in October. A black iron ball spitting flame rolls across the planks. It howls with fire.

Zerel drops the poker and grabs the cinder shovel from the hearth. She nudges the flaming iron ball toward the fireplace where embers glow orange and soft and small in a nest of ash. The ball rolls at her bidding and comes to rest, fire within fire. More fire.

Reuben's feet are rooted to the floor of sparks and blood and glass, and he watches her and knows she would cut him down from the tree, would scatter the vultures, would eat the fire . . . it will be all right now, because she is a monument, she is a mountain, Zerel is a match for death . . . it will be all right now.

"It will be all right, Zerel," he says, his voice small and soft.

He raises one foot and probes it with white fingers, picking glass slivers from his torn, bloody sole. But his eyes are on Zerel, towering over the fire with the raised shovel, and she cannot leave it alone, she is staring at the fire like it is a vulture and there are curses in the red and black and gold air around the memorial of her head, and he starts to say, "Never mind, it's all right. Leave it be. . . ."

But she can't, Zerel, she can never leave things be, and she stares at the fire, she dares the fire, and Reuben cries, "Never mind," but his voice is lost in the explosion of fire and iron and Zerel's curses. . . .

And the children are there now—how could he not have seen them before? The Negroes, too, their faces gleaming dark with terror.

The stableboy, Ambrose, lights a lantern, and it is like a miracle, a small brown boy doing something so ordinary and sane while fire and blood and iron and glass and curses fly around him.

The girls are screaming. John howls. But Archie does not make a sound. His mother doesn't either. Zerel is a monument.

Zerel and Archie are torn apart without a sound and Reuben says, as if remembering it after a long, long time, "I am a doctor," as his little boy Archie falls into the mire of sparks and glass and blood.

Even his head hitting the wood is silent, as if the floor has gone soft to cushion his small falling.

The explosion might have been muffled by sleep and distance, might have been conscripted into dreams, forgotten by morning. But the screams of the Samuels skirt the trees and skim the frozen pastures to reach the neighbors.

They come from the land to the south, brothers, a man and a boy. The breaths of their horses are white clouds in the frozen black air.

Ambrose, the hired boy, having given light, sees that he can do no more inside the shattered house. He takes a shotgun and another lantern and chases after the men, who flee through the woods from their own destruction. The bare feet of the boy are black against the ground. They leave a trail of blood across the hard-packed snow. He hears them scrambling through the frozen brush up ahead. He fires one shot, random, into the dark.

Inside the house:

Fannie and John Samuel weep, their bodies whole, untouched. "Where's Jess, you think?" John says.

Charlotte, the aging woman of color who helps with the cooking and chores, now boils two large kettles of water and tears strips of sheeting into bandages. There is a large bloody gash below her left cheekbone. Forgetting herself, Charlotte prays aloud. Her voice, over and over again, lifts on the word "Jesus." The rest of Charlotte's words melt into a mumble of pleas.

Reuben Samuel, too, mutters. He seems still dazed. His hands, accustomed to healing and comforting, lead him. Reuben moves back and forth between the two rooms where his wife and youngest son lie. His hands are swift and never still, never at a loss.

Archie Samuel is nine and a half years old, a fair and slender boy with large bashful eyes that change from gray to green like weather. His lips are white and pinched now, his eyelids lilac. A large chunk of hot exploding iron is lodged in his left side. He is bleeding to death.

From time to time Archie's eyes flicker open, looking past his father and his sister Fannie, who tend him. His gaze is on the doorway. Archie is passionately attached to his mother and seems to be waiting for her to come to him. But he says nothing. His mother has eight children. Archie, the last, is accustomed to waiting.

Zerelda Samuel, three days from her fiftieth birthday, might be twenty years older than that. Her body, too long for the bed, has been placed across the mattress on the diagonal. Her right arm has been torn by a searing iron strip that flew through the air at a vicious speed to find her. Her hand, wrist, and a few inches of her arm dangle by shreds of skin.

Zerelda tries to imagine the pain, because she cannot feel it. The pain itself is too great to be reached. She rages at its elusiveness. It is rightfully hers, the pain, a belonging. She will not stand for its being taken from her. Zerel stares at her torn arm as if her eyes can give her pain back to her.

The neighbors come, the man and the boy.

"Oh, my God," the man says. He covers his face with his hands. All he has seen is the oak kitchen floor. He leans against the doorframe and looks as if he will faint.

Reuben Samuel comes out of the small bedroom where Archie is dying.

"I need another doctor here," he says. "I can't do this alone. Find Scruggs."

The neighbor, James Hall, nods and quickly leaves, grateful to be able to offer some help that will release him from the devastated house. As he goes out, he sees the old nigger woman, Charlotte, crawling through the wreckage and scooping up bloodied broken glass in her bare hands. Her lips move soundlessly. James Hall echoes her as he mounts his horse and gallops toward Kearney. "Jesus."

His younger brother, however, remains inside among the injured. E. P. Hall is twelve. He is uncommonly brave because he is uncommonly curious. He studies the pattern of shards and bloodshed on the kitchen floor without blinking. He gets a dustpan from the hearth and holds it for Charlotte, bloodying the knees of his pants as he crawls along beside her. He picks up a scrap of charred iron and, when Charlotte isn't looking, he slips it into his pocket.

"Anybody dead?" he says.

The old woman looks away, shaking her head. "Not yet, they ain't."

"Who got hurt?"

"Little Archie and his . . . the missus," she says. "Oh, Jesus."

There is much else E. P. Hall would like to know, of course: What happened? How? Who did this? Why? How bad is it? But E. P. would prefer to discover the answers for himself. It is partly a matter of pride, of a curiosity best satisfied when it has satisfied itself. But there is also some delicacy involved: the old woman would clearly just as soon not talk about it.

E. P. has been watching Reuben Samuel run back and forth between two bedrooms. When the doctor has entered the larger bedroom, E. P. ventures to the smaller one.

His friend Archie lies on a narrow cot, blankets heaped at his left side, nearest the doorway. Blood is pooling in a valley made by the blankets. Archie's eyes are closed. He does not open them when E. P. speaks to him.

"Don't look good," the boy says softly. "Jesus." Then he slides back into the hall. Dr. Samuel passes right by him, heading for Archie. He doesn't seem to notice E. P. The boy crosses into the larger room.

Even when she's lying down, Mrs. Samuel is so huge a person kind of has to be afraid of her. She wears a yellowed muslin nightdress all torn and smeared with blood and ash. A nightcap covers most of her gray hair. Her eyes are wide open, staring at E. P. He sees her arm. It looks like a wolf or bear got after it. It's torn off, really, all but for a ragged strip of skin. A goner, that arm.

"It must hurt something terrible," E. P. says.

The woman smiles at him—smiles, imagine! "Maybe not as much as you think," she says.

"How'd it happen?"

She stops smiling and doesn't answer. E. P. feels like her eyes are burning holes in him.

"I mean, I saw how there must have been a . . . a blowup, like."

"A bomb," she says. "They threw a bomb through the window of my house."

"Holy Jeez—*who* did?"

She doesn't say a word, just burns her eyes at him some more. But when E. P. Hall backs out of the room, he has the distinct impression, almost like an echo, of her saying to him, "Well, now, why don't you just see if you can't find out." She thinks he couldn't.

So it's all pride then, his curiosity. It shoves him right out through the kitchen, where the old black woman stands waiting for her kettles of water to boil. Then he's out in the dark and the cold, and it's darker and colder than he remembered. He'd look foolish, ducking back inside the house the minute he got out, so he goes to the barn instead. He knows the place well enough. He and Archie are always hiding out in the Samuels' barn so Archie can get free of chores for a spell. Also, the older brothers, Jesse and Frank James, spend lots of time out there when they're home. Just knowing Jesse and Frank have been there gives the place a manful kind of magic, a whisper of sin that makes E. P. feel something like when he touches himself at night in bed.

E. P. finds his way easily to the tack room, and sure enough, there's a lantern. A flint, too, just like he's been expecting. He lights the lantern and heads back toward the house with it.

E. P. examines every inch of snow around the house, cataloguing footprints and shattered glass, wood splinters and snapped twigs. It's a mess out there, but nothing like inside. You can tell a lot of men have been there, though. He figures maybe nine or ten. Other than that, the tracks and leavings don't tell E. P. a thing he doesn't already know from the kitchen floor.

He starts following the tracks away from the house, through the woods. Fifty yards from the back door, maybe less, he finds the gun.

All those feet have beat a regular pathway through the sparse brush and trees. The gun's just lying there, beside a stump, on top of the hard-packed snow. It is black and oily. E. P. picks it up carefully, checks the safety before he sniffs it or anything. It's a pistol. Doesn't smell like it's been fired. Too bad. E. P. holds it close under the lantern and turns it over a few times, up and down and around. It's a Colt.

The letters "P. G. G." are stamped in relief on the butt. Well, E. P. knows what that means, all right. Who doesn't? "P. G. G." Pinkerton Government Guard. Mrs. Samuel won't hardly have to be wondering anymore, so she can just stop looking at him with those smoldery eyes, like he's some dumb kid who wouldn't be able to figure out the simplest thing.

E. P. wonders if he should go in and tell her right away . . . maybe he ought to wait until she's feeling a bit better?

The arm is gone. Mamaw knows it by two o'clock in the morning. It's still attached to her by slender strands of useless skin, Reuben's eyes are still clouded with a desperate man's hope of saving something that's lost. But it's dead. Zerel knows the life's gone because the pain is all concentrated now in what's left of her. The pain is sublime, familiar. She doesn't need to imagine it.

"I think I can sew it back," Reuben says. "It's just that it's going to hurt you so . . ." His eyes fill with tears.

"Cut it off," his wife says. "Or give me a knife . . . something. I'll do it myself."

"Don't," Reuben whispers.

"Oh, it's already done. What difference does it make?"

He turns from her fury and contempt.

"What about Archie?" Zerel says. "Don't you know that's the only thing I want from you?"

"He's not . . . it's . . ."

"Damn you, *tell* me. I married you for a doctor. I married you for a *man!*"

Reuben seems to take hold of himself then. He straightens up and turns toward his wife. "I don't think I can save him," he says.

"*Think?* You don't 'think' you can save him, but you stand there weeping over a hacked-off piece of my useless arm?"

"I've done all I can, Zerel. I've given him morphine. He's not in pain."

She starts to rise, then falls back on the bed, blood seeping faster from her arm. Her husband leans down and unties the tourniquet, then tightens it. Sweat breaks out all over her gray, haggard face, but she doesn't make a sound.

"Our son . . ." Reuben weeps. "Our child of peace . . ."

She turns her face to the wall. "I could kill you," she says.

"My dear, I can't . . ."

"His pain was all he had left of his life. You took it from him? I could kill you," she says.

In the smaller room across the hall, Archie Samuel's eyes change from a turbulent green to the pale gray of woodsmoke. His pinched lips grow lax. "Mamaw?" he says. His voice is small and soft.

"Sh. Mamaw's coming." His sister Fannie leans down, bringing her face close to his. "Mamaw's coming right away."

Archie smiles as if his sister has made a silly, forgivable mistake. He closes his eyes.

Fannie picks up Archie's hand, which has slipped into a pool of blood in a crease in the blanket. She wipes his fingers on the corner of a sheet. There are little half-circles of dirt under Archie's fingernails. He needs a haircut. He is missing a front tooth.

"Sh," Fannie whispers.

Archie makes a little gasping sound. Then he stops breathing.

The oil lamp beside the bed has been smoking. The chimney is all blackened on one side, so the light in the room is very dim.

Fannie doesn't realize what has happened.

E. P. Hall watches from the doorway. He understands. *Terrible,* he thinks. *This is death. Death is terrible.* He wishes he knew what it felt like. He wonders if he should tell Fannie, make her come away from Archie now. Fannie is only eleven. E. P. doesn't want to be the one to tell her. He wishes the light were better. He wonders what it feels like in there, where Archie is.

"Sh," Fannie says.

Reuben Samuel snips the tatters of skin with a surgical scissors, finally severing his wife's right hand from what remains of her arm.

It is nearly three o'clock in the morning, and Reuben knows by now that the child is dead. He has not told Zerel. He wants to take care of her arm first.

The scissors are sharp and fine. The skin cuts as easily as linen.

He has an idea that his wife's hand should be buried in the pine box with the boy. *Barbaric,* he thinks. The word twists around in his mind like it's trying to break free and find its way to something else. What? Reuben doesn't know.

"Forgive me."

Zerel doesn't look at him. She doesn't make a sound.

His white hands are steady as they lift up her severed hand, pale and bloodless by now. He wraps it in a clean muslin pillowslip. He looks around in bewilderment. Finally, he places the small white parcel, for now, on top of the cherry bureau.

"Zerel?"

"I didn't even feel it," she says.

"I'm so sorry, my dear."

"Never mind."

He wraps the ragged stump of her arm in the bandages old Charlotte has torn in the kitchen. He secures the tourniquet with tape.

Pain rages in fingers Zerel keeps forgetting she has given up. Their agony will not stay put on the other side of the room. Still, she does not cry out.

Reuben is crying.

"Be still," she says.

"I must tell you . . . Archie is gone."

She howls like a dog.

In the kitchen Fannie, John, and E. P. are drinking warm milk. Charlotte is boiling more water, though she doesn't know why.

They hear Mamaw's keening.

"Oh, Jesus!" Charlotte shivers.

The youngsters say nothing, but look away from each other as if embarrassed.

Reckon she knows about Archie now, E. P. thinks. He wonders what it feels like, and her hand gone, too. He wonders what they do with parts of bodies that people lose.

Charlotte is remembering a little boy she lost once. It was a long time ago.

Fannie tries not to think about the dirt under Archie's fingernails.

John Samuel is wishing Frank and Jesse would come home. So long since they been home and *I would know what to do if they was here,* Johnny thinks. *I am nearly a man. I would know what to do.*

Mamaw screams again, and what she says is: *"Jesse . . . Jesse!"*

———

Daniel Askew, his heart impaired by terror, sees the city men as far as the railroad tracks. Jack Ladd can't walk without help. The others could get him there, but Askew thinks *I signed on, I'm counted in this, I kept the boy under my roof and . . .*

"How is he?" the man named Tisdall asks.

Ladd's voice is weak; still he sounds like he might bust out laughing. "I'm all right, Dick. Who fired that shot, I'd like to know . . ."

Daniel Askew might be talking to himself, sternly. "It's bad, very bad."

By prearranged signal, the Burlington train bound for Kansas City makes its unofficial stop.

Daniel Askew, alone, returns to his house across the road from the James place. I ought to gone with them, he thinks.

But Daniel is not a city man, a stranger. This is where he lives.

Quiet as an Indian, Jack Ladd dies just about the time the train passes out of Clay County.

In a small room off the kitchen, Pappy shows his youngest boy to Dr. Scruggs, who finally got here from town.

"What happened?" says Scruggs.

Reuben, silent, looks down at the small boy's body. What happened . . . there was an explosion, fire within fire. Zerel dared the fire, stared into the fire with the hot embers of her eyes and dared it. A monument, Zerel . . . she could never leave things be.

"There was an explosion," he says, laying one fine, pale hand on his child's cooling forehead.

April 12, 1875

Daniel Askew dips a bucket into the spring that trickles down from the Samuels' land to his own. Snow hides here and there beneath the long skirts of firs, but the air is softening, the sun is warm.

Three explosions. The bullets shriek as they fly toward Daniel Askew from behind his own woodpile. Neighbor Askew drops the pail. It rolls and stumbles over bark and lichen, and the cool sweet water returns to the spring. Daniel lets go of the pail, but he still has too few hands to cover the holes in his body. His blood flows toward the stream.

The metal pail hits rock with the sound of an explosion.

Daniel Askew dies with the side of his face pressed to the thawing earth beside the spring, thinking *it was only meant for light, not death. But then there was the fire. . . .*

XVIII

Hell to Pay

1 8 7 6 — 1 8 7 7

September 7, 1876. Northfield, Minnesota.

Mamaw is not there, naturally. But it's in all the papers. Cletus
Birdsall doesn't bring the papers anymore. He doesn't come
around at all. The children all keep their distance now, as if
she can do more harm with one hand than she might have
done with two. People, even the grown ones, can't help but
stare at her stump. There really isn't anything to look at,
nothing much to see. But they'd rather look anywhere than
into Mamaw's eyes. Their squeamishness tickles her.

"What must folks think of us?" she says to Pappy sometimes. And then she laughs, for the part of her life that matters
has grown huge and unruly, has gotten away from her. "I
don't know what to think of us myself," Mamaw says.

Reuben always listens, though, considers her questions,
considers what folks must think.

"I am a doctor," he says.

Archie lies in the ground, where he cannot grow, but neither can he harden, or turn away from her. At least she knows
where he is.

It must be very peaceful under the soil, she thinks. Her

child of peace is as safe as any mother's son can be. Violets grow there, where Archie is buried, in the spring. Now leaves bright as stained glass litter his grave. Mamaw visits the churchyard twice each week, when she goes into town to pick up the papers. She doesn't brush away the leaves. Nor the snow, when it comes. Such signs and relics are all the child has now of life.

Susie in Texas with babies of her own, John growing tall and too fresh, Fannie coming about as close to beauty as any girl-child of Mamaw's conceivably could . . . but none of it matters. Sallie is almost eighteen. She wants to get married, too, and she surely will. Mamaw can't change anything even if she wants to, and why would she want to when life gets its own way with you in the end anyhow?

She understands Pappy when he says, "I am a doctor." He means: it just doesn't matter. Whatever you are, you can't change a thing. Ain't a heart among us don't get broke sooner or later, Mamaw knows.

Mamaw knows about Northfield before it happens, before she sees the papers, before there is anything to know.

One morning in the first week of September she wakes and senses danger. Like a big black boot heel, she thinks, something is about to come crushing down on us. . . .

She has not known for months, for certain, just where Jesse and Frank are. A few weeks after the explosion Jesse came once in the middle of the night. She woke up and he was just there, beside her bed, in the dark.

He was gone before dawn, leaving no tracks. No one but Mamaw even saw him.

She hasn't seen Buck for nearly two years. She doesn't blame him. It's not safe for the boys to show their faces around here, even in the middle of the night. She yearns for them . . . and prays they'll have the sense to keep away.

Sometimes they're in Missouri, sometimes not. Often the papers report them being in two places at once, places they've never been at all. But it doesn't matter. When they cross into Missouri, she knows it. She doesn't know how she knows, she just does. She senses when they are near her, and she senses when they are near danger.

They are cutting through Missouri the first week in September. She wakes one morning and feels them there, feels everything again: their danger and her desperate love. She is crippled.

There are eight men: Jesse and Buck, three Youngers—Cole, Jim, and Bob—Charlie Pitts, Clell Miller, and Bill Chadwell. Mamaw can't know all that, of course, wouldn't know the last three if she saw them, still can't tell the Youngers apart. She only knows her boys are crossing Missouri, a large, dark, reeking shadow cast before them.

There'll be hell to pay, she thinks.

And why shouldn't there be?

Something gnaws at Mamaw's roots, and what flows from her is a kind of hatred against them, against her own boys, yes, against them most of all. She doesn't want them harmed. She just wants them to pay. . . .

Mamaw wants her boys to enter the eye of the danger, to see the heart of hell, as she sees it. She wants it for their seasoning and their due, for her sons to enter the circle of fire, to endure and survive it, to be saved but not spared. . . .

And the eight men stretch forth like a shadow across Missouri, riding toward Northfield, Minnesota.

They attempt to rob the First National Bank, but they are driven off without a dime. They murder, in blood colder than any they've yet shown, one cashier and one bystander. The cashier, Joseph Lee Heywood, is already unconscious when he is shot through the head. No need. The bystander is a Scandanavian immigrant who doesn't speak English. He is gunned down because he keeps walking when commanded to halt. No need.

The local citizenry rises like trained guerrillas, firing on the robbers, shooting from rooftops and windows like snipers. They send up every manner of alarm. Bells toll. Pots and pans clang. Fire whistles hoot. Ladies holler. When the bandits ride out of Northfield, there are only six: Clell Miller and Bill Chadwell lie dead in the street. No need. Bob Younger has been shot through the arm, Frank has a bullet in his thigh. Jim Younger has had most of his mouth blown away. One of the horses is down. It is the heart, the heat, of a necessary hell.

And hell follows them. Danger sticks like glue.

By nightfall, wounded and weak, they are pursued by two hundred armed men.

After five days they have moved only fifty miles, and nearly a thousand men are in pursuit. They are trapped and stranded. They are starving. They are fighting among themselves, despair poisoning what was kinship. They have nowhere to turn. They can know no peace.

In a couple days' time every paper in the country bleeds black and white with the news.

"They're in real trouble this time," Reuben says.

She nods. "Reckon they are at that."

Reuben sees what looks like a gleam of satisfaction in Mamaw's eye. But then she must be frightened half-crazy. Who wouldn't be?

She smiles at him. "Cut my meat for me, Pappy?"

Yes, Reuben thinks, madness was bound to touch her. Sometimes a mind just can't bear to hold on anymore. We been through so much. He wishes he knew whether Dingus and Buck had good horses.

The slice of smoked ham covers her plate, its edge fluted with fat. A pale ring of bone marks its center like a target. Reuben starts cutting the meat into small bite-size pieces. Before he has finished, Mamaw is spearing the chunks of flesh on her fork three at a time, pulling them into her mouth. Her jaw works like a thresher.

She says something with her mouth full.

"How's that?" he says.

"I said, never mind about the damn horses."

His hands, still at work over her plate, begin to tremble. He hates it when she reads his mind this way. Seems lately she does it more and more. It isn't fair. It makes him feel like crying.

He smiles at her.

She knows he feels like crying.

"They'll be all right," Mamaw says. She lifts another forkful of ham. "Ours will, I mean."

Reuben believes her. Zerel knows things. He blinks to dry the tears on his lashes.

Pappy, it seems, knows a thing or two himself:

The James boys would give a considerable cut in the year's take—this most recent disappointment notwithstanding, it has been a good fiscal year—for a pair of decent mounts.

When the eight jaunty bandits entered what they took to be a sleepy one-horse town, they sat astride honest-to-God racehorses. Thoroughbreds, Kentucky bloodlines and all. But the horses got as bad a beating from Northfield as their riders did. One of the poor critters got blown to pieces. The stallion that carried Cole and Bob together out of town will be lame for life. Horses, it turns out, are The Boys' biggest trouble.

They steal a few replacements along the way—as they've always done, when pressed. But nothing seems to work out too well.

"Be a fine howdy-do if we wind up in jail for stealin' a miserable field nag," Buck says.

"Shut up," says Cole. It is his usual prescription for every hitch. Cole likes to show Jesse ain't the only one can give orders.

After a few days of listening to Cole, Jesse's had about enough. "Maybe we'd best split up." He looks at his brother and raises an eyebrow.

"Good idea." The gang joins in like a chorus, all but Jim Younger, who doesn't have much of a mouth to assent with anymore.

That night, on a backwoods road too close to Northfield for comfort, in spite of wounds and hunger and cold and being lost and having horses that are about to drop, Jesse feels a surge of optimism. "Just you 'n' me, brother," he says. "The James Boys rides again."

An owl hoots and Buck grunts.

"Your company ain't the most charming I've known," Jesse says, "but it's a durn sight pleasanter than listenin' to the Bishop cuss, and starin' into the bloody hole used to be Jim's face."

"Don't drown in your milk of human kindness," Buck says.

"Hey, a full sentence . . . you're doing good."

"Leg pains me something fierce."

"Yeah." Jesse is looking off to the left, into what appears to be a dark, empty field.

"Mamaw must be prayin' for us, brother," he says.

"Where was she a couple days ago, while we was in that thunder-mug of a bank?"

"Never mind. I think salvation lies yonder. Hang on."

Jesse slides from the back of his horse and slithers into the darkness. Then he's just gone and Buck's too plain tired to follow him with his eyes.

When he comes back, Jesse's grin bobs through the brush like a gleaming lantern.

"What say to some fresh horses?" he says.

"Wouldn't say a thing to 'em, I'd just take 'em."

"It's like the papers say, Buck, you're the tactical genius."

The two field horses ain't a bit of trouble to catch and

bridle—probably ought to be a clue. But the James boys are so tickled to be able to unload the old horses, they don't ask questions of the new ones.

Jesse slaps the worn-out horses' flanks, sending them off. They take to the woods without a second suggestion.

"Don't reckon they're much sorrier to part with us than the Youngers was," Jesse says.

"Notice you didn't thank 'em no more kindly, neither," says Buck.

"Dumb beasts don't put much stock in courtesy."

On a dark pathway through the woods outside a small Minnesota town that vanishes at night, Jesse and Buck take to their newfound mounts. Jesse sings a little bit, as he often does when fate seems cooperative:

"Oh, there's Honey in the Rock, my brother,

There's Honey in the Rock for you . . ."

His horse stumbles and nearly pitches him.

Behind him, Frank curses the darkness.

The horses snicker softly, and both stumble again, like drunks.

It takes the James boys a bit longer to figure things out than it should, maybe. They are, for one thing, about done in. Their wits aren't as sharp as they might be. But they also, at first, plain can't believe their luck could get any worse.

The two stolen horses are blind.

"I'd say that just about caps it," Buck says.

"Buck?" says Jesse.

"Yeah?"

"Shut up."

A hundred posses tear Minnesota apart. Stouthearted men and nerveless boys: their horses are indomitable, their weapons oiled, cocked, phosphorescent. The first frost is trampled under hooves and boots; Indian summer is run clear out of the state. Rains are held off, harvests halted. There isn't room in Minnesota for another thing but posses.

Women and children line unmarked roads in unheard-of places: everywhere is a parade. Tin stars are handed out like wedding garments, multiplied like loaves and fishes. Sheriffs transform youngsters into deputies like Jesus turning water into wine. Minnesota is a living miracle.

But the paths of the righteous are not made smooth. The posses bump heads in the dark, shoot each other in broad daylight. Stouthearted men and indomitable horses meet terrible ends. The bodies of nerveless boys sink to the bottoms of lakes, hang from trees, roll down hillsides. Whole parties are lost, mistakenly ambushed, stricken with mysterious ailments. Limbs are lost as easily as coins. There is an epidemic of blindness.

Peaceable Minnesota fights back in ways Missouri never dreamed of.

The James gang, cut in two, slips through the cracks.

Mamaw is watching, seeing to things.

Minnesota has much grit, little luck. Whole posses die of self-inflicted wounds.

Jesse and Buck suffer more at the hands of survival and escape than they would in captivity. Their feet give out faster than thoroughbreds. The James boys grope and stagger and bicker and starve. . . .

Mamaw watches, waiting for them to make straight the path. . . .

Minnesota has them surrounded.

In a vile pit known as Hanska Slough, outside the town of Madelia, Minnesota, it all comes to a sorry conclusion for the boys taking Cole's terse orders. Charlie Pitts is blown to bits in the mud. The Younger brothers, smelling to high heaven, are hauled off for deposit in the Faribault jail.

The three Youngers have eighteen gunshot wounds among

them; eleven are in Cole. Jim will never chew again or be much of a conversationalist. Bob comes up short one lung.

Faribault has its first tourist season. The Youngers are patched up and placed on display. Visitors flock to the jail-house in droves so thick you can't tell the Pinkertons and marshals from the thrill-seekers and pilgrims.

Cole Younger is the star attraction. Costumed in bandages, the Bishop noisily repents, even cries real tears. He borrows hankies from visitors and wets them with his remorse. These damp swatches of linen are retrieved by their owners, carried off with the conviction that a freshly minted saint has been seen. The faithful would stick their fingers in his wounds if they could. And he would let them. But bars intervene.

Even Charlie Pitts gets a cut of stardom, of awe; his ear, in a glass case in a Northfield museum of eccentricities, draws crowds. His bones find their use as a physician's educational tool.

Jesse and Buck are spared such indignities, but are spared little else. They are kept on the dodge for hundreds of miles, sneaking through Minnesota, the Dakota Territory, hateful Nebraska. It is many months before their feet touch Missouri soil. Their bodies are ruins, their spirits given up for dead.

Of the eight men who set out for Northfield the first week of September 1876, only five survive, three of those in Still-water Penitentiary.

Of the eight only one—Jesse James—emerges from the ordeal without a single wound.

Mamaw's been keeping a real close eye on things.

She finds them one morning, a little after six, when she comes out to collect the eggs. It is the tag end of winter, the sharp edge of dawn. The boys are hunkered down behind the corner of the henhouse, leaning against each other in a shallow bunker of snow. Their faces are lean and gray, yet innocent as babies'. They've fallen asleep, their gloved hands resting on a single saddlebag between them.

"Boys," she says.

Buck tips backward, cracking his head against the weathered planking of the henhouse wall. Jesse has a gun in his hand before his eyes are open.

"Never mind now," she says.

"Mamaw."

A great rush of love rises up hot in her, boiling. A sickness of love, she thinks, and she will not betray herself, will not shame herself by spewing it out . . . no, it is a sickness. She chokes it down like bile.

"Little early for visitors, ain't it?" she says, her mouth bitter.

"She's playin'," Jesse says.

Buck glances at him. "How can you tell?"

"Mamaw knows better than to say 'ain't.' She can talk real pretty when she wants to be serious."

Buck studies his mother with narrowed eyes. "Don't reckon she's changed much, huh?"

Jesse grins. "Not a bit. Ain't she a beauty?"

"Amen."

She glares down their attempts at playfulness, will not be cajoled. She hugs herself inside Reuben's wool mackinaw. The jacket is a little snug. She jams its flapping right cuff into her pocket.

"What are you doing out here?" she says. "It must be below zero this morning."

"Yeah, we been following the weather right close," Jesse says. "You glad to see us, Mamaw?"

"I seen you lookin' better," she says.

"We're a mite road-worn," says Buck.

"I expect so. Why didn't you go into the tack room, at least? Mighta froze out here."

Buck mumbles: ". . . keepin' an eye on the road an' all."

Jesse's voice cuts above his, sharp and clear: "Seein' as how you keep the barn locked up now," he says.

Finally she laughs. Can't help herself. The laugh, deep and hoarse, feels fine as a cough that brings up something stuck in the throat for a long, long time. "The famous James boys wouldn't dream of breaking a barn door padlock, that right?" She bends at the waist and slaps her thigh.

Jesse bows. "Hear tell you and your family was defenders of the Confederacy, ma'am. We confine our outrages to the Yankee population."

"I read something to that effect," she says.

"In the light of our consideration, would it be too much for us to hope for some Southern hospitality?"

Mamaw sniffs "We're just poor farmers here, only young 'uns and old folks, you know."

"We'd be grateful to warm our hands by your fire."

"Next thing you'll be expecting breakfast . . . I don't cook much anymore, maimed as I am."

"Told you she was pullin' our leg," Jesse says.

"You best hope so, brother."

"Reckon you can come in," Mamaw says. "But don't get too comfortable."

They walk side by side up to the house. She is between them, taller than both. The boys are unsteady on their feet. She acts as if she doesn't notice. When they reach the kitchen door, the two sons step aside, allowing their mother to enter before them.

They are home and they aren't. They are in and out, vanishing and reappearing, hiding and venturing out again, perpetually leaving and inevitably coming back. They are neither here nor there; she doesn't half know where they are. She doesn't ask. The less they are home the better, the more they are home the better she likes it. But Mamaw knows the boys cannot stay. They shouldn't have come at all.

Zee and Annie are stashed Lord knows where. Jesse and Buck sneak off to see their own wives like it's a scandal. When they come skulking back to their mother, they wear sheepish faces and high color.

"Zee and that Annie," she says. "Them girls must have the patience of saints."

Buck looks ashamed. Jesse looks proud.

"Reckon they need it," Buck says.

"Reckon they love it," says Jesse.

"You have a son," she tells Jesse. Her face is an accusation.

His smile is a triumph. "Just wait till you see my boy, Mamaw!"

"You reckon I ever will?"

Then she's the one ashamed. Hurt and longing leak out in her voice as if she's split a seam and she's not, no, she's sworn she won't ever, *ever* be one of those old women who whine for what they want, weep for what they miss. She'll never ask, never *beg* for a thing.

Jesse looks contrite. "You will, Mamaw. I promise you'll see my boy soon."

"Likely just as well I don't get attached," she says. And she means it. She does.

"You can't stick around here much longer," she says.

"No, reckon we got to find ourselves a place where we can . . . you know, live."

The following summer, fitted out in wagons, with wives and household belongings and hired drivers, the James brothers light out for Tennessee. They are all got up as ordinary men, full of hopes and ambitions and unnatural cravings.

"We just want to live in peace and quiet," Buck tells her as they go.

"Hardest thing in the world," Mamaw says. Then she pats his rough cheek.

Buck worries her. Northfield put twenty years on him, and they still haven't fallen off. Buck ain't like Jesse. He don't bounce back, lose scars, don't forget slights or sufferings. Buck, after Northfield, will never be the same.

"I don't want that life anymore, Mamaw," he tells her. "I ain't cut out for it, shooting and running and hiding." He looks at the pastures, the henhouse and barn, the ramshackle house overrun with children and hollyhocks, chickens and weeds. His eyes are moist and greedy.

"No, son," she says. "I don't guess the life of crime suits you." She smiles as if she has never really believed it anyway, any of it.

Buck *is* an ordinary man, she thinks. No matter what he's done or seen. He lacks heart for the life he got caught up in. Maybe he'll find peace and quiet, after all.

It's different with Jesse. No matter what he says. No matter where he goes, what he does. Tennessee won't change a thing. Peace and quiet would be the death of him.

It ain't that Jesse's cold-blooded. People can think what they like, Mamaw knows what's inside these two—and what ain't.

Buck might not want to kill, but he's the one with the cooler eye, the clearer head, the steadier hand. Buck will have the cold heart if one is needed. He does what he has to.

With Jesse, though, every crime is a crime of passion. There can be no governance, no reprieve.

Jesse stretches forth his arms, as if meaning to waltz with her. "Look after yourself, Mamaw." Contrite, eager to go . . . the boot heel to crush her, the light in his eyes to keep her from being snuffed out.

Mamaw slaps him smartly on the flank. "Best git then, if you mean to go at all."

Mamaw watches her boys go, old losses crunching under

their wagon wheels, peace and quiet glittering up ahead like fool's gold. Frank waves. Jesse lets loose a hee-hah.

She doesn't know which of them should worry her most. They've never seemed more doomed to her than they do at this moment; setting out, too late, after ordinary lives.

"I hope they get there," Pappy says.

XIX

Assumed Identities

1 8 7 7 — 1 8 8 1

The boys are in Tennessee, mostly in Tennessee, for four years, and living, mostly, respectable.

Jesse runs through a whole medley of names before he settles on one he likes the sound of: Tom Howard. So *plain*, Mamaw thinks. *Like he was just anybody.* Frank, as B. J. Woodson of Nashville, sounds more like a party to be reckoned with. And likely he is. Frank'd do well, Mamaw imagines, at acting respectable, living peaceful.

When her sons left, Mamaw had only one grandchild, Jesse, Jr.—except they're calling him Tim now, like the tyke already got tracks to cover, disgrace to live down. The year after he settles in Nashville, though, Frank has a son, too. Robert. Letters from Tennessee are few and far between, and when one comes, it's more likely to be from Mr. Woodson than Mr. Howard. (Mr. Howard was never, his Mamaw recalls, much for spelling and sums and putting things to paper.)

Buck, though, he's got a downright wordy streak sometimes. Seems Nashville lies within shouting distance of his dreams: farming, earning extra income as a teamster for a lumberyard, living in a regular house with his own wife and child. His penmanship and grammar ain't half-bad, and he gets right poetic now and then, boasting on his hogs. The Poland Chinas took a ribbon at the State Fair, and Buck's been hired as a starter for the Blood Horse Racing Association. Out at the Flats on a Sunday afternoon, about everybody knows him—he's even listed in the city directory.

"Oh, I can just see . . . kinda tickles me to picture it, you know?" Mamaw says. "A solid citizen."

Buck's letters are a pleasure to read, but in late 1878 when Mama recognizes Jesse's uneven block printing on an envelope Johnny carries from town, trouble and sorrow are like a postmark that's bled from the rain.

"You open it," Mamaw says.

Johnny takes out his pocketknife and slits the envelope. "Can I read it?"

"Give it here. I'll look at it later." She slips the letter into her pocket and gives her son a forbidding look that clears him right out of the house.

It is bad, sorrow and trouble, but not the sort she'd have guessed. Jesse tells her of the birth of twins, baby boys so weak that they lived for mere days.

"Zee crys most everyday still thow shes tryin hard to keep things goin and I help her best I can. The twins is burryed here out back of the house and Im carvin stones to show there names."

He forgets to tell her what the names are.

"What did Jess have to say?" Johnny asks his mother at dinner.

Mamaw's eyes escape the kitchen for a moment, retreating to the framed square of noontime, the glare of an ice-glazed pasture. Something in her wants to hoard this small particular sorrow, keep it for her own. They are all looking at her—Pappy and John, Fannie and Sallie and her new husband, Will Nicholson. The family waits for Mamaw to lower the boom.

"They're fine," she says. "Both the boys is fine."

Well, they *are,* she thinks, understanding neither her lie

nor her shame for it. Why stir up grief for two mites this family will never even know? Can't do a bit of good. And she keeps the loss to herself, like a small, hard precious stone wrapped in the paper she carries, still, in her dark pocket.

The following year Zee gives birth to a healthy little girl.

Yes, things is going pretty good, though Mamaw keeps the thought—like the loss—to herself. Why remind disaster of their whereabouts? She ticks the children off at night, counting them before she goes to sleep, starting always with the two she can be sure are at peace: Robert . . . Archie . . .

Susie with a houseful of babies now out in Texas . . . Sallie plump and married and living right up the road . . . Fannie seventeen and right pretty and can't hardly wait to find herself a husband, too . . . the girls, none of 'em, never caused her a lick of trouble, and Mamaw tries not to wonder: *If they had, would I love them more?*

Johnny give her some trouble, though a small enough kind. The boy is lazy and vain, too handsome for his own good. But he's all right. Just needs some more growing up, maybe.

And Frank . . . well, it appears Buck's finally found a life to suit him. Each night Mamaw holds her breath here for a second, hoping Frank's contentment can last.

And Jesse?

She acknowledges it: she plain doesn't know. The only thing certain is holding her breath won't do a snap of good. She strings together dreams, praying they're large enough for him to fit into. But she knows, Mamaw, it's just a trick she uses to lull herself to sleep. And it don't work, most nights, near so well as she wishes it would.

The second year of the boys' absence, 1879, there's a story going around that Jesse James has been out in New Mexico, that he took Sunday dinner with Billy the Kid. The papers make a big to-do about it, print the names of folks who swear they saw Jesse out near Santa Fe . . . Las Vegas. . . .

The rumor is never proved true about New Mexico. Might be only a tale. But Mamaw can't help believing it. Things been too quiet, she knows her boy, he's bound to be getting restless. Buck's letters gotten mighty sparse since he wrote how Jesse and Zee showed up, moved in with him and Annie lock, stock, and barrel. Two more youngsters in the house . . . poor Buck, getting everything just about the way he likes it, then along comes his brother to pilfer his dreams like he used to filch his Christmas candy.

Awhile later, in September, there's a big train robbery in Glendale . . . *right here in Missouri. Well, I ain't surprised, I swear I can feel when my boy sets foot on Missouri soil, Frank not with him, alone right here in the neighborhood almost, but he didn't come see us.*

And she knows it's just as well, knows home has become the unsafest place in the world; still, *he might have . . . a body'd think Jesse might have tried to come.*

Jesse and Frank face each other, their two poorly padded armchairs squared off in the shabby parlor of a rented house in Nashville. The drapes are drawn. In the next room their wives chat idly as they prepare a meal. The odor of boiled onions fills the air.

Each of the men holds a child. Frank's three-year-old son is squirming almost violently to escape from his father's arms, but Frank holds him tight against his chest, like a shield. Jesse, his baby daughter asleep in his lap, is staring from a yard away.

"We got it good here, Dingus. Why can't you leave things be?"

"Using what for money, meanwhile?" Jesse keeps his voice low.

"I know it's a a novel notion, brother, but you ever think of working?"

"Say, there's a idea, just march myself down—where? The

city police, maybe? Say, how-do, name's Jesse James. You figure you fellas might have a job for me? I'm right handy with a pistol, you know—"

"You were doing all right in Waverly, sellin'—" Frank grins. "Whatever it was you was sellin'."

"Sellin' cows and makin' beans. That sound like much of a bargain to you?"

"Aw, fi-nances got nothin' to do with it, anyhow. You just got ants in the pants like always. But I'm telling you, Jesse, you spend much more time with Ryan, you'll wind up with manure up to your moustache. The fella's got a big mouth when he drinks and drinkin's all he does."

"Whiskey Bill . . ." Jesse laughs softly. "He ain't the smartest fella we ever put to work, but he tells one hell of a story."

"I'm right glad to hear it—" Frank sighs and lets his son, who has bitten his wrist, slide from his knee and run to his mother. "It's a good thing Ryan can tell a tale, brother, 'cause when the two of you pull this dumb Muscle Shoals job, a good story's exactly what you're gonna need."

"Buck, you're getting timid as a virgin at a orgy, boy. Ain't been a easier setup since we went into the business. A couple dumb messengers on a couple horses ain't been treated right, and a government payroll the size of a moose."

"Sure, and the whole Federal government, which I'm pleased to say we've managed to avoid right well since the War . . . the Feds are just gonna say, 'Well, I guess you win, boys,' and we won't hear from 'em again?"

"Sweetheart?" Annie James calls in a soft voice from the kitchen. "You and Uncle Jesse ready for supper?"

"We'll be right along in, Aunt Annie. You girls just make sure ain't a lump hiding in the gravy." Jesse raises the baby in his arms, preparing to get up, and winks at Frank. "Ain't we got tame, brother?" he whispers. "Don't it make you kinda heartsore?"

"Yeah, well, they'll put you in a cage anyhow, you and Ryan go ahead with this stunt."

Mary James, a year and a half old, opens her mouth and begins to whimper. Jesse swings her gently back and forth in his arms. "Daddy's gotta go risk his neck, darlin', and you'll likely wind up a pore orphan child"—he is singing the words to her, sweet and soft—"just 'cause your mean Uncle Buck won't take one nice little horsy-ride into Alabam' with Daddy . . ."

"Aw, shut up," Frank says.

Jesse grins. "Then again, Whiskey Bill'll probably come through fine. Maybe I oughta sign a paper 'fore we go, make him guardian of my pore children?"

"Didn't like Tennessee all that much, anyhow," Jesse says. "Quiet as a tomb."

"So was it here," says Mamaw, "till you boys show up again."

"Seems like peace takes to this family pretty much the same as oil to water." Frank looks like he's been trampled.

"Where's the rest of you?"

Jesse stares at his mother, mystified.

"Like my grandchildren, as a for-instance?"

Jesse's face smooths out in relief. "Oh, they're—"

"Never mind," Frank cuts in. "Fewer know the better."

Mamaw opens her mouth to protest, outraged. Then her glance brushes Johnny, slouching in the corner of the room, all ears, "Reckon you're right about that," she says. "This place got to be a regular haven for magpies."

"Had the same problem in Tennessee, Mamaw." Frank looks hard at Jesse, then stalks out to the barn.

"Jesse, I got a feeling you been making things hard on your brother."

He shrugs, then laughs softly. "I don't know how to break

this to you, Mamaw, but I fear our Buck's getting a tad middle-aged."

"If by that you mean sensible, I pray you're right."

Jesse winks at Johnny. "May hafta look around for a new pardner while I'm in fair Clay County."

John Samuel straightens up, gazing at Jesse with a hopeful expression.

"Don't even *think* about it," Mamaw says.

"Mamaw?" says Johnny.

"What?"

"It be all right if me and Fannie invite some friends over . . . tomorrow evening maybe? Everybody's been wanting to see Jesse and Buck—"

"This ain't no damn shivaree," she says. "What's wrong with you?"

Jesse hoots.

"Be still."

"But—"

Mamaw gives her youngest son a look that could curl his hair.

"I's you, little brother, I'd drop the subject. Our Mamaw seems to be sufferin' a spell of the spring crankiness just now."

She doesn't look at Jesse, seems like she doesn't even hear him or recall he's in the room. Her eyes are narrowed on John Samuel.

"You want to be just like him," she says. "You think you are like him. But you're not. You hear me, Johnny? You're *not!*"

Suddenly, unaccountably, her eyes are filled with tears. She turns away quickly so the boys will not see, and she stumbles, half-blind, out the door.

Mamaw finds Frank sweeping out a stall that already looks passably clean. He starts at the creak when she opens the door. Swallows swoop and twitter in the rafters, and a field mouse dives into a stack of bales. Mamaw lingers in the doorway for a moment, wiping her eyes with the back of her hand . . . as if she's just tired.

Frank rests his broom against the stall rail. "Just looking for something that needed doing," he says.

She smiles, moving toward him. "We got plenty of such," she says. "Son, what happened?"

He shakes his head and looks away.

"I never asked to know everything, Buck. You know that. But the way things is now . . . it's something different, isn't it?"

"I don't know, Mamaw. It feels different to me, too." He smiles sadly. "You reckon we're just getting too old for all the hell-raising? That's what Jess tells me."

"Jesse . . . I'll get around to him, I always do. But I come out to ask what about you?"

He shrugs, picks up the broom again, rolls the handle back and forth between his calloused palms. "I just got a deep streak of fool in me, I guess."

"Well, you come by it rightly," Mamaw says.

"It was good in Tennessee, Mamaw. I missed you and Pappy and the homeplace and all, but still—"

"I know. It's why I don't understand . . . why I need to know how you come to leave."

Fiddling with the broom, looking down at the barn floor, Frank tells her about Muscle Shoals, how they made off with the government payroll easy enough; he went along only because he feared what would happen to Jesse if he didn't. But then the government detectives were all over the respectable B. J. Woodson, everything was falling apart.

"Had me a friend down there, Mamaw. A real friend of my own—not Jesse's, not some hotfoot wants to get in good with me so's he can learn how to rob a train. To this friend I was just Woodson, and Woodson was a good man." Frank steals a shy look at his mother, as if he expects her to laugh, but Mamaw is looking at him tenderly. "Truth is," Frank says, "I was getting kinda fond of this fella Woodson myself."

"How come you give him up so easy, then?"

"Not easy, Mamaw. Not easy at all."

"All right," she says. "I'm listening, son."

"My—Woodson's friend, his name was George, and I went to him and told him I was in a bit of trouble and I needed somebody to say they seen me around home a certain day.

"Well, George, he didn't even ask what kinda trouble. He just marched down and let the police know Woodson been with him that day."

"So you're in the clear, then?"

"I was . . . for a spell. But see, Jesse . . . Jesse had him a friend, too. Name of Ryan. . . ."

And Mamaw can just see him, Whiskey Bill, a bad penny if ever was one, drinking himself to a braggart's pitch and telling everybody in the barroom how he'd rode with the famous outlaw Jesse James . . . got the cash right here to prove it, boy, you hear about Muscle Shoals? Say, let me buy you a drink. . . .

"Wasn't easy, Mamaw, leaving Nashville. It just wasn't possible to stay."

"I see." Mamaw presses her lips together and turns so Frank can't see her face because she's afraid she might start to cry again. Guess I really *am*, she thinks . . . getting old.

"Mamaw?"

"Yes, son?"

"Feels like I'm about eight, trying to tell this. You know I ain't a snitch—"

"No need to tell me that."

"Jesse . . . something inside him's different now. He might look the same, but something ain't right."

"You don't have to tell me that, neither."

Mamaw knows, all right. She just doesn't know what to do about it is all.

XX

Seasons of Usefulness

1 8 8 1

Home is an empty house now, Mamaw thinks. Fannie just married and Johnny gone off to Kentucky to spend the summer with Reuben's people. Even Charlotte ain't around anymore. Got so skittish after that Pinkerton business, she just got to be no use, had to be let go. Now Mamaw's the only woman for miles.

Reuben, whose hands seem to grow more deft as his brain gets more feeble, has built a platform swing in the yard, under the branches of the coffee bean tree. He stays out there most of the time now, sometimes even when it rains. He stares up at the tree with a rapt, bemused expression, swaying back and forth. His lips move from time to time.

Mamaw pauses on the porch and watches him. He goes through it again and again, she knows, hoping it's going to come out some other way. The scars on Reuben's white neck have faded to the color of weak tea. No matter how hot it gets, he wears a shirt with a high collar to cover the marks, but he doesn't fasten his collar button. He can't stand to feel anything tight around his neck.

"What are you doing out here?" she says, crossing the yard.

His eyes seem to descend from the coffee tree one limb

at a time. "I'm a doctor," he whispers. "I've done all I can."

"I know," she sighs. She leans down and presses her lips to the bald spot at the back of his head. "Reckon we've all done all we can," she says.

A garden snake slithers around the trunk of the tree into the high grass. Reuben doesn't notice. He is studying the tree again, listening to the leaves whisper.

"Why don't you come inside with me, out of the hot?"

"It's only summer," he sayd. "It will pass."

"That's right. But it's cooler in the house."

"Will Zerel be there?"

"Zerel will be right there, Pappy."

"Everyone's always going off somewhere," he says, getting tearful.

"Never mind. Everyone always comes back," says Mamaw.

He is looking up at her, eyes round and washed clean, like a baby's.

"I'll tell you what," Mamaw says. "You come inside now like I tell you, you and me'll have us a cool bath—you know, how you like?"

Oh, Pappy likes when Mamaw takes her bath with him. She leans close, her strong fingers rubbing the soft, soft soap into his skin. Her breasts hang like great brown-speckled pears, sweet and ripe above his face. Sometimes Pappy lifts his chin to get his mouth around the fruit, his tongue touching the small hard stems, and she lets him. . . .

"What say, Pappy?" She smiles.

Slowly, as if afraid he's falling for a trick, Reuben nods. "Everyone will come back?" he says.

The summer is hot and lush, wet and fetid. Mushrooms of fantastic size and color spring up like fists breaking through the soil, clutching at the gnarled roots of trees. The mushrooms are buttercup yellow and blazing scarlet, some of them orange as pumpkins. When Zerel looks more closely she finds

others, more subtle and complicated: grayish-white config-
urations like brains, brown lumps like entrails. She studies
and names them.

Mamaw knows some of the mushrooms must be poison-
ous. If the children were here she wouldn't allow them to
touch a single one. But she will not come to harm. She breaks
the moist chambered stems tenderly and sinks her teeth into
the rich earthy flesh and feeds.

Her appetite for the food she serves at table grows lax,
indifferent. Meat seems unbearably crude. She can't, after a
while, even put it on her plate. She nibbles at cheese rinds,
craves the bluish mold that decorates stale bread. Mamaw
eats her vegetables out in the garden, soil still clinging to
them.

Reuben doesn't notice, of course. Reuben scarcely minds
what he eats himself. Mamaw can see to herself.

She expects emptiness to overwhelm and defeat her—
children gone, Reuben too absent in his way. Even the crops
seem to rear themselves this year, thriving on heat and nightly
rainstorms and an atmosphere of neglect.

And in this season, suddenly—no, she corrects herself:
finally. In this season, finally, the bleeding stops. What
matter . . . what loss but for the shame, the bother, the rags
to soak and scrub or burn? I ought to be rejoicing, Mamaw
thinks, yet she feels bereft. Ain't worth thinking about . . .
didn't expect you'd bring forth another baby or two before
it was done, did you? But the fingers of loss are tight and
chilling, and she cannot pry them loose. She longs for a woman
to talk to. Or, at least, to huddle with, hover near. She remembers Old Louisa, who explained the bleeding the first
time it visited her . . . realizing only now that her own mother,
who should have been the one, never even warned her.

To hear Aunt Mary tell it, womanhood was all a matter of
ruffles and curling irons and manners, though she loved me
right enough, Aunt Mary did.

Were it not for that old nigger woman, though, *I wouldn't hardly know what I am.* Then Zerel thinks of Charlotte, sent off so easily . . . a season of usefulness ended . . . dismissed . . . now I'm the only one here.

But solitude embraces her like an old friend. In ways she hasn't done since she was a child, Zerel is filling herself, feeling a prodigious strength. The rich soil, the heavy heat, the fantastic things that spring from the ground as she sleeps banish loss and longing and nourish her.

Mamaw weighs two hundred pounds and still has her full height. Her hair, severely parted and plaited and pinned, is the color of iron. Each feature of her face has found its final form. Her eyes are set in a permanent squint. Many of her teeth are gone, and her mouth is small and tight-lipped, as if stunted by the perpetual shade of her domineering nose. Mamaw's face is as alert, implacable, dangerous as a steel trap.

She sees it one day, this face, as if she's never seen it before. She is crouching beside the pond to watch a catfish in the stagnant green shallows. The fish (a beast, really—it hardly resembles a fish) is tangled in some weeds. Mamaw thinks the creature struggling to free itself is the homeliest thing she's ever seen.

Then her own face appears, rising to the scummy surface of the water like something thrown up by the mud. For the first time in her life she sees what other people must see when they look at her.

They are right, she thinks. *I am terrible.* Her laugh is small, surprised, delighted—as if a dim memory has returned, unbidden, to reclaim her after many years.

She reaches into the water and pulls at the slimy, dripping clump of weeds. The catfish is freed, and Mamaw's face floats away in widening circles of black and green. *I know just what I am.* That night she is wakened by Reuben's weight upon her.

"There," she says. "There . . ."

His mouth is at her breast. She takes him in and he is so small and warm and smooth between her great thighs, it is almost like giving birth again.

Reuben sucks in air, struggling to breathe. Something quickens inside her, breaks free, and ripples out in wider and wider circles. Reuben collapses on her. His weight is nothing at all.

"There, there," she says. She strokes him with her fingers. He is small and soft. "Never mind." She is mighty and filled. She touches him where he is damp and tender. She smells earth, and sinks her teeth into flesh that tastes like mushrooms.

In late August the boys are back. In early September John returns from Kentucky, and Buck and Jesse are leaving again, and the air grows cool and dry. Mamaw feels flush. Winter is striding forward like a bully . . . *I'll know what to do when the time comes,* she thinks.

September 7, 1881: It is exactly five years to the day since the disastrous raid on Northfield.

At Blue Cut, a few miles from Independence, a Chicago and Alton train is halted by warning flags and an obstruction of rocks and logs across the track. Bandits fire Henry rifles into the air and beat the express messenger senseless. They grab twelve hundred dollars. No great shakes.

As the band is about to depart, the leader, the only man whose face is uncovered, tells the engineer he's about to meet his Maker and forces him to kneel on the track. Then the bandit starts laughing, pulls the terrified engineer to his feet and hands him two silver dollars, "Drink to the health of Jesse James tomorrow morning," he says. Then he rides away with a laugh like a scream: Jesse James, the perfect symbol of his own imagining.

The engineer, Choppey Foote, slips the silver coins into

his deep pockets and wipes his palms on the legs of his overalls. "Feel like I been handlin' a rattlesnake," he says.

"You fellas best start clearing this rubble off the tracks so we can git. Tarry here much longer, we're apt to have the next freight rammin' up our backside."

Choppey rests a minute, trying to put the brakes on his heartbeat, before he joins the crew on the tracks. He pulls the silver dollars out of his pocket again and studies them. Seems like they still retain heat from the bandit's hand. Hotter than a fireman's shovel, that fella.

Jesse comes home and struts and prances. Flush, "Whaddya know, Mamaw?" he says.

"Enough," she tells him. "More than I care to."

But there are also days when he pales, languishes, cowers, and curses. "I hardly know what I'm doin' anymore," he says.

"Hush," she says. "Never mind, now. Don't work yourself into a spin."

"I feel lost," he says.

"I know . . . I know."

Jesse, her bright, blinding one, is darkening. He dwindles and dims. He tosses and turns. He mutters about nature-doctoring in his sleep, and dreams of deadly viruses attacking him. He broods.

He is not extinguished, oh, no, Jesse will never be snuffed out. But he smolders, smokes.

"Ten thousand pieces of silver," he says. "They mean to betray me."

"Who does, who means to betray you, son?"

"All of them," he says.

He does not know, then:

Who?

Mamaw knows her new season of usefulness is at hand.

———

Mr. Tom Howard has moved to St. Joseph, Missouri, with his wife and son and his little girl, Mary. They live in an unremarkable house, not their own, set high on a hill like a fort, fortified like an arsenal.

"I can see the Pony Express barns below, Pappy'd like that, and clear across into Kansas," Mr. Howard writes his Mamaw. "I can see anybody so much as *thinks* about starting up here to look for me." He underlines "thinks" three times.

He can see betrayal everywhere, and doom, and she, his Mamaw, can see the edges of all he is and has been and is thought to be and might become: eaten away by greedy, vicious dogs. It seems to Mamaw she should go to St. Joe, hover near his hill, protect him. She imagines herself astride a summit, mighty and irrevocable as rock, his fortress beyond which no harm might pass. But to go would be to betray him: in St. Joe he must be Tom Howard and cannot be her boy.

Mamaw stays put at her kitchen hearth and conjures his safekeeping and vanquishes his enemies with the might of her seeing and the omnipotence of her hating. She is wondrous, insuperable.

He lives in St. Joseph, Missouri now, Mr. Howard does, high on a hill. But Jesse keeps coming home to Mamaw.

One night she is awakened by a weight upon her, and it is not Reuben, no, not Reuben, who sleeps curled in a tight warm ball at the far edge of the mattress. The darkness darkens to a deeper-than-dark and the weight-not-Pappy presses her down, down. The darkness swallows her breath and sucks the light from her eyes, and she thinks, *He is here again. He has come.*

She turns back the comforter, pushes off the pressing weight, and rises. Her bare feet ache with the cold touch of the floor as she struggles against her stone-heavy bones and fights past darkness. She finds her boots and a shawl. She takes them to the kitchen, where she lights a candle. She forces the boots over her feet. Her stiff fingers grapple with the laces but cannot win; she cannot tie them. The shawl is an ephemeral warmth about her shoulders, a bother. When it slides to the floor she tries to catch it with the hand she keeps forgetting isn't there. She leaves the shawl on the floor and goes into the night.

The wind gives her a sound thrashing as she stumbles toward the barn. Her nightdress and boot tops flap. The mud has frozen into shapes of hooves and wheel rims. Her ankles twist and crack, lapped by the loose leather tongues and laces of the boots. Her heavy, unfeeling feet pilot her straight into the wind, push her weight toward the barn, where a frail lightglow beckons, warns: *He is here. He has come.*

He is singing.

The lantern is set in the tack room. His bedroll is spread out, a Bible beside it on the rude planked floor. The Holy Book lies open, face-up, in a litter of hay and rags and bits of broken strapping. The pages seem turned toward the light like petals. The yellowed page is Ecclesiastes:

"There is an evil which I have seen under the sun, and it lies heavy upon men . . ."

And down the dark passage in one of the stalls, Jesse curries a great white beast with wide, wild eyes, and sings: "We Will Wait Till Jesus Comes."

"Son," she says, no music in her voice, but prayer. "Son?"

He does not turn around. His hands, like a lover's, caress the horse's flank. "Mamaw comes," he says. "We waited."

"I was waiting for you," she says.

He chants, his fingers drumming a tattoo on the soiled white of the horse's bulging haunch. "Couldst thou not wait one hour with me in the garden?"

"Stop," she says. "Blasphemy won't help."

"Stop?" He laughs. "I don't know how to stop, Mamaw. I

am a speeding ball of fire and so is this horse and this world, and this firmament shall spit fire and . . ."

"Jesse."

"I'm so tired." He drops his head to rest on the high curved back of his horse. The animal whinnies and shuffles a bit, but doesn't truly resist him.

Nothing can truly resist him, she thinks. *He will be slain because he cannot be resisted. Unless I . . .*

His eyes are closed. She holds the lantern close to his face. His cheek is sunken and pale beneath his dark, luxurious beard. His eyelashes are tipped with gold. His mouth is a delicacy, its sweetness childish.

She touches her shoulder to him, nudging gently. "Come to sleep," she says.

He rests another moment before he raises his head from the horse's back. He looks at his mother with the confusion of someone waking in an unfamiliar room.

She hands him the lantern. "Come rest. I'll sit with you."

"Will you sing to me?"

"No."

"Will you tell me things?"

"What on earth can I tell you, son?"

"Tell me how to be saved."

"By God, you mean?" She sees the Book, laid open amid stubble and trash.

Jesse laughs softly. "From man," he says. "Be practical."

He walks to the tack room beside her, his eyes riveted to the light he carries between them.

"Lie down," she says. "Be still."

He stretches out on the bedroll and moves close to the wall, making room for her next to him. She crouches slowly, hearing a crumbling sound in her ankles and knees, her hips.

"You need some oil, Mamaw."

"Reckon I need more than that."

❖

She sits with her back propped against the cold wall.

Beside her Jesse closes his eyes. She places her hand on his forehead.

"Tell me," she says.

"They mean me harm."

"That has always been so, son."

"But there is money now, and vengeance. There are more of them and —"

"And what?"

"And less of me," he says. His voice is soft and bewildered. "Less now of me."

She nods.

"You know?"

"I know, son," she says.

"Help me, Mamaw. What can I do?"

"Tell me who they are, the ones are a danger to you."

"Some I don't even know. It's them I fear. There are men I never even seen who eat and live and dream my killing." He is whispering now. "They want me so, and I can't even imagine 'em." he says.

"But that's what you must do. Imagine them."

"You're talkin' nonsense. Turning into an old woman on me. Don't."

"I *am* an old woman," she says.

"Save it for the newspaper stories, Mamaw. I know what you are."

She laughs softly.

He opens his eyes and looks steadily into her face, with effort, as if he is reading. "You used to call me 'little brother,' " he says.

"You recollect back that far?"

"I don't forget nothing, Mamaw. Never."

"That's good," she says. "Forgetting is blindness."

"I been feeling like a blind man lately."

"Forgetting who you are," Mamaw says. "You let them

276

trick or talk you into that, son, you may's well put a hot poker to both eyes."

Jesse turns his head away from her, toward the light. He squints. "I know it," he says.

"Tell me what else you know."

"I know the trouble I'm into now is deeper than any I recall."

"It is."

He turns back in her direction. "I'm good as dead."

"Don't say that."

"Well, it's true. If it ain't today, it's tomorrow . . . ain't next week, it's next month. The best I can do now is move quick enough to buy a little more time. But, Mamaw, I'm slowing down."

"Talk like that, boy, you might as well *lie* down."

"My Mamaw. You ain't much changed since I was hurt so bad at the end of the War. I was dying and you knew it plain as me, I guess, but you just wouldn't have it."

"And I won't have it now."

"You got another subject you want to raise?"

"What I want is truth, facts. And I expect to hear my son talk like a *man*." Her voice is low and full of fury.

"Facts." He sits up, nearly spitting the word in her face. "Fine, Mamaw. Here's some facts for you:

"There's probably half a million dollars in reward money on my head by now, and somewhere upwards of a hundred Pinkertons on my tail. Buck is tired and so scared he don't hardly give a damn anymore. We got no money—despite the newspapers' way of accounting what we manage to lay hands on, we can hardly feed our families. We got no gang. We had no gang worth shit since Northfield, if truth be told. . . ."

Northfield, she thinks. I wanted . . . I prayed for them to pay then and I thought they did . . . hell to pay. But *the paying is now*.

"Jesse—"

He raises his hand. "No, Mamaw. Wait. You want the facts, you say. Well, you listen to 'em.

"We got no gang, like I said. But we got friends. So many boys comin' around wanting to join up with us, me and Buck can't hardly beat 'em off with a stick.

"Who means me harm, you ask me. Well, never mind the Pinkertons, the sheriffs, the damn Governor of Missouri. Let's just start close to home. I figure probably four outa five of these boys saddled up and ready to ride behind us to the nearest bank vault or caboose is just volunteering so they can get a clean shot at the back of my head, then carry it into Jeff City on a dinner plate."

Mamaw lowers her head and covers her eyes with her hand. Merciless, now, Jesse's voice follows her into the darkness:

"You got enough facts to suit you now, Mamaw? You got what you need to know?"

A few seconds pass before she raises her head. "I don't know," she whispers. "Do I?"

"Well, let's see. Am I leaving anything out? Nothin' big, I don't guess. But maybe you'd like a few names . . . a few examples? Like Ed Miller—take him. A good ol' boy, Ed— his brother Clell went all the way with us at Northfield. So Ed is surely an official gang member and blood brother, you know? Only lately seems like Brother Ed got dollar signs for eyes . . . and looks like he'll puke for shame whenever I say how-do to him.

"But you don't know Ed Miller, Mamaw, do you? Let's pick somebody you're real well acquainted with, say Wood Hite—"

"Wood's your cousin, Jesse. He wouldn't harm you for—"

"Right enough," Jesse says. "Or so I always figured. Well, you tell me, Mamaw—how come Wood don't show up when he's supposed to these days? How is it we ain't seen hide nor hair of Cousin Wood in more than a month now?"

"Might be he come to harm himself." Mamaw's voice sounds ill and weak.

"Might be." Jesse lies down again on the floor. "Cousin Wood mighta died for my sins, for all I know." He laughs softly.

"Sh. Son," she says, "listen to me now."

His eyes are attentive, wary.

"Don't distract yourself, seeing enemies where there ain't none."

"I just finished telling you—they're everywhere." Jesse closes his eyes again. "A body gets tired enough, dying don't sound half bad."

He waits for her to assault him with objection, but when Mamaw replies, her words are soft and calm. "I been that way," she says. "But, son?"

He opens his eyes.

"I always woke up again," she tells him. Then she smiles and places her hand on his brow. "You rest here now."

"You'll stay with me?"

"I ain't going nowhere," Mamaw says.

Mamaw's feet are asleep, her legs cramped. Jesse is gone.

She presses her hand to the floor, rises stiffly from the stone-cold planks. Hay and rubble and dirt drift from her clothes as she walks slowly out of the barn.

The sky is still black, but a silver rim is widening along the eastern edge of the land. The wind whips her again, lashing the folds of her thin nightdress to her knees as she goes back to the house.

She is breathing hard, as if she has covered a vast distance, and she pushes back at the wind with the mechanical resistance of a person whose destination is yet such a long way off that it is incalculable.

XXI

The Burning

1 8 8 1 — 1 8 8 2

Mamaw dreams for several nights of deep woods: fathomless drifts of dry powdery snow, a black tangle of branches against a silvery sky, more snow in the air.

Mamaw approaches the woods, catching scents of snow and fear, blood and silver. The sky is weighted. She does not enter the woods, but glimpses from its edge a man with lacings of ice in his beard and hair and eyebrows. He falls from the back of a silver horse, diving headfirst into a deep bank of snow. Blood soaks red into the white pillow of snow beneath him. As he dies, the man reeks of fear, not silver. He would have killed for cowardice, not greed. But he would have killed. Would have lent himself to Death.

When she wakes, Mamaw remembers only woods and snow, yet her knowing tells her there is one less wolf in the pack that drives Jesse deeper among the frozen trees, farther from home. Jesse has killed Ed Miller, but he can never be truly safe now, for the scents of fear and blood and silver surround and give him away.

Wood Hite is still missing. Mamaw leans into the hearth, trying to conjure him, and whenever she does, smells of blood and rotting and dirt arise from the embers.

❖

Wood Hite, Jesse's cousin and accomplice and disciple, has been dead since early December. He was killed by Bob Ford, who had to prove he was a big man, butting in on a fight between Wood and Dick Liddil.

Wood Hite has been dead for more than a month, his frozen body tossed away under snow and brush and a filthy blanket on Martha Bolton's farm near Richmond. Wood Hite smells of blood and rotting and surprise, but no fear. Who'd think to fear little Bob Ford? Wood never knew what hit him.

Wood is dead, unburied, frozen: a surprise in the dirt waiting for spring to unearth him in a filthy blanket of snow and moth-eaten wool and treachery. Bob Ford is small and hard and cold as a coin. Bob Ford smells of fear and blood and silver. Bob Ford stinks of terror. Because having killed Jesse's cousin, he knows Jesse will eventually kill him. Unless he can kill Jesse first. "Besides," he tells his brother Charlie, "there's all that money."

"Dream on," Charlie says. "You think a couple guys like us could get the draw on Jesse James?"

"You think on it," says Bob. "Then think on it some more."

Charlie does, and what he sees in his mind makes him walk over and throw up on a bush.

Mamaw don't know Bob Ford. Or Charlie. Never heard of them. She only knows beyond knowing that Wood Hite would never, for fear or love or money, betray or abandon Jesse, so he must be dead or in terrible trouble. It's likely too late to save Wood, but not too late to heed him.

"Heed Wood," Mamaw whispers. When she says his name, she smells blood and rotting and a fear that is her knowing.

Is this all her knowing amounts to now, she wonders— fear? Perhaps that is why its power has so utterly failed her youngest son. Mamaw never thought to fear for Johnny, to take him in hand, to warn him.

John Samuel is now twenty, a man. That seems impossible.

It isn't that she wonders where the time has gone. No, if anything her life seems longer than her years. Mamaw is not amazed to find her children grown. She is simply astonished that they can remain children after they're grown.

Johnny's the most childish of all, though Fannie is two years younger. The boy is impetuous, unstable, handsome, ticklish, charming. He has come by his share of Jesse's good looks and wit. But John drinks whiskey, has no grasp on gravity. He gets into trouble plenty, always has, but always a child's troubles. Mamaw never thought to fear a man's troubles for him.

Jesse goes out to hold up a train or a bank, to kill a traitor, and he comes back safe and whole, the blood being shed elsewhere.

While his beautiful half-brother John, so eager to imitate, so like Jesse in so many ways, goes out to a New Year's Eve party with his sister, starts a fracus, and is carried home on a bloodstained comforter with a bullet hole in his right lung.

Mamaw never thought to fear a man's troubles for this silly boy, and now he is dying. Even the newspapers say John Samuel is dying.

Mamaw tends young John with her good left hand and her stiff upper lip, her horse sense and experience honed by decades of deathbeds.

Reuben is there, but not there. "I am a doctor," he says. He no longer tries to prove it. His deft hands are helpless. His beautiful white fingers hang at his sides, ornamental and impractical as fringe. After the first night, chilly vestibule of an unfamiliar year, Reuben won't even look at his boy, his only living son, living so tenuously now. Reuben lurks in the kitchen, staring out at the naked coffee tree and the thick canopy of snow spoiling his lovely swing.

John lingers for weeks, not fighting off death, it seems, but flirting with it. A doctor comes almost daily from town. Mamaw tends John. But the boy seems to have gone quite mad in a silent way; he does not lend himself to comforting. Mamaw feeds and bathes and rebandages him. Because he is still a child and can make no use of it, she kills his pain by teaspoonsful. She wishes she had heeded him more. But she doesn't blame herself, no. Even now it's impossible to see how this child could have had a man's dangers coming to him.

The weeks of winter pass into March, still winter, John still dying but no closer to having done with it. She tends him, waiting, speechless. And she thinks, *For once this house is prepared for death.*

And after a time, Mamaw absorbs that, takes it in: *prepared for death.* Then the phrase is transformed into knowing:

John will not die, of course. Not this one. Not this time. Death comes by stealth and seeks resistance. Death avoids a ready welcome.

Everyone looks at John Samuel and says, "Death is near," yet Mamaw knows death is skulking off, miffed. It will find some other way to this house, some unprepared way, some way around her knowing. Death despises Mamaw's knowing.

Near midnight, March a wet howling and hurling against clapboard, a rattling of glass.

John's friends and Fannie's friends and the Samuels' curious neighbors crowd the house, hoping to be there to see death when it comes, sure it can come any time now, not knowing what Mamaw knows: death has changed its plans.

She wishes the damn lot of them would clear out, but she leaves them stay because while they look at her mad malingering child she can look at them and needn't look at him. John: she's sick of the sight of him and his parody of death, mere petulance. He doesn't know the first thing about dying. . . .

John's in cahoots with it, she thinks—death, trying to distract her with this frivolous playacting when her knowing tells her it is Jesse, whole and unbloodied and endangered, who should have her entire attention now.

And then he is there. Jesse.

He doesn't come into the house. Well, he wouldn't, of course, finding all that light and movement at midnight, all those horses standing about in the yard. He must think she's hosting the Sheriff's Ball, another reception for Pinkerton men. Why else would a crowd assemble here at the home-place late on a raw night if not in the name of Jesse James?

And so he will lay low, will watch and wait. She knows that, when she senses his nearness. Knows, too, that he hasn't come alone. Who's he brought with him this time? Not Buck. She smells blood and silver, cold and rotting and fear.

John holds his audience until near dawn, with his silent histrionics, his pale mask of suffering, his shallow cough. And she can't clear them out, can't show her eagerness, for she must not draw their suspicion. Mamaw serves them tea in chipped cups, rude cakes on raveling napkins. As she waits for them to go, she pretends to doze in her chair by the fire so she won't have to talk to them

The sun crackles pink and orange against the whitened sky then, and John sleeps, and the curious and guilty creep away with their disappointment and irritation at having missed death again. One of the girls takes Fannie along to town, "to get her mind off things for a day or two."

"Go," Mamaw says.

Finally they are alone: Pappy and John in their own beds, dreaming, having what Mamaw imagines as melancholy but orderly dreams. And Mamaw, with a melancholy order of her own, rising from her chair by the fire, pausing to stir up the embers and place another heft of pine on the grate before she steps out onto the porch.

He'll be watching. She knows he will be watching: possibly from the woods, more likely from the barn.

She pulls a soiled handkerchief from her pocket and shakes

❖

it out like a crumb-littered tablecloth. She is watching the barn. The door opens slowly, just a crack at first. She can't see him. She waves the square of grayish linen again.

Jesse comes out, followed by two smaller, grubby-looking men. All three are bundled to the ears, bulky with flannel and felt and wool and sheepskin and leather and the cold, cold metal of guns she cannot see but smells. The guns smell of silver and fear and death.

Mamaw stuffs her handkerchief into her apron waistband and raises her hand in what seems more a salute than a beckoning. Then, without waiting for Jesse and the two men, she turns and goes back inside the house.

She does not like those men. They are not to be trusted. The odor of treachery precedes them into the kitchen. But Jesse is here. Jesse will be safe as long as he is here. *If only he could stay. He can never stay.*

"Mamaw, sweet Mamaw!" He kisses her forehead and dances her past the stove. He tears off his wide-brimmed hat and, bowing, sweeps the floor with it. "My one true sweetheart, boys. This here's my Mamaw."

"How-do, ma'am. Pleased to make—"

She nods coolly. "Don't belive I got your names," she says.

"Charlie," the taller one says, shuffling his huge, sodden boots.

The other one, young and very small, smiles too disarmingly and looks past her shoulder. He stinks of something she is sure is blood.

Jesse hoots. "Names! Why, Mamaw, you want these boys to think I ain't brought you up right? Where's your manners, askin' a couple desperadoes their names? You don't ask a lady's age, do you?"

She turns away to the stove. "Reckon you could do with a hot breakfast," she says.

"What's got you in a snit? And while we're on touchy subjects, what in tarnation's been going on in this house, with

286

visitors all night long? I thought the law was here, till I got a look at 'em. We been freezing in that barn since midnight, you know."

"I know," she says. "It couldn't be helped."

Then she tells him about John's mishap. "Figured somebody would have told you."

"We been on the road a lot." Jesse doesn't look her in the eye. "How is the crazy kid?"

"Likely about to make a miracle recovery," she says. "Now that you come to see him."

She shoos them like chickens from her kitchen, and they go, all three of them, down the hall to the sickroom. She begins frying sausage, boiling coffee, heating cane syrup. The odors of cooking food fill the room, but sweetness and salt don't mask the reek them boys carried in the house with them.

She is frying green apples, showering them with cinnamon, when the little one sidles up to her. She didn't hear him coming. He makes her jump. She glares at him and stands up very tall. He is puny, sneaky, so smooth and hungry-eyed. Reminds her of a weasel she killed this fall down by the coops.

"Reckon I give you a start, ma'am. Beg pardon." His voice is soft and high, both threatening and confiding. Obscene almost. The hair at the back of her neck prickles.

"You want something?" she says.

"No, indeed," he says. "Can't believe I'm actually in your house is all."

"It's like any house," she says.

He laughs in a way that says clearly, *Well, now we both know that ain't true.*

She stirs the apples with a wooden spoon. Some of them stick to the buttom of the cast-iron skillet and she can't get them loose. The pan keeps sliding off the burner because she hasn't got a hand to steady it.

The boy reaches out quickly (such liberty, such violation in his so-familiar ways!) and holds the hot handle of the skillet in place for her as she scrapes. The slices of apple in the bottom are burned some places when she works them loose. A scorched smell rises, sweet and sharp and terrible.

"Thank you."

"My pleasure." The boy sucks his hand, fastening his ravenous little mouth to the pad of reddened flesh inside his thumb joint, and she thinks, it's him that's burning, *the burning is him*.

"Reckon you might want to put some ice on that hand," she says.

"It ain't nothin'."

Oh, but it is. *It is*. It is burning and rotting and fear beyond hurting. He means for her to see it and to mark it. It's not nothing. He means for her to see his burning and smell his burning and know that his burning is apart from his fear and not subject to it. His burning is not subject to anything. His burning is everything.

"I come out here to . . . well, to tell you my name," he says to her. "Reckon it ain't right to sit at a body's table without them knowin' who you are."

"Who are you?" Her voice is a rasp. Grease sputters and spatters her hand and she draws back. Oh, *she* is not unafraid of the burning. Her voice is a whisper and hot like the sputter and hiss of grease when she asks him, "Who are you?"

"Bob Ford," he says. "Name's Bob Ford. Don't reckon you heard of me."

"No."

"That's Charlie in there, my brother." He smiles, his face defeating innocence.

"Bob Ford," she says. "You're Bob Ford."

She has never heard of him.

"That's me," he says.

She knows Bob Ford beyond knowing.

The grease spits and hits the flame beneath the coffeepot. The flame rises and licks the black-speckled metal. The coffee starts to boil over. The hot, dark liquid spits on the fire. The flames recoil, hiss, then spring up. A bolt of dark smoke, unrolling, wraps around her face.

Mamaw, turned to stone, stands at her stove, all burning and rebellion before her. Her left hand, holding the wooden spoon, is raised high, as if frozen in the act of striking. The crook of her half-arm covers her eyes.

The boy's voice is high and thin with excitement. "Well, I'll be!"

Bob Ford reaches into smoke and flame with his bare hands. Sparks fly.

"Say, you ought to be careful here," he says.

Mamaw smells flesh, burning. Death hovers near the ceiling like black smoke.

They sit through an uneasy meal, too much food, little stomach for it. There isn't a hearty appetite among them. Bob Ford nibbles the crisp rinds of two baking powder biscuits, leaving their centers on his plate. His brother looks plain sick. Reuben worries sausage gristle between his tender gums and stares out the window. Mamaw picks charred apple skins from the skillet and takes them for herself. The rest of the dish sits in the middle of the table like decoration.

Jesse can't seem to sit still. He is coy and volatile as a young girl with her first suitor. His eyes dart endlessly around the table, pausing longest on Bob Ford, who seems to repel, worry, amuse, and fascinate him.

"You boys ain't eating much."

"Been so long since we seen decent food, reckon we don't know what to do with it," Jesse says.

Charlie picks up his fork and makes a path through a pile of grits. "Sure is good," he says. Then he lays down his fork again.

"Well, it will all be over within a month or two anyway," Reuben says.

The others look at him with wide, shocked eyes. Charlie coughs.

Then Mamaw blinks and shakes her head. "He means winter," she says. "Don't you, Pappy?"

"Winter?" he says. "Yes, I suppose so." Zerel must know. Zerel always knows better than he does what's in his mind. "Don't forget to tell me when it happens."

"How you been keeping yourself, Pappy?"

Reuben looks at Jesse, squinting. "You used to be Dingus, right?"

"Can't fool you for a second, can I?"

"Never mind, now," Mamaw says.

"I used to be a doctor," Reuben says.

Jesse turns to the Fords. "Pappy's saved my life more than once."

"That right?" Charlie mops his pale face with his napkin.

Bob grins. "Reckon you had more lives than a cat, Jesse."

Pappy laughs.

The boys are sleeping, Jessie beside Charlie in the large room, Bob Ford alone in the loft. They sleep straight through the afternoon as Mamaw listens for a groan in the floorboards, the creak of a ladder rung. She listens all day, but the boys are dead to the world.

Finally, around four o'clock, Jesse comes out, more rumpled and tired looking than he was at dawn.

Mamaw sits at the table, her eyes fastened to the bottom of the ladder showing in the bedroom doorway. *He will not get past her, Bob Ford will not get past her.* She's so absorbed with Bob Ford that she doesn't see Jesse.

"Mamaw, you look like you're in a trance."

"Oh." She stiffens, blinks, then sinks back in her chair. "Thank goodness," she says.

"Something ailing you?"

"Sh." She listens for a moment. There is no sound overhead. "Sit down," she says. "I got to talk to you."

Jesse seems to come fully awake now. "What's the matter?"

She leans toward him, dropping her voice to a whisper. "That Bob Ford," she says.

"Funny kid, ain't he?"

"No, he ain't. He ain't a bit funny."

"Don't take to him, huh? Not many folks do, I guess."

"Listen to me."

"I'm listening."

Through a closed door, they hear John Samuel moan, then Reuben's voice, vague and sibilant, soothing him.

"Pappy ain't sat with John in weeks," Mamaw says.

"Well, Pappy ain't been hisself for a long time now, Mamaw. We all know it."

"But why do you suppose he's in there now?"

"How would I know?"

"Bob Ford," she says. "He makes a person want to hide from his eyes."

"Now that's—"

"I'm telling you true, Jesse. I am warning you."

"You're serious," he says.

"More serious than I got words for. You watch him."

"I do, Mamaw. I know Bob's slippery, maybe even a little crazy, but—"

"And puny and foolish and fearful, I know. But . . ."

Mamaw's head falls back and her eyes close, as if she's fallen asleep in the middle of her own sentence. Her exposed throat is pallid, pulsating like a bullfrog's.

"Mamaw?"

Her lips barely move. Her eyes stay shut. Her face, very white, appears transparent in the dimming light of late day. "Ask Bob Ford," she says. "He knows."

"Ask him what?"

She opens her eyes now, but she is staring through Jesse, beyond him. "Ask Bob Ford about your cousin Wood, for instance."

"It won't do any good."

"No," she says. "I'm afraid it won't."

Then her eyes refocus on her son. "You think I am mad."

"Aw, for Pete's sake!"

"Don't turn your back for a second," she says.

The floor above them creaks.

"Do you still pray, Jesse?"

"Of course I do."

She nods, listening to Bob Ford's feet starting down the ladder.

She is trembling all over.

"You're worrying me, Mamaw."

"I mean to be," she says.

Bob Ford comes into the room then. "Ever'body rarin' to go again?" he says.

Mamaw and Jesse study him, their eyes troubled and dark.

"Reckon I'm interrupting somethin'." He starts to back out.

"Stay right where you are," Mamaw says.

"Sit down, Bob," says Jesse. "Sit down and make yourself to home."

She feeds them again. Then they bundle to the ears, arm to the teeth again. Next thing she knows they are going.

Charlie Ford mumbles thanks and looks down at the floor as he darts out the door.

Bob grabs her left hand and works it up and down like a pump handle, nearly drowning in his own compliments.

"You look after my boy," she says, trying to pin down his eyes with her own, trying not to sound as if she's pleading.

"Yes, indeed. That's what I'm here for." He gives her a

high, thin laugh, a wink, raises his hat. But his eyes strike a mark wide of hers.

Charlie and Bob Ford and the three horses wait in the yard. It's started to snow again. A lantern on the porch railing casts a film of light across the snow. The two brothers stand just outside its reach, stretching like shadows, waiting, their backs to the house.

Jesse pauses in the doorway and kisses Mamaw's forehead. His lips are strangely cool.

Mamaw disgraces herself: she cries right in front of him, cries because her boy is about to go.

"What's got into you?" Jesse tries to smile, but his face gets so twisted he looks like he might cry, too.

Mamaw brushes the hair from his forehead, her fingers like ice. "Please," she says.

"What, Mamaw?"

She cannot answer him. She is stopped by her knowing, left mute. Mamaw knows what she knows, knows beyond question, knows beyond knowing:

It would do no good.

Bob Ford is a burning, a fire beyond fearing, a fear beyond killing.

The snow floats down in the lantern light. Large flakes, almost weightless, touch down, a littering of pale yellow paper.

And a few weeks later winter is over and the word Mamaw awaits floats down on a scrap of yellow paper, the black words blinding and known beyond knowing:

Her boy is dead. He turned his back, and Bob Ford burned and turned and exploded and flamed and burst . . . oh, it only took one spark, Bob Ford, and the whole world goes up in smoke and floats down in ash, and she knew it, saw it coming, heeded, but it just didn't do any good.

Even knowing did, at last, no good at all.

PART III

... though you plant pleasant plants and
set out slips of an alien god, though you
make them grow on the day you plant them,
and make them blossom in the morning
that you sow, yet the harvest will flee away
in a day of grief and incurable pain. . . . Ah,
the roar of nations . . .

—Isaiah 17:10

Antiphony

A mountainous woman stands, alone, on the rough edge of a fractured planet. The sky behind her is a sheer granite face, her dark face like a shadow upon it. Grief is the air she breathes. No other life forms survive here.

The woman's legs, wide apart, rise from this alien ground like ancient stone columns excavated by catastrophe. Between them she holds a thunderous pain. Faster and faster the pain crashes upon her, then recedes only to resume. She does not make a sound.

At last her legs crumble and she falls to the ground like a landslide. Her thighs straddle and clasp the ravishing pain, her thick gray skirts thrown up over her face to smother what might be cries of anguish or ecstasy. The broken planet does not admit to time. Perhaps an age goes by. There is no counting, no manner of reckoning here. The woman outlives several generations of pain, and then brings forth her offspring, a son.

The child is born to the shape of a man and the size of a world and the color of precious metal. His light is an insult to granite and grief. It extinguishes constellations, her child's light. But he bears in jeopardy the birthmark of a jealous deity: a fist-sized hole glistens red in his chest like an accursed jewel.

The woman struggles to rise from her stony childbed and stands again, leaving her son in an embrace of ancient rock. She strides to the jagged precipice where the planet ends and, reaching into oblivion, she snatches a small pale bird from another world. It is a dove. Its wings beat against the imprisonment of her fingers, and she squeezes until its longing to escape weakens.

When the bird is still but for its faint breathing, she raises it to her mouth and tears its breast open with her teeth. Inside a small heart pulsates, garnet-red.

The woman crosses the planet swiftly, returning to her marked child. Astride the ground where she bore him, she bows and covers the wound in his breast with the fast-expiring bird.

As the small bird stills and stiffens, her son's light begins to grow brighter. Soon he becomes so blinding that the woman must close her eyes.

When she finally opens them and looks at her child again, his light has gone out. A fist-sized hole in his temple glistens red. His eyes are closed. His skin is the color of granite. Then she hears a frantic rustling sound like the beating of wings, and she watches, still as stone, while a flock of small pale birds without number fly from the riven head of this newborn man, her child.

There is no light. The birds peck at her hair, her eyes. They devour her flesh and pick at her bones. She does not fight or drive them off, but stands still as a statue, a mountain. Her gaze is fixed on the granite sky. Just before her eyes are plucked out, the woman sees a dark shape soaring overhead, then plunging into an abysmal distance. She believes it was a hawk.

And then she is blind, and alone again on the fractured planet.

XXII

Beyond Where the Breakable
Heart Ought to Go

1 8 8 2

She is met by a crowd, hailed and scrutinized.

Her beautiful boy, her tender and perishable child, not quite ripe, has been dead twenty-four hours when the train pulls into St. Joseph, Missouri, and spews her into a maelstrom of curiosity and disbelief, pity and satisfaction. Fate, that mob, she thinks. *A legendary fate before which knowing comes undone.*

Her black silk dress is new, but wrinkled already, streaked with the dust of travel. She is alone. Pappy's feeling poorly, and Fannie stayed to look after him and John.

Mamaw carries a black umbrella, a fringed black shawl, a reticule of petit-point: primroses on a field of black. Reuben's old black doctoring bag serves for a valise to hold a change of underclothes and an extra pair of thick black stockings, her heart medicine, and the Book. A tintype of Jesse, from when he was a child. A vial of smelling salts. Mamaw carries grief as if she were born to it, as some are born to royalty, some to unfounded pride. Her dignity, within such knowing, is a kind of madness.

The crowd teases, parting for her, then pressing in again.

She is carried, sailing, through the depot on a wave of their words:

"It ain't true, ma'am. Don't you believe it."

"Sorry for your trouble."

"Them what lives by the sword shall die . . ."

"It ain't him. You wait and see."

"They'll pay for this. Someone will . . ."

"Vengeance is Mine, saith . . ."

Vengeance? Perhaps.

But first she has to get through the necessary hell beyond her imagining.

She doesn't even know where she is going. Her arm is weighted down with all her dark belongings, and she hasn't another hand to lift. Her sense of direction falters before the awesome throng that parts for her, then embraces her again. Grief passes down, but she holds up her head and keeps walking, not knowing where she's going, knowing only that for her head to stand so high above them, for her steps to follow one upon the other, for her eyes to burn such a steady flame amid drowning: she knows her own madness then.

Someone is touching her shoulder, perhaps saying her name, but they are all saying her name, all of them.

"Mrs. Samuel? This way, ma'am, if you please. . . . Here, let my men carry those things for you. Don't worry."

Worry? She smiles. "I think I'm going to be sick," she says.

"Hold on just a second now, we'll have you out in the air." Her arm is freed of its burdens, and she remembers the tintype, its black case embossed in gold just like the cover of the Book . . . *an evil which I have seen under the sun* . . .

"My things," she says.

"They're right here, see?" the marshal says. "Now you just give me your arm," and Mamaw thinks: *How odd, being rescued by the law that hated him and wanted him dead, to be saved from the mob that loved him so* . . .

It is the first Tuesday in April, the air summer-balmy, the

sunshine wanton, an unseemly climate for grief. The marshal
grips her elbow firmly and guides her over the crowded pave-
ment. At the curb he helps her into a small black covered
buggy. A pair of horses impossibly white. "I don't know
where I'm supposed to go," she says.

The marshal climbs in and sits beside her.

"My things . . ."

Her belongings are handed in, and he places them carefully
on the seat between them. "Everything's going to be fine,"
he says.

"Of course," she says. "Thank you kindly." Not laughing.
Not keening. Not striking his kind, stupid face. Not vomiting
her grief on the plush seat of the carriage, not splattering the
hot stink of her hatred out into the gutter at the feet of the
yearning, straining crowd. They would be pleased to lick up
her despair, that starving mob. *But it is not theirs,* Mamaw
thinks. *I will not let them get near enough to lay a finger on my
grief, my madness, my son.*

"Are you taking me to claim my boy?"

"Well, to *see* him, ma'am. . . . We'll go first to the mort—
to the funeral parlor?"

Mamaw nods, biting down.

The marshal leans out the side and gives a signal she cannot
see. The carriage jerks forward.

"They got him over to Sidenfaden's," he says. "On Fourth."

She turns, her face wan and mystified.

"Best undertaker in St. Joe," he says.

"Yes, fine."

The crowd is there, too, the same hungry faces, as if the
crush at the railway depot has been flushed ahead to pool on
the street outside the mortuary. The welcome, the fanfare,
questions and condolences waved like beggars' hands before
her frozen face. She is impervious to their wanting, their
touching.

She disregards her things, left lying on the carriage seat.

❖

Neither the street nor the crowd, the marshal's steady arm nor the solid building they enter impress themselves on her now, Mamaw is striding forward to where her boy waits for her. To claim him.

She moves in close, to see, to block him from the view of those she has left behind.

He is packed in ice.

His body is stretched out, looking dwarfed and misshapen. Block ice is piled under and all around him. The room is very cold, but her boy is melting the ice. The steady drip beats stern as a march into metal tubs below the platform where his body rests.

The cold, the ice: she shakes, feels herself sliding. "Oh, God." Where now the madness to keep her from slipping?

Someone takes her arm again—the marshal? the undertaker? She does not look to see. Someone is there to keep her from going down. Someone is holding her fast, steadying her.

"Leave me be," she whispers. "Just leave me with him."

The arm is still there, fastened on her, but she doesn't look, she doesn't believe anyone's there now, just Mamaw and Jesse, frozen, locked together apart from everyone else in the world. And she knows the place. It seems to her that each moment from the moment of his conception has been a step toward this room, this terrible hour.

"Mrs. Samuel?" She hears but doesn't heed the voice. "Is this your son, Mrs. Samuel? Is this your son Jesse James?"

And she hears another voice then, a voice of pride and blasphemy and every deadly sin, the voice beyond heeding: *This is my beloved Son, in Whom I am well pleased.*

"Oh, God!" Her cry falls beside his blind and frozen face like a splinter of ice, melting. . . .

"Mrs. Samuel, forgive me, ma'am, but we need your word on this."

"My word?"

"Is this your son?"

"But how did he get so stout?" she says.

Then she begins to sob. The roll of flesh around his belt, his stomach a hump straining the buttons of his white shirt, a clean fresh shirt he couldn't have been shot in, the swelling in his neck and fingers: the false, unseemly flesh on him breaks her the way the bullet wound in his temple could never do. Mamaw has seen his chest laid open, has seen blood and poison pour from him. But she has never seen her beautiful boy blown up this way, like an ugly toy.

"Jesse ain't stout. You ought to know better."

"It's the . . . forgive me, ma'am, but what must be done to preserve the remains, you know . . ."

"Why couldn't you just leave him be?" She leans over the body, her hand stretched flat above his forehead, but she is not touching him. "Why couldn't you leave him . . . decent?" she says.

Then, still weeping, she brings down her hand, her fingers clawing the ice beside his head, as if the freezing is burning and she wants to suffer it, to submerge herself in it. But she doesn't feel anything, not the burning or the freezing, not the madness or the knowing, not even the sorrow.

She shudders, once, violently. Then the weeping stops and she simply stands there, her hand pressed to the ice. Mamaw looks as if she is waiting for something, but she is not, because all she has waited for has come now and has been done and it is over.

"Please, Mrs. Samuel."

"What is it?" she says.

"We must ask for your word—official identification. Is this man your son Jesse James?"

It ain't him . . .

"This was my son," she says.

"And you will swear to that in a court of law?"

She feels, for a split second, the burning. It sears her fingertips. She pulls her hand from the ice and presses her fingers to her eyelids.

"I will."

Mamaw makes a small choking sound, which the man behind her takes for a sob. He touches her shoulder, feels her shaking with what he will always believe was a mother's grief, what he could never know, would never believe:

Mamaw is laughing. Because what they got here, this is their creation, not her Jesse.

It ain't him.

Mamaw towers above the two marshals who escort her to the courthouse. Her walk is straight and swift, her eyes dry and haughty. She looks at no one.

Inside, the air is thick with cigar smoke and whiskey and whispering. Newspapermen brandish pencils like guns. Tin stars glisten and leather holsters creak and vest buttons strain. Everyone is sweating. Mamaw is cool and smooth as ice.

The coroner's jury is waiting when she enters the circuit courtroom. One juryman rises to his feet when she appears, his country manners responding like a twitch to the majesty of her bereavement.

"Remain seated," the coroner says. The man sits down in haste and embarrassment. Mamaw surreptitiously smiles at him.

She is led to the front of the room, where the coroner, a portly man of late years, stands before a window at a long oak table with a green felt cover. His bald, bullet-shaped head and the gold rims of his spectacles catch the sunlight from the window, creating a glare. Mamaw cannot get a sense of his face. His bearing is pompous and stern.

"Raise your right hand and be sworn," the coroner says.

She holds up the stump which is the unnatural conclusion to her right arm. She fastens her gaze on the glittering lenses of his glasses. His jowls tremble slightly.

"Please state your name."

"Zerelda Samuel."

"Where is your residence?" He clears his throat. "That is, where do you live?"

"Clay County."

"In the State of Missouri?"

"Yes, sir. Three miles from Kearney station."

"What is your age?"

She hesitates for a moment. She really cannot remember, and why would it matter anyhow, and now they will think it woman's vanity that she just doesn't want to tell. . . .

She grips the edge of the table, calming, concentrating, working out the sum: *Jesse is thirty-four. . . .*

"Fifty-seven years," she says.

"Are you the mother of Jesse James?"

"I am." *Jesse is . . . Jesse will be thirty-five in July. Jesse was . . . Jesse?* "Oh, God, I am," she says.

A murmur rises like a wind in the courtroom, and there is a sound of weeping, but Mamaw knows she wouldn't, she isn't, she couldn't . . . not before strangers.

"Please try to calm yourself, Mrs. Samuel."

She gropes in the dark of her mind for the madness they will take for calm. Her head is lowered, not abjectly but in resistance. They must wait for her. *They'll just have to wait.*

The madness slips into place then like a garment, and she fastens it about her. "Very well," she says.

"You are the mother of Jesse James."

"I am."

"Do you know where he is now?"

The question almost makes her smile because she has heard it a million times, has answered it a thousand times, almost never with truth; she rarely even knew the truth and wouldn't have told it if she did. Only now she does know and knows no reason not to tell, to lie. Such temptation, though, such powerful temptation sweeps over her, almost like physical

desire. Mamaw wets her lips, feeling a succulent lie on her
tongue.

Argentina, she will tell them. *Him and Buck got into ranch-
ing down there, doing right well, thank you kindly.* And the
very notion of her tongue, her lips, caressing the word, "Argentina," spreads a heat of pleasure down through every part
of her. Her knees go weak.

"Do you know where your son Jesse James is now?"

*Argentina . . . red meat at every supper, and horses so fast and
beautiful they put Kentucky to shame. You got to come, Mamaw,
you and Pappy. You got to come on down . . . so fast and beautiful. . . .*

"I just saw him," she says.

"You saw him?"

"His body."

"When?"

"Right before I come here."

"Whereabouts?"

"In that undertaker's place, I don't recollect the name."

"Sidenfaden's?"

"There, yes."

"Did you recognize the body of your son?"

"Not hardly," she whispers. "They made him look so stout."

"But the . . . the body you viewed was that of your son?"

"Jesse," she says. "Jesse James."

Her knees are buckling now. She needs to sit down. Her
fingers clutch the underside edge of the table, pressing into
something sticky.

"There is no doubt?"

There is always doubt, she thinks. *Even with the knowing,
there is doubt.* She shakes her head.

"Mrs. Samuel?"

"Sir?"

"I must ask you to state aloud for the record of the court.
Is there any doubt whatsoever that the body you have just

seen before coming here was that of your son Jesse James?"

Silent, waiting, she looks at the coroner.

He, too, is waiting for something. He turns, eager and impatient, moving a step closer to her. His face escapes the sunlight for a moment and she can see, behind the smudged lenses of his glasses, his eyes: a boy's eyes, blue as bachelor's buttons, innocent—for all they have seen—as a new day.

"Is there any doubt in your mind?"

"Would to God there were," she says.

Then someone in the courtroom is weeping again and Mamaw wishes they would stop her, silence her, but the weeping is a storm and cannot be stopped.

People press up around her, try to touch, to hold her, when all she wants to do is flee.

What do they want? Simply to comfort her, most of them, to lay a hand on her in a joining, a healing. Their fingers mean to speak a consolation their tongues have yet to learn. Mamaw understands this, a kind of mob kindness, but she cannot bear it, the touch of strangers. She shakes off their hands, glares down their pity, would run if she could.

She is plunging ahead of the marshals, nearly clawing her way out of the courtroom, when she sees the man sitting alone, off to the side, on a wooden bench. He is dirty, unshaven. He holds a battered felt hat on his knees, its black crown gone gray with fading and dust.

Mamaw stops in her tracks, forgetting the crowd, the reaching hands. The man is gazing at her with sorrow and knowing and a terrible fear. She falters, staring back at him. His face is familiar as kin.

Though he is perhaps eight or ten feet from her, she picks up his scent: silver and betrayal. *Filth,* she thinks. And she sees in his eyes that she terrifies him.

A voice behind her says, ". . . Dick Liddil, the one been over to the Kansas City jail?"

"What'd he do?"

"Don't hardly matter now. The Governor had him there for safekeeping. Liddil's the one meant to collect all that reward money by telling 'em where to find Jesse. Only them Fords'll get all the money now, looks like."

"You." Mamaw raises her arm and points at Dick Liddil.

The crowd draws back in a sudden and single movement, as if her fury is contagious, as if the thunder of her voice will be followed by lightning from her finger. . . .

A marshal steps into the intervening space around her and tries to hold her back, but she is straining toward the man now.

He cowers and raises his hat as if to stave off blows.

"Murderer!" she roars.

His eyes are wild as those of a fallen horse. He is down and broken and in a panic. "It wasn't me," he says. "I swear it wasn't."

"That's not Bob Ford, ma'am," the marshal says, trying to calm and capture her.

"I know that." Mamaw pulls away, panting, her arm raised to strike, though Liddil is still too far away. "I know who he is."

Her words are a curse and an indictment.

The second marshal reaches her. She submits and is pulled away, her feet dragging.

At the doorway of the courtroom, Mamaw wrenches around to look back.

Dick Liddil is crouched at the far corner of the bench, watching. His hat is clutched against his lap, as if to protect what is between his legs. His eyes are terrified. Twenty feet away now, she smells his terror.

Her voice is pitched low, tranquil and private. There might be nobody but him and her now in the hot, noisy, roiling room.

"You will meet a terrible end," she says.

He has no trouble hearing her. Dick Liddil draws his head down into his shoulders and shuts his eyes. He is shivering.

"You understand me," Mamaw says.

Then, led by the two lawmen, she goes out.

Zee has been in the courtroom, though Mamaw scarcely noticed her. Their first meeting, on the courthouse steps, is public: wife and mother-in-law, aunt and niece, acolytes in the same devotions.

Zee is weeping. She leans slightly on Mamaw. They do not speak. Their hands touch, then withdraw quickly, as if even this intimacy is untoward in the sight of strangers.

Zee has the children, Jesse, Jr., and Mary, with her. Both are dressed up, as if for church. The boy is not quite seven, the girl not quite three. Mamaw barely knows her own grandchildren. She studies them now, openly, plaintive with desiring. She is seeking her own son in them, but she does not find him. They are beautiful children, but only as all children are beautiful. What resemblance they bear to their father is slight and inconsequential. These are Zee's children, Mamaw thinks, full of the fearing, empty of the burning. Dragged into things they will always suffer from and never understand.

And they are afraid of Mamaw. They draw back and cling to their mother's skirts.

"I won't bite you."

"I know," the little boy says. "You're Daddy's Mamaw."

Zee presses a handkerchief to her mouth, and a shadow flickers across the child's face. "My daddy—"

"Never mind, now," Mamaw tells him. "It's all right."

"Are you coming to my house?"

They are helped into the same black carriage that brought Mamaw to the courthouse. Her things are still there, piled on the seat.

"I don't know where I'm going."

Zee nods. "Aunt Zerel, come with us." Her voice is trance-like, her mouth pulled down at one side as if she has suffered a stroke.

Mamaw is gathering inside herself, pitching toward the house she has never seen but knows . . . the house where everything, finally, was taken outside the field of her usefulness, her power.

The crowd is there, too, at the house. The narrow street that cuts smartly up the hill to Jesse's small fortress is thronged with people.

A policeman, hardly more than a boy from the look of him, but firm and efficient, is holding people back from the fence.

The house is white, two-storied, green-shuttered—as unremarkable as she imagined it. Although Mamaw has never been here, it is she who leads, hurrying the children along, steering Zee toward the door. *There is going to be blood,* Mamaw thinks, *I am going to see his blood now,* and she steps inside the house.

She studies the parlor the way she has examined his children, seeking relics from which she can begin to reassemble and retrieve him.

The room, unremittingly ordinary, defiles her memory of Jesse. It is vague and colorless, mildly disorderly, like Zee. The shapes on the patterned wallpaper, shadows of flowers, might be taken for waterstains were they not so uniform. The carpet is an arbitrary green, the furniture battered and brown. Antimacassars are draped here and there, like swipes of whipped cream on lumps of gingerbread. Mamaw runs her hand idly over the humped back of the settee, thinking how his hair pomade might be, must be, soaked into the horsehair.

But it doesn't help. It doesn't even hurt. Jesse is not in this room except as a lingering aroma of a meal cooked and eaten days ago.

"Oh, my God . . . dear God!"

Zee's wail cracks through the room like a whip. She seems

to have gone straight from a stupor to a frenzy. She is wringing her hands, stamping her feet, moaning, almost dancing, as she stares at the floor in a corner of the room.

The children stand close together, watching their mother. Their small faces are horribly white.

Zee grasps the lace collar of her black dress and it tears. Her hair comes unpinned and is flung across her face.

"Zee, child, what is it? Calm yourself. You're frightening the little ones."

"Oh, my God, will they leave us nothing of him?"

She points to the floor, where a corner of the green carpet has been hacked away. And then Mamaw knows. Zee doesn't need to tell her. *I am going to see his blood now....*

They have stolen his blood.

Zee screams, a litany of syllables that cannot be deciphered until they coagulate into a great choking "No!"

The children cry out, too. They keen and rage, until their own terror drives them from the room.

Mamaw's loosed tongue squanders a wealth of obscenity on the impoverished room that held her son, embraced but never knew him . . . no, no one but Mamaw ever knew him. She dips into hell for her language, makes free with Satan's vocabulary, while Zee screams and screams.

And they finally run out together, Mamaw and Zee, Jesse's sweethearts. They are finished.

Zee crumples to the floor, touching her forehead to the exposed oak. Scattered around her head, her hair covers the rent in the carpet.

He's going to tear my heart out, isn't he?

Yes, and bring you to your knees . . . but you couldn't oppose him, couldn't resist him, no.

Mamaw slowly crosses the room and lowers her tremendous, unbalanced bulk to the floor. She pulls Jesse's wife to herself, cradling her. "There," she says. "I know . . . Mamaw knows." She brushes back the strands of hair that stick to

❖

Zee's tear-washed face, strokes her head until the hair lies flat and smooth.

Zee presses her mouth to Mamaw's shoulder, weeping. Her body is tremulous and insubstantial as a rabbit's in her mother-in-law's arms.

Mamaw knows.

XXIII

Oddments

1 8 8 2

Mamaw recalls herself at the scene of death: a remnant.

"I don't guess I need to tell you"—she fixes her eye on Timberlake, the Kansas City sheriff—"I don't mean to leave here without my boy. And you got my guarantee, sir: you won't be pleased to have me stay."

Seems Kansas City thinks the remains of Jesse James is something they got a claim on. Then St. Joe gets riled up: he's here, he belongs to us. Finders keepers.

"He belongs," Mamaw bellows, "to *me!*"

Zee looks up, all tight-lipped and big-eyed.

"Which is to say, to his *family*," Mamaw amends.

The sheriffs and police, the coroner and politicians all gape at Mamaw like she's some rare specimen of raving radicalism.

"Is that a peculiar idea to you fellas, letting the loved ones do the burying?"

They hem and haw and call conferences in offices and corridors and alleyways. Seems Mamaw's word ain't good enough. They decide they got to call in another two, three dozen witnesses to swear it's really Jesse they got in there on that dwindling pile of ice. Mamaw tries not to picture what's becoming of her son's body as the controversy rages over its disposition.

It takes a whole day till everybody's satisfied it's Jesse they got. Then the Governor steps in to settle the question of who gets to keep him and—wonder of wonders—who but the Governor of Missouri himself lands down on Mamaw's side? He orders the remains released to the family. Then they can start arranging for a train.

"Bad enough, all this ghoulishness and pure politics," Mamaw will tell Frank later. "Then in the midst of it, I got a daughter-in-law's completely lost her wits. You shoulda heard Zee, talking about money from morning to night and how she's got to provide for these youngsters until a body'd think it's a bank book she lost, not a husband."

Zee is, evidently, afflicted with sudden and terrible visions of a rainy day. While others fight the battle for Jesse's body, she calls in an auctioneer and arranges for the immediate sale of the household goods: the feather duster Jesse held at the instant Bob Ford shot him in the head, the picture of a racehorse whose frame he was dusting. Even the family dog goes on the block. Brings a big price, too.

"Selling Mary's highchair?" Mamaw grabs Zee's shoulders and shakes her none too gently. "What are you thinking of, child?"

"Should I keep the coal scuttle?" Zee murmurs. "Or let it go . . ." Her hands run over a chair seat, anxious, calculating, covetous; the furniture belongs to the rented house and isn't hers to sell.

"Zee!" Mamaw shouts. "What are you doing? I want you to stop this business—you're making yourself sick."

Zee looks at her with cool depthless eyes resembling Pappy's. "Jesse would want me to be businesslike, Aunt Zerel, don't you think?"

"You aren't using your *mind*, child—"

Her son's wife spins around, eyes snapping. "I'm no child. I'm learning to look after things."

"But, Zee, there's time."

"Oh, you are *wrong*. Now there's no time at all. . . ."

Mamaw knows when she is licked, keeps still. Zee is finding her own way through this, she thinks. I musn't tamper with her ways. Zee has always been frail.

Mamaw sits in the parlor, her size overpowering the brown horsehair settee. She pulls little Jesse to her side, holds Mary on her lap. As Zee and the auctioneer dispatch used items and souvenirs across the porch railing and down the long, steep hill, Mamaw tells stories. Her protagonist is a brave boy with bright blue eyes, in a land of long ago.

"What was his name, Gramaw?" young Jesse asks.

"A secret name the forest give him on the day he was born."

Mary looks up, bashful, trusting. "What?"

"Little Brother," Mamaw says.

"No-o." Her grandson is skeptical, let-down.

"Yessir," Mamaw says firmly. "Little Brother was his secret name."

Things are sold and things are stolen. Jesse's belongings, and Zee's, disappear without a trace. Zee's hasty inventory points to losses without compensation: watches, chains, pins, one earring . . . the coral shirt studs Buck give his brother last year.

"Gone," Zee weeps.

Then a sheriff gently tells her she must surrender her diamond ring.

"But my husband gave this to me!"

"He stole it off a girl on a stagecoach in Arkansas," the man says. "Beggin' your pardon, ma'am."

An empty exposed place on Zee's finger, like the bald

patch of floor . . . like the gap around the bullet hole where the plaster's been chipped away . . .

"Never mind." Mamaw keeps her heft poised between the children and their hysterical mother. A bulwark, Mamaw. "You can't be worrying about a piece of jewelry now."

On the still-jammed streets of St. Joe, the festival of commerce continues, Jesse James changing hands like currency gone soft. The guns of his reputed ownership are prolific and much prized. Hundreds claim to possess Jesse's actual Colt, his favorite Remington. One newspaper reports: "Two Wagonloads of Weaponry Removed from James Hilltop Arsenal."

Occasionally a visitor with an especially compelling story for the police guard at the front door is admitted. An attorney with an engraved business card and a bowler hat offers to defend Zee.

"Why, how kind of you." Zee goes pale.

"Can I talk to you a minute?" Mamaw yanks her into the kitchen. "Defend you from *what*? You ain't charged with anything."

Zee blinks. "I'm not?"

Mamaw tells the lawyer, "You git on your way or it's you'll need defending."

A publisher wants Zee and Mamaw to collaborate on a book . . . with a ghostwriter, of course.

A promoter famous for displaying Garfield's assassin has a nationwide tour mapped out for Jesse.

"Ain't you ashamed?" Mamaw's voice is like chalk.

"But you'll be burying a fortune—"

"Out." She wields her stump like a club. The sideshow impresario hastens to the nearest exit.

Oddments: wondrous-strange, rare and fanciful proceedings, transactions, conclusions . . .

The baroque particulars of a public life and death, the bequests of a legend.

But, having nothing to do with her Jesse, they won't—
once the hubbub dies down—leave a mark on Mamaw.

Finally, toward sunset on April fifth, the third day Jesse is
dead, his remains are hoisted onto a Hannibal train pointed
toward home.

Mamaw, surrounded by Zee and the children, sheriffs,
marshals, deputies, newspapermen, slants her face away from
the crowd—not ashamed, not shy, not trying to hide. No,
not Mamaw. *The poor always ye have with you,* she thinks.
How odd, hearing those words in her head without quite
knowing what they mean. Poor? Yes . . . yes, poor, she thinks.
Folks with lives so impoverished they'd starve to death without the legend, without . . . her boy. Desperadoes: them, out
there along the street, the tracks, Mamaw thinks. *What are
they going to get by on now?* A man leaps at the hearse and
slices wood chips from the box with a knife. *Starved.* As
Mamaw alights from the carriage outside the depot, another
man fires a pistol . . . at Mamaw, imagine! Misses by a mile.
So drunk he can hardly stand up. A sheriff wrestles him to
the ground. Another takes Mamaw's arm and hustles her
through the throng. "You sure you're all right, ma'am?"

All right? What a question. "Never mind," Mamaw says,
thinking, *Starved, that poor man.* Who, now, is going to feed
this wretched mob, who?

It is 1:30 A.M. on April sixth by the time the special train
reaches Kearney Station. It is Holy Thursday. Jesse, his face
under glass, lies in state at the Kearney House. The coffin is
banked with candles. Throughout the night and the next
morning, hundreds come to see him. Trains make unsched-
uled stops so passengers can run into the hotel and wonder
at the beauty of his remains and the awful glory and . . . *it
ain't him, it can't be . . . because there's just got to be something
won't die, won't, no matter what. It cannot be.*

Through what is left of the night, Mamaw stands beside her son's body, cordial and dignified, dry-eyed. Two blood blisters are raised on her hand from the hundreds of times it is pressed. And still they keep coming, the poor, breaking their nags and their budgets and their arches to get there. They stagger, bless them, in from Gosneyville, from Lathrop and Holt and Lawson, from Missouri City, all the way from Vibbard. "Walked all that way, did you?" The newspapermen jot down mileage on small note pads, seeking a record. "One for the books," they say.

A couple of The Boys, who are going to dig the grave, drive Mamaw out home finally. It is just past dawn, and the fields sparkle with so much dew they seem to be moving on their own, an exuberant flexing after months of being frozen stiff.

"Looks like the dogwood's trying to bloom itself in time for Easter," Mamaw says.

"Yes, ma'am."

Mamaw steals a glance at him sidelong, the one who's driving. Can't recall his name, but he fought with Jesse at Centralia. He's gone fattish and slow-moving, but she remembers him . . . had a laugh like a donkey, maybe still does. His face is slanted away from her, but she sees him reach up every couple of minutes to wipe his eyes with the back of his hand. She wants to touch his arm, maybe say something to him, something comforting or at least kind. *But I can't,* she thinks. *I need to keep everything I got now . . . can't start trying to carry other people's sorrows, too.*

Mamaw closes her eyes, doesn't even open them for a look at the homeplace when she feels the turn of the wagon into the drive. *Even the earth will fail this need,* she thinks. *To open my eyes would be to seek a consolation that does not exist.*

Reuben is alone, sitting at the table, when Mamaw walks into the kitchen. A pot of coffee is boiling over on the cookstove, hissing, and Reuben is staring at it. There are crumbs of food in his long, white-streaked beard.

"Pappy?"

He is still for another moment, then shakes himself like a wet dog. "Where did you come from?" he says.

Zerel pulls a chair beside his and sits down heavily.

"I been with Jesse. Fannie told you about Jesse, didn't she, Pappy?"

"I don't recollect." He thrusts out his chin.

Mamaw looks him steadily in the eye for a minute. Finally he nods. "Jesse, yes."

"I need you to help me today, Reuben." Mamaw whispers it, almost to herself.

"I know, Zerel. I will." He smiles sadly. "You tell me when, all right?"

"All right."

"Zerel?" His voice wavers. "What does he look like?"

"He looks beautiful," Mamaw says softly. "Unconscionably beautiful."

Reuben gazes out of the window. In the yard six men, some of The Boys, take turns with three spades, digging Jesse's grave beneath the coffee tree.

Mamaw brushes the crumbs out of Reuben's beard, then gets up and goes outside.

"Cut extra-deep," she tells them, "you hear?"

"Yes'm." They shuffle their feet, waiting for her to go.

"Seven feet, at least," she says. "I wouldn't put it past 'em to come around and try to take his bones."

They think she's gone a bit off, of course. Mamaw don't care, long as they do like she tells them. *Dig down deep because there ain't a place so low they won't crawl there to get you.*

The funeral is held at a quarter past two in the Mount Olivet Baptist Church, where Jesse James was once welcomed to the fold and then run off like a black sheep all inside half a year. Robert's church, one of them. The president of William Jewell College was lined up to make the eulogy until somebody had to go and remind him about that poor student shot down at Liberty. . . .

The one-story brick church hunkers under its plain little belfry in Centreville, the old part of town. It seats three hundred and fifty, but more than twice that number have come.

As the funeral cortege makes its heavy-footed way from the hotel to the church, onlookers press knots and sprays of wildflowers on Mamaw . . . golden seal, trillium, Star of Bethlehem. Mamaw accepts the tributes with silent nods, passing the nosegays to Reuben and the girls as fast as she can take them . . . more than a single hand can hold.

Zerel's brother, Jesse Cole, walks behind her close as a shadow. Major Edwards hovers where he can watch her with his swollen, stricken eyes. She hears people whisper, "Here somewhere, he is, mark my words . . ." and she knows they are talking about Buck . . . and she knows they are wrong, wishes they were right, thanks the Lord they're not.

"Keep your head down," she whispers.

"What?" Reuben looks alarmed.

Mamaw shakes her head a little: *don't mind me.* She presses her lips together, throws her shoulders back, and walks the fine straight line to the church.

The service is brief, tense, and terrible. There are two preachers, one Mamaw doesn't know, the other she doesn't care for. One of the hymns is "What a Friend We Have in Jesus." The scriptural sources include Psalms, Matthew, and Job:

"Man born of woman is of few days, and full of trouble."

In the late afternoon Jesse is finally set down beneath the coffee bean tree in the corner of the yard at the homeplace.

Once again there are delays, complications, detours. The casket is carried into the house so John can lay adoring eyes upon his half brother one last time.

And Mamaw, then, breaks. Everyone knew she would, sooner or later . . . everybody but Mamaw. John looks at Jesse and lets loose a wail, and Mamaw cracks right in two. Zee is in pieces. The children shriek. For a few moments Pappy seems like the only one who's got his wits about him. "There, there," he says.

"He ain't all in there!" Mamaw cries. "I know he ain't."

"Zerel, what on earth—"

"You didn't see how they took things . . . not just things laying there. They come with knives and hatchets, with chisels . . . ain't nothing they wouldn't wrest from us . . . from him . . . oh, God!"

"Sh, Mamaw."

"I won't have it. You get the Major in here . . . some of The Boys. We got to open that box."

Fannie and her husband enclose Mamaw like parentheses. "Now, Mamaw, you can *see* it's Jesse . . . you can see his face plain enough here through the glass."

Zee sobs.

Mamaw slaps her hand on the iron lid at the foot of the coffin. "What about his legs?" she says. "His hands . . . you think they wouldn't help themselves to those, put wax pieces on him and —" She releases a wrenching scream.

Inside the house everyone weeps, covering their faces. In the yard a hundred hungry eyes crawl over the house.

John Samuel loses consciousness.

Mary crawls under his bed, where, unnoticed, she rocks.

Only Reuben . . . only Pappy . . .

He walks up to face Mamaw, standing so close that her breath shivers through his beard. "Zerel," he says. His voice is low and very firm. She quiets a little, looks, steadying her eyes on him.

"That's enough now," he says.

Mamaw gives one deep shuddering sign, then she nods.

The sun is beginning to sink through layers of delicate mauve vapor as Jesse James is at last lowered into the ground. The Clay County soil is moist, rich, teeming with life and spring. As the mourners sing his favorite hymn, "We Will Wait Till Jesus Comes," Jesse is buried down deep, his head turned toward the South.

XXIV

Last Rites

1 8 8 2 – 1 8 8 5

She no longer speaks to God. Using no intermediary, no code, Mamaw addresses Death directly now: "You win. Everything I had worth saving you got. And if you want the rest, you'll take that too, I know it."

She stares blindly into the rim of the rising sun.

"Well, I'm still here. You ready to make something out of that?" She spits. "Go ahead," she says.

Mamaw waits on dawn, pacing the edge of the grave, still raw, as she wonders where her knowing, her seeing gone to. Then she thinks, *What good would they do me now, anyway? Ain't a God-given gift I'd know what to do with now. And Death ain't interested in a body's prepared for it.*

Jesse's been gone . . . she counts over and over the same five fingers. Today will be the nineteenth day. In nearly three weeks she has slept for only minutes at a time. Her dark eyes are so deeply shadowed they resemble coals. Soon it will be May. Clumps of black mustard bloom everywhere, sweetening the earth's breath, and soon their heavy seed pods will burst. . . .

No, I ain't completely blind, Mamaw thinks. *I can still see what I care to.* She casts her eye upon the rich coverlet of soil laid over Jesse. Must be crawling with life this season, beetles and earthworms and grubs. And the idea of all those live things sharing her son's grave bestows on her a small, exquisite satisfaction. She bends down and sifts a handful of loose, faintly moist earth through her fingers. *Look close, I could see 'em right enough*, she thinks. *If I cared to.*

Mamaw does not care to sleep: she is convinced if she does, they will come and take the last of Jesse from her.

"Who will, Mamaw?" Fannie asks gently.

"You never seen what they done in St. Joe." Mamaw's voice breaks. "Pulled pieces out of the wall, the floor . . ."

Fannie's fingers softly digging into the flesh of her shoulder. "Don't, Mamaw, please. You're destroying yourself."

Zerel laughs, thinking, *Destroy? Ain't I dead? Can the destruction go on? Yes.*

"You think they'd stop short of stealing his bones?" she says.

The effluvia of human grief—words, tears—elude her. And even if they did not, she knows they would fail her. Mourning is the marrow in her bones.

Morning after morning, while inside the family sleeps, Mamaw is out in the southeast corner of the yard, watching, waiting for dawn. Huge, bulky, bent.

She looks, from a distance, like a scarecrow.

Mamaw sits in the porch rocker, her head pressed to its high back, her feet rooted to the floor. Two rosy finches bicker in a nearby gooseberry bush. Dish towels are spread out to dry on the shrubs below the porch railing. Some cottonwood froth captured in her hair is set loose by a breeze and drifts down to tickle her nose. She slaps it away like an insect. The gesture is absent, instinctive. She is, this year, oblivious to the onset of summer, to all sight and sound, light and motion. She is imagining herself wedded to this chair, to freeze or disintegrate or petrify here. Only her eyes would go on living, eternally paralyzed, riveted age after age on that swath of ground that is the repository of all her hope and belief, her boy.

A sound from the road breaks into her trance. She looks up, reluctantly drawn outside herself, yet instantly wary. A shoddy-looking mule cart turns in from the road. As the cart comes closer, she sees a man and two boys. All three are thin, weathered brown, dressed in faded blue overalls. The man has on a black felt hat sun-tainted to a greenish cast like spoiled meat.

She waits until they draw up before she pushes herself from the chair to take the few steps to the dooryard gate.

"Somethin' I can do for you?"

The man looks embarrassed. It takes him a minute to get his voice operating.

"This the house where Jesse James was born?"

The simple question seems to pierce her, sharp and hot. She reaches out to steady herself on the gate. *Not before strangers . . .*

"Might be," she says.

The two boys are looking at her, eyes glowing like jack-o'-lanterns with candles inside their skulls.

Mamaw stares back at the children. Finally a strange tight smile slices her face. "You got twenty-five cents, it is," she says.

The man nods slowly. The children squirm with excitement.

What is she doing? What is Mamaw thinking of? She's not sure herself. She hears a voice inside her: they come all this way . . . come to lay a finger of their sorry lives on Jesse, what they *think* is Jesse; well, then they are pilgrims and there is a kind of holiness in them. . . .

But it's a lie, and she knows it. Mamaw don't give a damn for them and their sorry lives and their hard trips.

There is something for me in their coming here. For me. Somehow she knows it, without knowing what it is.

Mamaw gives the visitors their money's worth, though.
Shows the whole house and everything in it: Jesse's school
reports and old targets and baby teeth. She don't hold nothing
back, except her reasons.

Johnny and Pappy are sitting in the kitchen, drinking buttermilk. Mamaw points them out and names them, as if they
are statues. Pappy seems delighted. John stares at his mother,
his mouth gaping to show the yellowish- white coating on his
tongue.

She saves the grave for last, and it makes a grand finale,
that eight-foot shaft of white marble gleaming in the sun like
it burns with a light of its own.

The two boys get down on their hands and knees, pawing
the ground, combing it with acquisitive fingers. The smaller
one scrambles back to his feet and sidles up to Mamaw, a
smooth rose-veined pebble in his grubby palm. "You reckon
I could keep this, Ma'am?"

Mamaw chuckles. "If your daddy got another quarter you
can."

The man, looking stricken, digs into the pocket of his
overalls.

"What the hell's got into you, Mamaw?" Oh, Johnny's mad
as a tick. "Come troopin' through the house with a pack of
seedy strangers so's a family can't have a bite without feeling
like a damn sideshow!"

Mamaw don't have a thing to say for herself. Just smiles
like a person's overheard a large and unsavory secret.

And Johnny, though still put out considerable, backs right
down. What is he to make of it, Mamaw's spectral smile?
He's sure he don't know, but it's the first sign of life been
seen in her in weeks. Why raise a fuss now, anyway, with the

shit-kicking sharecropper and them two scabby kids already long gone?

The girls, though, they give her a little more trouble. Sallie and Fannie come over together to speak to her in a few weeks. Make the visit seem so formal that Mamaw serves tea in the china pot.

"This business with the visitors, Mamaw, it's got to stop."

"I don't see why," she says. "Ain't been but a dozen or so."

Fannie, who has the stronger temper, glares at her mother. "Because it's making a spectacle . . . not just of you and this family, but of Jesse!"

The girls are taken aback—indeed, stunned—by her guffaw. "Jesse never minded making a spectacle of himself."

Well, grief has ransacked her mind, her sense . . . that's clear as daylight.

"Mamaw," Sallie says gently, "Jesse belongs to *us*. It's not a public—"

Mamaw leans into the table and sets her cracked teacup down hard. "Listen, it's two different things, the part that's ours and the part folks want to see."

"But our *home*," Sallie murmurs, wringing her hands.

"And taking *money*!" Fannie slaps her own cup down. "Mamaw, think how it looks!"

Mamaw's eyes glow with a new vitality, which her girls take, naturally, for madness. "Never you mind. You don't like it, it ain't got to be your concern. Don't neither of you live in this house anymore."

"And what about Pappy. I'd like to know?"

"Your Pappy's always right pleased when we have company."

"This ain't company, Mamaw!"

"It is to us," she says.

She has her reasons, does Mamaw, reasons aplenty. She knows just what she's doing now . . . she has found her niche, her way, her livelihood, her calling. Mamaw is launched in a new endeavor . . . seems like her whole lifetime has taken pains to prepare her for it:

Mamaw is making a mockery of Death.

They come in droves to watch her do it . . . and depart ignorant of what they have seen. The big hit is always the gravesite. Each week Mamaw scrubs the white marble marker with a special paste she concocts: soda, soft soap, and whiting. So many folks wanting to buy a pebble from the ground out there, she has to keep carting a new supply up from the creek bed. Oh, she earns them quarters, penny by penny she earns them. Her apron pockets are full of weight and noise.

And Pappy gets right in the act, standing beside her, telling in a rambling kind of way how Jesse shot off his own finger in the War and how The Boys give him the name Dingus after that . . . then telling how he saved Jesse's life, him being a doctor and all, and Pappy smiles like a house on fire and everybody's plumb crazy about him, such a sweet little man. . . .

"Y'all come back, now, hear?"

Pappy waves and Mamaw reaches inside her apron to count the house.

It's a living.

On the drowsy August afternoon when she sees the claret-colored phaeton approaching the homeplace, Mamaw thinks it's merely another curious visitor. A paying customer.

Johnny is slouched on the porch step, watching the fancy carriage turn into the drive. Mamaw grins at him. "Well, now, 'pears we're starting to attract a better class of clientele."

John makes a sound of contempt and goes inside, slamming the door. Mamaw stays on the porch, admiring the high-stepping gait of the chestnut filly as she nears the yard. The man who is driving, the phaeton's solitary passenger, is dressed in smart city clothes: a fawn-color suit, a high-crowned hat the shade and texture of fudge.

"Well, I'll be," says Mamaw. "Got us a true pilgrim this time."

John Newman Edwards alights unsteadily from the carriage and loops the traces around the gatepost. As he lopes toward her, he is removing his hat and doesn't notice he steps into a fresh horse-dropping. Mamaw starts to laugh, but as he gets closer, his face is so tragic she is overcome with gravity. . . .

And genuine emotion, too. *If ever a soul loved Jesse as much as me, if ever a soul struggled to keep my boy afloat, it's this thrashing dreamer.*

She hasn't seen the Major since the day of the burying. From the look of him, his mourning has been as deep and heartrent as her own. Edwards looks old enough to be Jesse's father, she thinks. Then she's caught by surprise, hearing herself say, "Hello, son."

He offers her a shy, wounded smile. "Ma'am." He smells of whiskey.

Mamaw holds out her hand, making it easy for him to kiss it, for he would anyhow. Then she keeps hold of his wrist and leads him up to the porch. "Sit down," she says. "You come all this way, I reckon you got time to sit with me some."

Edwards, tongue-tied, takes the buggy seat and leaves the rocker for Mamaw.

"You look like you been through another war," she says.

The Major looks down, ranging his fingers around his hat brim. "Yes." He nods absently, then sets his hat on the porch floor.

"Folks say it gets easier," Mamaw says, "but I don't guess it does, you think?"

He looks up at her, lamblike, his innocence pilloried but still pure, Mamaw thinks. "Some days I feel like I can barely walk," he says.

Mamaw reaches over and pats his arm.

"But there is one thing. . . ." Edwards, flushed, stops to clear his throat. Then he looks at her steadily. "There is still Frank, Mrs. Samuel."

Frank . . . got so's I barely give him a thought. What kind of unnatural mother . . . but he can't come here, I know it, and to hope would only be to give Death another opening, another—

"You heard from Frank?"

Edwards' eyes are evasive. "We've been in touch."

"You seen him."

He looks at her and doesn't answer.

"Well, all right, I don't need to know as much as that. Is he all right?"

"Your son is healthy and safe but for the afflictions of loss, dear lady."

Mamaw smiles. "I'm surely pleased to see you still got the silver togue inside that sad face."

"Forgive me, Mrs Samuel, I—"

"I know," Mamaw says. "It's all right."

"I come here because, as you know, Frank needs help. I believe I am the one who can provide it. But I may need your help . . . convincing him."

"What can you . . . what can anybody do?" Mamaw leans toward Edwards. "Every price, every accusation was on Jesse's head is still on Frank's. We both know that."

"Yes," Edwards nods. "But as in a war . . . forgive me, Mrs. Samuel, if what I am about to say seems indelicate to you or even heartless. I am not a cynic. But in a war the enemy often tires after the major battle. Much fighting remains to be done, yet . . . "

"I know what you're saying." Mamaw squeezes her eyes shut and feels for a moment as if her own voice will go no further with her. She draws a deep breath, lets it out slowly. "You mean now they got Jesse, they might not fight so hard anymore."

The Major nods.

"How can—"

"The center of it is, Frank will have to surrender."

She knows the word before it's out of his mouth. "Surrender." Mamaw shakes her head fiercely. "Like Appomattox," she says.

Edwards lowers his eyes.

"Or like Jesse surrendered?" she goes on, her voice getting shrill. "Reckon you know what they done to Jesse when he turned himself in."

The Major seems dismantled, but as she watches, she can see him pull himself together, ignite. His eyes blaze with appeal, with hope. "It doesn't have to be that way this time, Mrs. Samuel. It *won't* be like that, I promise you."

"Never mind," Mamaw says. "Ain't a thing you got to say that I mean to listen to."

"I love Frank like a brother."

"I reckon I know that, I don't doubt it at all. But if you mean to get your 'brother' to turn himself in to those bloodthirsty men been hounding him these many years, you sure ain't going to have his mother's help in coaxing him into it."

"It's his only chance, Mrs. Samuel."

"Then he got no chance at all."

John Edwards gets up and paces the length of the porch several times. Then he stops before her and bends low. "I beg of you, ma'am, do not consider me your enemy."

Mamaw's smile is grim. "I couldn't, Major," she says. "You and me have loved the same, and truly, and I'm bound to remember it. But don't you, in this business with Frank, consider me no ally."

"Surrender is the only way to save him."

"I don't believe in surrender," Mamaw says.

The boat Frank rows upriver is barely as long as his legs, scarcely as wide as his hips. His head and back bow with grief, hopeless, as he lowers the oars, then pulls against the water with all his might.

The river is smooth and dark, like something molten and thick, a tarnished color. Frank's head lifts a little as the oars come out of the water, a small moment of alleviation. Then he is bowed and straining again.

Mamaw hovers on the bank, waving her arms above her head, calling out to him over and over. He is all alone out there, solitude a peril, the boat so frail, the placid water so fraught with unseen things. The current mightily fights the pull of his arms . . . I'm here, son, right here. . . .

Mamaw flails, pummels the sky with her fists, calls out in such a fury that his name pounds against the water, a curse. Frank . . . Buck . . . oh, my son . . .

But he just keeps on, alone, fighting the perverse, dark, spangled water. He dwindles to a point of dim light on the horizon. His little boat leaves no wake.

"Zerel?"

Mamaw bolts upright in the bed, pummeling the daylight advancing through the shutters, creeping over the folds of the comforter.

"No," she says.

Reuben catches the stump of her right arm on the downswing, holding her still, struggling against her might, her frenzy.

"All alone out there in that puny little boat." Her throat is thick with disgust and tears.

"Never mind, Zerel," Reuben says. "I have bad dreams, too. It's all right."

In September Frank comes in from the cold, surrendering with great prearranged pomp in the Governor's office.

Mamaw hasn't seen Buck for more than a year when they are reunited on the steps of the courthouse in Independence. She has come to this, his first of several trials, alone. John

Edwards spots her in the crowd on the courthouse steps and
takes her in tow, gets her over to Frank.

"Mamaw."

"Son," she says.

They do not embrace, do not even touch. Avid onlookers
enclose them. Mamaw and Buck speak to one another, barely
moving their lips.

"You look good," she says.

"I'm all right."

"What's going to happen to you?" She asks the question
as if it comes of idle curiosity.

Frank glances at Edwards. "We got things in hand."

She nods.

"Let me get you settled inside, Mrs. Samuel." The Major
takes her arm.

"Reckon I'll be seeing you." She smiles at her son grimly.

As Edwards leads her off, she looks back once. Frank's
white shirt is dazzling. People are pressing his hands. He
looks like a solid citizen.

The trial at Independence comes to nothing. The prosecu-
tion's evidence shakes out like a blanket the moths been into.

In August of '83 Frank comes to trial in Gallatin, charged
with three murders, as well as two robberies. Mamaw keeps
out of sight for this one.

The Gallatin trial has an eight-day run, a staggering cast.
Frank's defense keeps eight prominent lawyers strutting, calls
thirty-nine witnesses to the stand. Their ace-in-the-hole is Jo
Shelby, the only Confederate General who never surrendered. Shelby's so drunk he has to be helped into the witness
box, but he vouches for Frank James in no uncertain terms,
and applause breaks out in the courtroom till the judge's
gavel might be pounding dough.

The second week of September 1883, Frank is acquitted
in Gallatin astride a volcano of public delight, then tried in

❖

Huntsville, Alabama . . . in Booneville, Missouri . . . Mamaw can hardly keep track.

The last charges are dropped on February 21, 1885. Frank James is a free man. Ain't even spent so much as a single night in a jail cell.

He comes sneaking in on her, just like him and Jesse used to do, startling the life out of her as she bends to stir up the fire so she can start breakfast. His temples and moustache are threaded with gray. The merriment in his eyes is guarded, halfhearted.

"Guess who?" he says.

"Frank . . . Buck!" Her lips twist, resisting his name. "Son."

It is a frozen morning in March, and his eyes water from the cold wind. "I'm home, Mamaw."

"So I see." She looks him up and down. "You look a mite pinched."

"And feel it. But I'm here."

"Welcoming committee mighta been bigger if you warned us you was coming."

"I wasn't sure."

"Well, I figured you'd be along soon enough. Don't guess you got all that many places else to go, now all the tom-foolery's done."

He laughs softly. "Sentimental like always, Mamaw, ain't you?"

"You had enough folks to drool over you without me," she says. "Where's Annie and young Robert?"

"I left 'em to stay with Annie's people in Independence for a spell . . . till I get more of a bead on what I mean to do."

"Them Ralstons must be tickled to death, what you dragged their girl through." Mamaw half-turns and stirs up the cook-stove coals with a poker. "What *do* you mean to do?"

"Damned if I know." Buck sighs. "I feel like a soldier been

fighting so long it half scares me to death now the firing's stopped."

Mamaw grunts, and Frank can't tell whether she means disdain or understanding.

"I seen Zee." Frank's voice is neutral, cautious. "A few weeks back. I was in Kansas City, so I figured I'd look up that boardinghouse where they—"

Mamaw's face turns frosty. "How is she?"

"About as good as she's likely to get, I reckon." Frank takes the poker out of his mother's hand and starts fiddling with the fire. "Truth is, Zee's more dead than alive, Mamaw. Inside. It's like talkin' to a ghost. But she gets by, looks after the youngsters real good."

"Good?" Mamaw presses her lips together. "Being reared in a boardinghouse ain't my idea of good."

"She does the best she can."

"She and them children ought to be here . . . at home."

"Zee don't look on this like home. You can't hardly expect her to."

"What I expect is for her to do what's best for your brother's children, but Zee, she—"

"You ain't gonna change her, Mamaw."

"No, I know I ain't." Mamaw stares bleakly into the fire. "You seen the grave on your way in?"

He shakes his head, his eyes dimming.

Mamaw grasps his arm. "Come out. I'll show you."

As they cross the frozen grass and mud, Mamaw, still holding her son's arm, feels him start to tremble as they near the grave. The white marble marker is a startling white against the colorless early morning sky.

When they reach the corner of the yard, Frank shrugs off Mamaw's hand. He walks over and reaches up toward the pointed top of the marker, but he is not tall enough to reach it. His hands drop to his sides. His face is pale, drawn, and dazed-looking.

❖

"You picked a good place," he says.

After another moment Frank backs up a few paces, as if he's just realized he is standing on the plot. When he's beside Mamaw, he removes his hat.

She waits.

"Almost hard to feel anything, coming so late to stand here, Mamaw." His voice is choked.

"Does it look like you pictured it?"

"I been trying pretty hard not to picture it, I guess. I just keep wondering—"

"What, son?"

"Which of him is down there, Mamaw?"

She knows just what he means. Buck ain't talking about all the rumors and tales, how Jesse never really died at all, nobody coulda got Jesse James, must be some other body's in that grave down there by Kearney. *It ain't him.* Scandal sheets reporting every couple months how the real Jesse's been found at last, not a mark on him . . . in New Orleans . . . in Chicago . . . in San Antone. . . .

Ain't none of that Frank means.

"I wonder at it, too," Mamaw says. "All these folks come by, so hungry-like. I tell 'em what they crave to hear. But all the time I'm going on thataway, the wondering's like a bell clanging at the back of my mind till I can't hardly hear myself talk. Is it their Jesse down there . . . or mine?"

Frank nods, then shakes his head. "Don't hardly matter now, though, does it?"

Mamaw rears her head. "That's the only thing that matters now at all."

Frank rubs his knuckles into his eyes.

Mamaw takes his arm again. "Let them have their Jesse," she says, more quietly. "They'll never get ours."

Buck puts an arm around Mamaw's shoulders. In the sky above them a line of mallards fans out into a dart-shape, pointing west. Dark smoke trails from the chimney of the house, and a train can be heard clearly in the cold, still air, passing through Kearney. . . .

Signs of life. But it seems to both of them, Buck and Mamaw, that they inhabit a frozen piece of ground broken off from the rest of the earth, nobody on it but them.

XXV

Relics

1 8 9 3 — 1 9 1 1

Ten years now she's had folks pitching her to buy the house, wanting to lift the planks right out from under her. Hucksters selling snake oil and schemes. They don't give up. What a body won't stoop to'd make a short list.

But by the spring of '93 the old wing is a wreck and the price is right.

So half the house is sliced off and carried away to the Chicago Exposition: "See the Birthplace of Famous Outlaw Jesse James!"

Mamaw is caught off guard by the hot core of pain that bores into her with the surrender of three decrepit rooms . . . another piece of her hacked off. *I am dwindling,* she thinks, *on the wane.*

Another of her children gone—Susie died in Texas two years ago, bearing her seventh child. *Stillborn. Fully half my babies gone now,* Mamaw counting her losses.

Then, not long after Susie, John Edwards died in Jefferson City while covering a legislative session. Just fifty years old. "One of the oddest and best of men." the papers said. "What he could not otherwise endure, he idealized."

"Almost like one of our own," Mamaw says to Frank. She

remembers the Major's mournful face, the loyalty that burned in his eyes hot as lust.

And she doesn't say, not to Buck or anybody else, how the adoration in Edwards' eyes frightened her sometimes. She saw something just like it one other time . . . all that hot dangerous love; it was in Bob Ford's eyes, too.

Still, Mamaw feels like another part of herself has disappeared.

The homeplace has shrunk something awful: acres gone to each of the girls when they married . . . other parcels sold off to get through hard years . . . can't hardly bear to think what it comes down to now, the homeplace. The house was never the thing. It's just that you start feeling there's so little left on earth to hold onto . . . until the whole damn world don't look familiar anymore.

In 1895 Zerel's brother Jesse Cole, not quite sixty years old, walks out into his yard one noontime, neatly folds his coat and vest, and places his gold watch on top like a paperweight. It is a breezy day.

Jesse stretches out on the scratchy grass and, holding a revolver in his right hand, he shoots a hole in his heart.

John Samuel carries the news to the homeplace. Mamaw lifts her shoulders, lowers her head, counts numbness for a blessing. "What on earth could he have been thinking of?"

Torn flesh and smashed bone like a birthright, she thinks, parentheses of violence enclosing her life before she ever had a say in the matter . . . and her brother's too, that golden boy she knew in her blood but not her mind . . . *a likeness a body can't do without,* she thinks, *even when they got to. And here Death coming to get the jump again, and me not paying any mind* . . . not even the knowing a thing she can keep hold of. . . .

———

Mamaw looks out from the front door at Reuben, rocking slowly in his swing beneath the bare branches of the coffee tree. It is starting to snow. His head is bent. He isn't wearing a hat. He resembles a tree himself, thin and gnarled, as if he has taken root out there in the soil of his humiliation.

She throws on a shawl and goes out to him. "You best come in now."

"No," he says.

"Pappy, it's snowing. You can't stay out here."

"Jesse can," he says. "You let Dingus do anything he wants."

"Now don't start getting all-overish. You been real good so far today."

Reuben looks up at her and smiles peaceably. When he stands, she thinks he is about to follow her into the house. But when she turns to start back, he jumps her from behind, knocking her flat on the frozen ground.

She has more than a little trouble getting him back inside, and she has what feels like it plans on becoming a black eye.

Pappy gets like that sometimes. He can't help it, poor soul.

"What am I going to do with you?" she says.

Reuben smiles.

Mamaw warms some milk, adds a spoonful of honey, a drop or two of laudanum to help him sleep. She tries to remember if any fresh meat is left, something to lay on her eye. . . .

Pappy will not drink the milk, just won't have it.

Mamaw rubs the bald spot on the back of his head. "Who's my boy?" she says. She rakes her fingers playfully through his chin whiskers. "Come on, now, who—"

Pappy covers his eyes and looks at her through his fingers. His hands are blue with cold.

"That's right," she says. She stands beside his chair and holds his head to her breast, as she spoons the warm sweet milk between his lips.

———

"He's just getting to be too much of a handful, Mamaw, and ain't a soul in town but you don't know it."

"Franklin's right, Mamaw," Annie James says timidly. "You got to know he is?"

Mamaw has quite a shiner. She knows the cornstarch she dusted it with don't hide it a bit. She keeps that side of her face slanted away from them, for all the good it's apt to do.

"What I know," she says, glaring at her son with her good eye, "is what maybe all them busybodies in town forgot but you oughtn't: Pappy raised you like you was his own, and loved you, and even set his own life right down in the path of what meant to harm us. He saved your brother's—"

"Life. I know, Mamaw. But you're talking about love and gratitude, which I got, believe me . . . only that don't change the situation now. Pappy's getting to be a menace—"

Mamaw hoots and hollers. "That puny old man? I can keep him in line with one hand. And I do."

"Right. And you come up with a black eye for your trouble."

"This eye ain't flea-droppings," she says.

"Maybe so. But who's to say the next time won't be worse?"

"*I* am."

The battle is waged off and on for several years, and Mamaw holds her own, holds her ground. Frank and Annie are all over the place—Louisiana, Texas, New Jersey, as well as every part of Missouri a body could think of and a few they couldn't. Frank sells shoes, clothing, produce, and theater seats. He tends horses, drives wagons, and starts races at the St. Louis Fairgrounds. For a while he guards the door at the Standard Theatre in St. Louis and even has a brief theatrical career himself, in a Wild West Show. Annie is patient and mobile and game, but nothing ever seems to settle right, so they keep turning up back at Mamaw's. Each time they do, Frank starts in again: Pappy needs to be put away.

Like something we outgrew, wore out, Mamaw thinks.

But finally, in 1900, her defenses crumble. She is seventy-five years old, though she doesn't go around pointing that out. Reuben's spells have become so violent that Mamaw can't quell them.

It is a freezing day in midwinter when John Samuel drives his father from the homeplace to the Missouri State Hospital. Mamaw has Reuben well-bundled and wonders if she ought to tie down his arms under his coat the way she's had to do sometimes when he's got obstreperous.

But Pappy appears meek and vague this morning and John says never mind.

Reuben stands beside the door, scuffing his feet like a youngster waiting to be set free.

"You just hold on, now." Mamaw goes to the ashwood chest in the next room. It takes a few minutes to find what she wants, because it's all the way at the bottom, under blankets and Pappy's tattered shirts that she saves for rags.

When she returns to the kitchen, she loosely winds a blue scarf twice around Reuben's neck. The wool is misshapen and ragged, the moths have been into it. "I made this for you once, Pappy. Remember when Mamaw used to knit?"

He watches her face with mild, vacant eyes.

Mamaw lifts up his long white beard, pulling it carefully outside the folds of the muffler. "Reckon you best be going on, then," she says.

John takes his father's arm and leads him out to the wagon.

Mamaw stays inside where it is warm and watches through the window, as Reuben sits docilely on the wagon seat. Then John wraps a horse blanket around the old man's legs. The ends of the scarf are lifted up, flapping like bright blue wings, as Reuben is carried away.

Mamaw stays looking out the window a long time after the wagon is out of sight. She watches the empty swing by the coffee tree tossing back and forth before Jesse's grave . . . back and forth, as if it just can't figure out how to escape from the strong and bitter wind.

It's like one of them bull's-eye things, Mamaw sometimes thinks, the way life keeps turning so's you find yourself inside smaller and smaller circles. Young folks got all that wide rim to move around, but they're always worrying how they can get to the center of things . . . never realizing what the center comes down to is next to nothing.

There is, though, a kind of rightness to it, a symmetry you can spot if you keep your eye on the whole circle, not just the dwindling spot where you stand.

In 1900 Zee dies—barely remembered, scarcely seen—in Kansas City. She lived only fifty-five years, but they were long and hard ones.

And within the same year that their mother passes quietly out of existence, both the James children marry. Mamaw starts thinking about great-grandchildren . . . the circle spinning wider and faster as she becomes hardly more than a speck. . . .

Above Jesse's grave the branches of the coffee tree are bare and fragile-looking. The grass that covers him is yellowed and patchy. Each year, in this dying season, Mamaw imagines herself stepping up to his resting place to lay a soft quilt over her child. He seems so unprotected these weeks when the leaves are first gone, before the snow comes.

She knows such thoughts are fanciful. But for twenty-odd years Mamaw has never got over the fear that someone will come and steal the last of Jesse. The homeplace might fall into anyone's hands in that dark unforeseen time when Mamaw's gone. . . .

In 1902 she makes up her mind to have Jesse moved into the graveyard in town. She has to let him go, for safekeeping.

On March 1, 1908, close to his eightieth birthday, Reuben dies in the Missouri State Hospital.

His delicate white hands are kept still with restraints, even when he is near death: never know when the flashes come upon him, and he can be downright dangerous for such a very small and soft old man. There is a tea-colored scar like a ring around his neck.

A man who looks nearly as old as Pappy is sweeping in the ward near his bed. The fine, strangely youthful hands twitch and Reuben's voice, mumbling for the past quarter hour, suddenly goes strong and clear.

It is perhaps more curiosity than compassion that causes the other man to set his broom against the iron bed railing and lean over the dying man. A fortunate accident that Pappy's last words are heard:

"I am a doctor," he says.

Sallie is appointed to come and break the news to Mamaw. She tells her gently, in a low voice, as she kneels beside her mother's rocking chair.

Mamaw has not seen Reuben in the eight years since he went to the hospital. He wouldn't have known her had she come, and St. Joe is a place Mamaw hoped to never again set foot in.

When Sallie finishes, Mamaw, dry-eyed, simply nods.

She's in shock, Sallie thinks. I'm not reaching her.

She leans close, peering into Mamaw's tranquil face with big wet eyes. "You all right, Mamaw?"

Mamaw's voice sounds perishable. "I just wish I could have kept him by me," she says.

A popular legend

She wanted to go home to die.

Mamaw has made the trip to Oklahoma—by no means her first—to pass part of the winter with Frank and Annie. They've made a big fuss over her eighty-sixth birthday, a cake and everything. Frank sang "Hang Old Jim Lane" to her in a voice like a rusty hinge.

The winter landscape out there, all tumbleweed and mistletoe and cloud-sculpted skies, never fails to excite Mamaw. "It's like seeing Creation before the Lord got it half figured out," she tells Frank. And he grins because when Mamaw talks about God, somehow it always seems a mite suspect.

At night the wind rages like a violent argument just beyond the window of her small snug room. Mamaw enjoys listening. And she sleeps better, dreams more, in Oklahoma, her mind an empty slate for things to be written on.

Yet after only a couple of weeks, she feels restless. She can't truthfully say why. She just knows in her bones that she's got to leave, get home.

"I wish you'd wait, Mamaw. Or let one of us ride along with you, at least," Annie says.

"Buck and Jesse never come to no harm on a train, ain't hardly likely I will." Mamaw winks at her son and squeezes her daughter-in-law's hand. "Them two brothers at Kitty Hawk a few years back? Now, that's a way of travel to worry a body."

Buck laughs. "I'm surprised you ain't tried it."

"Pains me some I ain't likely to get the chance."

"You look after yourself, now, Mamaw."

She cuffs Frank's ear. "You keep out of trouble, boy. Your Mamaw's running pretty short on alibis."

The train pulls out, screeching. Mamaw, a crocheted mitt on her hand, waves behind a sooty window.

A fact

Mamaw don't want to go home to die. She just wants to go home.

A memory

Indian summer on the prairie, warm and bright; the air is shot with gold. The hawkweed, brazen, slinks right up to the edge of the dooryard, and Mamaw, flush, can see for miles.

The creek is high and rambunctious with early autumn rains. The stripped-naked trees won't hide her now, but Mamaw don't care. Mamaw's got nothing to hide.

She drapes her dark dress on a spindly sapling shaped like a hall-tree. She wastes no time getting into the water. The shock of it against her skin is cathartic, infusive, aphrodisiac. The cold bites her breasts, her thighs, playful, libidinous, and Mamaw laughs so loud that the prairie buckles a little bit. She warps the land, Mamaw, when she cares to.

And there in the icy ink-dark water, Mamaw is surrounded. The children, slick and limber, writhe like snakes around her neck and waist and shoulders, submerge themselves and slither between her legs, entwine her ankles. Rocks tumble down the bank, obeying the implicit authority of her joy. Throwing her weight around, Mamaw, as she chases the countless children, catching hold, then letting them go, with her two good hands.

A memory

It couldn't be. Surely this is no more than a dream?

Mamaw don't split hairs, never did. Mamaw knows: ain't a memory worth keeping that's much more than a dream, anyhow, if you take a close look.

Fact

February 10, 1911.

Zerelda Samuel, born in Kentucky on January 29, 1825, dies late at night in a Pullman berth on a Burlington train near Oklahoma City.

The cause of death, according to a coroner's report, is "heart failure." Which goes to show how much stock a body can put in fact.

A personal legend

A mountainous woman stands, alone, on the rough edge of a fractured planet. There is no light. She is blind. But her heartbeat is irrefutable.

Grief is the air she breathes. She opens her mouth and inhales, drawing deep.

Death is a knowing, the very marrow of her bones. She waits, alone, a monument etched on the gray granite sky. And when her bones tell her that Death, no stranger, is finally come, she gulps in one last draught. . . .

And she spits.

A legend: Mamaw.

Author's Afterword

Four years after the death of his mother, Frank James died in Kearney of a heart attack. He was seventy-two. His widow occupied the homeplace until her death in 1944. Annie James, shy and reclusive, would hide in the house when visitors came.

Today there is a prominent highway sign on I-35, not far from Kansas City—"Birthplace of Jesse James." The James Farm is open to the public as a museum.

My first visit to the James place, on a fall afternoon in 1986, came of a most idle curiosity. "Outlaw" was the sum total of my knowledge about Jesse James, and I was mildly surprised to find him in Missouri—I'd have imagined him farther west.

Several portraits of Zerelda Samuel hang in the James farmhouse. Her face is . . . remarkable? extraordinary? unforgettable? Language falls short of it, Mamaw's face. From the instant I saw it, I knew that I would write this book. . . .

I have had, in the ensuing months, a great deal to learn. I have tried to remain accurate to historical fact. But for me the real truth was, and remains, Zerelda Samuel's face. I have, above all, tried to be faithful to that.

349

❖

In May 1987 I visited Mamaw's grave. Although I had gone to the James Farm several times by then, I had never stopped at the town cemetery. Perhaps it was because she seemed so alive to me that I had never felt any desire to see her burial place.

I pulled into a service station at the Kearney exit. The older gentleman who tended my car seemed very friendly, so it was easy to ask. And he was pleased to give directions to the family plot.

I started to thank him, but he held up his hand, an addendum.

"Jesse ain't there, you know."

"He's not?" My voice was a little faint.

"No, ma'am. A long while back they come and took the body. Jesse's not in that grave. . . ."

It ain't him. . . .

If you keep company with the James gang, you find out soon enough that legend's grip is a good bit stronger than history's. You try to learn to live with it. And perhaps you come to a different kind of knowing. . . .

Osage Beach, Missouri
October 1987